THREADS OF MAGIC

Mike Jefferies was born in Kent but spent his early years in Australia. He attended Goldsmiths' School of Art and then taught art in schools and prisons. A keen rider, he was selected in 1980 to ride for Britain in the Belgian Three Day Event. He now lives in Norfolk with his wife, Sheila, working as a full-time writer and illustrator.

Voyager

MIKE JEFFERIES

Threads of Magic

HarperCollins*Publishers*

Voyager
An Imprint of HarperCollins*Publishers*
77–85 Fulham Palace Road,
Hammersmith, London w6 8jb

The *Voyager* World Wide Web site address is
http://www.harpercollins.co.uk/voyager

A Paperback Original 1997
1 3 5 7 9 8 6 4 2

Copyright © Mike Jefferies 1997

The Author asserts the moral right to
be identified as the author of this work

A catalogue record for this book
is available from the British Library

ISBN 0 00 648262 7

Set in Postscript Goudy and Fenice by
Rowland Phototypesetting Ltd,
Bury St Edmunds, Suffolk

Printed and bound in Great Britain by
Caledonian International
Book Manufacturing Ltd, Glasgow

TO MY WIFE SHEILA
who helped me weave these slender threads
and brought the magic to life.

I

The Runesgate Gorge

THE GREAT DAYLIGHTS of magic have stolen away and silence fills the brooding night. Nightshapes weave their shrouds amongst the whispering treetops and moon shadows softly dapple the forest floor or shimmer in silvery, liquid ripples upon the surface of the swift mountain streams. Rainbow-fish trap the moonlight in their incandescent scales as they leap and play across the waterfalls that plunge into the dark, secret depths of the Runesgate Gorge. High above those vanishing plumes of icy spray where the sweet, heady scent of jasmine blossoms, wild rosemary and nightflowers perfume the dark and the rush and gurgle of water running over stones is heard; above the dense, impenetrable briars and tangled blackthorn bushes that guard the Runesgate at the starlit head of the thickly wooded gorge, high upon a promontory of silver-veined marble, the ancient magician's tower stands, etched in albescence against the hunter's moon.

Once it was the place where legends were hot-forged upon the anvil of time and so steeped in the myths of magic that it held sway over the lives of all it touched, both kings and common folk. The Runesgate Tower was the fountainhead of all knowledge, absolute and terrible in its power, where Nevian, the Master of Magic, watched over the world and moved the people of Elundium to chase their fate. But with the passing of King Holbian, the last of the Granite Kings, and the dawning of the new age of men who could control their own destiny, his magic began to fade along with the beautiful colours of his rainbow cloak. Gradually his powers shrank until they were lost in fairy tale.

Forgotten in the schemes of men the tower endured, isolated upon its high promontory. Sometimes wreathed in mist or racked by sudden, unpredictable storms, its ice-clad, granite walls were weathered smooth by the changing rub of time and circumstance. Its once-great beacon lamp diminished and was now no more than a fragile, flickering light that clung precariously upon the brink of night, a fallen star lost amongst the black monoliths of the Emerald Mountains.

Night had drawn its mantle over the Runesgate Gorge; but a soft candlelight and the hint of magic still dwelt behind the shuttered windows of the tower and a single, spiralling ribbon of applewood smoke hung above its chimney hole. Orundus, Lord of Owls, sat high amongst the smoke-blackened rafters, his battle daylights long forgotten, his feathers ruffled against the cold. He slept soundly, oblivious to the magician's mumblings as they echoed in the vast, shadowy, circular room below.

Nevian was bent over almost double, engrossed by his new storm engine, his long, thin fingers poised upon the polished spindle of the huge brass windwheel, its curved crystal sails unfurled and trembling, waiting for the slightest breath of air. Suddenly the old man straightened his back, his ancient face creased into a troubled frown.

'Who's there? Who calls me?' he called out, uncertainly, twisting and turning his head from left to right, hunting the gloomier recesses of his chamber for the faint cries and echoes of despair that seemed to fill the air around him before vanishing tantalizingly into the shadows before he could grasp their content.

'Who is it?' he called again, bleakly remembering that

4

his eyes were too weak to delve into the ways of man and that to the people of Elundium he was almost a transparent wraith, powerless to intervene or stop the dark canker of fear that relentlessly tightened its grip upon them. His daylights of meddling into the lives of kings and crooked chimney sweeps were truly over, but still he glanced once more around the smoky chamber, chasing those fading echoes before letting his hands fall to his sides.

'It will do you no good – you waste your breath trying to call me, whoever you are. I cannot do anything to help you.' He returned his attention to the huge storm engine whose mesh of cogs and wheels and forest of levers climbed up into the darkness, almost filling one half of his chamber. 'Ah, there's a wind to raise – a fierce rainstorm to try to break across the Emerald Mountains ... Now, where did I put that bucket of water? A rainstorm won't be much without water will it? No that won't do, it won't do at all.'

He started to search the untidy room, muttering to himself, until he caught sight of a brimming bucket just where he had left it, near the threshold. He hurried across, held the handle carefully with both hands, making sure he didn't spill a drop as he retraced his steps, treading over his discarded rainbow cloak where it lay half-buried amongst the paraphernalia cluttering the chamber. He placed the bucket exactly beneath the crystal sails. Everything was now ready. Nevian replaced his hand upon the spindle of the windwheel, the cares and troubles of Elundium forgotten.

Nothing now disturbed his moment of expectant silence save for the crackle of the flames that leapt and twisted between the apple logs burning in the fire hearth. Fat-bellied cauldrons hung side by side there from iron chains, and hot crucibles of precious metals bubbled and frothed, forgotten upon the glowing coals. Softly the firelight reached out with shifting, flickering fingers to illuminate the long, ebony tables and high-backed walnut chairs ornately carved with coiling serpents and mythical beasts. Each receptacle was crammed to overflowing with mountainous piles of manuscripts and scrolls of spells, the flames from the fire illuminating the spines of the thousands of books that crowded the shelves and rose haphazardly to vanish into the raftered darkness.

Grannog, Lord of Dogs, who had once run at the stirrup of the Granite Kings, yawned, his grey-flecked muzzle twitching as he dreamed of far-off daylights when he hunted the Nightbeasts in the black Gates of Night. The dog stretched, deaf to the moment of magic, and rested his huge paws among the blackened fire tongs, the long-handled salamanders and leather bellows that had been left to clutter the ash-choked hearth, making them rattle. Nevian, momentarily distracted by the noise, glanced across to the enormous Border Runner sprawled in front of the fire and smiled.

'The Nightbeasts have all gone, save in your dreams, Grannog, gone forever.' He gave the maze of wheels and giant cogs a final polish, trickling oil of myrrh and sneezewort from a glass phial onto the brass spindles and working it carefully into the teeth of the cogs. His quick fingers made a number of last-minute adjustments to the trembling crystal sails and then all was ready. There was magic to make. His thick, white, bushy eyebrows rose into owlish arches of anticipation as he pushed with his fingertips, setting the huge windwheel into motion.

Cogs clicked and meshed together, trammels whirred and spindles turned as the great wheel gathered speed. It began to turn faster and faster. The leather bellows creaked and expanded, bright bilious liquids bubbled through the spiralling copper tubes. The crystal sails clattered and hummed to become a spinning blur of shimmering light.

'It works! It really works!' Nevian exclaimed, clapping his hands with delight and making Grannog grumble and yelp in his sleep.

An eddy of air stirred in the ashes of the hearth, combing through the dog's rough coat before crossing the floor to tug at the hems of the magician's silken azure gown. The first faint breath of air became a piercing draught that caught in the crystal sails and rifled through the untidy piles of manuscripts, scattering them across the flagstone floor. The draught grew stronger, picking up forgotten quills and heavily-woven strings of black tourmaline; peacocks' feathers fluttered and spun; golden runes and hammered, silver numbers fell heavily from where they lay upon the shelves. The draught became a howling wind. It shrieked through the tower, tearing painfully at Nevian's hair and spinning him round, upsetting bottled hares' ears and jars of aromatic juniper and saffron seeds. The wind grew. It overturned chairs and tables, gathered up pewter bowls and vellum scrolls and sucked them up into a swirling tide that raced towards the fire.

Orundus rose in a gale of disgruntled feathers to seek a higher, safer perch above the eye of Nevian's storm and Grannog awoke, snarling and snapping in startled anger at the sound of the approaching hail of debris which was racing across the chamber towards where he lay in front of the hearth. Growling, he slunk away, tail curled down between his hind legs, and disappeared into a secret corner only moments before the wind whipped up the surface of the water in the bucket where Nevian had placed it beneath the crystal sails. The spinning sails drew up the water, separating it into a million glittering raindrops that soaked the magician's gown and left puddles on the floor before scouring through the embers in the hearth, scattering them into a swirling cloud of dust that roared up the chimney in a blaze of sparks and fire.

'Oh dear, I think I used a little too much of everything in this storm.' Nevian threw open the shutters to watch the lightning fly from the fire and crackle and flash across the Runesgate Gorge, throwing it into stark silhouette. Ball lightning shot up from the chimney in a blaze of sparks and raced across the stars to fall hissing and spitting amongst the trees. Burnt fragments of manuscripts drifted in the air and broken pots and pans clattered to the ground. A sudden deluge rattled the roof of the tower and gurgled throatily in the gutter spouts, streaking long, wet fingermarks down the weathered stonework. The rain thrashed and beat the undergrowth, bending boughs and breaking branches, while the swift mountain streams boiled and overflowed their banks, flattening the dense bracken fronds and drowning the knapweed and woundwort that grew there in profusion. The flooding torrents dislodged rocks and boulders and carried them in a thundering avalanche down into the gorge.

'That's quite enough for one night. I must be more careful what I use next time,' Nevian laughed, reaching for the long ironwood brake lever beside the windwheel.

He was delighted that his storm engine had really worked. Now there was no need for the weather to be so unpredictable. It was just a matter of making the right calculations and, of course, ensuring there wasn't a fire burning in the grate unless he particularly wanted lightning. One quick glance around the shambles of his chamber was enough to tell him that he would have to tidy things away and make sure everything was safely under lock and key before he set the storm engine in motion another time. But what an asset it would be, to have wind or rain, perhaps even snow – maybe if he put ice in the bucket beneath the crystal sails – whenever he wished it.

Grasping the brake lever with both hands and throwing his weight against it he pushed it forward. There was a screech of hot metal as the brake bit against the wind-wheel and bright sparks jumped and danced between the meshing cogs. Smoke and steam erupted in hissing spouts from every joint in the maze of spiralling copper tubes. The bellows sighed and gently collapsed, expelling their last breath of air as the crystal sails slowly turned one final time before hanging limp and trembling as the huge storm engine came to a shuddering halt.

Nevian stepped back, rubbing his hands together in satisfaction and looked up at the gleaming apparatus as the smoke and steam drifted away. He was well aware that creating storms was small magic compared to having the fate of kings at his fingertips but beggars, even magical ones, couldn't be choosers.

'Yes, I'm sure it's just a matter of balancing the elements. I have to create the right updraughts and down-draughts – whatever they might be. Now, where have those calculations got to?' He stooped to gather the scattered remnants of his manuscripts from where they lay floating in the puddles upon the floor. He righted the chairs and began to gather up books and overturned bottles and jars in his search for those particular scribblings that referred to the storm. Suddenly he paused and frowned, catching sight of his rainbow cloak which lay, half-buried amongst the chaos the wind had left in its wake.

'Why that's odd, very odd, very odd indeed,' he

muttered darkly, touching the crumpled sleeve with suspicious fingertips.

The colours of his cloak had dimmed with the weakening of his powers. The once-brilliant topaz, peacock blues, rich indigos and mulberry hues had been reduced to little more than soft, translucent shadows. And the vivid images of moments past, the great battles they had once fought to win the daylight, the proud warhorses, stoops of battle owls; the fortress wreathed in smoke and fire as hordes of Nightbeasts assaulted the walls, all of which had once dwelt within its magic threads, had all faded away to nothing. Then suddenly, quite unexpectedly, the colours started to glow again with bright, vibrant light that filled the gloomiest corners of the chamber.

'By all the spells I can engrave upon a grain of sand – what magic has caused this?' He gathered his cloak up in his hands and tentatively crushed its weave between his fingers, feeling the power that had once dwelt in each coloured crease and voluminous fold slowly regrow, making his hands tingle with warmth as it travelled through the fabric, infusing each faded thread.

Shaking the cloak, he pulled it thoughtfully around his shoulders. It fitted as perfectly as it always had, making him stoop slightly beneath its weight. He glanced up at the huge, silent storm engine. Glistening beads of condensation were forming on its cogs and wheels and were dripping, hissing, to the floor.

'Surely such an invention – such small magic – could not have caused my cloak to glow with such fresh colours? Grannog, come here, look at what's happening. Grannog – Grannog – now where has he got to?' He stared frantically around the chamber, momentarily worried that he might have been sucked up the chimney during the height of the storm.

The old dog emerged slowly from the shadows, his hackles raised along his back, his lips drawn back into a snarl as he padded protectively towards Nevian's side. Orundus hooted a shrill warning as he left his perch high up amongst the rafters and stooped to the magician's shoulder, talons unhooked and wings outstretched. The ancient Lord of Battle Owls faced towards the doorway, beak ready to strike, prepared, as ever, for the Nightbeasts that might lurk and threaten from the darkness outside.

'What is it?' Nevian asked in alarm. 'Surely nothing should disturb your rest. The age of the Granite Kings with all the unnatural creatures spawned in Krulshards' darkness have gone forever. There is nothing left for you to fight.'

Orundus hooted again and Grannog advanced towards the door, growling, filling Nevian with concern. 'What far-off echoes of catastrophe have pricked your instincts? If it comes from the new age of man we are powerless to intervene: we can do nothing, I'm afraid. Sometimes I also imagine I can hear the echoes of the new Elundium forging its fate but I cannot help: I am trapped here by the weakness of my magic.'

Nevian sighed deeply. There were times when it was so frustrating, tinkering with the weather and a host of other inconsequential things while chaos and desolation were spreading across all that he had once helped King Thane to achieve; and the worst of it was not knowing what was happening because since his confinement in the tower, past and future had become such an elusive blur. His memory was so unreliable that he wasn't even sure where the last of his powers had been used. He had vague memories of attempting to rally the few loyal Kingsmen who were scattered through the villages, and it had taken a lot of his residual strength to appear in a vision in the forge in Muddle, and then to convince the blacksmith. Now what was his name? Nevian searched through his failing memory; oh yes, of course, Quencher, such a simple name. Yes, convincing the blacksmith to gather the loyal Kingsmen and their families together and take them on a journey through the Emerald Mountains in the depths of winter had been a considerable feat of magic, but had it helped the King? Had they re-armed the Knights of Cawdor? He knew they had arrived safely, for he had provided for their ragged, starving company as they travelled through the high passes and he had kept a careful watch over them until they entered the ruined fortress. That should have been the end of it. His powers had diminished but he couldn't be sure; there was a nagging image at the back of his mind of being drawn back to Cawdor, but by what or by whom? There had been voices, people screaming, folk calling for help, and he thought he had glimpsed them fleeing for their lives, pursued by strange, shadowy figures and a darkness that had covered the ruins ... But the memories dissolved whenever he tried to focus on them. But one image from that awful scene always stayed clear. He was trying to enfold the fleeing people with his rainbow cloak, trying to help them escape. Were the faint echoes that troubled Orundus and Grannog coming from the ruins of Cawdor or were they the sounds of the fall of the Granite City and the end of Thanehand's brief rule? No, surely not: the Lords of Battle Owls and Border Runners were from the time of the Granite Kings – the affairs of men, no matter how disastrous, would not have disturbed them. Unless ... unless ...

Nevian looked quizzically down at the old dog and rubbed his hands reassuringly through the thick coat, feeling the low, vibrating, threatening growl rumbling in its throat, looked more closely at the shifting new colours in the flowing folds of his rainbow cloak.

'I wonder?' he murmured. 'Could some dark spectre of Krulshards' evil have survived and arisen from the dust of ancient battles? That would certainly explain why the colours have come to life again – but what unnatural evil could it be? What could possibly have been overlooked as King Thane slew the Master of Nightmares? Surely I would have sensed it.'

The old man looked thoughtfully towards the well-worn stairway that climbed up around the outer edge of the chamber through each floor and gallery until it reached the top of the tower. If there was new magic in the worn-out threads of his cloak then what other of his powers had been restored? Had his power to foretell returned?

'I must look into the high windows of the tower!' he cried. 'I must look to where the future was once foretold and images of the truths of yesterday were shown to me. If the darkness that has shrouded their surface has cleared then they may already reveal what has caused this strange phenomenon. I may yet see what fate has befallen Elundium.'

Gathering up the billowing hems of his cloak, Grannog at his heels, Nevian raced up the circular stairway. The draught made reed lamps in their iron baskets gutter, shadows leaping ahead across the walls. On he ran, through narrow, curved galleries, past rooms crowded with forgotten relics. The quick scrape of his footsteps echoed in the vaulted, windowless corridors as round and round, up and up he climbed until, with rasping breath, he reached the final stairhead and paused at the entrance to his observatory. Anticipation tingled in his fingertips as he lifted the latch. Dare he look – dare he hope that something would be revealed?

Grannog nudged past his flowing robe and, standing on his hind legs pushed the door ajar with his forepaws before padding almost soundlessly across the threshold. Starlight silvered the silent observatory, casting soft, velvet shadows across the magician's starwatching chair and lit the clutter of his astrological instruments and charts that had been left surrounding it. Cautiously Nevian entered the room. Wrinkling his nose at the musty scent of so many discarded yesterdays he hurried to the nearest window.

'Look, Orundus – Grannog, look . . .' he whispered, gazing out at the bright canopy of stars sewn across the night sky. 'The shrouds that dimmed my sight have melted away. Look how the mountains stand out in stark relief and march away to the edge of tomorrow where the first thin finger of light strokes the night. Look how the trees in the gorge below us are etched in such leafy detail, see how the starlight glitters on the hidden streams, but . . .'

Nevian frowned, his voice trailing away as he peered quickly from left to right, pressing his nose against the glass, gently misting its cold surface with opaque beads of condensation. Grannog looked up expectantly, staring at the magician with ears pricked.

'This is no good, no good at all,' Nevian muttered, his voice heavy with disappointment.

The glass was crystal clear, clearer than he remembered it in all his daylights of magic, but it revealed only the commonplace panorama of starlit mountains and the dark depths of the Runesgate Gorge. There was nothing more, nothing of what once had been and nothing of what might come to pass. The power of second sight, so vital in the art of magic, still eluded him it seemed, despite the new, vibrant colours that had come to life in his rainbow cloak.

Sighing, he turned away, absently brushing his sleeve

through the beads of condensation that smeared the window, unaware that in doing so he left a thin line of wet colour upon the glass. Orundus hooted and dug his talons into the magician's shoulder making him pause upon the threshold and glare back to the window. Something was happening: the beads of moisture on the glass were moving, they became a shimmering spectrum of colour melting into the surface of the window. The starlight dimmed and faint, hazy images began to appear.

'By all the riddles of the golden circle ... by calcite and mockwood ... my powers must indeed be returning ...'

Nevian hurried back to the window, clutching at the stone sill as the pictures swirled and merged together faster than he could blink. It became a jumbled pageantry of warhorses, citadels and spires, faces and places he barely remembered. For a long moment he stared in confusion: then he glimpsed King Mantern raising his arm to drive that fatal hammer-blow into the ground, greedy for the rare silver-veined marble that lay in the depths of the marble valleys, ignorant that he was about to fracture the surface of the world beyond repair and release Krulshards, the Master of Nightmares, with all the unnatural creatures of the night eager to plague the sunlight.

Nevian watched as the nightwinds screamed around inside his observatory and he heard cruel laughter mocking his attempts to return things to what they once had been. The mountains outside seemed to tremble and shake, sending avalanches thundering down into the valleys, choking them with debris. The images became a shifting, murky kaleidoscope of shadows; ruin and devastation seemed to stretch wherever the vision took him, covering Elundium. The Granite City appeared grim and silent, wreathed in gloom without a single light burning in Candlebane Hall. Then the shadow of the fortress of

Cawdor briefly filled his vision. It looked empty and desolate as the wind pulled at the branches of a single, ancient gnarled tree that clung to the bleak marble cliff. But another image started to grow: there was movement. Nevian leaned forward to see more clearly, but what he saw made him gasp and draw back hastily. Misshapen creatures, half-beast half-human, loomed towards him and then shrank into a haze of darkness. Suddenly the black Gates of Night filled the glass and from deep within the bowels of the earth he thought he caught the sound of something stirring. It was, as yet, faint and far away but he could hear the smallest echo of footsteps, the whisper of voices, rising up towards the light.

Grannog barked and snarled, leaping up suddenly at another of the windows which overlooked the entrance to the gorge. The commotion made Nevian spin round. 'What is it? What have you seen?' he cried, looking quickly back towards the dark, elusive shapes that were ghosting across the windows, casting lurid shadows across the room before they faded away into the night.

The magician rubbed the glass furiously but the images had disappeared leaving a dark, forbidding gnawing in his mind. What omens of disaster had he glimpsed? Grannog's barking grew more persistent, cutting through his troubled thoughts and making him hurry across the room and peer down into the night-shrouded gorge. Faintly, from far away, he caught the sound of a horse approaching.

'Who can have breached the Runesgate? Who has the power to penetrate my shroud of spectres? Was it one of the creatures I glimpsed in the glass?' Nevian opened the window directly above the gorge a mere finger's crack as he pressed his ear against the gap. Listening to the familiar nightsounds of cascading water and the wind combing gently through the treetops he caught the clatter of iron-shod hooves on the moss-wet rocks and the movement of stones in the river bed from the dark depths of the gorge. The sounds grew gradually louder and eventually he could hear the soft musical jingle of bit rings and the creak of leather.

'It can't be evil, it doesn't sound evil,' he muttered, throwing the window wide open and reaching up to stroke the owl perched on his shoulder.

'Fly, Orundus, fly and hunt the shadows – see who dares to come to my tower uninvited,' he urged.

The Battle Owl flew silently through the open window, spreading his flight feathers in the chill updraughts of night air and wheeled above the gorge, searching the darkness below with sharp eyes for the slightest sign of motion. Suddenly he shrieked and stooped, vanishing from sight amongst the treetops.

Nevian stood for a moment poised on tip-toe, peering down into the gorge. In better daylights, when real magic still coursed through his veins, he wouldn't have hesitated to step out onto the narrow window ledge and launch himself into the thin night air to descend in a blaze of rainbow colours through the trees to confront the intruders, but not now. Now he had to be much more circumspect. Drawing back in frustration he snapped his fingers at Grannog and strode towards the door of his observatory.

'Come, we must hurry down and be ready to defend the threshold. There is no knowing who it might be. Oh, why hasn't Orundus come back: he must realize how anxious I am to know who it is. Now where did I leave my sword?'

The old man hurried down the stairway, pausing to throw each door open in turn and rummage through untidy cupboards or to delve beneath the haphazard clutter of furniture and long-forgotten debris in search of his sword.

'It has to be here somewhere! I can hardly defend the tower with my bare hands. What can we do, Grannog? Ah, yes, I know, it would have been different in the time of my magic . . .'

The dog padded along at his heels, seeming to listen to every word, but there was an edge of exasperation and regret creeping into the magician's voice. He couldn't even remember all the words of a finding spell without first searching out the parchment that dealt with such commonplace magic.

Grannog suddenly pricked up his ears, his pale, amber eyes reflecting brightly in the flickering lamplight: the sound of the horse was directly below the tower now. He lifted his muzzle, scented the air and growled, his hackles raised as he bounded down the last flight of steps to position himself in front of the heavy ironwood outer door.

Nevian sniffed, wrinkling his nose at the pungent odour of rotten leaves and moss that wafted through the tower. What in all Elundium could cause such a smell? He hurried after the dog, all thoughts of finding his sword forgotten.

Seven-fingered Umm, the Yerrak, kept a light but strong hold upon Sparkfire's bridle to prevent the horse who was carrying the unconscious body of the small boy sprawled in the strangely-shaped saddle from slipping on the treacherously steep mountain slope as they reached the summit of the rocky ridge and stopped. Umm squatted down and stared anxiously ahead, trying to remember by leaf, branch, rock and stone the way to the magician's tower. His brow was furrowed with concentration. Only once before, as a youngling, had he ventured this far away from the paths that his people followed through the high, inaccessible passes of the Emerald Mountains and then only by accident had he stumbled upon the deep gorge where the tower stood. Drawn by the sound of the waterfalls and the scent of the wild gooseberries, thornapples, jasmine and rosemary he had trespassed. The magic had jumped from between the trees and the moving colours of the rainbow cloak that the magician wore had terrified him and made him run for his life. He was still afraid now but need drove him; for the fate of all the Yerrak, he believed, rested upon his finding that place again and pleading with the magician to save this boy's life.

The Yerrak, whose people were once the proud rulers of Cawdor long before the time of the Granite Kings, had fallen into shadow and been almost forgotten with the fall of the citadel, save for mention in old legends and fairy tales. They had been reduced to shy, secretive, nomadic gatherers; simple, gentle creatures who lived on the edge of subsistence by harvesting the fruits of the forest. They knew each tree by name, each rock and stone, and all the secrets that were hidden amongst them. They moved slowly with each season, barely leaving trace of their passing – merely a broken twig or a footprint, as they travelled from the high passes in the mountains down through the petrified forest to feed on the black seaweed that was thrown up by the restless surf that boiled along the dark margin of their world. They had long lived in peace, shunning the world of men, until Umm had accidentally come upon the boy in the forest and stolen his hand. That terrible act had angered the Eretch, the grave-wraiths that infested the ruins of Cawdor, and he feared that they would never leave him and his people in peace without the boy's forgiveness.

Below the spot where Umm squatted in the cold

starlight, velvet shadows lay on a thickly-wooded valley. Tall, straggling pines and dense copses of mountain ash and silver birch fell away to a sheer crack between the mountain's shoulders. Could this be the place he sought? He leaned forward to scent the wind and stare down at the thick tangle of undergrowth that seemed to choke the head of the valley. Could that be the dark mouth of the gorge? Faintly he caught the cascading roar of the waterfalls and the sound of water rushing over stones as it fell into secret rock-pools, and there was a hint of wild rosemary, jasmine, nightflowers and pine resin in the air which stirred up memories of that last visit to the magician's tower.

'This must be the place,' he whispered in soft, musical tones as he rose quickly to his feet, spreading the seven toes of each foot to find a safe path down into the valley.

Suddenly, Sparkfire snorted with alarm and threw back his head, causing Drib to rock in the saddle and fall to one side. The whites of the horse's eyes were clearly visible in the starlight as his hooves skidded on the steep slope of debris left by the winter's avalanches. Loose shale, disturbed by the horse's feet, clattered and rolled down into the trees. Umm tightened his hold on the bridle and soon had the horse calmer as he used his considerable strength to slow the frightened animal down and together they climbed, step by step, down the steep path into the trees. Sparse clumps of mountain grass gave way to a thick carpet of pine needles as it grew darker and darker beneath the canopy. Ferns deadened the horse's hoofbeats and unseen branches brushed against them, snagging in Sparkfire's mane. Gradually the sound of rushing water grew louder as they descended towards the mouth of the gorge. Livid patches of moss and lichen covered the rocks and speckled the bark of the trees that crowded in on either side. Umm hesitated, scenting the night air, unsure of the path as the undergrowth became thicker. He didn't remember the valley being so choked with unkempt wildness when he had strayed beneath its trees as a youngling: then there had been lush grasses between his toes instead of sharp stones and the trees had grown in well-kept groves. He could remember birds singing in their branches and everywhere there had been succulent fruits that he had gorged himself upon – until the magic had frightened him away. But it *had* been *this* place, *this* was where the magician lived!

Sparkfire felt Drib's unconscious body begin to slip further and further to the right despite the two curved leather horns that Flock, the saddler, had sewn into the saddle to keep his crooked legs securely in place. The horse snorted in alarm and nudged the Yerak's furry arm with his muzzle, making the bit-rings jingle. Umm glanced back just in time to see the boy about to slip and fall to the ground. With a soft grunt of concern he caught the boy's limp body and set it straight in the saddle, draping him forwards with his arms on either side of the horse's neck. He touched the ugly wound on the back of Drib's head and bent down to listen to his shallow, thready breaths. The boy sounded much weaker now and his skin was growing colder.

'We must hurry, he will die!' Umm cried, forging ahead and pulling aside the low, overhanging branches only to be brought to a sudden halt by dense elder bushes, blackthorn and silverspikes with long, razor-sharp thorns that blocked their path and stretched away into the darkness – an impenetrable barrier for as far as he could see.

Umm bellowed with frustration, making the horse shy away as he attacked the wall of thorns, pulling and tearing at the tangled mass of branches, trying to force a path.

He had to break through, to find a way to the magician's tower and beg for his help. He couldn't bear to think what would happen to his people if he failed and the boy died. But with a yelp of pain he was forced to retreat, the thick, leathery skin of his forearms and hands cut and bleeding. The tangle of branches rustled and sprang back into place as though he had never tried to tear them apart.

Umm sank down onto his haunches and licked at his sore hands. Tears of despair began to well up in his gentle eyes. He didn't know what to do now. Somewhere in the darkness away to his left Sparkfire whinnied softly, calling to him. The Yerrak looked up, realizing that the horse must have wandered off while he was trying to break through the thorns. Umm followed the horse's hoofprints through the undergrowth. The sound of a mountain stream rushing its way down towards the gorge grew suddenly louder. With a rustle he pushed his way through a dense clump of giant bracken fronds and found the horse standing up to its hocks in a high bank of knapweed and woundwort on the edge of a stream.

'You must not wander off like that: it won't help our cause,' Umm grumbled, reaching for the horse's bridle only to pause and stare at where the stream narrowed in racing ripples between high banks before disappearing beneath the barrier of thorns. The lower branches hung a good hand's span above the water's glistening surface.

'I think you have found us a path. Look, there is space beneath the thorns: all is not lost,' whispered Umm, his wide mouth splitting into a smile as he caressed the horse's neck. He let go of the bridle before slithering down the bank, ploughing a wide break in the nettles and brambles and crushing the bracken flat before calling the horse to follow. With a splash he entered the icy water and waded out.

Sparkfire slithered down the bank with a snort, his ears flattened as the water quickly rose to his flanks. He followed Umm out into the swift-flowing current. The stones and boulders on the bed of the stream rolled beneath his hooves making him flounder. Umm reached out with a strong, steadying hand and calmed the horse as they slowly moved towards the impenetrable barrier of thorns. He was forced to sink lower, bending his knees. First his broad, muscular shoulders and then his squat neck disappeared and finally his chin was below the surface of the water before he was able to wade beneath the overhanging tangle of branches. Sharp thorns caught in his thick mane, pricking and gouging his scalp painfully. The Yerrak paused in the confined space and reached ahead, running his fingers over the mass of thorny branches. Most of them trailed so low that they almost touched the water. Shuffling a little forward and peering ahead he thought he caught a glimpse of starlight reflecting on the ripples of the stream beyond the dark bulk of the tangled thorn branches.

'I think we can force our way through under here. Follow me!' he called, tightening his grip on the horse's reins and inhaling a deep breath as he sank even lower.

The water swirled up around his flat nostrils as he tried to step forward but the reins suddenly became taut in his hand as the horse pulled him backwards making him lose his balance. Umm clutched wildly at the branches above his head and sharp thorns pierced his skin as he turned awkwardly to struggle against the current and retrace his steps.

He emerged from beneath the thorny barrier and tried to pull Sparkfire forwards but the horse neighed fiercely and repeatedly threw up his head in refusal, ears flattened, nostrils flared as instinct warned him that the gap was too narrow and the current too strong. The water was already washing against the saddle-flaps and was close to breaking over Drib's knees: if it became any deeper and the boy slipped, he would drown.

Umm couldn't see why the horse wouldn't follow and he scratched his forehead as he stared at the barrier ahead of them. There was no other way he could see of getting to the magician's tower. Then he remembered what the elders of the tribe had once told him and he realized why Sparkfire wouldn't follow him through the gap: horses were afraid of putting their heads into water.

'Wait,' he whispered to the horse as he moved forward and stood beneath the thorns to reach up with bloodied fingers and untangle the lower branches. One by one, using all the skill of leaf and branch that he knew, he bent and wove the trailing twigs and razor-sharp spikes together into a tight, secure archway that rose above the centre of the stream, just high enough for them to wade through side by side, both their heads above the water.

'Stay close, we will get through safely, I promise,' Umm reassured the frightened animal as he tried once again to coax him forward, but Sparkfire still refused to move. He hadn't understood much of what the Yerrak had said to him ever since they had caught up with him and Drib in the petrified forest after their flight from the destruction of Cawdor, but he had understood enough from their musical voices to know that they didn't mean any harm and he had let Umm lead them into the Emerald Mountains because he sensed that he wanted to take Drib to somebody who would save his life; but he still feared that Drib would slip beneath the water and drown.

'We must go on, there is no other way!' cried Umm in exasperation, pulling hard on the reins: but that only made Sparkfire snort and shy away.

Umm couldn't understand what was wrong. The arch-way was high enough for both of them and he could see no other danger. He moved in close to the horse's shoulder, keeping a firm grip on the reins, and lifted Drib's head up from the horse's neck to cradle it in his arms, holding it safe above the rushing water. 'No harm will come to the boy, I promise,' Umm promised.

Sparkfire whinnied softly as he saw Umm lift Drib's head and he let the Yerrak lead him forward. At last they seem to have understood each other. They moved slowly beneath the barrier of thorns. Night insects swarmed around their heads in the dark, stifling space and the water frothed against them as the current eddied dangerously, threatening to topple them over where the stream nar-rowed between the high banks. Sparkfire floundered and Umm staggered as ribbons of snakeweed curled around their legs. The Yerrak spread out his toes amongst the shifting, slippery stones on the streambed and held on tightly to Drib as they fought to keep their balance. One giant stride began to break through the snakeweed and then two more and the dark, tangled mass of branches above their heads began to thin out. The starlight reflecting on the broken ripples ahead was getting brighter.

Umm gave a gasp of relief as they waded out from beneath the thorny branches and eased his hold on Drib, letting him lie forward against Sparkfire's neck as the treacherous current slackened and the stream widened out between low banks of lush vegetation. The air was heavy with the scent of wild garlic and rosemary; jasmine was intertwined with pure white nightflowers that bloomed and trailed in the water. Above their heads the stars were visible between the branches of the tall, black ebonies and ironwoods that grew in dark groves beside the stream. Shoals of rainbow fish and swordtails dived and darted through the shallows, reflecting the brilliance of the starlight in their phosphorescent scales, scattering amongst the weeds as they approached. Umm brought them to a halt and looked ahead at the sheer cliffs that rose from behind the trees on either side of the mouth of the gorge. They seemed to reach halfway to the stars. A single, high span of rock arched between them, carved with strange, contorted figures, signs and symbols that were almost obscured by a thick, hanging tracery of flowering vines and brilliantly coloured orchids. The air was moist and full of the thunder of unseen waterfalls. He had not been wrong; the mouth of the Runesgate Gorge was almost exactly as he remembered it, heady with the scent of wild blossoms. The shadows between the trees were softly silvered and mysterious but his heartbeats suddenly quickened and a cold shiver tingled along his spine as he caught a glimpse of the magician's tower on a high promontory, silhouetted against the night sky. For a moment his courage failed him. What if the magician were to strike him down for trespassing where he should not wander? He would have turned and fled but he looked down at Drib's unconscious body and remembered what disaster would befall his people if he did not beg the Master of Magic to save this boy's life. Another glance at Drib was enough to convince him that they had to hurry.

'Come on,' he urged the horse, catching at Sparkfire's reins. 'I'm sure we will be able to follow this stream down into the mouth of the gorge, and from there a steep, winding path should take us up through the trees to the tower . . .' Umm hesitated and then added slowly, 'not that I have ever dared to come this close . . .'

He hurried forward, keeping to the shallows and reaching out with his free hand to brush aside the giant bracken fronds and the purple-fruited brambleheads that hung down to trail across the water. Sparkfire splashed along wearily beside him, head down, hooves clattering over the loose stones and shingle on the streambed, kicking up plumes of spray as he moved along. Together they were forced to scramble over slippery weirs and wade through deep, still, silent pools, sending out widening ripples that disturbed the clouds of iridescent insects hovering across their starlit surfaces. At last they reached the dense shadows cast by the towering cliffs which guarded the entrance to the gorge. Umm brought the horse to a halt and stared up at the cliffs. They were far too steep for him to scale and he couldn't see a path for Sparkfire. Immediately ahead the stream tumbled over a weir and disappeared beneath a thick veil of vines and creepers. Clearly the Runesgate was blocked, the way ahead shut, and it obviously had not been disturbed for ages.

Umm realized that he would have to try to break through, for there was no way of getting underneath. Swallowing a nervous breath he glanced anxiously over his shoulder: there was no way of knowing when or where the magic might appear, or what it would do to him. But he had to try to reach the magician, it was the only way.

'Wait here,' he whispered to Sparkfire as he waded cautiously forward until he reached the weir. Bracing himself against the slippery rocks, up to his waist in the water, he pushed both his hands into the mass of vines and tried to pull them apart. Nothing happened. He paused and then tried again, this time pulling harder. Gradually the thick veil trembled and parted a finger's breadth. It stayed open just long enough for him to glimpse steep wooded slopes with waterfalls plunging down beyond the cliffs into the depths of the gorge, and there was a clear path – flat rocks risen above the bed of the river in the bottom of the gorge – that they could follow; and by the look of it a winding track led up through the trees. The tower high up on its promontory of rock looked so tantalizingly close. So close that he could see a curling thread of smoke rising from its chimney. So close that he felt he could almost reach out and touch it. But it might as well be beyond the dark side of morning if he failed to break through the Runesgate.

'I must ... I must,' he muttered over and over again, summoning all his strength to try once more. The muscles across his shoulders and along his forearms knotted and bulged. He ground his teeth together and grunted with the effort, violently shaking the vines as he attempted to tear them apart. Loose stones broke free from the arch high above his head and rained down, splashing into the water around him, but he wouldn't give up. The interwoven stems trembled and shook in his hands and delicate, brilliantly coloured flowerheads broke off to drift down as thick as snowflakes around his shoulders before settling on the water, bobbing and turning as the current took them over the weir. Umm's muscles were burning and his lungs felt as though they were going to burst. He was just about to give up when the vines began to snap and break as they tore apart.

'Quickly, come on, there's no time to lose. The magic may strike us at any moment when it sees what I have just done. Come on!' Umm urged, pulling the creeper apart until the gap was wide enough for Sparkfire to follow. He clambered over the rim of the weir and reached up for the horse's bridle to steady him as he scrambled down into the deeper water. Three huge, crumbling steps through the cascading water and they were in the gorge. Umm broke into a long, loping gait and Sparkfire trotted beside him through the shallower pools as they crossed the river that meandered through the bottom of the valley.

Slowly they climbed up onto the narrow, rocky path that passed behind the waterfalls and edged their way through the shifting curtain of spray only a handspan from the rushing water. The air was full of swirling silver rainbows and the deafening roar and thunder of the falls that soaked through the Yerrak's coarse fur. The water trickled coldly down the back of Drib's neck, beading into glistening droplets on his armour and soaking through his clothes. The small, unconscious boy shivered and groaned as he shifted slightly in the saddle before lying limp and still again. His weak movements went completely unnoticed in the roaring darkness behind the falls as Umm hurried them up onto firmer ground.

'It isn't far now. Look, you can see the magician's tower up there above us. I only hope he isn't too angry with us for trespassing here.' The Yerrak paused and frowned, tilting his head. 'Listen,' he hissed, fear widening his eyes as he stared up at the tower. 'There is a wild wind rising, in the tower. The magician must be very angry. What are we to do?'

Suddenly a flash of lightning leapt up out of the chimney and crackled across the starlit sky, vividly lighting up the gorge.

'Forgive us for trespassing, please, we only came here because of the boy. Help us, I beg you, help us,' Umm wailed, collapsing in terror, losing his grip on the horse's reins as he fell to his knees, but his pleas went unheeded.

Stinging clouds of dust, hot ashes and pillars of flame spat out of the chimney. Brilliant orbs of ball lightning shot up into the air, rising in a blazing arc that raced across the night sky and fell hissing and spitting amongst the trees where Umm cowered. Sparkfire neighed in terror, spinning round and shying into the undergrowth as dozens of balls of fire landed all around him, exploding into millions of white-hot sparks that fizzed between his hooves. Cantering wildly, he broke through the trees, his bit-rings jangling madly, as Drib's body jolted roughly from side to side while the horse followed the steep track up towards the tower.

'No, come back, Sparkfire, come back. Don't go any closer! Can't you see that we have angered the magician enough, he may kill us for trespassing here. Turn and run for your life – escape while you can . . .' Umm's voice was drowned out by the sudden, ferocious deluge that thrashed the undergrowth, flattening the bracken fronds and breaking off branches as thick as his arms before hurling them to the ground all around him. Torrents of water suddenly flooded down the steep sides of the gorge, racing towards him and making Umm leap to his feet and cling on to the largest tree that he could reach, climbing up into its lower branches only moments before an avalanche of rocks and broken trees swept down past him in a rush to reach the bottom of the gorge.

The storm abated as abruptly as it had begun but Umm remained, trembling and hidden in the branches of the tree, barely daring to uncover his eyes. It was only worry for Sparkfire and Drib's safety that eventually made the Yerrak curl his toes securely around a stout branch and reach up to part the thick canopy of leaves above his head to search the gorge for any sight or sound of them. He heard the creaking rattle of the shutters from the tower as they were thrown open and he looked up, holding his breath. He caught a glimpse of raw rainbow colours streaking across the pane as the window swung open. The magician's ancient face appeared in the gap, pale and sunken with shadows, but there was a glint of a piercing eye on either side of his beak-sharp nose as he bent forward to stare down into the gorge. Umm heard the distinct clatter of Sparkfire's hooves as they crossed the loose shale that the deluge had deposited amongst the trees to the right of the tower. An uneasy combination of emotions – relief that he had survived the terrible storm and terror that the magician would see him at any moment – swept through the gentle Yerrak.

'Sparkfire – stand, stand perfectly still, hide amongst the trees until the magician's eye has passed over you,' he hissed as loudly as he dare, but his warning came too late.

The figure at the high window turned in the direction of the sound of hooves and a dog snarled and barked within the tower, making Umm's blood run cold. At that moment the huge, dark shape of a Battle Owl flew silently out through the open window to soar and hover above the gorge. Umm shrank down, letting the leaves close over the top of his head so that he vanished from sight as its shadow passed slowly over his hiding place. Owls were different from all other birds; they could see in the dark and there was a touch of magic in their silent flight-feathers that he feared. He remembered how an owl used to sit on the boy's shoulder or follow him everywhere. Orundus suddenly shrieked and flew away from where Umm was hiding to vanish amongst the treetops. Umm scrambled down and silently followed the bird's path.

Orundus, Lord of Owls, had once, in times long forgotten, known the names of all the Nighthorses who had been gathered on the dark side of morning, just as he had once known all the names of the riders who had been mounted upon them to keep the last lamp of Underfall burning during the darkest daylights of the Granite Kings. Spreading his flight-feathers in the chill updraughts of the night air, the owl looked down and recognized Sparkfire as one of their descendants. He saw that the horse was gaunt and weary from a long journey and that he carried an unconscious rider in battered armour. The Battle Owl knew that great need must have driven the horse to bring his rider into the Runesgate Gorge to seek Nevian's help. He stooped swiftly to the cantle of the saddle, calling out to the horse to tell it that he would guide them to the threshold of the tower.

'No . . . no . . . come back, don't let that owl show you the way . . . don't listen to it . . .' Umm whispered in dread. He held his head in his hands and rocked back and forth in despair. It was his fault that they were here in the magician's gorge: he had brought them and he knew he would have to follow Sparkfire up to the tower to plead with the magician not to take the boy's life. He would have to surrender himself to the Master of Magic as punishment for trespassing and it was with leaden footsteps that he slowly climbed up through the trees.

II

A Remedy for Sore Heads and Broken Bones

NEVIAN gathered up the folds of his rainbow cloak to stop the hems trailing through the puddles on the flagstones in the main chamber of the tower as he hurried towards the heavy, ironwood doors. He muttered to himself, trying to reawaken forgotten memories, and pulled the cloak protectively around his shoulders. There was something so familiar about that pungent odour of rotten leaves and moss that had suddenly wafted through the tower as the intruder drew closer, something hovering on the edge of his memory that should have given him a clue to who it might be. New, magical colours might have mysteriously infused the threads of his cloak, giving it weight and substance but they certainly had not shown any signs of improving his memory, so far. What was it about that smell? He frowned irritably: there was more to it than damp, autumn leaves, wet bark and mushrooms, he was sure of that.

Nevian almost tripped over Grannog who had positioned himself directly in front of the outer door. He cursed, grabbing at a high-backed chair to keep his balance, scattering the untidy pile of scrolls that filled its sagging seat. Grannog edged closer to the door, crouching, his hackles ridged along his back. A low growl rumbled in his throat and his lips were puckered and stretched tightly back to expose his blunt, yellowing fangs. The magician glanced down at the dog who was now ready to leap in his defence and remembered how, when the dog had been in his prime, he had fought savagely to defend him against a swarm of Nightbeasts in the mouth of night. Tears filled his eyes as he smiled and shook his head.

'Stay close to me, old boy, and don't attack unless I tell you. I have a feeling that whoever it is out there doesn't pose a threat.'

Grannog reluctantly moved in close to the hems of the magician's cloak and his growl softened but did not altogether die away as Nevian drew back the ornate metal bolts one by one. A firm turn of the key and the door rode open, creaking on its hinges.

'Now let us get to the bottom of this mystery and find out what this smell of wet leaves and mushrooms is all about, shall we?' Nevian muttered, reaching up for the guttering reed lamp hanging in its iron basket beside the door jamb.

'Trespassers indeed,' he grumbled, trimming the wick.

Holding the lamp aloft he strode out of the tower. 'Show yourselves! Come forward, whoever you are! Who has the audacity to trespass inside the Runesgate? Come forward this minute!' The magician moved the lamp from left to right and peered out into the darkness.

Sparkfire snorted in alarm when he heard the anger in the old man's voice and saw the strange-coloured lights that reflected from his cloak in the lamplight. Bright topaz and saffron with soft, mulberry hues spilled out across the threshold where the Master of Magic was standing. The light flooded towards the horse, illuminating every pebble, rock and tuft of grass, weaving in amongst the branches of the trees that surrounded them until the light seemed to trap him in the swirling, shifting colours. The horse arched his neck, eyes white with fright as he tried to shy away, but Orundus hooted, telling him to stand still, that he had nothing to fear from the magician.

'Walk towards the tower: let Nevian see the wounded rider upon your back.'

The owl spread his wings and lifted from the cantle of the saddle to fly to the old man's shoulder, informing him in low hoots that the trespassers posed no threat but were merely a weary horse with an injured warrior lying across the saddle.

'Yes, yes, of course, I can see that quite clearly for myself, but they don't have that strange smell about them do they?' Nevian replied, sniffing the air around him.

'Are you sure they are alone?'

'I am the Lord of Owls! None would have escaped my blinkless eyes as I flew over the gorge!' Orundus shrieked. His feathers ruffled with indignation as he flew up to perch in the branches of a white oak tree that grew close to the tower.

'I'm not so sure,' Nevian muttered to himself, hurrying down the tower steps with Grannog close to his heels.

Sparkfire threw up his head. The muscles rippled across his gaunt flanks as he backed away.

'Be easy. I'm not going to hurt you,' the old man smiled, reaching out slowly and touching the horse's trembling neck gently with his free hand.

Sparkfire whinnied and lowered his head, reassured by the magician's soft voice and sure touch. He rubbed his muzzle against the man's arm, feeling the warmth of the cloak against his skin.

'Now what have we here?' Nevian murmured as he moved closer to the saddle and leaned over the small, unconscious body of the rider. His eyebrows drew together with concern as he lifted his lamp and saw in its light the battered armour and the ugly wound across the back of the boy's head. He brushed away the tangled fringe of hair and rubbed away the dirt and the leaves hiding the rider's face and then let out a startled gasp. The rider was a mere boy, barely old enough to bear arms, let alone stand up to the shock and sway of the battle which had left him severely wounded. As he got closer he realized that there was something remarkably familiar about the boy's face; but where in all Elundium had he seen it before? And by what improbable twists of fate had this boy found his way to the Runesgate – to the threshold of his tower? Nevian frowned and absently stroked his chin. Nothing, he knew, ever happened by chance: there was a greater scheme to things, there was a sway and purpose to fate as it trod out the future. So why was the boy here?

The old magician sighed. Questions would have to wait. The sooner he got the boy into the tower and applied oiled cottons of black amber and soothing lotions of rose-hip and camphor to the wounds and bound him up with a healing liniment of jalap, coriander seeds and nightflower petals, the sooner the boy would regain consciousness and then he would have the answer to the riddle. Nevian was sure he could not have come alone. There wasn't a horse in all the world who could have found its way into the Runesgate Gorge, except, perhaps the Lord of Horses and the one that carried the boy was certainly no lord. Nevian looked into the dark depths of the gorge. The smell of wet leaves and mushrooms was getting stronger. Grannog snarled and edged protectively forward.

'Stay close. Watch the trees, but don't attack. Don't move unless I tell you,' Nevian whispered, reaching up to hang the lamp from one of the branches of a tree where it swung slightly in the chill night breezes, its pool of light shifting backwards and forwards across the limp body of the boy.

'Now, let's get you inside,' he muttered, bending down to gather the lad in his arms.

With a grunt of effort the old man tried to straighten his back only to find he couldn't. The boy looked small and light enough for him to lift with one hand but he couldn't move him at all. He appeared to be stuck fast in the saddle.

'That's very odd.' Nevian moved closer and changed his grip to try again, only to feel the boy's out-turned leg and twisted foot catch against his leg and snag in the folds of his cloak.

'Perhaps someone has tied you to the saddle to prevent you from falling off,' he frowned, carefully pulling the boy's unconscious body upright.

The magician paused and stared down at the boy's crooked legs and the way they were held securely in the saddle by two curved, leather horns that had been cleverly sewn into the knee rolls. Seeing the boy's crippled legs suddenly nudged the magician's memory.

'You're Drib, aren't you? You are the penniless chimney-sweep's apprentice. Yes, of course, I remember you now!' At once he realized why it had taken so long for him to place their meeting: it had been a small matter of no real consequence – or had it?

With the passing of the last Granite King his power had begun to wane, and for some inexplicable reason he had been prevented from using the last of his shrinking magic to help Thanehand, the first King of Men, consolidate his victory over the forces of darkness after the Battle of the Rising. The King had had to find his own way through the chaos of government in order to build himself a new world while, by some perverse twist of fate, the magician had been increasingly drawn into the insignificant troubles of the ordinary folk of Elundium. He had been called away from his tower by the clamour of so many of their voices as they wished for him to settle silly arguments or see that common justice was done that it had become quite wearisome. They had been exhausting, irritating times of triviality that had all too quickly squandered the last of his magic and, he had thought, served little purpose. But now, seeing Drib so totally transformed from that ragged chimneysweep's apprentice, dressed in armour and mounted upon a fine horse, he wondered: what magic had he nurtured that night in the cellars beneath Candlebane Hall? What tiny ripple had he touched to widen and spread out across the liquid surface of fate?

He could remember Drib's voice all right. That cry of sheer, dark despair and hopelessness that had drawn him out of his tower and across the night-shrouded leagues of Elundium into the damp, gloomy cellars beneath the Candlehall. He could remember where the boy had been imprisoned, falsely accused of beating a pony almost to death in the breaking yards. Drib had cried out for the truth to be heard because nobody would believe in his innocence. He had been driven to the brink of despair to think that anybody could believe him capable of laying a hand on the pony. But there had been more to it than that. The boy had been tormented and cruelly treated, mocked and cursed because of his crippled legs from the day he had been born and yet never once had he complained or become bitter. He had never indulged in self-pity even though poverty overwhelmed him and circumstances forced him to become a chimneysweep's scramble. Quite the contrary, throughout all this crushing misery that he had been forced to endure he had held onto his secret dreams, his love of horses and the impossible idea that one daylight, despite his crooked legs, he would ride. Unfortunately it had been that simple dream that had driven others to conspire against him and fuelled all that hateful jealousy. Anger had stirred in the magician's heart as he had listened to the boy's story in the cellar. Enough anger for him to reach beneath the folds of his rainbow cloak for the small, sky-blue pouch that hung there stuffed full of the seeds of doubt. He had let Drib cast a handful of those seeds away into the darkness to make Breakmaster, the King's horseman who had once befriended the young lad, think again and realize how impossible it would be for Drib to commit such a crime.

Nevian had never given much thought to the outcome of young Drib throwing the seeds, but his face softened into a smile as he carefully eased the boy's legs out from beneath the curved leather horns and gathered him up in his arms. He had certainly come a long way from those dark, hopeless moments in the cellar and the seeds must have done their work. Nevian felt sure there were other vague images of Drib on the edges of his memory but they would have to wait. He was about to turn and hurry up the steps into the tower when Grannog suddenly leapt forward, barking furiously at something in the dense undergrowth just beyond the circle of light cast by the lamp. The pungent odour of rotten leaves, moss and mushrooms filled the air.

'Come out, whoever you are. I command you to come out and show yourself, before I slip the leash and set Grannog on you! Orundus – be still, stay where you are,' Nevian commanded as the owl spread his wings to stoop.

The bushes rustled and moved apart as a huge, dark, hairy figure stood up and slowly shuffled forward. Umm knew they were in black trouble for trespassing in the Runesgate. There could be no doubt about it now. The magician had sensed their presence the moment they passed beneath the last waterfall and it had angered him. Why else would he have conjured up that ferocious storm

41

if not to wash them away? And he had known instantly that the storm had failed. That was why he had sent out the owl to scour the gorge and find them. Umm had been lucky enough to spot the owl as it flew from the tower and quick-witted enough to duck back beneath the thick canopy of leaves and stay out of sight while it soared over him; but Sparkfire either hadn't heard his whispered warning or had not realized the danger they were in, for the owl had spotted him almost immediately and had swooped down to perch on the cantle of his saddle, pecking at the boy's armoured arm and hooting and shrieking as if to tell the whole world that he had found the trespassers while he forced the horse to climb up to the tower.

All Umm's plans to save his people lay in ruins, but he could not slink away unseen and undiscovered. He could not abandon Sparkfire and the boy: his simple sense of honour would not allow him to. No, he would have to surrender himself. His shoulders sagged with bleak despair as he followed in Sparkfire's hoofprints up the steep side of the gorge, but deep down a spark of hope flickered. Perhaps if he threw himself down at the magician's feet he would relent and put aside his anger just long enough to listen to his plea and spare the boy's life. But as he drew closer the tower rose sheer and terrible through the thinning trees and the open door was filled by the magician's silhouette as he stood with a huge, savage dog at his side. Both figures were haloed in such dazzling, magical light that Umm's courage faltered and failed and he sank down, trembling, amongst the dense undergrowth. He wanted to draw his arms over the top of his head and cover his eyes in despair but he could not. There was something about the soft sway of the magician's lantern and the warm pool of light that surrounded him as he descended the steps of the tower; his voice was fierce but not terrible as Umm had imagined it would be. He crept stealthily closer to the tower, irresistibly drawn by the beautiful lines of light that shimmered in the folds of the magician's cloak. He crouched behind some undergrowth on the edge of the clearing, only a hand's span from the circle of light that was thrown out by the lamp. He was afraid to take another step. He parted the thick brambles and bindweed with his leathery fingertips to watch with bated breath as Sparkfire shied at the old man's approach and then stood still and submitted to his gentle words. Umm watched Nevian's face soften into a smile as he caressed the horse and bent to examine the boy before gathering him up in his arms. The Yerrak felt a shiver of apprehension run up his spine as the Master of Magic turned to carry the unconscious body of the boy up to his tower.

Umm knew he had to act quickly, had to surrender himself and make the magician understand why he had brought the boy here. He half-rose and opened his mouth to cry out but fear strangled the words in his throat and froze him to the spot. The huge dog crouched beside the magician and turned his head in his direction as he moved. Umm glimpsed snarling fangs as Grannog leapt forward. In the light of the lamp Umm saw the owl spread its wings to stare down, unblinking, to look at him from a branch high up in the tree beside the tower. He was discovered. He knew from the sound of the magician's voice that he was being told to come forward and show himself. Umm swallowed and stood up, trembling from head to foot and shuffled slowly into the light. He would only have one chance to plead with the magician. Keeping a watchful eye on the snarling dog the Yerrak held out his empty hands as a sign of submission and began to speak, his deep, musical voice rising and falling, but panic began to tighten its grip upon him as a look of bewilderment spread across the magician's face. He spoke faster, his voice rising now into shrill notes that echoed the wind thrashing through the trees and the roar of water tumbling over waterfalls. He tried to gesticulate with the seven fingers of each hand, to act out the destruction of Cawdor. He drew weird, shadowy shapes in the air to mimic the Eretch who had brought about the citadel's ruin and caused the terrible wounds to the boy.

Nevian frowned and shook his head in confusion. Of all the peoples of the world he could not put a name to this strange, hairy, seven-fingered figure who had emerged from the undergrowth and yet he felt there was a remnant of a lost culture in its simple gestures. There was something about him that was as old as time itself and he was sure that the soft, musical sounds it made were the echoes of a once beautiful language. There was a gentleness in its jet-black eyes that tugged at ancient memories.

Nevian studied the Yerrak's simple but frantic gestures for a moment longer. It wasn't too difficult to understand from the way he kept pointing at the wound on the back of Drib's head and then gingerly touching the boy's sword-arm, cowering back between each movement and drawing his arms over the top of his head before covering his eyes and his hands in an obvious sign of despair, that he feared that Drib was about to die of his injuries. Nevian glanced down at the hand Umm had been touching and wondered how he could have missed such an injury. He eased back the torn and bloodied sleeve, pulling it away as far as he could, and his eyebrows rose in dismay. The skin was blackened and bruised and the raw, splintered ends of the bones had ruptured through the skin just above the wrist. It had clearly been a savage blow that had caused such damage. He carefully pulled the sleeve back into place.

44

'You want me to heal Drib? Is that why you have brought him here? You want me to save his life?' The old man smiled, Drib was getting heavy and he gathered him more securely in his arms, but as he turned back towards the tower he looked quizzically at the Yerrak.

'But why here? How did you know about my tower? Surely there must be healers much closer to where the boy received these injuries, healers with more skill than I have for setting broken bones and mending sore heads?'

Umm held his breath, listening intently to the tone of the magician's voice. He didn't sound as angry as he thought he would: perhaps he wasn't going to kill them for trespassing after all. Suddenly Umm remembered the purpose of their journey and he rummaged in the pouch hidden by the coarse covering of hair that hung down over his flanks. He held out the crumpled battle glove that he had once accidentally stolen from the boy, still believing it to be his hand.

'No, no, that won't be necessary,' Nevian laughed, shaking his head at the offered glove. 'I think it will be some time before young Drib will be putting anything on that hand, don't you? But we have wasted quite enough time out here in the cold: follow me and I will see what I can do to heal his wounds and set his broken bones.'

With a rustle of soft silk and with melting colours flowing out around him Nevian retraced his steps and walked to the door of the tower, pausing only when he realized that the creature had not followed him. He glanced back across his shoulder to see that the simple creature who smelled so strongly of the forest was still crouching in the dirt beside Drib's horse where he had left him.

'Come on, hurry, there is nothing to be afraid of. Bring the horse up to the tower: you will find stables to the right of the steps. You can unsaddle him there and then come in out of the cold and warm yourself up by the fire while I tend to Drib,' he called out, making slow, deliberate gesture to show that Umm should follow him.

The Yerrak hesitated. He had delivered the boy into the magician's care and from the tone of his voice and the way he had carried him up into his tower he was sure he would make him well, but he did not wish to go with them into the tower. He had never been inside a dwelling in his life and he was afraid, but he couldn't just run away, not yet, not until he had made the magician take the boy's hand and made him understand that his people needed his forgiveness for stealing it from him. When he had done that then he could leave. Umm looked wistfully back across the gorge to the distant mountain. He could just make it out in the starlight, through the gap in the cliffs that formed the Runesgate. His home in the forest with his own people seemed so far away.

'Come on, we haven't got all night,' the magician's voice cut into Umm's regrets, making him rise reluctantly to his feet. He took a hesitant step forward, but fear of the magician's dog who crouched in the path ahead of him and of the owl who still stared down at him from the tree beside the tower brought him to a halt. His people had always feared dogs and with good reason. The huntsmen who lived high amongst the mountains above the petrified forest hunted his people mercilessly with huge, savage leash-hounds whenever the changing of the seasons forced them to travel through the forest in their search for food. Whenever they travelled to the surf that thundered along the dark margin of their world to feed on the seaweed that collected below the haunted, shadowy ruins of Cawdor, they would be savaged by these dogs. Umm stopped and sniffed the air suspiciously. His hair ridged and pricked across his broad, muscular shoulders and rose on the back of his squat neck. The scent of Grannog was too powerful: it sapped his courage. The dog was growling softly, fangs bared, and Umm retreated, knees trembling. Sparkfire sensed the Yerrak's fear and whinnied, stepping between him and the dog as Umm sank to his haunches and covered his eyes, his voice rising and falling with a sound no louder than a weeping child begging not to be hurt.

Nevian watched the Yerrak's hesitation with exasperation. 'Now, what's the matter? Surely he can see I won't harm him? He let me take the boy off the horse – why won't he come into the tower?' the old man muttered with impatience. 'As if I haven't got a thousand more urgent things to do.'

Patience was not, and never had been, the magician's strong point, being quite unnecessary in most things magical; that was why his crumbling memory was so tiresome. He grew weary of having to read all those simple spells that had once been his to command, let alone the more complicated ones. 'Come along, come along,' he cried, motioning as slowly and clearly as possible to encourage the Yerrak to follow him into the tower.

Almost anybody else who had trespassed into the gorge would have received the sharp edge of his tongue for the interruption and would certainly have been left outside to cool their heels until he found time to grant them an audience, but he didn't want this strange, simple creature of the forest to wander off and disappear while he was attending to the boy's injuries. So much of Elundium was his creation. His spirit dwelt in the wind that rustled the leaves in the trees, the swirling eddies of dust at the start of each road; in fact everything held a little touch of his magic, so how had he overlooked this simple, seven-fingered people? Who and what were they? He couldn't just let Umm vanish until he had at least attempted to learn a little of his beautiful language.

'Grannog – Orundus – bring our reluctant guest into the great chamber, but be gentle. He is obviously very frightened. See to it while I heal this boy.'

Nevian hurried into the tower and climbed up the winding stairway to a small bedchamber on the first galleried landing. Grannog growled softly and circled around behind the Yerrak, keeping low to the ground as Orundus stooped to hover above his head, hooting softly and beating his wings. Umm tried to turn and flee but found the savage dog snarling and advancing towards him as the owl's outstretched talons raked through the coarse, matted hair on the top of his head. Umm wailed in terror and ran towards the tower, stumbling awkwardly up the steps as he heard the dog snapping at his heels.

Nevian rummaged through the crowded apothecary shelves and cupboards on the first floor of his tower as he searched out the potions and apparatus that he would need to heal Drib's wounds.

'Now, where did I put the essence of cuckoo's spit? It should be with the oil of camphor and the gall of hare,' he muttered, sneezing as he wiped away the thick layers of dust and cobwebs that had accumulated on the rows of odd-shaped bottles and jars. He peered closely at the spidery inscriptions scratched on the thick, greenish jars that described the virtues of the thousands of liniments, embrocations and vile-coloured drenches and compounds they contained. Good sense told him that it would prob-ably be easier to set the broken bones while the boy was still unconscious and he carried everything he thought he would need into the bedchamber: two slender splints of fossilized ebony, no longer than the boy's forearm, and enough golden thread to bind them securely; a wide-bellied jar containing hundreds of tiny arach – silk-weaving spiders who were no longer than grains of sand – whose webs he would need to cover the wound and prevent it from turning septic once he had set the bones. He searched around and found the ingredients for a poultice and finally a large jug of ground chalcedony, peacock's ore and snow-water mixed into a thick paste that would set as hard as stone once he had rubbed it into strips of pure linen which he would wrap around Drib's arm to keep it immobile until the bones had knitted together again. Picking up the jar of tiny arachs he gave it a gentle shake and the spiders scattered, running around and around the inside of the jar, weaving their gossamer webs.

It was lucky for Drib that he did not regain consciousness before Nevian attempted to set his broken arm. The magician knotted a stout length of rope around the boy's wrist, turned it once around the newel post of the bed and then pulled hard, grunting with the effort as he stretched the damaged forearm. Blood oozed up around the splintered bone ends and out of the wound as he twisted and pulled on the rope. The boy groaned and shuddered. Suddenly the ends of the bone disappeared and they touched, grinding together. Nevian felt along the forearm, pressing both of the bones into the correct position before securing the rope to hold the arm while he fitted the splints on either side of the break and bound them together with the golden thread. Next he cleaned the injury thoroughly with oiled cottons before dipping his hand into the jar of silk-weaving spiders. The cool, delicate webs clung to his fingers and it took only a moment to make a sticky poultice using the essence of cuckoo's spit, starwort, camphor oil and loosestrife which he spread liberally over the wound, pressing it down over the ragged edges of skin. He wound the strips of linen soaked with the thick, stone paste he had mixed up, around and around Drib's arm from above his elbow to the middle of the palm of his hand, leaving only a small hole so that he could untie the rope from around his wrist once it had set.

Nevian washed his hands and returned the jars and potions to the apothecary's shelves while he waited for the stone paste to set hard. When he was satisfied, he loosed the rope from the bedpost, unknotting it carefully and removing it from Drib's wrist. 'Well, that should be as good as new once it has healed,' he smiled, slowly and gently moving each one of the boy's fingers in turn.

Humming a tuneless dirge he turned his attention to the ugly wound on the back of Drib's head, cleaning away the thick crust of dried blood and dirt with oiled cloths to reveal a ragged gash. His eyebrows rose in surprise as he discovered a large, blackened bruise about the size of the head of a battle-mace just above the gash. There were small, regular, darker indentations spread across the bruise that suggest to the magician that the mace had been spiked.

'You can count yourself lucky, my boy, that you were wearing a helm when that weapon struck you: without it a blow like that would have split your skull in two, there's no doubt about that at all.'

Drib groaned as his eyelids fluttered. He could feel gentle hands touching him and far, far away through the well of darkness and oblivion that had enfolded him from the moment he had been struck down in the courtyard of Cawdor, he heard Nevian's voice softly speaking his name. The voice seemed to be talking to him, but surely that wasn't possible. Nevian had come to him once, in his moment of despair when he had been imprisoned in the damp, gloomy cellar beneath Candlebane Hall but surely he couldn't be here in Cawdor, hundreds of leagues from the Granite City? Drib sensed that something was terribly wrong as he began to regain consciousness. The magician's voice was coming to him through a soft halo of beautiful light but he couldn't seem to open his eyes properly.

'Nevian? Nevian?' he tried to call out, but his voice was barely a whisper and he couldn't move.

'No, no, don't wake up yet. Let the poultice soothe you and begin to heal your broken bones. Rest a while and let the cool liniment ease the pain in your head. Sleep, Drib, sleep, stay quiet, remain oblivious to your pain.'

Nevian reached across the boy's trembling body for the small, crystal phial of crushed nightflower petals that he had lain upon the pillow just in case the boy should suddenly awaken. The petals had been harvested on a dark, moonless night when the wolves had howled and the Nightbeasts had stalked the roads. That was when their sweet, heady scent and the virtue they possessed to protect through sleep were at their strongest.

'Sleep, boy, rest easy,' the magician murmured, breaking the phial between his fingers and holding it beneath Drib's nose.

Drib convulsed, his back arched and ridged with pain. His sword-arm felt as though it were on fire and for an instant his eyes snapped open, wild and afraid, as strange images of the rout of Cawdor crowded in around him. The roar and clash of battle, the shouts and screams of terror, his people fleeing in every direction, briefly thundered in his ears. Slowly the scene melted away as the heady scent of the nightflowers wafted over him. A face appeared above him, creased and lined with wisdom and old beyond time.

'Nevian!' he tried to speak out but the image blurred and folded around him as he sank into painless oblivion. 'Nevian, is that really you . . . ?' Drib sighed as he sank in a deep sleep.

Nevian quickly dressed the boy's wound on the back of his head, covering it with liniment and then bound the whole area with linen bandages before stripping off the rest of Drib's armour and boots and covering him with a warm sleeping rug of softest swan-feathers. This done he slowly backed away and left him to sleep.

The soft jingle of bit-rings and the scrape of Sparkfire's hooves on the loose rocks close to the tower made the magician pause at the stairhead and peer down through a narrow mullioned window to see the horse still saddled and bridled, grazing unattended near the tower steps. The reins had slipped along his neck as he lowered his head to crop at the sparse mountain grasses instead of being looped securely around the stirrups. Nevian could see them trailing along the ground where they could become entangled with Sparkfire's forelegs at any moment. The magician sighed irritably, realizing that the forest creature must have abandoned the animal once he had carried Drib into the tower.

'As if trespassing here uninvited and taking up my valuable time were not enough. Tending to the boy's wounds is enough of an imposition – now it looks as though I am expected to be his groom as well!'

The magician muttered crossly to himself as he descended the stairway but he paused again halfway down at a twist in the steps and frowned as he searched the large, circular chamber below. He thought he had made it quite clear by his gestures that the creature was to come into the tower to warm himself by the fire, that Grannog and Orundus were to shepherd him in, but he knew he was somewhere in the room, he could smell the strong odour of rotting leaves and moss, but where was he?

'Grannog, what have you done with him? Where is he?' Nevian demanded of the old dog who lay stretched out across the threshold, guarding the open doorway, his watchful eyes half-open.

Orundus hooted, making the magician glance up at the owl perched on the topmost spindle of the storm engine, fussily preening his feathers. He listened to it for a moment and then exclaimed.

'I told you to bring him into the tower, not drive him underneath my storm engine. There's no knowing what damage he may cause there!' Then as an afterthought he added, 'And it's no way to treat a guest, even if he has trespassed!'

Nevian descended the last flight of stairs in a billowing swirl of rainbow colours and bent to search beneath the huge windwheel, but the shadows were too dense to see more than the vague shape of a figure pressed against the back wall.

'Come out, no one will hurt you. Come and warm yourself by the fire,' he coaxed, turning and throwing a huge log onto the flames, causing a ribbon of bright sparks to leap up the chimney, illuminating the room with their brightness.

Umm wailed and shrank even further back, his gentle eyes showing white rings of fear in the firelight. Seeing him so cowed and clearly frightened of the flames flickering in the hearth made the magician wonder if he had ever entered a dwelling before or even if he knew how to use fire. Perhaps he didn't understand about the unsaddling of a horse or even that the poor animal outside had been wearing a saddle and bridle; perhaps he didn't understand about any of the ways of men. Nevian decided that he had better see to the horse himself and retraced his steps to fill a bag with oiled cottons and liniments to treat saddle sores.

'Orundus, watch over Drib and call me if he wakes up. Grannog, make yourself useful, stop snarling at our guest and try to coax him out from beneath the storm engine,' he called out, stepping over the dog and hurrying down the tower steps to where the horse still stood.

III

A Dark Evil Unmasked

THE MAGICIAN'S FACE broke into a warm smile on his return to the tower after he had settled Sparkfire down for the night in the stables and tended to the ugly sores that were beginning to form beneath the heavy saddle. He discovered that the forest creature had emerged from his hiding place beneath the storm engine and was now squatting near the hearth, but from the way he was keeping a wary eye on Grannog, who crouched, watchful, in the centre of the chamber, Nevian was sure that he hadn't ventured out entirely of his own accord.

'I hope you were gentle with him,' Nevian muttered to the old dog as he settled himself into an ancient, high-backed, leather armchair on the other side of the fireplace.

'Now let us try to communicate a little,' he smiled to the Yerrak, slowly prodding his fingers into the folds of his cloak just below his collarbone, making the colours shimmer and expand in soft ripples of light. 'Nevian – I am Nevian, the Master of Magic. There is nothing here that you need to be afraid of. Now, tell me, what is your name?'

Umm stared at the magician in bewilderment, tilting his head slightly to one side, his low forehead creased into deep furrows as he watched the magician repeat the unintelligible sounds and motions. Perhaps, Umm thought, his heartbeats suddenly quickening, he was trying to tell him that the boy had awoken and he was going to forgive him for accidentally stealing his hand. That had to be it. That had to be why the magician kept pointing at him and then slowly drawing his hands back to touch his beautiful cloak with all its shifting colours. He wanted to give the hand back.

Umm's voice rose in hurried, breathless, musical tones of thanks as he searched out the crumpled glove from where he had hidden it beneath his thick fur and held it out towards the magician.

'No, no, no, I do not want the boy's glove, thank you. Keep it safe: return it to him yourself when he wakes up. It's your name I want, I wish to know who you are and where you come from. That's all I really want to know right now.'

Nevian sighed, waving the glove aside, but he couldn't help wondering what could be so important about the battle glove that every time he spoke to the creature he held it out to him. Slowly he started again from the beginning only much more carefully.

'Nevian . . . my name is Nevian . . . now tell me, what is your name? What do you call yourself? Everybody has a name – everybody has a name!'

Umm wasn't listening. His face had collapsed in wretched despair as he clutched the glove to his chest and rocked backwards and forwards on his heels, emitting a low wailing sound. Clearly the boy was never going to forgive him, which meant that the dark shadow of the Eretch would haunt his people forever.

'This isn't getting me anywhere is it?' the magician muttered impatiently as he threw another log onto the fire.

Umm cried out and shrank away from the hearth as the flames leapt up and ribbons of fresh sparks vanished up the chimney.

'Oh dear, I am sorry, I forgot, fire frightens you doesn't

58

it?' Nevian apologized, but seeing the simple forest creature's startled reaction to the flames gave him an idea.

'Fire ... fire ... there is fire in the hearth,' he spoke slowly, pointing his hand towards the dancing flames.

Umm looked up and followed the direction of his hand into the fireplace and a glimmer of understanding showed in his eyes as he traced the shapes of the flames into the air and uttered a long, deep, stuttering musical sound that held the echo of fire crackling amongst dry twigs. Nevian tried to repeat the sound the creature had made but it just came out as a strangled growl. Umm shook his head and then imitated the magician and sang the word 'fire' giving it a sharp, crackling sound – 'Fireck ... firek ... fire ...'

'Fire! Yes, that's right: flames are consuming the logs in the hearth. Fire is our friend – we use it to cook our food and to keep us warm. Look, I'll show you,' and Nevian leaned forwards, stretching out his hands towards the flames but stopped as Umm cried out and covered his eyes, peeping out through the gaps between his fingers and only removing his hands when the magician had sat back down in his chair.

Nevian looked at Umm thoughtfully and stroked his chin. They might have found their first common word, but from the way the creature reacted they were a long way from sharing a common meaning. He sighed. In the great daylights of his magic he would easily have bridged their differences with the light of knowledge. Ah yes, if the magic had not faded and deserted him he would have used it now to light that tiny spark and illuminate all the wonders of the world here in his tower for the Yerrak to see. He would have drawn simple pictures that would have hovered in the firelight while he put names and meanings to their existence no matter how large or how small.

A smile crinkled the old man's lips as memories of how he had once used that spark of knowledge to great advantage flooded back to him. He had journeyed secretly, deep into the City of Night, slipping silently past the watchful Nightbeast who guarded the gates. He had been following forgotten rumours and fragments of stories once gathered from long-cold, camp-fire ashes of a people that Krulshards, the Master of Darkness, had stolen from the daylight and condemned to be his prisoners. He had been told how these people had been kept for so long as slaves, forced to hollow out the City of Night and spread Krulshards' darkness under the world of sunlight, that they had forgotten the names and all memory of the beauty above the ground. But he had returned that knowledge, withdrawing the spark of light from the pouch hidden beneath his cloak, and in its illuminating light he had painted in the millions of stars that shimmered in the night sky above their prison. He had coloured the soft colours of the flowers as they swayed in a summer wind, the tall, sombre forest, the wooded hills and steep mountains that marched away beyond the edge of sight; he had even painted the stones that glistened wetly in the swift-running streams, the leaves upon the trees and the blades of grass; in fact everything that they had been denied. It had been a strong magic back at the beginning of their journey into the sunlight.

Nevian was about to push the memories aside when he paused. 'Perhaps . . .' he murmured, remembering that the colours of his cloak had been renewed and the windows of his observatory were now showing him new, if unpredictable, images. Perhaps it meant that other aspects of his magic had returned.

'Nothing ventured . . .' he frowned, rummaging beneath the folds of his cloak, feeling amongst the dozens of small leather and silken pouches that had once contained the artefacts of his magic. He searched through numbers of hidden pockets until his fingers found what he had been looking for and closed about the light of knowledge. Disappointment momentarily clouded his eyes: the spark had felt so small, so ice-cold between his fingertips, lifeless and barely longer than a grain of sand. But as he brought it out and held it up, it began to glow blue-white.

'Let us start with the trees,' he smiled at the startled Yerrak who would have turned and fled as the bright light burned suddenly between the magician's fingertips; but one growl from the huge dog just behind him kept him crouching where he was, trembling in terror.

He watched as the magician drew a beautiful ironwood tree in the firelight. Sunlight and shadows seemed to dapple its rustling leaves.

'Tree,' Nevian spoke slowly, pushing the images towards the Yarrak. The branches of the tree bent and swayed.

'Go on – touch it, it won't hurt you – it's called a tree,' Nevian coaxed, brushing his hand through the leaves once or twice to show the creature how safe it was.

'Tree ... tree ...' Umm sang in reply, tentatively touching the leaves and then drawing his hand away despite Nevian's reassurances that there was no harm in it. The image changed slowly to a spreading, black ebony and Umm cried out in excitement as he recognized it. Gradually as the dead hours of the night crept towards morning Nevian painted a thousand pictures of Elundium, spelling out each thing, explaining its meaning and closely watching the creature's reactions.

Quite suddenly, as the first smudge of the grey hours had lit the horizon line, Umm saw a way of telling the magician about the stolen hand and he took the tiny, glowing point of light from Nevian's hand. He reached across and drew a chaotic tangle of trees, dark groves of hanging vines and creepers.

'Stooone fooreeest,' he sang, attempting to draw Spark-fire beneath the trees.

Nevian leaned forward, his eyebrows raised in surprise as he stared at the weird, four-legged creature that Umm had drawn amongst the trees.

'Is that Sparkfire, Drib's horse, by any chance?' he asked, pointing to the strange image of a horse.

'Aaaah, aaaah, Sparkfireck!' Umm cried, and with rapid strokes he attempted to draw the bleak ruins of Cawdor that stood upon the black marble cliffs at the wild margins of the world.

'Cawdor!' Nevian exclaimed, recognizing the fortress immediately and half-rising from his chair. But what had Drib to do with that wild place, a place of legends situated on the dark side of morning? What trick of fate had taken such a boy there?

'Yes, yes, Cawdor . . .' Umm's voice rose frantically. Perhaps here was his first real chance to make the magician understand that he had never meant to steal the boy's hand in the stone forest close to the ruins. If he could only make him believe that it had been a terrible accident, that he had not meant to stir up the wrath of the Eretch who, for as long as his forefathers could remember had infested the place and shadowed it with their darkness, then the boy would be able to forgive him.

'Please . . . please . . . you must make him understand that it was an accident – a terrible mistake – I was only following the smell of the purple fungus – our people crave the taste – and we could smell the scent of it on his hand – he must have touched it. I did not mean him any harm,' Umm's voice wailed hauntingly in his own strange tongue. He held out the crumpled glove once more while with his other hand he tried to draw images of the grave-wraiths that his people feared so much.

Nevian peered into the dying firelight, 'Slow down . . . slow down . . .' He let the words fade and he frowned as he stared at the ghostly shapes, barely able to believe that the simple, forest creature could have drawn such images. Where could he have seen them? What did he know of the evil they had once carried? Surely he couldn't have seen them in the ruins of Cawdor? A shiver of dread crept up the old man's spine. He would never have allowed the Tunnellers to flee to Cawdor if he had known that the ancient evil still haunted its ruins. Nor would he have used the last of his fading magic to gather together all those who were still loyal to the King and lead them through the high passes of the Emerald Mountains into Cawdor had he known. Another chill ran through him. Those images in the windows of his observatory – he had glimpsed ruin and devastation everywhere: he had seen the Granite City grim and silent, wreathed in gloom without a single light burning in Candlebane Hall – were they clear pictures of what had come to pass while he remained contented to tinker with the weather here in his tower? Had he really witnessed the downfall of King Thane and the end of everything he had tried to achieve? Surely it had not all been brought about by the unseen resurrection of that ancient evil?

A silent shadow passed over the stairhead and glided across the flagstone floor of the chamber, silently arriving beside where the magician sat lost in black speculation. Umm cried out and shrank away as Orundus stooped to Nevian's shoulder.

'Drib's stirring, is he? Well, perhaps now we can get some real answers about the fate of Cawdor!' Nevian quickly rose from his chair and, beckoning to the Yerrak to follow him, strode towards the stairs in a swirl of billowing, coloured cloak-tails. 'And bring that glove with you. I know you want to give it to the boy!'

Umm hesitated, holding the glove to his chest. Clearly the magician wanted him to follow, but how? He had never climbed such a steep, wooden slope as the one the magician was now climbing – it vanished right into the roof. What was he to hold onto? There were no branches to help him. Grannog moved in close, snapping at the Yerrak's heels, and with a wail the forest creature ran across the chamber and scrambled, tripping and stumbling, up the stairs as he followed the magician along the low, vaulted corridor. Crouching down so that he would not hurt his head on the rough stone and stooping at the open doorway of the small chamber, Umm peeped in at the boy who lay groaning on the bed.

Drib felt safe and warm in the enfolding darkness as he gradually woke up. He thought he was floating, drifting along on a soft feather bed, but as the effects of the phial of nightflower petals wore off his senses sharpened. Gradually he became aware of faint, unfamiliar sounds, a splash, a jumble of running water, the wind running in the tree-tops, distant voices he didn't recognize and a strange, aromatic smell in the air. He felt so drowsy he couldn't seem to open his eyes. He moved his hand and the softness of the bedcover beneath his fingers felt too real to be a dream: but he had to be asleep – there were no feather beds in the house of Sweepscuttle, his master, in the lower circles of the Granite City. A lowly chimney-scramble like him would never expect to sleep in such a bed. No, it didn't feel at all like the meagre pile of threadbare rags that he had become used to sleeping on, spread out on the bare earth in a corner beneath the stairs that he shared with a jumble of rods and brushes with which they swept the city chimneys. Even the creak and scrape of approaching footsteps on the stairs was coming from the wrong direction. It came from below where he lay instead of the stairs above his head. As they came closer he didn't feel the fine shower of dirt and dust that constantly fell from the stair-treads onto his face warning him to wake up. Something was definitely wrong – he had to wake. He tried to open his eyes but his eyelids seemed to be glued together.

He felt a hot, searing pain in the back of his head as he tried to raise himself onto his elbows and look around. His right arm felt heavy and almost as though it were on fire. He sensed it was daylight beyond his closed eyelids and the footsteps were almost at his door. Panic seized him. At any moment his master's blows would rain down upon his head and he would be punished for over-sleeping. Sweepscuttle would curse and beat him for being late for work. He tried to raise his arm to protect himself but he couldn't – something heavy was holding it down. He cried out and tried to shrink away, but he couldn't move.

A voice he half-recognized whispered his name and told him to stay still as a gentle hand touched his shoulder. It couldn't be Sweepscuttle.

'Nevian? Is that you?' the boy asked in confusion.

A cold, wet cotton gauze dripping with camomile and snow-water was carefully dabbed upon his eyelids to dissolve away the crust of dirt and tears that had dried there while he slept.

Drib gasped and shivered, ignoring Nevian's command as he tried to twist his aching head away from the ice-cold cloth. He shuddered as the lotion stung his skin and escaped in wet rivulets to run down his cheeks and soak into the pillow. But the treatment worked: he blinked again and his eyes opened. Lifting his head from the pillow he stared wildly around, but everything was a blur of light and shadow, all out of focus. He could vaguely see a tall, thin figure standing beside the bed, enveloped in a soft haze of shifting colours.

'Nevian, is that really you? What has happened to me? Where am I? Why can't I see?' he cried, his voice rising in panic as fresh tears streamed down his face.

'Patience, Drib, dear boy; don't be in such a hurry to overwhelm me with questions,' Nevian laughed, grasping the boy's left hand to comfort him. 'Here, use this cloth to dab away your tears and give your eyes a moment to clear.' With that, he pushed a small square of white linen between the boy's fingers and guided his hand up to his face.

'There, that's better, isn't it?' The old man smiled as Drib stared around.

'But ... but ... where are we? I don't understand – how did I get here?' he frowned, pulling away from the magician and looking around the white-washed bed-chamber with its tall, ornate cupboards whose shelves were crowded with jars and bottles and books of every shape and size. He looked through the high, vaulted window in the wall directly opposite where he lay in the hope that the view would give him a clue to where they were, but all he could see were the tops of pine trees restlessly bending and swaying in the wind and between them a view of distant mountains. At the foot of his bed he caught sight of a pair of armoured boots and pieces of dirt-streaked, battered armour lying on the floor. There was something very familiar about this. He glanced down at his right arm where it lay upon the soft, swan-feathered sleeping rug. It looked strange. For a moment the swollen fingers protruding from the grey-white, dusty stone cast that encased his forearm didn't look or feel as though they belonged to him, except that his fingertips had started to tingle. Tentatively he tried to move them but winced as hot needles of pain shot up his arm. His head ached and throbbed and felt so heavy. He frowned and reached up with his other hand and to his surprise discovered that his head was swathed with bandages. He felt the tender spot through the dressings on the back of his head and wondered what could possibly have happened to him. How had he received such injuries?

'Nevian . . .' he began, but the words faded away. His face turned a deathly shade of white as memories of the fall of Cawdor, the roar and clash of the attack, the helpless shouts and screams of terror as his people fled before their shadowy, hideous attackers, flooded back.

'Sloeberry! Sloeberry . . . I must save her!' he cried suddenly as a clear image of her unconscious body, bruised and bleeding, dangling by her hair from the Chancellor's son's clenched, armoured glove filled his mind. He had to save her, nothing else in the world mattered. He had to save her, he loved her so much.

He grasped at Nevian's sleeve with his one good hand and tried to pull himself upright, gritting his teeth against the pain, but fell back, dizzy and exhausted against the pillow. 'I have failed her,' he sobbed in black despair. Fresh tears welled up and escaped, unchecked, from the corners of his eyes.

'Drib, tell me what happened. Tell me: were you at Cawdor with Berioss and the Tunnellers? Is that where you received these terrible injuries? Do you know what happened to the others – do you know who it was who attacked you? It is very important that you try to remember.' Nevian sat on the bed beside the small, crippled boy and put his arm around his shoulders to comfort him, but still he pressed Drib for an answer.

'What happened to Sloeberry and the others? Did you recognize your attackers? Start at the beginning – start at the moment I left you in the cellars beneath Candlebane Hall. It seems as though those seeds of doubt I let you sow amongst those who accused you must have contained some very strong magic indeed. Tell me how you came to be at Cawdor, and leave nothing out.'

Drib nodded bleakly and wiped away his tears.

'Well, it all started that night in the cellar beneath the Candlehall only moments after you disappeared. Eider Greygoose, the Captain Archer's son, was thrown in with me: he had been falsely accused of some crime or another against Loremaster Grout. Of course, Eider didn't believe you had appeared in the cellar, especially to the likes of a penniless, crippled, sweep's scramble. He saw that I was always making up my ridiculous stories and chattering on too much – at least that's what he accused me of, and that's why all the other boys in the Learning Hall persecute me and tease me all the time but . . .'

'Yes, yes, yes, I'm sure he did, and we both know how wrong he was,' Nevian interrupted with a smile. 'Now tell me how you came to be at Cawdor. It's a long way from the Granite City. And how did you meet the Tunnellers? How did you escape?'

'Why, in the cellar of course. The Tunnellers were thrown in with us later that night. There was a terrible commotion going on as they were brought into the city – we could even hear it in the cellar. The city folk were going mad to get at them. They were hammering on the doors, circling the walls that surround the Candlehall and howling for their blood. Berioss and Ustant, the two old Marchers, were travelling with the Tunnellers, trying to protect them: they were worried that they wouldn't survive the night.'

Drib paused and fresh tears brimmed in his eyes. 'That's when I first met Sloeberry.' He blinked and turned his head away as a tear escaped down his cheek. He was filled with such a gnawing emptiness when he remembered that first meeting – her beautiful, slender face with its large round eyes as she was thrown into the cellar. He remembered the delicate tips of her ears showing through the silken strands of the dark hair that fell about her shoulders. He remembered her voice and how it held the echo of skylarks flying on the wind high above the summer fields, or perhaps the musical whisper of windbells ruffled by an evening breeze. She had been the first person in his life who had not looked down at his crooked legs with disgust or given him a cold glance of dismissal. A love had grown up between the two of them and it was more wonderful than anything he had ever hoped for. Drib rubbed away his tears on the corner of his sleeve. Putting into words everything that had happened since he had been locked up was not easy. He didn't understand half of it himself.

'I know the Tunnellers didn't want to escape. Ustant was convinced that the King would judge them innocent of all the crimes that they had been falsely accused of, but somebody else certainly wanted it to appear as though they had escaped. They killed the guard and skewered his body to the outside of the cellar door and then they unlocked it and took away the key. Both Berioss and Ustant were convinced that they would be accused of killing the guard, but it was a trap. There were Nightbeasts or something very like them waiting hidden in the court-yard of Candlebane Hall: they were waiting for us to emerge through the door at the top of the cellar steps. Ustant died keeping them back, while Eider picked the lock of a door that Damask had noticed halfway down the stairs. We only just managed to escape by the skin of our teeth and we went into an old disused, underground tunnel that lay behind the door and led us to the armoury. Berioss made us choose warm winter clothes and take some weapons and armour with us and then we only escaped from the city because the Nighthorses came to our rescue when those creatures attacked us again in Tallow Finger Alley.'

'Did Berioss or the Tunnellers have any idea who was behind it? Do they know who was making it look as though they wanted to escape?' Nevian interrupted abruptly. He had heard so many rumours in his travels across Elundium and now there was a chance to get at the truth.

Drib shook his head. 'No, I don't think so . . .' Then he paused. 'Why, yes, I remember. Sloeberry said she thought that she caught a glimpse of the boy who attacked them in the inn at Deepling – you know – where all those troubles are supposed to have begun. Yes, I remember now: she said she saw him lurking in the shadow of the courtyard at Candlebane Hall just as the Tunnellers were being unloaded from the prison cart and herded down into the cellar. Berioss was convinced that he was behind all the troubles and unrest being blamed on the Tunnellers. I often overheard him muttering his name after we got to Cawdor.'

'The name! What did he call him?' Nevian cried, grasping Drib's good arm fiercely.

'Snatchpurse – I heard him: he called him Snatchpurse,' Drib replied, recoiling from Nevian. 'He was Ironpurse's son, Ironpurse, the Chancellor. And he was the one who drove the Tunnellers out of Deepling and then burned down Ustant's hut . . .'

'The Chancellors!' Nevian exclaimed, his face darkening with anger. 'Berioss thought it was the Chancellors who were at the root of all the upheaval and chaos that is spreading across Elundium. But he said nothing to me when I appeared to him in the ruins of Cawdor on the daylight of your arrival.'

The magician rose from where he had been sitting on the edge of the bed and paced the room, muttering to himself about how much disaster could have been averted if only Berioss had had the sense to speak up when he had the chance.

'I . . . I . . . I don't think Berioss was all that sure about the Chancellors – not in the beginning. He did say something about it being too much of a coincidence that Snatchpurse should be hiding in the shadows of the courtyard at Candlebane Hall when they arrived there as prisoners, but it was only after seeing those travellers you guided through the depths of winter arrive at Cawdor that he began to put two and two together. He realized then, from what they told him about the state of things in Elundium, that it was probably the Chancellors who were behind all the unrest. And then they told us about the Honourable Company of Murderers – some secret society who seemed to have a hand in everything bad that happened all over Elundium.'

Nevian's face creased into a smile. 'Be at ease, boy. Berioss was a brave Marcher and he was not to blame. Caution is a virtue, indeed, a wise prudence.'

The old man sighed and seemed to sink a little as he strode slowly back to the bed. 'Once I held the threads of fate in my fingertips, Drib. I held sway over both Kings and common men but now I can't be sure of anything. If there is blame to measure then its weight should lie squarely across my shoulders for not considering the Chancellors a threat. Yes, I have been a complete fool for overlooking them, for thinking that they would sink beneath the yoke of disgrace they earned for themselves during the last daylights of King Holbian's reign and the great siege of the Granite City.'

Nevian saw that Drib's eyes had grown wide and round with interest, his fear forgotten as the magician spoke of such things. 'Yes, boy, the Chancellors have nothing to be proud of. While the city folk were close to starving and the King, and all those who could fight, strove to keep back the horrors of the dark that swarmed against the walls, battering the gates with ironwood trees, the Chancellors stole the last of the meagre supply of food and fled from the city by a secret road that they had learned of through Loremaster Pinchface. But as if that wasn't enough treachery, they slipped the bolts on the great gates moments before they vanished to let the Night-beasts into the city. Yes, oh yes, I am a fool to think that they would dwell in exile in the depths of Meremire Forest and keep to their own business.'

Nevian rose to his feet again, clasping his hands behind his back and paced restlessly to the vaulted window. In the great daylights of his magic truth would not have eluded him so easily. He stared long and hard at the distant snow-capped mountain peaks now bathed in morning sunlight before turning to look back towards Drib, murmuring thoughtfully, 'What convolutions of evil are set to snare the unwary.'

After a moment he retraced his steps to the bed and sat down beside the boy. 'I also heard rumours of that Honourable Company on my last hurried journey through Elundium, Drib, but I was far too busy gathering together those still loyal to King Thane to pay them much heed. But, I confess, they did kindle a certain hope in my heart. They made me believe that the King's plight had not been

72

entirely overlooked by the Marchers and Gallopers who, in the generosity of victory at the end of the Battle of the Rising, King Thane had released from their pledges. I imagined that it was they who had gathered together to protect the people.'

The old man sighed.

'I thought there were rumours of an Honourable Company gathering, the beginning of an army coming together to come to the King's aid in these troubled times. I thought they would need no more help from me, but, from what you have just told me, clearly I was wrong.'

'From what Berioss has told me of the Chancellors they were not very nice people,' Drib ventured timidly.

Nevian nodded, 'Not very nice ... you are certainly right about that, my boy. Their hands were dirtied with intrigue and politics long before even King Holbian came to the throne. Now I come to think back on it, there was a darker side to the rumours of the Honourable Company of Murderers; even the name doesn't seem quite right, does it? How can murderers be honourable? And there was always a hint of fear, something left unsaid in the voice who spoke out about them. They were shrouded in secrecy, too much secrecy to be up to any good. Do you think it was Snatchpurse and the Chancellors who attacked Cawdor?'

Drib shrugged his shoulders helplessly, forgetting, for a moment, his injuries, and winced at the sudden, hot stab of pain that shot up his arm and the throbbing ache in the back of his head as he moved. 'I can't really say for sure, but ... but ... inside I know it was him. It had to be. Not because Berioss was convinced that Snatchpurse was behind all these troubles but ...' Drib hesitated, letting his voice die away into silence. He didn't know how to explain his feelings, but he was certain, absolutely certain it was Snatchpurse and the conviction was gnawing away in the pit of his stomach.

'If only I had allowed my doubts about that Honourable Company to rise to the surface instead of trying to suppress my fears, then Cawdor may never have fallen. Start at the beginning, tell me why you are so sure it has to be him . . .' Nevian coaxed gently.

'Well, I never actually saw Snatchpurse's face, or any of the others who attacked us during our escape from the Granite City, but as we emerged from that cellar beneath the Candlehall I managed to loose a lucky arrow into the leading Nightbeast's chest. I don't think the arrow-strike could have done more than pierce the armour but it certainly slowed up their attack and helped us to escape. The thing is Berioss was sure they were not real Nightbeasts; he thought later that they were Snatchpurse and his friends in disguise. Well, on the morning that Cawdor was attacked Berioss had taken most of the Tunnellers with Eider and myself on a hunting expedition into the stone forest. Cawdor would have been razed to the ground and everybody we left behind murdered where they stood if Silkstone the owl, who always stayed with me, had not sensed something was wrong and warned us.'

Drib paused and shivered as the memories of that desperate ride back through the forest flooded into his mind. He heard again the horses' bit-rings jangling madly as they streamed down across the headland and saw before them the thick pall of smoke and the fire billowing from the three towers they had laboured so hard to rebuild. People were fleeing in every direction with blood running down their faces. Some were limping and crawling, and all were in a desperate panic as they tried to escape. With a brief roll of thunder their hoofbeats had echoed on the causeway as they galloped through the river doors of Cawdor, but they had come too late. Boiling black shadows filled with half-human shapes engulfed them. One thought had filled Drib's mind on that fateful ride as he hurled his spear into the seething mob who tried to block his path – he had to rescue Sloeberry: nothing else mattered. Drawing his sword, he had spurred Sparkfire forward, forcing a passage through the horde.

'What happened, Drib? What happened when you fought your way into the fortress that made you so sure it was Snatchpurse?' Nevian pressed, making Drib blink and look up into the magician's eyes.

'Well, then the mass of shadowy warriors who had over-run Cawdor drew back as I fought my way into the main courtyard. They jeered and shouted at me but none of them raised a blade against me. Eventually I reached a spot where I faced their leader, a tall, hideous creature with armoured scales growing out of his skin in numerous places. He was holding Sloeberry – she was unconscious and he gripped her hair in his armoured glove. He goaded me, calling out my name, as if he knew all about me and wanted to take his revenge. He kept pointing, he kept pointing at this scar on his chest.'

'Do you remember exactly what he said to you? Think back, try to remember his exact words.'

'I can remember quite clearly how his eyes had shrunk to mad pinpoints and his voice gloated with victory as he cast poor Sloeberry aside. "How long I have waited for this moment" he said, and then . . .' Drib paused. 'And then he said "your king is siege-locked and starving to death in his Granite City. All your friends are dead: you are done for. Listen, cripple, listen to the silence. We have thrown that old fool of a Marcher over the cliffs. There is nobody left to help you now, nobody at all. Even that precious owl of yours has been chased off by Squark, my magpie. You are all alone."'

Drib fell silent and bowed his head. A huge tear escaped to run unchecked down his cheek.

'What made you stand your ground against him, Drib? Something made you stand up to him despite being surrounded by overwhelming odds – what was it?'

Drib wiped away the tear and looked up, nodding slowly as a ghost of a smile touched the corners of his lips despite the tragedy and loss he had suffered.

'Berioss – Berioss forged us into the Knights of Cawdor – how could I back down?'

Drib paused, the knuckles of his good hand suddenly tingling on the swansdown sleeping rug as he remembered seeing Sloeberry groan and stir when Snatchpurse had thrown her aside so roughly onto the cobblestones before advancing upon him. And there had been something else that had fuelled his courage on that dreadful morning—

'She was still alive. Sloeberry was still alive when I fought my way into that courtyard! I saw her move, I know she was still alive. But that wasn't all: one of those hideous creature's followers burst through the mob surrounding us and shouted out that the people were escaping, that they were using the shadows and webs of fear they had brought with them to destroy us and they were reaching the safety of the forest. Yes, and he called out that Eider had somehow managed to break free and gallop away and was hidden by the trees as well. They said they couldn't find any trace of Damask, Mistletoe and the Tunnellers who had been thrown from their mounts as we galloped through the gate arch and into the outer keep. The mob went silent then and a surge of uncertainty seemed to ripple through them. Then another voice called out that they had driven the old Marcher over the cliff edge, but nobody could see any sign of his body on the rocks below. They could see nothing except a gnarled, old tree clinging to a narrow ledge halfway down. Their leader's gloating sneer of triumph seemed to vanish instantly and Snatchpurse's face quivered with rage as he cursed his followers and shouted at them, telling them to follow Eider and the others and scour the ruins for the Tunnellers. Knowing that Sloeberry was still alive and hearing that some of the others had managed to escape gave me the courage to raise my sword and spur Sparkfire on.'

Drib looked down at his injury, touching the hard, cold stone cast that encased his sword arm. The futility of that moment's defiance flooded back into his memory. Echoes of Snatchpurse's cruel voice as it jeered and taunted him seemed to fill his ears, but nothing had deterred him. Snatchpurse had stepped so easily out of Drib's path and then he had brought his battle mace swinging down onto his sword, shattering the blade into a thousand shards. The blow had numbed Drib's fingers and sent shivers of agony up his arm as Sparkfire pirouetted, kicking out to keep space around him.

Snatchpurse had sneered, 'Come on, crooked boy, surely you can do better than that!' then he had swung the battle mace again, striking Drib's forearm before he had a chance to draw his dagger. Drib winced, even while lying in his bed: the sound of the bone cracking and the pain that flooded through him were engraved into his memory.

'Do you remember what happened then? Do you remember how you managed to escape?' Nevian asked.

Drib shook his head carefully. 'The last thing I remember was that Sparkfire suddenly reared up and leapt for a gap in the crowd just about where the messenger had burst through to bring news of the others' escape. The mob seemed to scatter in front of Sparkfire in confusion and I saw the shadows at the gate arch pass above us as we galloped out onto the Causeway. Then everything went black. I am sure I would have fallen off if it hadn't been for the two leaping heads that the saddler had sewn onto my saddle to keep my crooked legs in place. But . . .' Drib stared around the bedchamber, '. . . how did I get here and where am I?'

Nevian laughed softly and patted Drib's shoulders as he rose from the bed. 'You are in my tower at the Runesgate Gorge; but how you got here, that, my boy, will take some unravelling. I hope you can help me with that question. But first let us meet the guide who brought you here. He has got something he is very anxious to give to you. Umm, come in here. Umm . . .'

Nevian crossed to the door and out into the corridor to where the Yerrak was squatting on the floor and beckoned to him to come into the room. Umm grunted and scrambled to his feet, stooping to follow the magician and reluctantly squeezing his broad, powerful shoulders through the door frame. On seeing Drib sitting up in bed he gave a cry of joy and hurried forwards, falling on his knees beside him and holding out the crumpled battle glove for him to take. Drib gave a startled cry of surprise and fear as Umm appeared in the doorway and shrank back against the wall, raising his good arm as if to ward off the huge, hairy creature as its shadow fell across the bed. Nevian frowned. He had not expected Drib to be afraid of the creature; in fact quite the opposite – after all, the Yerrak had brought the boy all the way from Cawdor or at least from somewhere very close.

'It's all right, Drib, he is not going to hurt you. Relax, he's gone to a lot of trouble to bring you to me.' Nevian motioned the Yerrak to move a little away from the bed.

'I thought you must know this simple forest creature, for clearly he thinks he knows you. Since your arrival he has been trying to give me that old battle glove that he's holding. Do you recognize it? Is it yours?'

Drib blinked and rubbed his eyes, wrinkling his nose and cautiously sniffing at the strong odour of rotting leaves and moss that the creature had brought into the room with him. 'I don't know: I'm not really sure of anything that happened after the attack on Cawdor,' he replied uncertainly. So much of his memory was still a haze. But surely, he wondered, looking at Umm, surely he couldn't have forgotten meeting such an enormous creature, no matter how hard the blow to the back of his head. And he would never have forgotten such a pungent odour. As for the glove he was offering to him, it looked about the right size to fit his hand, but it just couldn't be his, he was sure he had caught a glimpse of both his gloves just after he had woken up. Yes, he distinctly remembered how odd the armoured fingers looked sticking up from amongst the jumble of his clothes and pieces of battered armour that lay scattered on the floor near the foot of his bed.

Umm saw the boy looking quizzically at him and renewed his efforts to make him take back his glove, pleading with him in his soft, musical voice, telling him how sorry he was that he had stolen it from him in the snow. Drib sensed a sadness and a regret in the soft, lilting tones of Umm's voice and there were words woven through the music, words he could almost understand. He sensed an urgency and a warning: something terrible had happened or was going to happen if he didn't take back the glove. But what – and why?

Trying to decipher what the creature was telling him was not at all like listening to Silkstone. When he had first spoken to him on the roof of the Prancing Warhorse Inn in the Granite City the owl's voice had been much clearer, the words easy to understand as he had offered to show him a way down. Drib reached out to take the glove. It was the least he could do in the circumstances; but he hesitated for there was something very odd about the hand that was holding the glove towards him: there were too many fingers – seven in all curled – and that touched on forgotten memories. It had something to do with purple fungus – but what? He frowned and looked up into Umm's face. Where had he seen those small deep-set, gentle, jet-black eyes before? There was also something familiar about the thick orange tufts of hair that sprouted from his broad, weather-beaten, leathery face. Suddenly he shivered. The sooty, cold smell of snow seemed to fill his nostrils as the memories sharpened.

'Nightboar!' he whispered in a dry voice, looking up at the magician as his fingers closed around the battle glove in Umm's hand. 'Yes, the glove is mine – I remember now. Eider and I had gone hunting for food on the daylight we first arrived at Cawdor and we killed a Nightboar. Well, actually Eider killed it – I was much more of a hindrance, falling off my horse and . . .' Drib let his voice trail away as he saw a frown darkening the magician's face that reminded him to keep to the facts of the matter and not go rambling on. 'The only way we could get the Nightboar's carcass back to Cawdor was by making a sledge out of fallen branches and yoke the horses to it. A blizzard suddenly swept down over us and I couldn't keep up with the sledge: I tried but then I just collapsed, exhausted, in the snow. Eider put me on the sledge beside the Nightboar and the next thing I remember was waking up to find – Umm – that's the creature's name isn't it! – leaning over me and pulling at my glove. I particularly remember seeing that he had seven fingers before I fell back in a black faint just as the glove came off. After that I don't remember anything else until I woke up beside the fire in the ruins . . .'

'I expected there to be much more to it than that!' Nevian muttered in disappointment. 'After all the fuss he's been making about giving it back to you – and it still doesn't explain why he was drawing the shapes of shadowy, evil figures in the firelight downstairs. Have you met anything like that in the vicinity of Cawdor? Can you think how they can be connected with your glove and why he should have taken it in the first place? How do you know his name? I've been trying to get him to tell me all night.'

Drib smiled and shrugged. He turned the glove over in his hand. 'He told me his name just now when he offered me the glove. I'm afraid I can't understand much but I can sort of make out a bit of what he says.'

Drib paused. The answers the magician wanted were so tantalizingly close, if only he could remember. He glanced down to the glove and to his surprise he found that there were traces of a purple stain all over it. It certainly was not rust, and it had come off the glove onto his fingers as he handled it. Cautiously he brought the glove up to his nose and sniffed, catching a faint odour, an earthly perfume that he had smelt somewhere before. The scent brought a host of memories rushing back. He could remember touching the purple fungus on the fallen oak tree – could remember how the bright puffs of purple dust exploded from the thousands of tiny, bell-shaped toadstools beneath his hand, staining the leather fingertips of his gloves. He had not realized then that he had covered his glove with a scent that the Yerrak prized so highly they would follow it for leagues.

On their return to Cawdor with the Nightboar carcass Eider had insisted that Umm and his two companions had attacked the sledge because they had been after meat; and although he had no idea at the time that it was the pungent odour on his glove they had been after, he had still had the distinct impression that the huge, hairy creature had been searching for something. It was only much later, on the daylight when Cawdor had been attacked that he had guessed why the creature had taken his glove. He had seen gouge marks all over the rotten trunk and high up, way beyond where any of them could have reached, he had seen seven-fingered marks through the thick patches of purple fungus.

'I do know why Umm took my glove! Yes, I remember now: it was because I had touched the purple fungus. They eat it, you know. It didn't have anything to do with the ghostly figures we caught sight of amongst the trees, the ones who haunted Cawdor. No . . . wait . . .' Drib frowned, turning his attention to Umm.

As he listened to Drib the Yerrak slowly realized that he could understand some of what the boy was saying – but it wasn't the truth, not as it should be told. He gesticulated wildly, waving his arms in the air, scraping his knuckles roughly across the ceiling beams and his voice rose in urgent cries. They had to know the truth! Drib listened intently, letting the urgent, melodic cries fill his head, discovering that he could understand more and more of the strange creature's words until eventually Umm reached the part of his story where they had entered the Runesgate Gorge and he fell silent. Drib turned slowly towards Nevian, a look of confusion in his eyes.

'Well, boy, what has he told you? Enough, I hope, to get to the bottom of these riddles?'

'I'm . . . I'm not really sure. Perhaps you can make some

sense of what he has just told me,' Drib frowned. 'Umm says he never meant to steal my hand, although how he could have mistaken that battle glove for my hand I don't know: but I was right about the purple fungus. He called it musk-sponge. But what I don't understand is how taking the glove could have cast such a terrible shadow over Umm's people, or how it could have brought about the destruction of Cawdor. Berioss was always worried that Snatchpurse and his murderous friends would follow us to Cawdor – that was partly why he was trying to teach us how to defend ourselves. That and his plan to ride back to the Granite City after the snows had melted, to serve the King. He used to say that it was his pledge to make us into the Knights of Cawdor, to fight for justice. Not that we seemed to have been much use when the fortress was attacked. But what mystified me is why Umm should think that when he accidentally took my glove it could have had anything to do with stirring up the evil spirits that attacked us. What do you think?'

Nevian smiled as Drib described how hard Berioss had worked to make them into warriors. Pledging the old Marcher into service to forge Drib, Eider and the Tunnellers into warriors had certainly not been a wasted effort, despite what Drib said. They seemed to have fought back valiantly before being overwhelmed; and most of them, it seemed, had survived – although where they were now was anybody's guess. But his interest had sharpened at the mention of the evil spirits. 'It's important, Drib, that you get Umm to tell me exactly what he knows of this evil that haunts Cawdor. The fate of Elundium may well be revealed in his answer.'

Drib spoke slowly to Umm but the mention of the ghosts in the ruins made the Yerrak cry out and cover his eyes. It was difficult for Drib to make head or tail of what he said. He shrugged: it all seemed a terrible muddle, but he was careful not to move his injured arm too much, for his fingers were beginning to throb painfully. 'There is not much to tell, but I get the impression that the Yerrak are really afraid to go anywhere near the ruins. He said something about it being a very ancient evil that steals people's hearts . . .'

'He told you nothing more?' The magician frowned, a little exasperated that the boy seemed to be able to understand the creature when he was at a loss. In the days of his magic there wasn't a language in the whole world that had eluded him. 'Are you sure you have asked the right questions, boy?' Nevian fretted.

'Yes, yes, of course I did!' Drib cried. 'He told me lots of other things about taking my glove and finding me in the forest unconscious, lying across Sparkfire's back, only I thought you would be cross and accuse me of chattering on if I told you everything.'

'Chatter, boy – chatter, and let me sift out the gems of wisdom, if there are any amongst the chaff.'

'Well, he said it was hunger that had driven him and his two companions down out of the inaccessible passes of the Emerald Mountains and into the petrified forest. They were foraging for food when they caught the scent of the purple fungus that I had disturbed when I climbed up onto the fallen tree trunk – normally the fungus is hidden beneath the snow in the winter. Anyway, Umm had not the slightest idea we were sheltering in the ruins of Cawdor when he took my glove. The Yerrak are very shy of people and keep well out of their way. They saw the marks of the Nightboar hunt and the blood of the kill in the snow and from the track we left they knew there were only two of us and the scent of the fungus was too strong for them to resist. Umm never meant either of us any harm, but when my glove came off, he thought he'd torn off my hand and he knew that his people would be persecuted and hunted for what he had done – unless he could get me to take it back and forgive him. He was horrified to see our sledge disappear into the ruins of Cawdor. Apparently the evil that slept there had been woken and it was gliding restlessly through the crumbling walls, sweeping through the blizzard. Umm retreated into the forest before it saw him, sure that his reckless act had stirred it up – and now his quest to return my glove became even more urgent, but his courage deserted him. He hid in the forest for daylight after daylight, watching, waiting for an opportunity, and during that time he began to realize that we are a part of the evil. He became convinced of this after Snatchpurse and his followers arrived and hid in the forest above the fortress the night before they attacked. All night long it seems, there were ghostly shapes pouring out of the ruins and sweeping up across the headland to converge on our attackers, fusing with them, possessing them, changing their bodies into hideous shapes. They grew claws and armoured scales and were fuelled with a terrible evil that swarmed down on Cawdor as soon as Berioss had led us into the forest on that hunting expedition. Umm had watched all this take place and had been about to flee to warn his people that all was lost when he saw Sparkfire with me lying on his back as he broke free from the seething crowd. He caught up with the horse, thinking that this was his last chance to return my glove, but he found me unconscious and thought that I had magically grown another hand in place of the one he had torn off. Fearing that I had even greater powers than he had first imagined, he brought me here. He had trespassed into this gorge as a youngling once when in search of fruits and berries and caught a glimpse of your magic. He thought you would be able to save my life. That's just about everything that Umm has told me so far. But I could ask him to elaborate if you want me to.'

'No, no, that won't be necessary at the moment, Drib: this has given me more than enough to riddle over for the time being, thank you.' Nevian rose stiffly from where he had been sitting on the edge of the bed. He frowned and began to pace the chamber, deep in thought. Umm had confirmed his worst fears about what the evil that haunted Cawdor might be, although the name of it still eluded him. Much more worrying than remembering its name was finding out what had become of it since the fall of the fortress. Was it still there, or, as he feared from those dark, unsettling visions of the desolation of Elundium he had glimpsed in the windows of his observatory, had Snatchpurse and his murderous followers taken it back with them? Umm had said that his people feared the ancient evil because it stole hearts. Had he meant that it had the power to possess? That was exactly what it seemed to have done when the Chancellor's son and his followers arrived in the vicinity of the fortress, and, given Drib's description of the ferocity of the attack, through the possession of the evil their strength had obviously multiplied. But why had it not attempted to possess Berioss or the others when they had arrived at Cawdor? Surely it was such a malignant power that it would have done more than appear as translucent, ghostly shapes?

Nevian stopped abruptly, mid-stride. What had he been thinking of, spending half the night and the best part of a new morning chasing blind riddles when he'd had the answer all along, right there in his tower? What had he been doing pursuing wild speculation and expecting sensible, intelligent answers from a mere boy and a simple forest creature? Why had he not looked into his books of lore the moment Umm had first drawn those ghostly shapes in the firelight? Was it not to solve a problem such as this that everything had been written down, no matter how large or small since the sun first rose to shed its light upon the world?

'I've been such a fool. Wait here and don't move, either of you, I have the answers!' he cried, vanishing through the doorway in a swirl of rainbow colours.

Drib half-rose in the bed, propped himself up on his good elbow and stared at the empty doorway in confusion as he listened to the clatter of the magician's footsteps on the stairs. Faintly, from somewhere far below, he heard Nevian's voice muttering impatiently, 'I know the answers are here somewhere . . .' and then he caught the sound of a heavy thump, as though books were being pulled out of the crowded shelves and dropped onto the floor.

Nevian was the Master of Magic: he knew everything – he held the fate of kings in his hands – well, that is what Drib had been taught in the Learning Hall, and Nevian certainly seemed to fit his description the first time he had appeared to him in the cellars beneath Candlebane Hall, although now he seemed quite different. He did not appear and disappear into thin air as he was supposed to, but climbed the stairs like any ordinary person, and he seemed forgetful and erratic, taken with sudden moods, just as if his magic had deserted him. Drib shook his head: no, surely that was just not possible.

Nevian reappeared in the doorway, slightly out of breath, with a large, leather-bound, book of ancient lore clutched to his chest, just like the ones Loremaster Grout used to read from, except that this one was much older. 'Now, let us get to the bottom of the evil that is said to haunt Cawdor,' he said, depositing the book onto the bed in a thick cloud of dust that made Drib sneeze and his head throb with pain.

Nevian squinted at the closely-written script that covered the thick parchment pages and then pushed it aside in exasperation. 'Where did I leave my spectacles?' he muttered angrily, searching through his voluminous pockets, turning all manner of wondrous things out onto the sleeping rug; but they were nowhere to be found.

Drib craned his neck awkwardly and looked down to the open page, tilting the book slightly towards him as he began to read it aloud, faltering only slightly as he came to the more difficult words: '. . . and in the daylights of the first Granite Kings, Elundium stretched far beyond the Emerald Mountains and the last lamp of Underfall, through groves of hanging orchids and star-flowers, through the petrified forest and onto the shores of the limitless ocean. And on those shores Cawdor stood, a place of sunlight and beauty rising proud upon sheer, black marble cliffs.'

Drib paused and looked up, 'There isn't any mention here of Cawdor being on the dark side of morning, none at all.'

'You can read boy!' Nevian exclaimed in surprise. 'But that's quite extraordinary. I never expected . . .'

'. . . that a crippled sweep's-scramble like me would be able to read. Is that what you meant?' Drib's voice was full of hurt and huge tears were brimming in the corners of his eyes. He had never imagined that Nevian should have considered him so worthless and he had to quickly turn his head away.

Nevian frowned with concern, upset that his words of surprise had unintentionally pricked the boy and he thought he could catch the glint of a tear drop trickling down his cheek as he turned his head away.

'No, Drib, no, you misunderstand me,' he spoke softly, trying to reassure him as he reached out to touch his shoulder with gentle fingers. 'To be able to read, my lad, is a triumph that most boys, with a much better start in life than you have had, fail to achieve – and I am very proud of you.'

Drib blinked, suddenly ashamed of his outburst, and slowly looked up into the old man's face, rubbing away his tears with the corner of his sleeve. He had never divulged the secret of his ability to read before, he had been so afraid of the mockery. 'I . . . I . . . I had to learn to read,' he stuttered. 'It was the only way I could find out what happened in all those wonderful stories about the Warhorses and the Battle Owls – and how King Thane won the daylight. Loremaster Grout never seemed to want to read those tales to us, and even if he did he would never finish them.'

'But Grout taught you to read?' Nevian queried.

'Oh, no, he wouldn't teach me – he only taught the high-born merchants' sons to read. They would stay in the Learning Hall after the noon-day bell was struck. The rest of us learned the stories by reciting them. Loremaster Grout never seemed to like having us in the Learning Hall at all. I used to try and get a seat at the front of the room close to the Loremaster and follow the words in the Books of Lore as he read them to us. That's how I learned.'

'But that's quite amazing! Then there is even more reason to congratulate you, for you taught yourself!' Nevian raised his eyebrows: there was certainly more to this little crippled boy than met the eye.

'Now, perhaps, since I have temporarily mislaid my spectacles, you could read the passage about Cawdor to me.'

'Why yes, of course I will, but . . .' Drib hesitated.

Loremaster Grout had never worn anything when he read to them – surely the Master of Magic, somebody with so much power at his fingertips, didn't need to bother with spectacles.

Nevian laughed softly, guessing the reason for the boy's hesitation. 'Magic has its limitations, Drib. Age, my boy, with all the infirmities that attend it, eventually catches up with us all, even magicians. Now, read for me: the morning is wearing away and there is still so much to do.'

Drib felt the colour rising in his cheeks and he pulled the ancient Book of Lore closer. He had never read aloud before and he was not sure he could do it properly. Finding the place where he had stopped he placed his finger on the line of closely-written words and began. 'The citadel of Cawdor rose in soaring spires, battlements and towers. Its quiet, shaded courtyards and vaulted halls were festooned with rare and beautiful stone orchids gathered from the petrified forest. It was a place of song and laughter, of great wealth and power, where the golden ships of Carth and the vessels full of silks and spices from Minios traded their wares. It was where the huge, reed boats from Gnarlsmyre rode the waves with swarthy Marshlords at the helm, haggling as they bartered on the harbour walls. But . . .'

Drib's eyes followed the line of words and he paused, his face growing pale as his finger faltered on the crowded line of script. His eyes filled with fear and terror.

'Well, boy, don't keep me in suspense: read on!'

Drib swallowed and continued in a hushed voice, 'But then, one moonless night while everyone slept, the Eretch invaded the great citadel. They crept out soundlessly, coming from the eaves of the petrified forest; they rose up out of the soft sea mist like elusive wraiths and engulfed everything, weaving their webs of shadow through the rigging of the ships in the harbour, darkening and possessing each person they touched. By the time the first fingers of the new daylight were lightening the sky the Eretch had shrouded Cawdor in the dark side of morning and nothing but the echo of what it had been remained in the thunder of the surf that beat against the black, marble cliffs.'

'The Eretch!' Nevian cried, striking his forehead with the flat of his hand and interrupting the boy. 'What a blind fool I've been to have forgotten of their existence for all these suns.'

'But who are the Eretch?' Drib asked.

'Who are the Eretch?' the old man exclaimed. 'Why, they are the most ancient evil that has ever stalked this earth. They are grave-devils, the remnants of the gaborewraiths, the very first evil that Krulshards released from the deepest chambers of the City of Night to destroy the Granite Kings. Their purpose was to devour everything they encountered and to shroud it in shadow, and from what you have told me and from the pictures that Umm drew in the firelight downstairs, they still infest the ruins of Cawdor. If only I had known, I would have urged Berioss to take you far away from there.'

'But they didn't do anything horrible to us except to give us the creepy feeling of always being watched. Oh, I have a suspicion that they somehow tainted the carcass of the Nightboar we killed on that first daylight at Cawdor. It stank and became alive with maggots in no time, despite our hanging it outside in the cold.'

'I am sure they would have possessed you too, if they could, Drib,' Nevian muttered seriously. 'You were in mortal danger, my boy – all of you were. You see, the Eretch are an ancient, very specialized, evil. They appear to be without any real form or substance, merely weak, almost indistinct, ghostly shapes, no more than pools of darkness or fleeting shadows. But don't for one moment be fooled by that, for their power is awesome and terrible once they have found a host.'

'A host? What is a host?' Drib questioned.

Nevian thought for a moment, how could he explain something so complicated? He sighed and continued, 'The Eretch strength comes through the people or creatures that they possess. If, as in your case, there is nothing for them to feed upon, no evil thoughts, no greed or envy, then they will pass you by. You see, their power lies in their ability to scent out those hungry for power: they can smell corruption, rage and anger; they can feel those eaten away by greed or secret envy from leagues away, and then they possess them silently, filling their minds with evil darkness, compounding all the nasty things going on inside their heads. You won't know anything about it until they start whispering, prompting you to do terrible things. From what you have said about the maggots infesting the Nightboar's carcass I wouldn't be surprised if the Eretch hadn't possessed the beast the moment your first arrow struck its hide. The murderous rage the creature would have felt towards you would probably have been enough to let the Eretch in. Did it seem to swell and grow darker as it charged towards you?'

'Why, yes, that's right, I saw ghostly shapes crowd in all around it!' Drib cried. He was about to elaborate when Nevian raised his hand.

'Thank goodness you didn't eat too much of the carcass; there's no knowing how it would have affected you. But there are more important things to worry about than a rotting Nightboar carcass, my boy.'

The magician glanced thoughtfully across to where the Yerrak was squatting beside the doorway of the chamber humming softly to himself. From the boy's description of the way the ghostly shapes had poured out of the ruins and swept up across the heathland above Cawdor to converge upon Snatchpurse and his followers, it left little doubt in the magician's mind that they had found themselves a new host. And from Umm's description of the way the Chancellors' sons' bodies had changed, growing claws and armoured scales, and the way the shadowy darkness had shrouded them during their ferocious attack on the fortress, it seemed pretty certain that they were possessed.

A cold shiver travelled up the old man's spine. Suddenly the images he had glimpsed in the high window of his observatory began to make sense. His face became deathly pale. 'The situation is far worse than I could possibly have imagined.'

'Worse? How could it be worse than it already is? Tell me!' Drib cried.

'Telling you won't make a jot of difference, boy,' Nevian sighed wearily. 'What could you or anyone else do against such evil?'

He rubbed his hand across his face. Without his magic he felt so useless, so defenceless. How could he change the tide of events that had swept up around the ruined walls of Cawdor and was even now retreating back into Elundium?

'Tell me!' Drib insisted, ignoring the pain as he leaned forward to clutch at Nevian's sleeve.

Nevian answered reluctantly. 'The evil that I thought had perished in the ruins of Cawdor when time was young seems to have survived despite being starved of new hosts to feed on. It was no accident, Drib, that Cawdor was isolated from the world, locked away to be forgotten by all, and only remembered in myths and legends. The

Nighthorses were gathered from Cawdor and brought to Elundium to service the Granite Kings because they feared nothing of the dark and evil had not touched them. When they left, the road through the Emerald Mountains was closed forever. Time should have eradicated the Eretch's power and rendered them no more than restless shadows, but clearly it didn't. Now they found a new and dangerous host in the Chancellors' sons and thus also a way to escape from Cawdor. Who is there who can predict what disasters their evil will cause amongst the people of Elundium? Who can protect them against the black chaos they will bring? They will use the Chancellors' sons, will use them to journey into the very heart of Elundium.'

Nevian paused to ponder the awful consequences and wrung his hands. 'I fear we stand on the threshold of a new dark age ruled by greed and corruption. We seem to be powerless to stop it. I doubt if the King, even if he had a dozen battle-crescents, could stop their relentless onslaught now.'

'No, you are wrong! Not everyone will be touched by the Eretch. They had no power over us while we were living in the ruins and they didn't poison the Yerrak either, did they? I am not afraid to stand up and fight them and I am sure there will be plenty of others who will think like me!' Drib cried out as anger instead of despair suddenly stirred in his heart. He might have lost everything that had ever been dear to him to Snatchpurse and his murderous friends but he wasn't about to slink away into a corner, beaten by their evil. He wouldn't hide away while there was breath left in his body: if he still had the strength to lift a sword then he would use it. Marcher Berioss' lessons in justice,. honour and the skill to bear arms had not fallen on barren ground. Everybody else might be about to turn their backs on their king, but he wasn't. He had not forgotten how the King had come upon him in the gutter as he lay bruised and beaten by the older boys from the Learning Hall. King Thane had dismounted and lifted him up, despite his filthy, ragged clothes. King Thane had made his wildest dream come true by putting him on his horse. He had sat astride Esteron, Lord of Horses, and he had trotted up the lane. But there was something else that strengthened the boy's resolve, a fragile spark of hope that he had refused to extinguish. He was still clinging to the slim chance that Sloeberry was still alive, that Snatchpurse had kept her his prisoner rather than kill her. The thought of her being so cruelly dragged along in chains spurred Drib's anger: he had to get up and ride after them before it was too late. He struggled to rise from the bed, grasping at the swans-feather sleeping rug with his sword hand, momentarily forgetting about his broken arm, but fell back, gasping with pain, sighing weakly against the pillow. Fresh tears of helplessness brimmed in his eyes. It was all brave talk, but he could barely sit upright, let alone grip the hilt of a sword.

Drib's head slumped forwards until his chin almost touched his chest. His anger began to fade and bleak reality stole silently into its place. Doubt whispered and scratched at his ears. '*What can a crippled boy like you hope to achieve? The Knights of Cawdor are finished – give up, Drib, give up and creep away into the shadows. Go home and beg your master, Sweepscuttle, to forgive you for running away with the Tunnellers. You never know, he might even take you back if you plead with him and throw yourself at his feet.*'

'No, no, I will never . . . never give up. I have to find Sloeberry, I have to . . .' Drib muttered, shaking his head as he tried to shut out the whispers, but still they persisted.

'*Marcher Berioss is dead and your friends can't help you*

*now. Even if any of them survived the brutal attack on Cawdor
they will be scattered in the petrified forest. Eider, Oaktangle,
Mistletoe and all the others are lost to you forever. Give up
before you get yourself killed. Remember you are all alone
now: even Silkstone has deserted you – or worse, lies dead
amongst the ashes of Cawdor.'*

'No, I don't believe that: he's alive, I know he is. He
was lost in battle, driven off by the magpie Squark – he's
probably looking for me right now . . .' Drib sobbed to
himself but the belief was fragile. Even if Silkstone were
alive how would he ever find him? A tear ran down his
cheek. It all seemed suddenly so hopeless. Without the
owl's help he knew he would probably never be able to
find his way back to Elundium, and even if he did, Snatchpurse's trail would have long grown cold. Where would
he begin to search for Sloeberry? The world was a far
bigger place than the Loremaster's books had ever led
him to believe. His resolve began to slip away into black
despair.

'You're absolutely right, my boy,' Nevian cried, cutting
through Drib's despair, making him blink as he looked up
to find a new light shimmering in the old man's eyes.
'Your courage in the face of such adversity puts me to
shame.' He paused and leaned closer. 'If the truth be
known, Drib, I think I had come to rely a little too much
on magic and I was willing to let things slip because of
the lack of it.'

He threw his hand up dramatically. 'What has possessed
me to waste my time tinkering with a storm engine? Why
did I believe that my useful daylights were over when the
fate of Elundium hangs in the balance by such a slender
thread? There's much to do, my boy, and it is no coincidence that new colours are flowing through my rainbow
cloak: now I see its purpose, although it is not a magic

that I am at all used to. The one thing we must never contemplate is to give up. To surrender to the evil that now threatens to overrun Elundium is unthinkable!'

Nevian rose from the edge of the bed in a swirl of rainbow colours, ignoring the startled look of surprise on Drib's face as he began to pace the chamber, deep in thought, muttering to himself. 'Firstly we must form a strategy. Search the petrified forest for the survivors of the attack. We'll need arms and armour before we can march to the King's aid in the Granite City. And the boy's right, not everybody will succumb to the evil of the Eretch . . .'

He stopped abruptly in front of Umm and stared down into his gentle, black eyes, suddenly realizing who the Yerrak were and why they knew so much about the Eretch. Their ancestors must have been the original inhabitants of Cawdor, the ones who had fled from the evil that had engulfed it. They had gone to hide in the Emerald Mountains, losing themselves in the forest and becoming nomadic. They had obviously passed their knowledge down the generations and now there was unlikely to be anybody in the whole world who knew as much as they did about the Eretch. Maybe it was even possible that hidden amongst their stories there may be a way to destroy them. He glanced across to the small crippled boy who was again struggling to get up out of bed and he smiled. If the fate of Elundium now rested with Drib it certainly wove its thread in the most peculiar ways.

'If only Silkstone were with me . . . Or Berioss . . . or Eider . . . and I don't know where to begin to look for Sloeberry . . .' Drib gasped dizzily as he finally managed to get his legs over the edge of the bed and tried to stand up.

'And where, exactly, do you think you're rushing off to

in such a hurry? I have not yet given you permission to get out of bed, have I?' Nevian demanded fiercely, quickly retracing his footsteps until he reached the side of the bed and prevented Drib's attempt to take a faltering step. He pushed the boy back gently beneath the sleeping rug and tucked it in firmly around him.

'But I thought I overheard you say that I am to ride to the King's aid, and if Sloeberry is a prisoner I had better start straight away! Except that I may never find it on my own – or the way to the Granite City, for that matter. I am sure to lose myself in no time without Silkstone to help me and . . .' Drib let his words trail away into an uncertain silence as the magician shook his head severely.

'You are in no fit state to go anywhere, Drib. I was merely thinking aloud, mulling over strategies, something that Berioss obviously omitted to teach you anything about!'

The old man suddenly laughed harshly. 'What sort of a fool do you think I would be to let you go blundering off after the Chancellors' sons in the condition you are in? Why, I doubt if you would last a daylight before they either killed you or captured you. How would Sloeberry fare then, with you in chains beside her? You don't think I wasted half the night mending your sword arm for you to ruin the job at the first opportunity do you? Give the bones a chance to knit together and regain your strength.'

'But how will I ever find Sloeberry and rescue her if I don't set out now?' Drib asked in a small, desolate voice as he tried to shut out the awful images of her at the hands of her captors.

Nevian saw the look of hopeless despair shadow the small boy's eyes and he reached out a gentle hand to comfort him. 'Patience, my child, is the hardest task-master. You must use this time wisely, to grow strong and prepare yourself for the dark and dangerous daylights that I am sure lie ahead of us.'

Nevian patted the boy's arm and rose from the bed, turning towards the door, eager to look once more through the high windows of his observatory and, with what he now knew, attempt to riddle out the future and form a plan. Already the chaotic kaleidoscope of images he had seen made more sense. Those half-beast, half-human creatures who had loomed so threateningly in the glass and had then shrunk into a haze of darkness had to be the Chancellors' sons possessed by the Eretch, and the brooding silence he had glimpsed at Candlebane Hall could only mean that the King was indeed siege-locked. But what was the significance of the single, gnarled tree he had seen clinging to the bleak marble cliffs of Cawdor? He would not have seen it if it didn't hold some importance. He heard a sob from the bed and paused to glance back. Drib was wiping away tears. The old man's face softened into a smile of concern.

'You will find Sloeberry, Drib, and you won't be alone in your search, that much I will promise you. While you are here with me I will try to teach you everything I can.'

'But who is there who can help me?' Drib frowned.

Nevian laughed and called out for Orundus, the Lord of Owls, who silently stooped through the doorway much to Umm's discomfort and perched on the magician's shoulder. 'Perhaps if you ask the Lord of Owls nicely he will search for Silkstone and find him for you while you are resting. And while he is scouring the countryside he can alert the Border Runners and the Warhorses that Sloeberry is Snatchpurse's prisoner: they will more than likely find out where she is quicker than anybody else.'

Orundus hooted and alighted on the end of the bed

close to Drib's pillow and then haughtily preened his flight feathers.

'Oh, by the way,' Nevian turned as he reached the doorway. 'You don't remember seeing a gnarled, old tree clinging to a ledge halfway down the cliffs at Cawdor, do you?'

The boy looked up and shook his head, 'No, there were no trees on those cliffs. They are sheer, black marble.'

IV

The Invasion of Elundium Begins

THE GREAT FORTRESS of Underfall stood sheer and impenetrable to its attackers, wrapped in silence in the cold, grey light of dawn. Its galleries and battlements were thinly shrouded in wreaths of acrid smoke and the bright, crackling ribbons of sparks that rose from the smouldering ruins of Marshthistle, a small hamlet that had grown up along the brink of the wide drainage ditch beside the raised causeway road that led to the fortress.

Nobody in Marshthistle had expected the sudden and unprovoked attack. Thunderstone, the keeper of the great lamp of World's End, was busy trimming the lamp's wick while Errant, the first captain of the Nighthorses who guarded the fortress, was settling his mounts for the night when the terrified screams and cries of the villagers reached their ears. Errant had mustered what men he could but it was already too late to do more than save a handful of people who had managed to flee the massacre and reach the causeway. He rallied his men around them, protecting them until they reached the safety of the fortress. Thunderstone barely had time to slam shut the massive, iron-studded doors and siege-lock them in the face of the evil, shadowy creatures, half-human, half-beast, who had suddenly swept down from the direction of the Emerald Mountains, swarming across the Causeway Fields, killing and burning everything that lay in their path as dusk had fallen. Neither Errant nor Thunderstone had ever seen the likes of these monstrous creatures before, nor felt such a menace as evening fell and a long, dark night of fear had gripped the inhabitants of Underfall as they crouched in their high galleries and watched as the evil hordes burned the surrounding countryside, drawing ever closer.

A mournful wind began to stir the embers of the dereliction and black carrion crows strutted and squabbled over the dead in Marshthistle as Snatchpurse, surrounded by his followers advanced into the ruins. He scowled and kicked out at the crows, sending those closest to him flapping heavily into the air. Their harsh voices seemed to mock his victory, making him turn on Huxort and Girrolt, his captains.

'Look, look, you stupid fools!' he snarled, stabbing a trembling claw-like hand towards the burnt-out houses and the mutilated bodies of their former inhabitants as they floated, face down, in the stinking, muddy ditch. 'What possessed you to squander our element of surprise? Why bother to burn these hovels to the ground? What purpose did killing these miserable peasants serve, save to alert the guards of Underfall to our presence? Come on, tell me, tell me!'

Bright bubbles of spittle were beginning to form in the corners of Snatch's scaly mouth and the pupils of his eyes had shrunk to murderous pin-points of rage. His followers began to ease away from him, knowing how unpredictable their leader's moods could be. They watched with bated breath as Snatch frowned and shook his head, clutching at his temples as though to still the conflicting voices going on inside his head. Once his purpose had been crystal clear: he had formed the Honourable Company of Murderers to seize back the power and dignity that had been stolen from his father. He had formed them to destroy Thanehand the thronestealer and return the rule of Elundium to its rightful custodians, the Chancellors. The killings, intrigue and web of lies and deception that had enmeshed his followers had merely been the means by which to achieve the aim; an enjoyable interlude, no more. But now – now that the Eretch had possessed his men they seemed unable to discriminate between an orgy of killing for the sake of it and the winning of a greater prize. He had specifically given them orders to swarm through the doors of Underfall before the guards had realized that they were under attack, and all but one of them had deliberately disobeyed him. And yet he knew that a part of his anger was fuelled by the knowledge that he also had paused to enjoy the massacre of Marshthistle. He knew that the Eretch had also diverted him, although only momentarily, from his true purpose. But it had been enough, enough to lose them their advantage.

'Underfall should have been ours – our greatest victory! Its fall would have struck terror into the people's hearts but because of what you have done they will mock and deride us. And why?' Snatchpurse's lips trembled with rage and he took a threatening step towards his followers, raising his clenched fist in anger. 'Because you disobeyed my orders! Because you turned aside from your true purpose to rampage unchecked through these miserable hovels. Because . . .'

Girrolt sensed something was happening amongst the company as Snatchpurse berated them. He glanced anxiously around him and gripped fiercely at Snatch's arm. 'Be quiet!' he hissed, drawing him back. 'Your anger is somehow stirring up the Eretch. Look, they are deserting us.'

Snatchpurse spun around so quickly he sent Squark, who had been perched upon his shoulder preening his feathers, flying up into the air. In disbelief Snatch watched a ripple of doubt spread through those closest to him. The ripple grew wider and seemed to draw out the evil darkness the Eretch had infused into his followers. The darkness was seeping out through the armoured Nighbeast skins they had worn as a disguise to commit their atrocities before the Eretch had fused those rotting skins into their bodies making them truly half-human, half-beast. Their scaly armour was losing its livid indigo and deep nigrescence, losing its shadowy power; the spines and ridges in the armour were becoming pale and brittle and the evil was oozing out through the pores of their skin, through their eyes and ears. Voices screamed and cried out in confusion. The air above Marshthistle darkened with a cloud of thin, ghostly shapes. The Eretch began to drift away on the morning breeze, floating towards the fortress of Underfall.

'What's happening to me?' Huxort screamed, falling to his knees and grasping at the Nightbeast claw that had become fused with his left hand when the Eretch possessed him. The jagged horn of the claw was beginning to split open and pour with blood, exposing the raw flesh beneath it. The pain made Huxort shudder as he writhed and convulsed on the ground.

'No! No, you must not desert us. Those kinglovers siege-locked in their fortress are no better than the Tunnellers we attacked at Cawdor. They won't want your power. Come back! Come back!' Snatch shouted in panic as he saw the Eretch glide towards the fortress. His own power was weakening and doubt dogged his footsteps as he chased after them, reaching up to try to grab desperately at their elusive, twisting shapes. At the back of his mind he heard the echo of Loremaster Grout's warning not to meddle with the power of the Eretch until he knew more about it. He remembered Grout telling him that they were grave-devils, unpredictable wraiths, utterly steeped in evil. Which was all very well: but what could he do to stop them from deserting him now?

Girrolt was suddenly beside him shouting, trying to get his attention.

'I think the Eretch are deserting everyone because of the doubts you instilled in us about the massacre. You voiced your fears – that is why they are going in search of new hosts.'

Snatch came to an abrupt halt and threw his head back as he howled with laughter. Was that all it was? The Eretch doubted his capacity for evil. Well, good riddance to them: they wouldn't be able to find a better host in all Elundium. And his men didn't need the power of any grave-devils anyway. No, now he came to think about it, they hadn't been much use in the destruction of Cawdor: almost all of the kinglovers and the ugly little Tunnellers had got away into the safety of the forest – all except the crippled boy's woman, of course. They had used the very shadows and webs of darkness that the Eretch had shrouded them with during the attack. His Company of Murderers wouldn't have let so many of them escape if they had been left to their own devices. Why, they had virtually brought Thanehand, the thronestealer, to his knees through the murderous intrigues and treasons that he had devised. They could certainly finish off the job by themselves.

'Go on, I don't need you,' he sneered, shaking a defiant fist at the departing, shadowy wraiths. Then Girrolt's voice interrupted him again, only this time he sounded more frantic.

'Snatch, Snatch, our followers are fighting one another – you have to do something. Stop them, quickly, stop them before they kill one another. Look out!'

Snatch turned sharply on his heel as the sound of Girrolt's warning clashed with the shouts and clash of steel behind him. He ducked just in time as somebody struck out at him. Cursing, he grabbed at his attacker and wrenched a dagger out of his hand, knocking him to the ground as he did so.

'Stop it! Stop it all of you!' he shouted, striding in amongst them. But he was helpless to stop the senseless stabbing and slashing as they rolled in the dirt and ashes that had once been Marshthistle, consumed by a murderous desire to kill one another.

Cold regret, rage and anger churned inside him. He wished he had heeded Grout's warning not to meddle with the Eretch until he had found out why Krulshards, the Master of Nightmares, had been so quick to abandon them in the ruins they had created at Cawdor. Suddenly the awful realization of what was happening to his followers struck home. The Eretch obviously cared nothing about seizing back the throne that Thanehand had stolen. All the spectral images they had glimpsed during their possession in the petrified forest, the physical metamorphoses they had endured that had transformed them into the creatures of the night they had once imitated when they had begun their intrigues and murderous treacheries against the King, all the dreams of power beyond their wildest dreams – had all been nothing but beguiling tricks set to ensnare them and make them willing hosts for the Eretch to escape from their enforced imprisonment at Cawdor. No wonder Krulshards had abandoned them. Perhaps the Eretch were destroying his followers because they feared leaving a thread of their power in a host which might be used against them one daylight? He stepped hastily away from the others, searching for a way of stopping the fighting. Somehow he had to keep the Eretch with them, at least until he had found out a way to dispose of them safely, but how?

Already the first of their translucent, ghostly shapes were boiling up against the walls of Underfall, cloaking it momentarily in webs of darkness before vanishing, melting into every fault and fissure, no matter how small, in the sheer, impenetrable surface. Snatch ran back into the smoking ruins of Marshthistle desperately searching for something, anything, that would divert his men from trying to kill one another. Squark flew lazily past his shoulder and settled amongst the bodies of the villagers who lay sprawled in the dirt. His sharp eyes had spotted plunder that the Honourable Company of Murderers had missed in their haste to slaughter the inhabitants of the small hamlet. The bird began to work its way through the corpses, his small pile of trinkets growing rapidly. Earrings, fragments of barter, pieces of jewellery; nothing of real value, but things that the company would never normally have left on those it murdered before the Eretch had possessed them.

The magpie stopped at a large woman sprawled in the centre of the road, his beady, black eyes catching the glint of silver beneath her hair. He hopped up onto her head and the woman unexpectedly flinched and groaned as his sharp claws dug into her face. She regained consciousness. Squark, startled, drew his head back to emit a harsh, pitiless cry and stabbed at the prominent knot of her jugular vein. The woman's body convulsed but Squark tightened his grip on her head. She gave a scream of pain, her arms flailing wildly, as a dark fountain of blood gushed up from the wound in her neck and splattered the white magpie's chest feathers. For an instant before her life-blood ebbed away she stared at the magpie, her eyes round with helpless terror, then her movements became weaker and her head slumped sideways, eyes staring blindly into the distance. The massacre of Marshthistle was complete. Squark ruffled his sticky feathers and busied himself with tearing free the bloodied earring.

Snatch grinned down at the magpie as he watched him plunder the woman. He had given him an idea. 'Here, let me have that,' he whispered, crouching and taking it from the bird's beak.

He rushed out of the ruins, thrusting the bloodied earring up into the air in front of his brawling followers, twisting and turning it so that it glittered in the early morning light. He sneered and laughed in their faces, shouting so that all of them could hear him clearly: 'Go on, kill each other, and be quick about it: I don't care. I don't need you, you stupid fools, because once you're all dead I won't have to share out the spoils of this or any of our other victories!'

Hesitation spread silence among the company. Swords, strangles, daggers and spears were uncertainly lowered, the madness to kill one another briefly pushed aside. Snatch watched their eyes. Greed, he had calculated, was a powerful force and, he cared to hope, an equal to the evil that had possessed them and was even now trying to destroy them.

'Our secret storehouses in Meremire Forest are almost full to bursting with what you have already taken from the people of Elundium, and all of it will be mine once you are all dead!' he goaded, his eyes narrowing with cunning and his thin lips splitting into a leer as he watched his words take effect.

His followers began to move slowly towards the burned-out ruins. Mutterings of greed and anger at being cheated out of their share of everything they had stolen erupted through the company and in a rush of armoured boots they swept into Marshthistle, stripping its corpses bare. Squark was forced to rise from amongst the bodies in a whir of feathers and his small pile of worthless trinkets became scattered and stolen in the onslaught. He swooped to Snatch's shoulder, tilting his head to one side and stared accusingly into his eyes.

'Thief! Thief!' he shrieked.

Snatch laughed and stroked his long tail before whispering conspiratorially to the bird, 'You can have the pick of everything we have ever stolen once Elundium is mine and I have no further use for this rabble.'

A movement in the air, a swirl of shadows and a faint cry of voices distracted Snatch. He frowned and glanced up above the ruins to see the ghostly shapes that had so readily deserted them pouring out of the fortress and sweeping back across the causeway. The Eretch descended and smothered his company in pools of darkness, making them halt and look up fearfully. Their voices became muffled as the shadowy figures swirled around them, reaching out to touch and caress the brittle, scaly armour that had fused with their own skin in the forest above Cawdor. One by one the company fell to their knees, reaching up with outstretched hands and claws, some trembling, some crying out as the Eretch melted back through the pores of their skin to repossess them. Their bodies began to swell and darken. The spines and ridges of scaled armour began to glisten again and take on the hue of deepest indigo. Once more they were filled with menace and brutal savagery. They rose to their feet and continued to strip the corpses of Marshthistle, all thought of destroying one another wiped from their minds.

Snatch stood quite still watching the repossession, waiting for the moment when one of the ghostly figures would descend upon him. He muttered impatiently under his breath, 'So, those wretched kinglovers in the fortress wouldn't let you in and you have come back to us but . . . why not come to me?'

He frowned as the last shadowy shape vanished amongst his men.

Looking down at the scaly armour on his own arm, he realized that it had never lost its colour like the others had. When he glanced quickly around he saw that neither Girrolt nor some of the original followers of the Honourable Company were being repossessed either. What did it mean? Why had the Eretch stayed with them while deserting the others? He beckoned Girrolt, Kush and Thorograsp to come to him and asked quickly what they thought had happened.

'I don't know,' Thorograsp shrugged. He had kept well away from the others when they had started to fight amongst themselves.

'I don't think they possess us all in the same way,' Girrolt ventured, hesitantly.

'Of course we have all been possessed by the same evil – look, look around you – or have you gone completely blind? There isn't one of us who hasn't grown a claw, a ridge of spines or whose skin doesn't have some armoured scales fused with it – is there? All of us were drawn into the massacre of Marshthistle, weren't we? And while we were enjoying an orgy of blood-letting we gave those kinglovers time to slam shut the doors of Underfall. What I want is an answer to this question – why didn't *we* try to kill one another just now – you and me – why not us? What makes us different to the others?'

Girrolt stepped uncertainly out of Snatch's reach. 'But that is what I am trying to explain,' he answered defensively. 'Surely the claws, the armoured skin, the scales – they all make us look the same but they are only the outward manifestation of the possession. My guess is that the fusing of the armour only happened because we were wearing the fragments as a disguise when the Eretch entered us – it doesn't mean that we are all the same inside, does it?'

Girrolt was putting more than guesses behind his theory: he had watched the way their men had reacted to the will of the Eretch on the long journey back through the Emerald Mountains and he noticed that he didn't feel half as compelled to do their bidding as some of the others did.

Snatch opened his mouth to sneer at Girrolt. Didn't he understand the simplest thing about the Eretch? They controlled people's will: they had filled their heads with persuasive whispers. They created the urge to commit all kinds of evil whether you wanted to do it or not. He had seen it in everybody, everybody in the company: there were no exceptions. It was that compelling power that the Eretch held over them that was so dangerous, it could, without a moment's notice make them turn upon one another senselessly. Snatch suddenly realized that he hadn't felt compelled to murder his followers; nor had Girrolt, Kush or a handful of others. Perhaps Girrolt was right after all: perhaps they weren't all possessed to the same degree. Obviously he still controlled a part of his own will that the Eretch couldn't touch. And yet he knew that they were inside his head: he could hear them, whispering, goading him to join in the looting. The beginnings of a way to rid them of the Eretch began to crowd into that part of his mind not occupied by them. He glanced furtively over his shoulder at the smouldering ruins of Marshthistle. The ragged black carrion crows were beginning to settle in the wake of his followers, landing on the stripped, naked bodies of the villagers to pick and tear at their cold flesh. Which ones, he wondered, if any, could he depend upon? Which ones still retained a fragment of their own will? Who were still true to their quest to overthrow the Thronestealer? Which of them would not turn a dagger against him the moment he discovered a way to drive the Eretch out of them?

Drawing Girrolt and the others into a tight conspiratorial circle around him, he looked uncertainly from face to face. How much of this scheme dared he voice openly before the Eretch grasped his intentions? Could they read those thoughts in him that they could not control? He swallowed, knowing that he would have to take the risk, but he decided to let the others know no more than was necessary. He needed eyes and ears amongst his followers, people he could trust. Lowering his voice, he ordered them to watch for the slightest sign that the Eretch didn't have full control of any of the members of the Honourable Company. 'I want to know who didn't indulge in that murdering madness just now. I want you to just whisper the names to me, just a whisper, nothing more.'

'But why?' Kush asked. 'What does it matter now? The Eretch are back with us and we can continue our assault on Underfall the moment the plundering of Marshthistle is complete. I'll organize a party to cut trees for battering rams and we will fashion the wood for siege ladders from that last copse we passed through.'

Snatch looked past the ruins of Marshthistle towards the sheer, impenetrable walls of Underfall and slowly shook his head. The lower sections of the walls were as polished and smooth as glass; they had no fault or crack to catch a siege-hook, and even if they had, the lowest of the fortified galleries were well beyond any ladder they could fashion and so cleverly edged with sharp, iron teeth they would be impossible to breach.

'We could starve them out,' Thrograsp ventured.

'I don't know what you're all so worried about: there's nothing here to worry us, those kinglovers are as good as rats caught in a trap. They can't go anywhere,' Huxort laughed, rising from his knees. He had been clutching at his bleeding claw as the Eretch had deserted him, but now Snatch stared at it. It looked as good as new.

Snatch watched Huxort as he would have done a dangerous viper, cautiously through hooded eyes. Clearly the Eretch were still very much in control of him. He would never have been so ready to give up such a prize as the fortress of Underfall before they had possessed him. How much had he overheard? How much could he be trusted? Snatch suddenly laughed and put his arm around Huxort's shoulder in mock friendliness. 'Yes, you're probably right, old friend: Underfall is of little use to us and there isn't much that rabble who defend it can do to hinder our victorious sweep across Elundium. Go and see to the looting: organize the men for our triumphant march – go!' He gave Huxort a firm push towards the ruins.

The smile dissolved from Snatch's face the moment Huxort's back was turned. 'Tell him nothing of our plans,' he hissed threateningly to the others.

'But what are we really going to do about Underfall? Surely we are not just going to march away?' Kush frowned. He could see movement in the highest galleries, warriors crowding forwards armed to the teeth.

'Do? What can we do?' Snatch snapped back angrily. 'Didn't you hear what Huxort said? I doubt if there is a man possessed by the Eretch who would put his heart into attacking Underfall. And why do you think that is?' Snatch lowered his voice, glancing furtively around before continuing. 'Because the Eretch have been inside the fortress and there is nothing in there that they want. That's why they came back to us. For a moment I thought greed had made our followers come to their senses but now I think it had more to do with the Eretch coming back to repossess them. We have no choice but to march on, but not before we have piled all the dead of Marshthistle up against the doors of Underfall. That should prevent their wretched horsemen following us – at least for a daylight or two. But keep a sharp eye open for Gallopers once we are on the road: they will be trying to overtake us and raise the alarm. Make no mistake, next time we attack, no matter where it is, we will breach the defences and secure it despite whatever the Eretch compel the others to do. Is that clear?'

'I think you can rely on Crimp: he's one of us for sure,' Thorograsp whispered, nodding towards the tall, thin boy who was loitering on the edge of the ruins, standing slightly apart from the others. 'I saw him charge straight towards the doors of the fortress, running ahead of everybody else, and he didn't even look back when the others stopped to massacre the inhabitants of Marshthistle. He would have reached the doors if he hadn't been driven back at the last moment by a hail of sharp stones.'

'Did he indeed . . . Send him over to me,' Snatch muttered mistrustfully. Of all his followers he doubted Crimp's loyalty most. In fact he had been watching him closely ever since that incident in Blackbone Alley behind the Learning Hall the last time they were in the Granite City. Snatch had noticed the boy hang back in the shadows as the others crept in through the back door of the Learning Hall and he had his suspicions that he might have been about to desert. Crimp had sworn that he had only been checking to see that nobody was following them and doubt had made Snatch resheath the dagger, but his misgiving had been strengthened once or twice since then. He had noticed that the boy was reluctant to join in the killing and Girrolt had even caught him weeping after the destruction of Cawdor, although what he could have found to weep about Snatch could not imagine. He had been waiting for an opportunity to kill the boy, to use him as an example to the others not to step out of line, but now, after what Thorograsp had just told him he didn't know what to think. Crimp his most loyal follower?

Crimp, the blacksmith's son, was not brave by nature, but nor was he as thoroughly evil as the others in the Honourable Company of Murderers. A knot of panic tightened in his stomach as he saw Thorograsp leave Snatchpurse's side and stride purposefully towards him. He seemed to be singling him out from among the others who were still looting the ruins. Had his plan to escape been uncovered? Had somebody seen him running towards the open doors of the fortress and realized that he was trying to make a break for it? How had they known he had been trying to escape instead of attacking it as he had been ordered to? They must have reported him. Snatchpurse, he knew only too well, didn't let people leave the Honourable Company of their own accord: he had made it quite clear with his bloody dagger that there was no room for doubters and that death at his hand was the only release. Crimp bitterly regretted running away from his home in the forge of Muddle as winter had set in. Why had he not listened to his father instead of rushing off to join this evil band?

Thorograsp had definitely singled him out, there could be no mistake. Crimp began to tremble. Why hadn't he realized before it was too late? Why had he allowed his hands to become stained with the blood of so many innocent people? There could be no honour in murder. Why had he not suspected the sinister intentions that lay just behind the façade? Snatchpurse, Crimp had discovered, cared nothing for the people of Elundium: he was obsessed with power, eaten away with revenge. His single purpose was to overthrow the King and seize the throne for himself. Crimp knew he wasn't the only one to be drawn into this murderous company by their beguiling lies about protecting the villagers, and merchants who travelled the greenways bartering their wares; he wasn't even certain that he was the only one to doubt and still survive for he didn't dare to speak openly. How he had managed to keep his loathing of what they forced him to do a secret for this long was nothing short of a miracle. He glanced anxiously around him but there was nowhere to run.

He had tried to escape once before, in the Granite City. He might just have succeeded if only his own indecision and spineless fear of the consequences of being caught hadn't made him hesitate. How much he had hated that moment's pause in the dark, dank alleyway behind the Learning Hall. If only he could have summoned up the courage to make a dash for it when the others slipped in through the back door; but Snatchpurse had grabbed hold of his arm and pulled him in with the others and Crimp knew how lucky he had been that their leader hadn't realized what he had been about to do, or he would have slit his throat right there on the spot.

Crimp swallowed nervously as he tried to mask his terror of discovery with a grin as Thorograsp drew closer. He had come to despise himself for what he had done so much that he could not even bare to look into the still pools of water when he washed himself for fear of seeing the monster he had become. Death, he knew, would be better than this evil existence, but he didn't even have the courage to take his own life. And his position in the company had become ever more desperate since the

Eretch had possessed them: he had not understood why, but their evil had barely touched him. He had felt it trying to get inside his skin, their vile whispers assaulting his mind but, if anything, they had only strengthened his loathing of everything he had been forced to do. He had screamed out and cried with the pain in the smothering darkness as the Eretch had invaded the company. He had felt their touch as they squeezed and searched for a way through the pores of his skin, had felt the pain as they tried to find a way through his eyes, his mouth, everywhere. He had clamped his hands over his ears, collapsing to the ground, rolling over and over in the dust and leaves. Suddenly he had found himself crouching in silence, almost untouched by the Eretch, while all around him he saw the others had been transformed. The disguises they had once worn had gone: now they had real horns with scales and claws. They had become the hideous beasts they had once imitated. At any moment he had expected them to rush at him, to tear him limb from limb. He had raised his hands to cover his face, only to discover that the Eretch had left some mark of their struggle of possession on him. The fragments of Nightbeast armour that he had worn as a disguise had loosely fused with his own skin. It clung wetly to his forearms and the backs of his hands. He had scuttled quickly backwards away from the others and hid among the trees while he felt along his upper arms and up across his neck. There were soft fragments of the scales clinging to him everywhere. With a sob of relief he realized that he must look, at least outwardly, almost the same as the others. He knew he would be safe from discovery. But as he moved to rejoin the group he had felt some of the scales flake and peel away before falling to the ground. The evil in him was only skin deep, and he knew from that moment he would have to be careful not to dislodge his scaly covering until he found a way to escape.

He had kept in the background as much as possible since that moment and had worked hard to mimic everything the others did, but he expected to be unmasked at any moment. Desperate to escape before the last of his scales fell away, he had made that wild dash to reach the doors of Underfall before they were slammed and siege-locked. It was his last chance. He had hoped to slip away during the attack on Cawdor and hide amongst the ruins until the company had left but to his horror, during the early part of the assault, when he had been pretending to be like the others, stabbing and thrusting his dagger at the inhabitants of the citadel, he suddenly found himself face to face with his own mother. He had plunged his dagger into her before realizing who she was. As the blade had struck there had been an instant, a moment, when he knew she had recognized him but then she had vanished. He had been overwhelmed with remorse and had sunk to his knees, all hope of escape gone. He could not give himself up to the people of Cawdor, if any of them survived the attack: he could never surrender, not after what he had done.

'Snatchpurse wants to see you immediately – and be quick about it.'

Crimp flinched instinctively at the sound of Thorograsp's voice but the expected curses and accusations didn't come. The order to report to Snatchpurse had been spoken in an almost conspiratorial whisper. Thorograsp moved even closer to him and gripped his arm with his clawed hand.

'Don't let the others know he has sent for you. Go across discreetly, go on.'

Crimp hesitated and stared into Thorograsp's face as

he tried to find some clue, some reason for his unexpected behaviour. Why had he not knocked him down and sent him grovelling in the dirt of Marshthistle to crawl over to where Snatchpurse now stood waiting with the white magpie perched on his shoulder? That was how all the other doubters had been treated. But Thorograsp's face, a distorted, scaly mask with its leering mouth of jagged teeth and two deep-set, murderous eyes lost in the shadows beneath the bony growths that had spread across his fore-head during the possession, gave nothing away.

'Don't stand there dithering, you stupid fool!' he hissed at Crimp. 'What's the matter with you? You know Snatch hates being kept waiting.'

'Yes, yes, of course – I'll go this minute,' Crimp stuttered, hurrying away through the ruins.

Beads of sweat were beginning to form on his temples and the palms of his hands had become damp. Sweat began to trickle down the back of his spine despite the chill morning air. His mind was racing. What could Snatchpurse want with him except to publicly humiliate him and then murder him for attempting to escape? Yet he had been sent for so secretly, so privately. There couldn't be another explanation – could there?

Snatchpurse watched the boy approach through narrowed, calculating eyes. He didn't like Crimp and he was in a quandary as to what to do with him now, especially if Girrolt was right about the degree of possession in some of his followers. And what if what Thorograsp had told him about Crimp's actions in the attack were true? He couldn't afford to allow this act of bravery, to go charging on alone while others paused to loot Marshthistle, to go unrewarded. And anyway, he needed Crimp, if the Eretch didn't control his mind completely.

'You did well, boy. It's a pity more of the others weren't

so singleminded during the attack,' Snatch muttered through tight, thin lips. He was having difficulty suppressing his dislike of the boy, despite what Thorograsp had said. He hunted his face to search for those doubts that he felt sure he was trying to hide.

'Did well ... did well ... ha ... ha ... ha ...' Squark shrieked, his head bobbing up and down.

'Quiet!' Snatch hissed at the bird, putting his hand over its mouth.

Crimp could hardly believe his ears. He was being praised for charging ahead of the others towards the open doors of Underfall. He was not being berated for trying to escape. His actions had been completely misread: this was beyond his wildest hopes.

'I ... I tried to do my best, sire, but ...' Crimp began struggling to suppress the fear and relief he felt from showing in his voice.

'I know all about it. You need not go into any detail,' Snatch snapped impatiently, beckoning the boy closer. He didn't want any more words than necessary to be spoken out loud lest the Eretch overhear. Drawing Crimp so close his lips almost brushed against the boy's ear he whispered, 'Next time we attack you stay close to me. Do you understand – I want you at my right hand.'

Crimp nodded vigorously, although he was at a loss to know why Snatch should want him close by. It couldn't be because he suspected him of trying to escape – he would have slit his throat on the spot if he knew only half the thoughts going through his head. But the reason didn't matter, he wasn't going to kill him. He was safe, for the moment.

Snatchpurse frowned as he drew away from Crimp. He was never wrong in his judgments – never – and yet in this instance he had to concede, no matter how reluctantly, that he might have misjudged the boy. There could be no other explanation for his valiant assault on the fortress. He needed Crimp's loyalty, at least for the moment, and to keep it he knew he would have to reward him with some trivial gift. But such generosity was against his better nature. What could he give the boy that he would cherish but had little or no real value? Irritably he glanced across the smouldering ruins to where he could see that his men were beginning to drag the bodies of the villagers towards the fortress. Perhaps he should give Crimp a pair of boots from one of the corpses, a stolen twist of copper barter, some worthless trinket . . .

Girrolt appeared suddenly at his elbow to inform him that they were about to begin blocking the door of Underfall.

'Yes, yes, I can see that for myself. Do it quickly,' he snapped testily, waving Girrolt away while he dealt with Crimp, but Girrolt hesitated.

'What shall we do with the prisoner? Shall I find her something to eat and drink before we march? She has had nothing for two daylights now.'

'No, let her starve!' Snatch hissed, his face souring at the mention of Sloeberry, the ugly little Tunneller he had captured during the destruction of Cawdor. Using her as bait to lure that wretched cripple, Drib, she was so fond it, instead of slitting her throat on the spot had seemed such a good idea at the time. Snatch had a bitter score to settle with the crooked boy for daring to loose an arrow-strike at him in the courtyard of Candlebane Hall. He had inflicted a wound on his chest that had never quite healed despite scouring and leeching it every daylight. The plan had worked, for it had drawn the stupid cripple on that horse of his right into the main courtyard when he tried to rescue the ugly little goblin as Snatch had held her by the hair. How sweet the taste of revenge had been as his men had surged forwards to cut off any chance Drib had of escaping.

Snatch's lips tightened and small bright bubbles of spittle frothed in the corners of his mouth as he remembered how the cripple had stolen that sweet moment from him. Knowing he had gravely injured the boy, shattering his sword arm with his battle mace and smashing him down into the saddle, gave him little satisfaction. He had wanted to torture and kill him slowly. Snatch shook his head: he still couldn't understand how the boy had escaped. Why hadn't one of his men thrust his spear through the horse's heart? There had been enough of them crowding the edges of the courtyard, blocking the archway. That horse should never have been able to get away. And yet it had spun round so quickly before rearing up and leaping towards the archway that it had scattered his men as easily as chaff before a storm. He had watched as it galloped out onto the causeway. The cripple had got clean away but for how long? He would have been dead from his wounds by sunset; of far more concern were the Tunnellers and kinglovers they had journeyed so far to kill. They had all vanished deep into the forest above Cawdor where his men would never find them even if they searched for a thousand daylights.

Through the consuming anger Snatch managed to remember that at least one good thing had come out of the attack on Cawdor: his men had found that meddling old Marcher, Berioss, who had been with the Tunnellers since the very beginning when he had driven them out of the inn at Deepling and lain all the people's fears falsely upon them. They had hounded him out of Cawdor and driven him over the cliff to plunge to his death on the rocks below. But it wasn't enough: his appetite for revenge, his thirst for power, had barely been whetted. Snatch looked back across his shoulder to where he had chained Sloeberry to the burnt stump of a blackthorn. She was kneeling in the dirt, her head bowed. The only reason he had brought the ugly little goblin with them on the long journey home through the Emerald Mountains was to blunt his black rage by tormenting and beating her so that she could entertain his men with her screams, but he had grown tired of seeing her ugly face with its tear-filled, bulging eyes and her pointed, shell-shaped ears. Every time he raised the lash to make her dance she reminded him all too sharply that the sacking of Cawdor had been a dismal failure.

Snatch suddenly laughed out loud as he saw a way of using her to his advantage. He slapped Crimp hard between the shoulderblades, making him stagger lightly, and cried, 'You shall be rewarded for your valour in the attack on Underfall. I have the perfect gift for you!'

Luckily for Crimp, Snatch didn't seem to notice the fine shower of armoured scales that fell to the ground around him, although Squark's sharp eyes saw them flutter down and he quickly flew down to peck at their slimy, brittle edges.

'You, Crimp, shall have sole charge of our little prisoner. I elevate you to the rank of warder. You can enjoy yourself by beating her whenever you wish. Go, go, take my whip and use it, make her dance and perform little tricks now and then to keep us all amused.'

Snatch smiled magnanimously and thrust his irontail whip into the boy's hands and waved him away dismissively in the direction of the tree where Sloeberry was chained.

Of all the luck! Crimp could hardly believe what he was hearing. He had expected to be punished for trying to escape and instead he had been rewarded, given a task that would excuse him from joining in the butchering and plundering of the villages as they marched through Elundium. It might even give him another opportunity to make good his escape.

'Oh, thank you, thank you, sire,' he repeated, bowing and stumbling backwards away from Snatch as quickly as he could in case he changed his mind. Once he had retreated a safe distance and Snatch was deep in conversation with Girrolt, he turned and hurried to where the girl was tethered.

'Get up – get on your feet, you wretched creature, and be quick about it,' Crimp demanded as he came to a towering halt over Sloeberry. 'Do as I say now or I'll flay the skin off your back. Get up!' he hissed impatiently as he saw her struggle weakly and slump back down.

'I won't ask you again,' he snarled, coiling the whip tightly in his right hand and making a show of drawing it back in readiness to strike her just in case Snatchpurse or any of the others were watching. He knew he had to make a convincing impression if he wanted to keep the exalted post of her warder.

Sloeberry flinched instinctively, expecting to feel the cut of the lash and the searing stab of pain across her shoulders and back as soon as Crimp's shadow fell across her. She had been driven beyond the point of exhaustion, beaten and tormented so often during the long journey across the Emerald Mountains that she hardly expected anything else. She was dizzy and emaciated, starving from lack of food. She was parched, her lips cracked and bleeding, but her will to survive, her determination to cling to life for as long as she could, burned fiercely in her heart. She knew that Drib was alive. She believed that with all her heart. And she knew he would come to rescue her:

one daylight he would come riding through the morning mist and then she would be safe. Her captors had tried to suffocate her hope with their cruel mockery and sneering laughter. They had told her he had died along with all her friends during the rout of Cawdor, that she was all alone in the world and they would torment her until she, too, was dead. But she knew their words were false, for she had overheard the truth one unguarded moment when Snatchpurse's rage at hearing about Drib's escape had lent an extra strength to the cutting edge of his whip. She had also overheard that Drib had been severely wounded before Sparkfire had charged through the swarming ranks of their attackers and taken him to safety in the forest.

Sloeberry tried to climb to her feet, pressing the palms of her hands onto the ground to help herself up, but she was too weak and sank down again onto her knees. Tears of helplessness brimmed in her eyes. This time she just could not go on.

'Get up, damn you, get up or I'll be forced to hit you.'

There was a hint of mercy in Crimp's voice but he held the whip high above his head, sure that the others were still watching him. Why didn't the wretched girl just do as she was told? All she had to do was to get up. He looked down angrily at her, cursing her under his breath, but then he hesitated, letting the whip fall unused to his side. He saw her small, pitifully wasted body kneeling helplessly in the dirt and he felt like weeping. She was no bigger than a child and her long, thin, delicate fingers, bruised and blackened by repeated torture, trembled as she used them to try to rise. He could see that her small wrists and ankles had been rubbed raw by the shackles she had been forced to wear, but it was the sight of the bloody weals in the soft woollen jerkin and leggings she wore where the iron tail of the whip had cut through them and into her flesh more times than he could count that sent a wave of revulsion over him. He couldn't imagine what she had been forced to endure. Suddenly Crimp felt the anger boil up inside him at the thought of what they had done to her, but it quickly turned to shame that he had done nothing to prevent it.

'I'll take no part in hurting you, I promise,' he muttered thickly, close to tears. He was about to turn on his heel and walk away from her, throw the whip onto the ground in disgust despite the trouble it would get him into when it occurred to him that he couldn't just walk away and hide amongst the others while somebody else beat her. It would be as good as holding the whip and doing it himself. Bleakly he realized that fate was giving him one last chance to do something good and honourable, that by staying with her, protecting her, even helping her to escape perhaps, he could, in some way, redeem himself. If only he had the courage to do it. He glanced furtively across to where Snatchpurse was bullying and cursing the others to work faster in building the pile of corpses to block the doors of the fortress and he wrung his hands together in indecision. What could he do? It was an impossible task: he was having enough trouble keeping himself alive in this murderous company. Suddenly, for better or worse, he made up his mind.

'You have to do everything you can to help me,' he sobbed, grasping the whip and raising it high above his head.

Sloeberry heard her captor sob and whisper something but she didn't understand. Her frail body tensed in expectation of the blinding stab of pain as the lash snaked across her back, cutting once again into her flesh. She heard the whistling crack of the whip's tail as it sliced through the air above her and she screwed her eyes tightly shut, grinding her teeth together in readiness to receive the pain. But the iron-tipped flail did not touch her: instead all she felt was the soft puff of dirt and a shower of small stones which hit her leg as the whip struck the ground beside where she was kneeling. She blinked and opened her eyes, uncertain of what new tortures her tormentor had in store for her. She lifted her head cautiously, brushed aside the untidy tangle of hair that concealed her face and looked up at the tall, thin figure who was towering over her. There was something vaguely familiar about his face despite the covering of slimy scales that disfigured it, mottling his cheekbones and clinging in peeling layers to the bridge of his nose before travelling in shallow, prickly ridges up across his forehead. There was something strange about him, almost a look of gentleness about his eyes: he reminded her of somebody, but she didn't have a moment to wonder who he could be or why he was being so considerate for Snatchpurse's voice cut across the harsh cries of the crows squabbling over the dead and the noise of his men throwing the corpses up onto the pile that now almost blocked the doors of Underfall.

'Get her up, Crimp! Don't be too gentle with her, boy: beat her to her feet. Hurry up! We're about to begin the march. What's the matter with you, boy? Don't you know how to use a whip? Do you want me to show you?'

Crimp felt a wave of cold panic seize him as he glanced across to the ruins. Snatch was standing, watching him just as he feared he would. He would come across at any moment unless Crimp did something, and quickly. He thrust his hand down and made a grab at Sloeberry's arm. 'Quickly, take my hand, I'll pull you up, but you must stay on your feet and start moving forwards. If you don't, he'll come over here and I won't be able to do anything to stop him from hurting you.'

There was a desperate urgency in Crimp's voice that made her grasp at his hand and, using the last of her failing strength, she managed to struggle to her feet with his help.

'Keep moving forwards and don't let it look as though you're holding onto me for support. I'll have to make a show of beating you but I promise the tail of the whip won't touch you. Once we're on the move and the others aren't watching us I'll give you something to eat and drink, don't worry.'

With much shouting and cursing at the warriors siege-locked inside the fortress of Underfall, the Honourable Company of Murderers assembled on the causeway to resume their triumphant march into Elundium. Crimp wisely chose a place for his prisoner in the rear of the column and made a show of forcing her to keep pace with the others. Sloeberry would have fallen many times to be trampled underfoot or to have felt the sharp cutting edge of the whip across her back if anybody else had been driving her forwards. She was dizzy and faint with exhaustion by the time they had covered the first half a league of the march, but once the stinging clouds of dust rising from the company's feet had safely obscured them, Crimp lifted her up and carried her. Keeping his promise, he gave her all that remained of the water in his flask and the food in the pouch that hung from his belt. It didn't amount to much more than a few stale fragments of waycake and a handful of berries that he had secretly picked in the petrified forest because he hated eating the raw flesh the rest of the company so clearly enjoyed, but to Sloeberry it was a feast. She kept taking furtive glances at his face, trying to remember where she could have seen him before and wondering why he was risking his life to help her when everybody else tormented her at the slightest opportunity. He reminded her of somebody, but who? There was something in the angle of his nose, something in his eyes. Suddenly it came to her. He bore a striking likeness to Quencher, the blacksmith who had led all those people still loyal to the King through the high passes of the Emerald Mountains. Yes, and now she thought about it, Mather, Quencher's wife, had spoken often about their son. She had told tales of how he had vanished, running off a few daylights before they had started their journey to Cawdor, and how she constantly worried about him and wondered what had happened to him. Then Sloeberry remembered that she had seen him once before in his father's forge in the village of Muddle. It seemed so long ago now, almost another life, when the small company of Tunnellers she was with had stopped at the forge to ask the blacksmith to sharpen their tools in exchange for some fruits of the forest that they had gathered whilst tending the greenways.

'You're Quencher's son, aren't you? I remember seeing you once before in his forge,' she whispered.

Crimp caught his breath. The mention of his father touched a raw nerve.

'Your parents were at Cawdor. They journeyed through the mountains in the depths of winter to help us. Your mother often talked of you: she was really worried and often wondered what had become of you.'

'I hope they never find out what I have become – I am so ashamed of myself,' he muttered thickly, looking away as large tears formed in the corners of his eyes. 'So ashamed.'

'I know there's a lot of good in you,' she whispered, trying to comfort him. 'When Drib comes to rescue me I will ask him if you can come back to Cawdor with us. I'm sure if I tell your mother and father how much you risked your life to help me they will forgive you. They'll understand that you didn't want to do all the bad things those monsters have forced you to do.'

Crimp shrugged his shoulders morosely. He could never go back to Cawdor, not after what he had done. 'What makes you so sure that Drib, or anybody else for that matter, is coming to rescue you? Haven't you realized that you're on your own now. There's nobody to help you except me.'

'Oh, yes, he'll come, I know he'll come and rescue me. He wasn't killed or captured was he? No, he got clean away with some of the others. Why, he's probably on his way right now!'

There was so much hope, so much belief in her voice that Crimp didn't have the heart to tell her that Snatch-purse had wounded the cripple so badly, shattering his sword and splitting his head wide open with his battle mace, that it was very doubtful that he was still alive by the time his horse reached the safety of the eaves of the forest.

'He'll come, I know he will,' Sloeberry whispered to herself. But she was frightened and refused to listen to the doubt in Crimp's voice. She had to keep that one seed of hope alive in her, she *had* to.

Thunderstone, the ancient keeper of Underfall, Errant, the first Captain of the Nighthorses and the handful of warriors loyal to the King watched helplessly from within the fortress as their attackers stopped on the causeway beneath their black banners emblazoned with a clenched, grasping claw. The air above their monstrously distorted bodies appeared to darken.

'Never in all my daylights as the Keeper of the great lamp have I seen such a strange evil!' Thunderstone muttered grimly, his knuckles whitening as he gripped the hilt of his horsetail sword.

The eerie darkness was beginning to swirl and take on the form of shadowy wraiths and ghostly figures as it expanded in widening ripples that swallowed up the causeway.

'Stand your guard, men, shoulder to shoulder. Be not afraid! Lift your voices in praise of everything that is good and beautiful!' he cried out to his men, giving them courage as the ghostly shapes boiled up against the sheer walls of the fortress and began to pour in through every gap and culvert, every crack and crevice. The Nighthorses neighed as they reared and plunged in terror, driving the Eretch away from them. The shafts of sunlight streaming into the long galleries suddenly faded. The shadows thickened and merged, plunging the warriors into the deepest indigo gloom while each man was violated with his own fears, isolated by his own weaknesses. The darkness was full of whispering voices offering to satisfy every desire of greed and lust, envy and jealousy. Cold fingers touched and probed, searching for a way beneath their skin, for a way to their souls.

Errant sensed that the wraiths were trying to enter their bodies and cried out, 'I want nothing that you offer – nothing that I cannot earn by honest labour!'

The ghostly fingers scratched at his face and shrank away. One by one the others cried out, refusing to take what the Eretch offered: the darkness gradually lifted to let the sunlight stream back into the fortress. The ghostly shapes retreated across to the causeway, settled over their attackers and vanished back into their misshapen bodies.

After the darkness had gone Errant turned impatiently, spurs jangling as he paced from window to window in the long galleries striking a clenched fist into his other open hand. 'We can't stay locked up in here and do nothing while those hideous creatures – whoever they are – defile the dead of Marshthistle. Have we lost all our sense of honour? Can't you see what's happening down there?' he shouted in anger, grasping at Thunderstone's arm.

'Look – down there – can't you see? They are tearing off strips of the villagers' flesh and devouring it as they pile their bodies up against the doors of this fortress. We have to do something, we have to ride out and stop them before they block the doors completely!'

Thunderstone pulled him away; anger momentarily flashed in his eyes. 'I don't like it any more than you do, Errant, but I am not about to let you ride out and get yourself killed. There'll be risk enough of that once that barbarous band has marched on.'

'Marched on? But surely they'll try to batter their way in here or starve us out first?'

Thunderstone shook his head gravely. 'My guess is they sent those ghostly figures in here to find a weakness either in us or the fortress before attempting to break the siege. But they couldn't find one. They obviously know we have enough food to last until the winter so they are piling up those bodies to prevent us sending Gallopers out to warn the King or any of the Wayhouses who are still loyal to him. Look, they've planted that vile standard of theirs in the centre of the village and they're beginning to form into a marching column. Your task, Errant, is to find a way to ride out of here and through Notley Marsh and then to reach Stumble Hill before they do. Remember Queen Elionbel and Krann fled there from the Granite City. You have to reach Kyot and Eventine at Stumble

Hill and alert them. When you have done that you must ride on with all haste to warn the King. Be ready to leave the moment we have cleared the bodies from the gates.'

V

Forgotten Threads of Magic

DUSK WAS BEGINNING to deepen beneath the canopy of the petrified forest. The still quiet of eventime was gradually spreading from branch to branch through the tangled tracery of vines and creepers that hung down in endless, flowery archways and dense curtains of verdant foliage that muffled the hoofbeats of the lone horseman hurrying through the gloom. Brilliantly coloured flowerheads with long, brittle petals swayed and rustled in the strengthening evening breeze. As they touched each other they began to glow and illuminate the thickening shadows that the Nightshapes were silently weaving between the trunks of the trees.

Nevian cursed under his breath as he felt the pull of sharp thorns snagging for the thousandth time in the long, flowing sleeves of his cloak. He pulled them free from the blackthorn bushes that crowded in either side of the narrow path they were following through the forest. 'Surely it cannot be much further to Cawdor! I never realized that getting anywhere could take so long or be so uncomfortable,' he muttered irritably from the saddle where he rode Equestrius, the Lord of Horses.

He had felt compelled to journey to Cawdor with all haste the moment Drib had finished telling all he knew of its destruction. He had to find out everything he could about the new evil that had dwelt there, lost and foolishly forgotten by the wise for so long, which had now arisen to cast its shadow over Elundium. Clearly most, if not all, of the Tunnellers, and many of those loyal to the King who he had led through the mountains in the depths of winter to help them had survived Snatchpurse's savage attack – if what the boy had told him was true. The King had great need of loyal followers now, more than ever before: from what he had learned from the boy and from Umm, the Yerrak, the Eretch had not been able to enter them during the winter they had sheltered at Cawdor. They had not managed to stain them with their evil. There had been no doubt in the old wizard's mind that he must journey to Cawdor and find all those who had escaped, no matter how scattered they had become. But that had been before he had realized the severe limitations of the new magic that had so unexpectedly infused the faded rainbow cloak with fresh colours. Its purpose, he was convinced after hearing the boy's story, was to draw him back into the affairs of mortal man. Clearly he had to rescue King Thane from the brink of despair and help him to banish the new evil that Snatchpurse had awoken. He had to help Thane drive it back into the shadows where it belonged. Nevian's only thought as he had descended the winding stairways of the Runesgate Tower was to search for those survivors, and to gather them together. He had thrown open the outer door and snapped his fingers, filled his mind with an image of the crumbling ruins of Cawdor perched high upon the marble cliffs and wished himself there.

But nothing had happened.

There had been no roar of wind, no rush of mountains and blur of trees. He had remained earthbound with only the faintest breeze ruffling at the hem of his cloak and the sound of the distant roar and thunder of the waterfalls emptying into the gorge below. Doubts had crowded forward on every side. What was he to do? Was he to find his own way to Cawdor, to journey there on foot? He considered saddling the boy's horse but it was still sore and too exhausted to take on such a journey. He cursed with impatience and frustration as he scoured his books for travelling spells, but to no avail. He would have been in a complete quandary had he not stumbled upon an old summoning spell – though he had to try three or four times before he found the right mantra. It brought Equestrius, white with sweat, to the door of the Runesgate Tower and with a sinking heart the magician prepared himself for this primitive form of travel.

The horse suddenly veered sharply to the left beneath a low tangle of vines and took them on to a wider track. Nevian had barely the time to duck and raise his hand to protect his face as the thick branches of flowerheads brushed across the top of his head, enveloping him in their pungent perfume. The gloom around him seemed to be lifting and he felt a strengthening breeze upon his cheeks. Peering forwards he saw lighter patches between the trees. Equestrius carried him out from beneath the eaves of the forest and below them emerged the gaunt, charred ruins of Cawdor etched in nigrescence against a shimmering sea of burnished gold reflecting the rays of the setting sun.

Night had drawn its smoothing shrouds across the ruins. A pale moon hung low among the stars by the time the old man rode in through the broken gate and dismounted stiffly in the inner courtyard. He wasn't quite sure what he had hoped to find as he peered cautiously into the inky shadows. Perhaps he had secretly hoped to discover that some of the inhabitants of Cawdor had returned, that they had found their own way back from the depths of the forest. But the silence hung too heavily in the silvered darkness for that. Only the faint sigh of the restless waves breaking up against the black marble cliffs below the fortress and the mournful whispers of the wind combing cold fingers through the deep drifts of ash and debris broke the silence. Somewhere in the darkness a splintered door creaked eerily on riven hinges and then hung still in the moonlight: there was no doubting that the ruins were utterly deserted.

Nevian sighed wearily and shivered in the chill, night air. In the daylights of his real magic he would never have found himself at such a loss or in such an uncomfortable predicament. In those daylights there had always been alternatives for someone with his powers: a mere snap of the fingers and he would have scoured the forest, a sharp turn of his head and he would have caught the sound of the voices of those he sought, no matter how far away. But these were not the only failing of this new magic – if indeed it was magic that had renewed the colours in his cloak and not some cruel taunt of fate to make him realize the vulnerability of mortal men, and not just some mere trick of the light that had lured him out of his self-imposed exile in the safety of his tower. He had never, as the Master of Magic, had to suffer the discomforts of ordinary men. He had not known the gnawing ache of hunger or the shivering touch of cold. These were base sensations that clouded his judgement, distinct discomforts that he was growing to dislike more each day. Hunger pinched at his stomach and the cold night wind probed beneath his cloak. He knew there was no point complaining about his plight as there was nobody about to listen to him. There was nothing else for it – he would have to spend the night in the ruins and make the best of it. Equestrius' saddle would have to serve as a pillow and the shimmering canopy of stars as the roof above his head. He would just have to make do and remember to prepare more thoroughly for such a journey in the future.

Muttering and mumbling about his misfortune the magician unsaddled Equestrius and left him to graze on the windswept headland. He found his spark, crackled it alight and set about searching through the debris that littered the ruins for enough kindling to light a fire. Soon the flickering flames cast dancing shadows across the walls of the courtyard and Nevian settled down for the night, nibbling at the few stale crumbs of waycake that he had discovered in the bottom of one of the saddlebags. He sat hunched forwards over the fire, blinking his watery eyes at the acrid smoke that curled and billowed up around his face. The dancing flames warmed him and made him feel drowsy. He yawned and rested his head against the saddle to find that his face had become bathed in moonlight and he let the sighing murmur of the sea breaking on the rocks below the fortress gently lull him into sleep. Tomorrowlight seemed a long way off.

He was on the very edges of sleep when he became aware of a sound that shouldn't be there, that didn't belong to the soft sigh of the sea or crackle of the fire. It shouldn't be in these burnt-out ruins at all, but it was getting louder. Nevian sat up abruptly and stared into the dancing shadows. There was something so familiar about that sound. What did it remind him of? Where had he heard it before? Slowly he climbed to his feet, loosing the dagger he wore hidden beneath his cloak. Turning his head he listened and frowned. No, it was not possible. Fire had ravaged the fortress from end to end, so surely he couldn't hear the whisper of the wind stirring a tangled mass of vines and creepers? The charred, crumbling walls of the fortress were completely bare of foliage, whatever had once grown there had withered in the fire. But he could hear leathery leaves and flowerheads touching and rubbing together, but it couldn't be. The sound was very much louder now and it seemed to be coming from the cliff edge, way beyond what remained of the defensive curtain wall that had once surrounded the fortress.

The sound prompted the magician to remember the image that he had glimpsed from the high window of his observatory, the strange picture of the gnarled old tree that clung precariously to the sheer rock face. Now that he thought about it, Drib had said something about their attackers seeing a tree growing halfway down the cliff on a narrow ledge close to where they had driven Berioss over the edge. Nevian hadn't seen anything of significance about the tree: there was nothing unusual about seedlings sprouting in the cracks and crevices of rocky ledges – indeed some of them grew into quite substantial trees – but there was something very strange about this noise. Surely there was not enough wind to make the leaves rustle quite so loudly.

Curiosity drew him forward. He picked his way cautiously over the remnants of the curtain wall, squeezing through a narrow gap until he was only a footstep away from the cliff edge. The sound of the rustling leaves was coming from just below where he stood. Now he could hear the creak of bark, almost as if branches were being bent and rubbed together by a gale. He felt the ground tremble beneath his feet as loose stones and earth crumbled and broke away from the cliff edge, clattering into the darkness below. He hastily stepped back from the edge and pushed his way through the narrow gap in the wall, crackled his spark between his fingers and held it up, catching his breath as he did so. His eyes widened in surprise as a gnarled old tree with ancient scarred and thunder-cracked bark, its branches heavily clothed with trailing vines and creepers began to appear in the uncertain light of the small spark. The tree swayed and creaked, turning slightly to the left and then to the right as if looking for a way forwards. Nevian thought he could see two sea-grey eyes high up in the trunk as its two main branches reached out towards the curtain wall. The knobby twigs touched the wind-riven masonry: it was as if the branches were seeking a purchase on the wall. The magician took another backward step in shock. The twigs spread out across the crumbling masonry, scratching at its surface, and then disappeared into dozens of tiny cracks and fissures. Fine chips of stone broke and flaked off as the twigs bent and tightened their grip.

The tree creaked and jolted sideways. Nevian could have sworn that he heard a deep voice, one that he almost felt he should recognize, coming from within the tree trunk. It was repeating itself, muttering, 'While there's life there's hope . . . while there's life there's hope . . . if anyone survived that attack I must find them, I must . . . while there's life there's hope.'

A thick root with five long tentacles spread out and slowly began to burrow into the ground with a deep groan of effort. A shower of rock fell away as a second root appeared and buried itself in the earth close to the first. The mass of twig-like fingers gradually released their grip on the wall. The trunk straightened and the branches rose and spread out on either side of it as the tree began to move slowly and purposefully through the gap in the curtain wall, lifting each root in turn and placing it carefully on the ground before moving another pace forwards.

Nevian looked up to the tree as it moved forwards slowly and saw that there was a rusty dagger protruding from its trunk at about the height of a warrior's chest. The bark around the wound was swollen and blackened with a dark, sticky sap that had stained the trunk as it had dried. Trees, he knew, didn't move of their own accord unless they were infused with magic. Suddenly he realized who this tree must be. It must be Berioss, although how the transformation had taken place was a mystery to him as there wasn't a magician in all Elundium, save himself – and only then at the height of his old powers – who was capable of casting such a spell. He had certainly been unable to use such magic for an age of daylights.

'Berioss, Berioss, is that you, old friend?' he called out, trying to get the tree's attention, 'Berioss . . . stop . . .'

The tree paused, one root momentarily poised above the ground. Had he heard a voice? Had he heard Nevian's voice calling out to him? He turned his head stiffly, listening, trying to peer down into the shadows through the vines and creepers that trailed and hung down from his arm. But the foliage obscured his sight and each time he moved the persistent creak and groan of the thick skin of bark that encased him drowned out all but the loudest sounds. No, there was nobody there. There couldn't be – the ruins were deserted, and even the seabirds had vanished after the attack. It was just his imagination dredging up echoes from his past. Nevian, Nevian of all people, would not have come to him. He had utterly failed the Master of Magic, failed to keep the pledge he had given to him, failed to protect the Tunnellers and forge them into the Knights of Cawdor. He was all alone and the only way he could begin to appease the shame and disgrace he felt was to start searching. If any of the company had survived that terrible attack he had to find them and somehow had to protect them.

He began to shuffle forwards again through the ruins. The ground trembled slightly beneath each deliberate, ponderous footstep. He had to bend down to enter the main courtyard but still his upper branches scratched their way along the walls and scraped the high, vaulted archway. Berioss came to a sudden halt. The leaves rustled and the twigs on the end of his branches bristled. Embers of a small fire glowed in the far corner of the courtyard and a saddle and bridle lay with a crumpled blanket on the ground close to the ashes. He wasn't alone! He had really heard someone call out to him the moment he reached the top of the cliff. He hadn't been imagining it.

Nevian hurried after Berioss calling out the warrior's name, but to no avail. He would have to do something quite dramatic, but what? What could he do to get the tree's attention? Could he remember enough of the spell for conjuring up lightning? Stabbing his fingers up towards the stars he chanted, but nothing beyond a faint, flickering flash in the sky happened. He called up the wind to roar but nothing more than a gentle breeze responded, barely ruffling the branches of the tree. The magician cursed and muttered under his breath. Stumbling over unseen mounds of fallen masonry in the dark he hurried to overtake the tree before it disappeared through the archway ahead of him and vanished into the courtyard. He wasn't used to chasing after people and if he didn't want to spend half of the night blundering through the forest he knew he would have to find a way of stopping Berioss without attempting to use any more magic. But how? And with what?

'Think! Think, damn you!' he muttered to himself, only to laugh out loud as a sudden thought struck him. 'Of course, what a fool! The answers are probably all right here!'

He delved beneath the voluminous folds of his cloak and, moving aside the silver phials that hung from his belt, he felt amongst the dozens of small cloth and leather pouches. The laughter died and his eyebrows puckered into a frown. Had he had the good sense to bring the pouch containing the elements of quickfire with him or was it lying, discarded, near the hearth in his tower awaiting his next experiment that required a rapid fire? Some lesser magicians and doubtful alchemists, he knew, used quickfire to impress and frighten the common folk, pretending they possessed powers beyond their true abilities. They would mix the two compounds of quickfire together beneath their cloaks and then throw them up in the air to create sudden flashes of fire. In truth it was merely a lazy man's way to stir up a blaze beneath a pot or crucible, to bring a potion quickly to the boil before it spoiled or congealed. Aha! He found it: luck had ensured that he brought it with him. His fingers closed around the tiny pouch sealed with wax to keep the air out.

Breaking the seal quickly he drew out two liberal pinches of sulphur and saltpetre – much more than he would have used to boil the largest cauldron in his tower – and placed it into the palm of his hand. He spat on the mixture and mixed it together into a sticky ball before it had the chance to glow and burn as it came into contact with the air. Hurrying beneath the archway, his hand held tightly shut, he drew his arm back ready to throw the quickfire into the air only to collide with the tree which had come to an unexpected halt just a pace beyond the archway.

'Berioss!' the magician gasped, his breath knocked out of him as he struck the trunk of the old tree. He staggered and began to topple backwards, his hand flailing in an effort to save himself. The hot ball of quickfire shot out of his fingers and flew up through the branches. It briefly fizzed and sparkled as brightly as a newborn star before dropping back to earth and landing with a soft splatter of sparks in the gloomy embers of the fire. There was a moment of startled silence broken only by the gentle sigh of the waves washing over the rocks far below.

Berioss felt somebody stumble against him in the dark and he could hear Nevian's unmistakable voice behind him crying out his name. A shiver of dread passed through the old Marcher as a hot ball of fire arched through his upper branches and flew above his head. Nevian had sought him out to take revenge for his failure to protect the company. He barely had the time to twist around and catch a glimpse of the tall, thin figure of the magician as he stumbled against him before the dying embers of the fire exploded into a blinding flash of light sending a spectacular whirlwind of sparks and flames high into the darkness. Leaves shrivelled painfully and turned black in the heat and his bark was scorched as it was showered with sparks. Berioss shrank back, the next ball of fire, he knew, would land directly in the crown of his upper branches and he would be consumed by fire. The magician would not forgive his failure a second time.

'Nevian forgive me, I know I have failed you, I know that all I promised lies in ruins. I pledged to protect the company . . . I pledged to forge them into the Knights of Cawdor . . . I know I was not worthy of your trust. Please, please, I beg of you, give me one more chance. Let me search and find out if any of the company survived. Once I have found them and safely gathered them together then I will come to you for the punishment I truly deserve for failing you.'

Nevian took a stumbling step, grazing his knees, before saving himself with his outstretched hands. He returned to his feet as he heard the shame and anguish in Berioss' voice. This was something he had not expected. Looking up into the dancing light of the fire he could see the tears of regret and broken pride which had misted his sea-grey eyes and were trickling down the age-cracked bark that coarsely covered the old Marcher's cheeks.

'I have ·utterly failed you. I do not deserve to ask for time or mercy. I dare not ask for forgiveness. I shall die without honour,' Berioss wept. With much creaking and groaning as the bark on the trunk of the tree stretched, he slowly sank to his knees before the magician, bowing his head in readiness.

'No, no, you have it all wrong, old friend, quite wrong. Now get up ... get up. Enough of all this nonsense!' Nevian cried, grasping at one of Berioss' arms and closing his fingers around a mass of twigs and shrivelled leaves. With a great effort he tried to pull the Marcher up onto his feet.

'Drib has told me how tirelessly you worked to forge the company into the Knights of Cawdor and how you fought valiantly to protect them during the attack on the citadel. He told me how you strode forwards scything a glittering arc with your sword, carving through the boiling shadows that engulfed everything. He saw how you sent up showers of bright sparks into the darkness as your blade smashed against iron helms and brittle claws, how you fought to keep a clear space around Damask and Mistletoe after they were flung from their mounts. He watched while you guarded them until they were able to escape and how, step by defiant step, you were driven back through the ruined courtyards, building up a wall of dead around you until, with riven helm and a notched and bloodied sword you made your final stand upon the cliff's edge. He heard you cry out your love for your king and the beautiful sunlight as you fell. You, old friend, should be heaped with honours for what you did on that awful daylight.'

Slowly Berioss raised his garlanded head, hardly able to believe what he was hearing, and he stared at the Master of Magic. 'Drib ... Damask ... Mistletoe ... they are alive? They are really alive? You have seen them ... spoken to them ... but that's more than I ever dared to hope for! We were overwhelmed by those evil creatures, they were half-human, half-beast and shrouded in webs of liquid shadow, the likes of which I have never seen before in all my marching daylights. But ...'

Berioss hesitated and looked out uncertainly across the desolate ruins. 'What of the others? I know some of the people escaped, I saw them as we were galloping down across the headland towards the stricken fortress. I ordered Oaktangle to look after the ones who were fleeing towards the forest. Did any more manage to get out? Where are they?' he asked in a hoarse, crackling whisper.

'As far as I know almost everybody fled beneath the cover of those shadows. Your attackers shrouded themselves with the very thing that enabled our people to escape, much to the fury of Snatchpurse, their leader. The Company is alive, they all got away except for Sloeberry, who was taken prisoner. They are now scattered, lost somewhere in that infernal petrified forest I've just journeyed through. I have been able to piece that much together from Drib's account of the attack. He is, in fact, the only one I have seen and he was brought to my tower by Umm, the Yerrak but he was gravely wounded ...'

At the mention of Snatchpurse, Berioss suddenly became agitated. The leaves that clothed his upper branches shook and rustled violently.

'I had my suspicions from the very beginning. I knew that evil good-for-nothing Chancellors' boy was behind all these troubles. They started within a couple of daylights of the evening he attacked Sloeberry in the Inn at Deepling when he drove the company out. I knew it ... I *knew* it!'

He paused abruptly, the bark on his forehead appearing to crease and wrinkle, 'But how did he manage to cloak himself and his followers in those webs of shadow? And how did he become half human, half beast?'

Nevian shivered and pulled his cloak more tightly about his shoulders. The shadows seemed to be gathering again, pressing in around them. He glanced across the courtyard and saw that the fire was now dying back to glowing embers. 'Patience, Berioss, patience. I will tell you everything that I've learned from Drib about the fall of Cawdor and the dreadful implications that I fear it has for King Thane, who is even now siege-locked in Candlebane Hall; but first let us move nearer to the fire. My magic isn't quite what it used to be and it doesn't seem to keep out the chill night air that nips at my bones.'

Nevian laughed softly, glad to see the light of hope rekindled in Berioss' eyes. He heard the tree shuffle across the courtyard behind him as he stooped to forage for kindling. 'That's better,' he murmured, holding out his hands to the new flames. He watched Berioss settle on the opposite side of the fire, his branches drooping slightly and his long, tentacle-like toes spread out along the ground. He had a few pressing questions of his own he wanted to ask the old Marcher.

'Drib was certain you had been driven over the edge of the cliff to your death. He even heard one of Snatchpurse's captains reporting it when he tried, unsuccessfully, to rescue Sloeberry. But clearly he was mistaken. Tell me, old friend, what happened? How on earth did you manage to transform yourself into a tree? Was there a magician in your midst? I know nothing about any other magician in Elundium. I know I was the only man with the power to do that during the great daylights of King Holbian, but that power, along with many others I once possessed, faded with the passing of the last Granite King. Somebody has performed this and that somebody I need to know about – he could greatly help your King.'

Berioss looked uncertainly across the dancing flames. Surely the Master of Magic hadn't forgotten that he had once turned him into a tree for refusing to pledge his loyalty to King Thane on the death of King Holbian? Surely he must know that this magic was his, and his alone?

'Well?' Nevian persisted, an edge of impatience in his voice, 'out with it, who is this magician? Who is this sayer of spells more powerful than mine?'

'But it is your magic, Nevian, nobody else's, or at least the forgotten threads of it that have dwelt deep within my bones from an age ago. Don't you remember cursing me along with all those other warriors who refused to pledge their loyalty to King Thane upon the Causeway Fields? It was a powerful spell all right, and we were fools to have ignored it because no sooner had we set foot upon a greenway than we were transformed into trees just as you said we would be. We had to stand there hot and parched in summer and frozen to the core in winter as punishment for what we had done. We stood there upon the greenway's edge until the King called for us.'

Berioss paused and sighed, emitting a sound like the wind gently rustling leaves on a summer's day. He lifted his hands and looked down at the mass of twigs where his fingers should have been. 'Traces of that magic have always been with me. There were daylights when my skin felt as tough as bark and my knuckles would swell and my joints would creak and groan when I moved. The villagers feared me, insisting that once the magic had touched a person it never left them. This was true: I thought it remained in me as a punishment for abandoning my king.

I called out for your help as they drove me over the cliff, although in truth I didn't deserve it, and suddenly, as I plunged towards the rocks, I felt that magic within me stir and come back to life. My armoured boots swelled and split apart and my toes spread out into a mass of grasping roots that burrowed into the dozens of fissures on the sheer cliff face. It broke my descent and I clung there in despair and desolation. I heard an echo of your voice, Nevian, telling me not to give up and that while there was life there was hope. I vowed to climb the cliff, no matter how long it took me and when I reached the top I would search for any survivors of the company. That was the least I could do for having failed to protect them.'

Berioss looked across at the magician and dared to ask, 'You couldn't possibly change me back into my real self, could you? It's just that each footstep takes so long to complete and it will take me forever to search the forest. I might never find them.'

'Extraordinary, quite extraordinary,' Nevian muttered, rubbing his hands together, lost for the moment in specu-lation. He had always assumed that the magic that bound a spell, any spell, would dissipate into the ether forever once a spell was undone or broken. That was, after all, the Lore of Magic. But clearly his books were wrong: magic could endure beyond the powers that originally created it. That power had faded with the passing of the last Granite King, so what could he do? He coughed and cleared his throat as he looked apologetically across the dancing flames to the gnarled old tree. 'I am very sorry, Berioss, but I'm not at all sure there is anything I can do to change you back into who you were. You see the power I had when I cast that spell back there on the Causeway Fields has faded. I have been reduced to small magic, tricks and illusions. Why, I even had to ask Equestrius, the Lord of Horses, to carry me here.'

A look of despair crumpled the bark on Berioss' face. 'Then I must stay like this forever.'

The old tree groaned and slowly began to turn away from the fire and look towards the archway that led out of the ruins and onto the windswept headland. 'Perhaps it is for the best. Perhaps it is Fate's punishment, a constant reminder for failing to protect the company when they had such a need of me. I must begin my search for them.'

'Wait, Berioss, come back. I didn't say I wouldn't try did I? Come back!' Nevian shouted after the departing tree. But Berioss moved slowly and resolutely forwards, deaf to his cries.

'Why didn't I have the forethought to pack a few of my books on magic. Equestrius could have carried them in his saddlebags. Everything seems to be going from bad to worse!' Nevian muttered. He knew there was little chance of his remembering the correct words and he had no hope of breaking such a powerful spell without them.

A chilling thought suddenly struck the old magician: what if that particular spell hadn't come from one of his books? He knew his spell books contained a wealth of tree magic, but what if he had created *that* spell on the spur of the moment? At the time he had been fuelled by anger and was desperate to protect the King. He was only too aware how dangerous it was to tamper with magic you did not fully understand – he could make Berioss' predicament much worse if he accidentally chanted the wrong words. But he couldn't leave the old Marcher trapped inside the spell. He would have to do something, whatever the risk. If only he could remember the content of that particular spell. Exactly what form had it taken? Cursing his failing powers he delved deep into his memory, squeezing between a thousand irrelevant images of light and shadow, searching for that particular moment. Suddenly fragments of it came to him. He could see the dark lines of the battle crescent that would not pledge their allegiance to King Thane spread out, creeping forward relentlessly across the Causeway Field, drawing ever closer. He remembered Thane snatching up his standard of the sun and spurring Esteron out onto the clear ground to confront them. For a moment he had stood there all alone before that dark, restless sea of distrust, listening to the black whispers of fear and doubt that rippled through the warriors. At that point he realized what the men feared. They believed it had been his magic that had kept them safe throughout the dark, desperate age of the Granite Kings. They believed, foolishly, that his magic had put Thane where he was. Nevian remembered how angry he had been. They had no reason to fear and threaten Thane. King Holbian had chosen him upon his death bed, named him as his successor and the new King of Elundium. Thane did not have magical powers – he never had need of them.

Nevian sighed. Since the fading of his powers he had come to realize that the ordinary folk had a real fear of magic and that they wove superstitions around everything they didn't understand. In retrospect he would have tackled the situation very differently, but it was always easier to be wise after the event and it wasn't getting him any closer to helping Berioss. Words from the spell floated into focus.

'eko, arazark, pledge your loyalty or by ash and elder and dragon's snap . . .'

The scrape and rustle of the tree's upper branches as it touched the roof of the archway's vaulted roof broke Nevian's concentration. The magician stooped slightly, pressing his fingers into his ears to try and shut out the sound. He needed more if he was to attempt to break the spell. Much, much more. Words appeared in his mind.

'daydrum, daydrum, remain forever chained, bound and condemned to stand, frozen, watching, waiting upon the greenway's edge . . .'

Nevian frowned. From what he remembered the spell was clearly one of his own making, at a time when he was hot and impulsive and, unfortunately for Berioss, it contained very strong magic. Was it, he wondered, because he had inadvertently used the word 'forever' in the forming of the spell, a word he would never normally have used. Was it that which made it so enduring? Perhaps it was impossible to break the spell entirely.

Nevian took a deep breath, summoning up all the antidotes to true magic that he could remember, hoping for Berioss' sake that he would be lucky. He called out,

'By oak and hazel, root and branch, Eko, Arazark, Daydrum, by leaf and twig let the sap rise and undo this spell.'

Berioss halted as buds suddenly swelled and opened into new leaves on all his branches. The mass of trailing vines that clothed his trunk burst into flower, filling the court-yard with a sweet and heady scent.

'What have you done to me? I can't see a thing!' he cried, his voice muffled by the lush new foliage that completely obscured his face.

'I think the antidote to the spell is just beginning to work. Don't worry, Berioss, you have nothing to fear, I'll have you back to your former self in no time at all. I just have to make a few alterations to the mantra.' Nevian cried with delight: after the most recent experiences he was beginning to doubt if he still had any abilities left at all and almost felt that he should stop trying to wield any real magic. His moment of delight quickly turned to alarm. It wasn't only new leaves and flowerheads that were bursting open. The tree was actually growing, taking root beneath the archway. To his horror he could see fresh green twigs sprouting on every branch.

'Step back, Berioss. Get out from beneath that archway before it's too late! Take my hand and I will guide you back to the centre of the courtyard. Hurry man, move while you still can!' he shouted, rushing across the courtyard in a flurry of billowing coat tails to make a grab at the closest branches.

With the creak and groan of expanding bark Berioss swayed and slowly attempted to step backwards. Branches bent and scraped at the underside of the arch, dislodging a shower of crumbling soot and mortar. With a loud, tearing sound he managed to lift each foot in turn, pulling free the tangle of newly-formed roots that were growing rapidly out of his toes. The tree lurched wildly from side to side and at times almost toppled over as it moved.

'Just one more step,' Nevian urged as they got closer to the centre of the courtyard.

'I can't move any further, the roots are becoming too strong for me to pull them out of the ground and the trunk is growing up and around me, it's stretching my bones, tightening around my throat. I can't breathe. Help me, Nevian, help me . . .' Berioss' voice shrank to a faint echo, a strangled gasp from somewhere deep inside the trunk of the old tree.

Panic seized the old magician. He had got it wrong again. If he tried another spell it would probably kill Berioss, but if he did nothing the tree would strangle him. Nevian chanted again, this time radically changing the words, using phrases and language he had not uttered for an age of daylights.

The rapid growth of the tree slowed. The thick branches hung still, a dark, heavy tracery against the bright canopy of stars above the magician's head. Nevian held his breath anxiously, watching, waiting. Had he said too much? The leaves rustled and began to fold themselves back into light sticky buds that shrank and disappeared gradually, leaving the branches bare. The mass of flowerheads drooped and faded and began to fall, drifting down in a soft rain of perfumed petals. To Nevian's relief he had halted the tree's growth, but was the old Marcher still alive?

Nevian pressed his good ear against the trunk. The bark felt warm, and from somewhere deep inside the tree, he was sure he could hear Berioss' strangled gasps for air. The magician stepped back, deep in thought, and looked up at the tree that now towered over him. He would have to be very careful. This time the words he chose had to be exact if he was to reduce Berioss to his true stature.

'Eko, Eko, Dragon's snap. Unbind, undo this warrior, marcher Berioss, undo him from the curse that holds him. Reduce his girth, yet not to dwarfishness, release him from the green roots that grow and the garlands of flowerheads that crown his forehead. Make him once more human size. Daydrum, Gerrunissimus, Outoria, Outoria.'

The tree began to shake violently as the magic swept through it, penetrating every thundercrack, knot and fissure. Shivers of bark began to break off and splinter away from the trunk. It groaned and creaked as it began to shrink. Branches broke away and came crashing to the ground. Nevian saw the old Marcher's face begin to appear behind the strips of bark as they peeled away from his nose and across his cheeks. His mouth then split open and he inhaled a deep breath of air. Two of the stoutest branches established themselves as his arms, complete with large, knobbly hands and gnarled fingers. A long, irregular crack appeared with a snap in the lower part of the trunk and widened, releasing the Marcher's trapped legs. The mass of roots that had grown so rapidly and spread out across the ground to support the tree began to shrink and disappear as the magic penetrated them, leaving only two long, slightly knobbly feet with splayed toes in their place. Berioss gave a startled cry as he began to topple forwards. He staggered wildly from side to side. With arms flailing he strove to find his balance as the last of the roots withered and fell away from the soles of his feet.

'There, I told you I would do something to help you, didn't I?' Nevian exclaimed, stepping hastily out of Berioss' way as the warrior sought to keep his balance in the flickering light of the fire; but the magician could plainly see that he hadn't got the words of the spell quite right.

'What exactly have you done to me? I feel so unsteady and the ground looks so far away. I feel dizzy . . .' Berioss cried.

Nevian frowned. He didn't dare chant another mantra. He craned his neck to look up at the Marcher, he was at least twice his normal height, if not more. A giant of a man. And he hadn't exactly managed to get him completely out of the tree either. He could still easily be mistaken for a gnarled old beech if he stood perfectly still.

'I'm afraid my magic has become a little unpredictable lately, Berioss, but I assure you there is nothing to worry about. Once we rid Elundium of the dark shadows of evil and we travel safely back to my tower why then I will have the time to search through my books and find exactly the right words to break the spell and . . .' Nevian paused. There was a look of despair in the old Marcher's eyes.

'Be patient, old friend,' he smiled reassuringly. 'Try and look on the bright side. At least I have been able to give you back the proper use of your legs instead of you having to shuffle along with them trapped inside the trunk of that old tree. Think of the advantages of not taking root every time you place one of your feet on the ground and being so tall and powerful you will make your enemies quail . . .'

Nevian paused. He could see that the old Marcher was not at all convinced. 'Look at it another way,' he continued quickly, 'how many daylights do you think it would have taken you to cross the headland beyond the gatehouse of the fortress and cross the open land to reach the eaves of the forest if Fate had not chanced to cross our paths tonight? Don't you realize what a help it will be if you search for the others while I return to my tower to seek out remedies against the dark evil. Now that Snatchpurse has harnessed the power of the Eretch I will have to do something to stop them taking the Granite City and corrupting the whole of Elundium.'

A movement in the darkness behind Berioss' head caught Nevian's attention and brought his words to a sudden halt. His eyes narrowed and he reached beneath his cloak, closing his long, thin fingers around the hilt of his dagger and loosing it from where it hung at his belt.

'What is it? What have you seen?' Berioss hissed in alarm.

A shiver of apprehension rustled the leaves that had grown during his latest transformation. Two winged shapes were flying low towards them, stooping in over the crumbling ruins. He raised his arms to ward them off but hesitated as he heard the magician laugh and call out.

'Berioss, be at ease. It is Orundus, the Lord of Owls, and, if I am not mistaken, that must be Silkstone with him, the owl that befriended Drib.'

Much to Berioss' surprise both owls stooped and alighted on his shoulders. He called out Silkstone's name. He turned his head at the sound of Berioss' voice and pecked at the rough bark that covered the side of his head as if searching for where the voice was coming from. Berioss called out the owl's name once again and he began to raise his hand to greet the bird but Silkstone flew away to perch on the crumbling wall of the courtyard.

'Don't be disappointed if the owl fails to recognize you immediately, Berioss. Remember you have changed considerably since he last saw you, have patience,' Nevian reminded him gently before concentrating his attention on Orundus. 'I see you have found Silkstone, but what of the others who survived the destruction of Cawdor? Have you caught sight of any of them? What news do you bring of the wildwood and the high passes through the Emerald Mountains?'

Orundus ruffled his feathers. 'The dark evil that the boy spoke of arose here in Cawdor and has indeed swept through the mountains, leaving behind it a wide trail of ruin and desolation. Even as we speak more of Elundium falls beneath the relentless tide of its shadows and with each new daylight villages lie burned to the ground, their people slaughtered. Of the ones who survived the rout of Cawdor yes, I have caught a glimpse of them from time to time during my search for Silkstone. They are lost and wandering leaderless beneath the trees. They scattered and hid whenever I stooped close to them. They appear to be truly afraid, helpless with terror.'

'All Elundium will fall. Everything will be lost if we

don't do something quickly. But what can we do? We are powerless.' Nevian looked up to the Lord of Owls and suddenly cried out in inspiration. 'Drib has some part to play in all this, I know he has. Fly, Orundus, fly back to my tower and protect him for me, wait until I return.'

The Lord of Owls rose into the darkness calling for Silkstone to follow and the two owls vanished as silently as they had come.

'What was that all about? What was all that hooting and shrieking?' Berioss asked as the owls departed.

'Dark news!' Nevian muttered gravely before telling him Orundus' bleak words. Then Nevian fell silent. He watched the firelight, lost in thought, searching, trying for a way to figure out what they could possibly do.

'What our king needs is a new army, a battle crescent, true-hearted Marchers and Archers, squadrons of Gallopers,' Berioss murmured.

The old Marcher's words broke into Nevian's thoughts. He frowned irritably as he glanced up towards the interruption. 'How am I supposed to think if . . .' he began, only to laugh out loud suddenly. 'Yes, yes, of course, you are absolutely right, Berioss, our king does need an army. He needs brave-hearted warriors whose souls cannot be stained by the evil of the Eretch, and the beginnings of that army is right here, wandering through the petrified forest.'

Berioss stared in bewilderment at the magician. There wasn't the beginnings of any army that he knew of wandering through the forest.

'Don't you see, man?' Nevian cried, leaping to his feet and sweeping his hand in the vague direction of the trees. 'All those people I gathered, they are all loyal to the king. Then there is you, there are the Tunnellers, Eider, Drib . . . the Eretch couldn't get inside any of you could they!'

'But they are not warriors . . .' Berioss protested. 'They are loyal but they are blacksmiths, weavers, fishermen, tradespeople – they cannot fight.'

'I know, I know, but they are a start and Eider and the Tunnellers, once you find them, will help you. Remember you have already taught them the skill of arms.' Nevian paused and glanced out through a gap in the ruins, looking across the ebony sea to where the grey hours had already painted a pale finger of colour along the distant horizon line. The small beginnings of what might just turn the tide of history had already started. He turned back to Berioss.

'Your king needs you now more than ever before. Will you gather together those who are lost and forge them into warriors? Will you lead them triumphant into Elundium?' Nevian asked, reaching across the fire to clutch at the Marcher's gnarled old hand. He was about to pull him to his feet when Berioss answered uncertainly.

'Yes, yes, of course I will try. I am pledged to serve my king, but an army needs weapons, clothes, food . . . where will I find such things in the forest? There are no forges beneath the trees, no looms to weave cloth, no lasts to cobble boots. My sword was lost in the destruction of Cawdor. How can I expect anyone to follow me, unarmed and dishonoured? And even if they did where exactly in all Elundium am I to lead them to?'

Nevian frowned and looked over the dying flames of the fire to the old Marcher, pondering on the truth of his words. Where indeed? Where would they find even the most basic necessities for such a venture when everything they had brought to Cawdor had been utterly destroyed? Who could provide for them in such black times? Berioss saw the troubled look his questions had brought to the magician's face and slowly he began to climb to his feet. He had a long search ahead of him.

Nevian suddenly caught a glimpse of the rusty dagger that had been thrust into Berioss' chest by one of his attackers only moments before he was driven over the cliff edge. He realized that it was probably the threads of magic in that old spell which had fused the bark tightly around the blade, staunching the flow of blood and saving Berioss' life, but it was time it was removed and the wound cleaned before it festered. Now he could see a more important use for the blade, and perhaps an answer to at least one of the old Marcher's questions.

'Sometimes fate has a way of providing the things we need in the strangest ways. Hold still for a moment.'

The magician chuckled as he reached across the fire and gripped the hilt of the dagger and wrenched it free. Berioss gasped with the pain and slumped back. Nevian quickly staunched the flow of blood and forcibly stuffed an oiled cotton into the raw wound, closing the crack in the bark. Casting around he chose the stoutest, straightest branch that had broken from the tree and stripped it of leaves. Carefully he bound the dagger onto one end of the branch, muttering a binding spell while he did so, and the metal and wood fused together in a brief flash of white hot light.

'There, now you are armed again, and with the very blade that would have sent you plunging to your death if the forgotten threads of my magic had not saved you.'

Berioss rose to his feet and took the spear, holding it up above his head. 'I would dearly like to meet the previous owner of this blade. Perhaps one daylight he will chance to come across my path,' Berioss muttered grimly. He took a step towards the archway and paused, glancing back to Nevian. 'You have strengthened my resolve. I will find those who are lost, but where am I to lead them?'

Nevian closed his eyes and let his head sink to his

hands. He pressed his fingers over his ears to shut out the persistent sigh of the waves breaking on the rocks below and the rustle of the dawn breeze as it whispered through the leaves of the waiting tree. He had to concentrate, he had to try and open a window into the future. So much depended upon it.

Silent darkness seemed to strengthen the magician. Gradually he became aware of the smell of snow in the air and faintly, he thought he could hear the distant hum and bustle of a great city. The rumble of carts came to him, the shouts of the cryers on the streets. Slowly the image of the sheer granite walls of Candlebane Hall began to appear but it stood desolate, its doors siege-locked, deserted save for one single light that burned in its highest window. One fragile flame was all that remained: defiant, unconquered by the encroaching sea of darkness.

Nevian blinked and stared up at Berioss. 'Candlebane Hall. You are to lead them to Candlebane Hall! That must be where the final battle will take place but when . . .' he paused for a moment. 'Of course – the smell of snow,' he cried. 'Berioss, you must bring every loyal warrior, everyone you can muster, and meet me in the shadows of Candlebane Hall before midwinter's day!'

The magician gathered up Equestrius' saddle and hurried out through the archway. 'There is no time to lose, there is magic to conjure and spells to weave.' He glanced back at the old Marcher and called out, 'Remember, old friend, you must trust in fate and be there by midwinter's day!'

Then he vanished in a swirl of rainbow colours.

VI

The Sorcerer's Apprentice

DRIB SLEPT SOUNDLY beneath the swans' feather sleeping rug in the chamber at Runesgate Tower. He slept for two nights and two whole daylights, soothed by the powerful sleeping draught of crushed nightflower petals, starwort and jasmine seeds that the magician had secretly sprinkled onto his pillow. But on the third night the effect of the sleeping draught began to wear off and he tossed and turned in his sleep, crying out Sloeberry's name. He was troubled by a dark, recurring dream: Sloeberry was being taken away, a helpless prisoner, and he could do nothing to prevent it. He could hear her voice calling to him, begging him to rescue her but it grew fainter as she was taken further and further away. He tried to follow the sound – he made every effort to chase after her, but sinister, shadowy figures always crowded around him, trapping his arms and legs. Cruel voices mocked and jeered his futile attempts: the more he struggled the tighter they held onto him.

Drib woke with a start. He was bathed in sweat. Listening to the night silence, he caught the faint echo of her voice: it seemed so real. She had to be there somewhere, she had to be out in the darkness, but slowly the sounds faded and melted into the silence. 'Sloeberry . . . where are you?' Drib whispered. His voice broke into a sob of despair as he saw the grey stone cast on his forearm and the memories of her capture came flooding back. He felt overwhelmed by a gnawing sense of emptiness, a hopeless feeling that he would never find her.

Grannog was stretched out across the threshold of the chamber, guarding the boy as Nevian had asked. He heard the sobs and rose stiffly to his feet, his hackles rising along his back. He leaned forward and licked the boy's cheeks to comfort him. Drib gave a startled cry as the shape of a huge, ferocious dog suddenly appeared beside him, looming up silently out of the darkness, its eyes and teeth shining luminously in the moonlight. It seemed to have appeared by magic. Drib could do little more than gasp and clutch with the fingers of his good hand at the hem of the sleeping rug before he felt the beast's hot breath on his face and a rough, wet tongue licking away his tears. The dog growled softly and looked at him for what seemed to Drib to be an eternity before turning away and softly padding across the chamber to settle in the open doorway and continue his watch.

Drib swallowed dryly, his heart beating fast. It was certainly the biggest dog he had ever encountered, much more powerful than the leader of the pack of Border Runners who had, quite as unexpectedly, appeared in the petrified forest and helped him and Eider hunt and kill that Nightboar on their first daylight at Cawdor.

'Hello, I . . . I . . . I'm Drib,' he offered hesitantly, smiling at the dog, remembering how Nevian had once said something to him about confronting his fears even if he had to pretend to himself that he wasn't really afraid.

'Umm, the seven-fingered Yerrak, brought me here, although I don't know where he is now . . . and I don't really know much about him . . .' Drib continued breathlessly, glancing anxiously around the room looking for him. He was sure he had been crouched against the wall near the door before he had fallen asleep. 'I was injured in the attack on Cawdor, you see, and my sword arm was broken, but Nevian has mended it now and . . .'

Grannog growled softly, interrupting the boy's babble, and told him his own name. He also told him that he knew all about his injuries and that the magician had asked him to watch over him until his return. Drib blinked in surprise. He could understand most of what the dog was telling him, not in words exactly but in much the same way that he understood the owl, Silkstone.

'Grannog . . . did you say your name was Grannog?' the boy asked in a shocked whisper of awe. Grannog, he knew from the Loremaster's stories in the Learning Hall, was the Lord of Dogs. He had fought alongside King Holbian, the last of the Granite Kings, in the great battle beneath the walls of Underfall when Krulshards had been defeated. He had run at the King's stirrup as they pursued the Master of Nightmares to the very gates of night. But Krulshards had escaped into the darkness and the King could not follow because he feared the dark – it had been the one weakness that Nevian had, in his making, overlooked. Drib remembered being told how rage and anger had killed the King as he saw victory stripped from his grasp. He had raised his sword to strike Nevian but Orundus, the Lord of Owls, had snatched the blade from his hands. Grannog had leapt at the King and Equestrius, the Lord of Horses, had reared up, thrashing the air above the King's head with his razor-sharp hooves, ready to crush his skull. But Nevian had forbidden them to harm the King. His moment of anger cost King Holbian dearly: the magician had broken the bonds that had, for time beyond counting, held the warhorses, the battle owls and the Border Runners to fight beneath the King's standard, battling together against the terrors of the darkness. From that moment King Holbian stood alone. It was one of the best of Grout's stories, one that had held Drib entranced until lessons ended with the noonday bell every time he told it. But how, Drib wondered looking across at the dog, could he really be the same Grannog? Surely that bond-breaking took place so long ago.

'Yes, I am Grannog, the Lord of Dogs,' he yawned in answer to the boy's question as he stretched out and half-closed his eyes.

Drib caught a glimpse of his worn-down fangs and saw that there were, in fact, flecks of grey around his muzzle and in his thick, broken coat. The dog was very, very old, but it was indeed the same Grannog, the Lord of Dogs made famous by the Loremaster's stories.

'Just imagine it, Grannog looking after the likes of me . . . a mere sweep's scramble! Eider's never going to believe a word of this,' he smiled, pulling himself up into a more comfortable sitting position with the pillow at his back. The moonlight made the room almost as bright as daylight and he didn't feel the least bit sleepy now. He thought about Eider and the others and imagined them lost and scattered somewhere out there in the wilds of the forest – that was if they had all been lucky enough to survive the destruction of Cawdor. Then the smile began to fade as he remembered Berioss being driven to his death over the cliff edge and thought of Sloeberry as a helpless prisoner.

He sat bolt upright, ignoring the stab of pain in his sword arm. He had no right to be sitting there safe and warm in a soft feathery bed while his friends were suffering so cruelly. He had to do something about rescuing Sloeberry. It didn't matter what the magician said about the severity of his injuries – he had to go, he had wasted enough time already, letting the trail go cold. But what could he do to rescue her? He could barely lift his injured arm: it would do him no good in a fight. Gingerly he tried to flex the fingers that protruded from the end of the heavy stone cast. They moved slightly but a hot, tingling sensation shot up his entire arm. It made him shiver but it didn't hurt as much as he thought it would. Perhaps he would be able to grip a sword after all. He tried to grip the hem of his sleeping rug but he couldn't. The movement made him gasp with pain.

He swung his legs over the edge of the bed and put his feet onto the floor. After a moment he began to rise unsteadily to his feet. He would just have to think of another way of defending himself until his arm healed. First of all he had to find her. He had taken no more than one small, crooked step towards the door before the enormity of the task confronted him. He was overwhelmed by it. Even if Grannog allowed him to leave the tower, he had no idea which direction to take or whether Umm would help him to find the way. He wasn't even sure he could put Sparkfire's bridle on with only one hand and he normally needed both hands just to carry the special saddle that Flock had made him to hold him straight. He still had to dress himself. It all seemed so impossible.

'I will think of ways to do these things. I have to,' he said grimly, reaching down for his clothes as quickly as he could.

The dog, who had looked so soundly asleep, blinked and looked up as the boy rummaged through his pile of clothes and armour that lay at the foot of his bed. Grannog rose silently and gently nudged at Drib's arm.

'I have to go, Grannog, you must understand. If I don't start searching for Sloeberry now I might never find her. I can't just sit here doing nothing!'

'Patience, Drib, have patience,' the old dog growled. 'Nevian will find a way to help you. He has more books on magic, more knowledge of Elundium, than all the other magicians ever had. Have patience and wait for his return, I must not allow you to leave here.'

'So I have to stay here, your prisoner, while Snatchpurse tortures Sloeberry have I?' Drib asked in despair.

'No, you are not my prisoner. You are free to wander wherever you wish, but you must stay in the tower. I am sure Nevian won't mind if you look at his books. You can visit your horse in the stables or walk freely with the creature who brought you here but you must not leave the Runesgate nor cross the weir without Nevian's permission. Do you give me your word you will not try to leave?'

Drib nodded bleakly. 'Books? What good can books do? How can I rescue Sloeberry with books?' Drib exclaimed as Grannog padded out of the chamber, leaving the doorway unguarded.

Drib sat on the edge of the bed lost in black despair, fighting back tears of frustration. He had no choice but to give his word to Grannog and he would not go back on it. He would not be leaving the Runesgate until Nevian returned, he knew that. He also knew that sitting on the edge of the bed feeling sorry for himself wasn't going to achieve much either – he could at least salvage some pieces of his armour and clean them in readiness for his departure. He could also see that Sparkfire had enough fodder and a clean bed of straw, and there were a thousand questions he had for Umm once he found out where he was hiding. With a heavy sigh he stood up and struggled into his clothes. Buckling up his breeches and buttoning his shirt with only one hand wasn't all that easy and stamping his feet into his boots made him gasp with pain but eventually he managed to get dressed. He discovered that his broken arm didn't throb quite as much if he raised it so he fashioned a crude sling by tearing off the right hand sleeve of his shirt and fastening his arm across his chest.

He peered tentatively out through the open doorway. To his right a broad spiral stairway rose through galleries and balconies with dozens of doors and corridors leading off it. To his left the stairway led down into a vast, shadowy chamber. He turned to his left and, holding onto the wall, he slowly trod a dozen or so stairs, careful not to lose his footing in the moonlight. He stopped and looked down through the ornately carved balustrade and saw a huge infernal machine, the likes of which he had never seen before. There were ropes and pulleys, cogs and wheels, crystal sails and a forest of levers. The contraption half-filled the vast room. The walls were lined with rows and rows of books, thousands and thousands of them, enough to fill a hundred Learning Halls, and everywhere Drib looked – the floors, the long tables, the chairs and cupboards – there was the paraphernalia of magic. It filled everywhere to overflowing. Cleaning his armour was forgotten as curiosity got the better of him. There was so much to explore here in the Runesgate Tower. But the boy hesitated. Surely the magician would consider him very rude if he explored the tower without his permission. Sweepscuttle, his master, wouldn't have tolerated it back in the Granite City. He would have thrashed him for venturing one sooty footstep beyond the chimney he was sent to clean. But then this wasn't the Granite City, and Grannog had said that he could wander wherever he pleased. A grin widened across Drib's face in the darkness. Perhaps Nevian would forgive him for taking a quick peep: after all there were so many fascinating and wonderful things around him.

'I promise I won't touch anything,' he whispered to the

shadows, unable to resist his curiosity one moment longer.

Drib had descended no more than another three steps when clouds rode silently across the moon, plunging the tower into total darkness. He cursed under his breath, stumbling on the unfamiliar stairs and scuffing the knuckles of his good hand on the rough hewn outer wall of the tower. He had never been afraid of the dark but he wished he had a spark to light his way, he didn't want to fall and damage the stone cast. He felt for the next stair and unexpectedly collided with an unlit fire basket that hung down close to the wall. He struck the wrought iron basket with his forehead and gave a startled cry. He staggered away dizzily and just managed to stop himself tumbling head first down the remaining stairs. The iron basket rattled noisily: it was loud enough to wake up the dead. A tiny blue-white flame suddenly sprang up in the centre of the blackened, burned-down reed lamp: it must have been smouldering there since last the lamp was used. The flame flickered in the bottom of the basket and grew stronger, illuminating the stairway and sending a mass of shadows leaping away across the vast, cluttered chamber.

'Now how did that happen? It must be the magic,' Drib hissed in surprise as he stared up at the glowing reed lamp. 'I wonder if I can do it again,' he grinned, glancing around him before moving down the stairway to the next hanging basket.

Raising himself up on tiptoe and grasping the edge of the cold bands of iron he looked into the cold, crumbled fragments of reed stumps and grey-white ash that choked the bottom of the basket. The boy shook his head. There wasn't any way this one was going to light without being thoroughly cleaned out and a new reed lamp set inside it. But he tapped it firmly all the same, just in case there was magic there. After all this was the magician's tower. The fire basket rocked slightly on its long, iron chain as he struck it and a small puff of ash and debris rose and drifted out between the iron hoops that bound the basket together. It drifted down slowly and settled on his hand.

'It's just as I thought. There wasn't any magic in that first lamp – I just blundered into it. There was probably only a tiny spark still alight in the bottom and I disturbed it.' He wiped the back of his hand on his breeches, feeling slightly disappointed.

'If I was a magician I would cast a spell to light all the lamps at once!' he laughed, giving the fire basket a hard knock with his knuckles and calling out, 'Lamps, lamps burn so bright and give me illumination in the night!'

He laughed to himself as he continued down the last flight of stairs and didn't give the fire basket another glance. But there *was* magic in the tower. He came to an abrupt halt as his shadow suddenly darkened and leapt out ahead of him down the stairway, stopping only when it reached the flagstones of the great chamber below.

Drib was startled, and somewhat afraid. He turned to look up, catching his breath as he saw a blazing column of fire filling the basket.

'But that's not possible! Those were cold ashes, I saw them, they couldn't have burst into flame!'

Before he could utter another word lamps of every shape and size, some hanging on long chains, some left carelessly amongst the magician's books and papers, began to glow with light. Some shone with tiny blue-white flames, some orange and pink, while others burned so brightly, they almost hurt Drib's eyes.

'Oh my goodness, what have I done? Nevian's going to kill me or turn me into something horrible for this!' Drib gasped, seized with a sudden panic. Everywhere he looked more lamps were bursting into life and ribbons of sparks were rising from the untrimmed wicks to twist and dance in the air. Suddenly the sparks drew together and swirled around the tower, dipping into the cold ashes in the hearth before vanishing up the chimney in a roar. But there was worse to come. The lamps that had been left amongst the magician's books were about to set the books alight. Drib felt cold with dread. He could see long, thin, untrimmed flames beginning to curl and lick dangerously close to the open parchment pages. He had to do something – and quickly. He didn't dare risk uttering another word in case it made the situation worse, although it was difficult to imagine a worse situation at that moment.

He ran down the last few stairs and raced backwards and forwards across the chamber on his crooked legs, stumbling over upturned fiddle-back chairs, unseen pots and kettles and a mass of experimental apparatus that cluttered the floor in his effort to snuff the lamps. He pinched out the hot, dancing flames with his fingertips, paying little attention to the pain it caused him: it had to be done as quickly as possible and he was handicapped by only having one good hand. Grannog, who had been asleep, leapt to his feet, snarling and barking, as the blaze of sparks roared over his back and up into the chimney. He growled as he watched the boy rushing about the chamber. Gradually the light dimmed as Drib managed to extinguish all the lamps that had been left amongst the books and papers and as many of the hanging ones as he could reach. Blinking his eyes in the haze of acrid smoke, he attempted to tidy up the books that he had accidentally knocked onto the floor in his haste to save them. He quickly gave up when he saw the dirty marks his sore and blackened fingers were leaving on them.

'I'll be more careful, much more careful, in the future, I promise,' he muttered, afraid of doing even more damage as he caught sight of Grannog watching him.

The dog growled softly and shook himself but he didn't return to his place by the hearth: instead he moved closer to Drib, following the boy as he made his way across to the outer door.

'Perhaps it would be safer if I went to see Sparkfire and try to find Umm,' he smiled sheepishly as he slipped out of the tower with the dog at his heels.

For a moment he stood there on the tower steps watching the hunter's moon riding through the clouds, smelling the resin from the dense groves of pines that grew on the steep sides of the gorge and listening to the thunder of the waterfalls emptying into the Runesgate Gorge far below in the darkness. He realized that he would have to be especially careful wherever he went in the Runesgate because there was so much magic woven through everything. He could smell it in the pine-laden air, hear it whispering in the sound of the water and taste it on his tongue as he swallowed in awe. He found the stables and called out to Sparkfire. As he lifted the latch the horse whinnied and made a great fuss, happy to see Drib on his feet again, but snorted with fear as he saw the stone cast on the boy's arm.

'It's all right,' Drib whispered, reaching up to caress the horse's neck with his other hand, 'Nevian is mending my arm, but we have got to be patient and wait. I have promised Grannog that we won't try and leave here until the magician has returned.'

Sparkfire tossed his head and snorted as he pulled at the sparse remains of the hay in his manger. Drib spent a long time in the stable talking to the horse and fetching fresh hay and water and cleaning himself up in the spring beside the yard before he set out to find Umm. Grannog suddenly pushed at him, darting off to the right and bounding into a dense clump of rowan-trees. The Yerrak immediately broke cover, retreating away from the dog, his deep, musical voice raised in cries of alarm.

'It's all right, Umm, Grannog's not going to hurt you. Come over here and sit down on the tower steps beside me. Come on, there are so many things I want to ask you. Come, he won't hurt you.'

Umm made his way reluctantly to the tower steps but not without repeatedly glancing over his shoulder to the dog who followed his steps silently.

'Come on, sit down.' Drib smiled and gestured to a spot beside him, moving along to make more room for Umm's vast, hairy bulk.

Umm gently touched the stone cast on Drib's arm in silent question and sniffed it, his forehead wrinkling with concern.

'Nevian's mending my arm, that's what the stone cast is for. It hardly hurts at all now, don't worry about it, we have much more important things to concern ourselves about. Tell me everything you know about those evil shapes, Umm – the ones we used to catch sight of in the ruins of Cawdor. Were they responsible for its downfall? You have to tell me, I think they've got inside Snatchpurse and they'll make him hurt Sloeberry. I have to know all about them so that I can fight them when I go and find her.'

At Drib's mention of the Eretch Umm wailed and covered his head with his long arms, hiding his face in fear. 'They are evil – they brought the dark side of morning to Cawdor. We never speak of it. You must never call it by its name unless you wish it to come to you. You must never enter the ruins of the great fortress lest it steal your heart.' Umm then rocked backwards and forwards with his long arms wrapped around his body.

'But we did enter the ruins, and we lived there. We were all right, the Eretch didn't steal *our* hearts did they?'

Drib tried to ask again but Umm only wailed louder, pressing his fingers into his ears. 'Evil did befall you and your friends. They are all scattered, lost in the forest. The evil will find you here if you speak its name. You must not talk of it any more.'

'But I wasn't killed or captured was I? I will never be able to find Sloeberry without your help,' Drib persisted. 'So tell me, why haven't they hurt me?'

'Because you have magic. You have the magic to grow a new hand, the magic to stay upon your horse even when you are asleep. That is why I brought you here, because of your magic,' Umm cried, turning away from Drib.

'Magic?' Drib sighed, patting the Yerrak's arm to comfort him, 'If only that were true, we wouldn't be in this predicament now, would we?'

Drib shivered and rose slowly to his feet. The night air was chilling his bones. 'I am going inside, it's warmer in the tower. Are you coming with me? I might be able to find some answers in the magician's books. I'm sure he won't mind me looking.'

Umm looked up through the door to the softly illuminated chamber and fiercely shook his head before hurrying away into the trees. Drib sighed with frustration as he watched the Yerrak disappear. How was he going to find anything out if the creature kept running off? He turned and paused on the threshold of the tower, looking in horror at the mess that confronted him. Surely he hadn't scattered everything onto the floor and upset so many chairs and tables as he tried to extinguish all the lamps.

'It must be magic!' he muttered darkly, wondering if secret forces hadn't had a hand in making the mess worse the moment his back was turned. Perhaps it would have been better if he had stayed put in the small sleeping chamber up the stairs. At least there he would have stayed out of trouble. He was quickly coming to realize that magic was a dangerous thing to meddle with and he could easily imagine the trouble he would be in if he didn't try to get everything cleared up before the magician returned. A small grin puckered the corners of his mouth as he pushed his untidy hair out of his eyes. Magic might be dangerous but it was also very exciting. He reached for the latch and pulled the door shut behind him, only to sneeze and wrinkle his nose at the stench of burnt reeds, wax and untrimmed wicks that still hung in a thick, blue haze in the great chamber.

'I had better get rid of that smell as quickly as I can,' he frowned, pushing the door wide open and hobbling across the chamber to throw as many of the windows open as he could reach.

'I'll have this room neat and tidy in no time at all. Even with only one hand I can do it, you'll see if I don't,' he called out to Grannog who had now stretched out on the top step of the tower. The dog yawned and didn't seem to notice the doubt in Drib's voice at the realization of the daunting task that confronted him.

Dawn had painted fresh colours across the distant mountain peaks surrounding the Runesgate Gorge and the morning sun shimmered on faraway drifts of snow before Drib had finished his task in the chamber. He had taken great care not to touch the huge machine with all its crystal sails, but every other piece of apparatus, every pot and vessel, quill, book and scroll that littered the room had been found a place, even if they didn't normally live where he had put them. He had filled tiers of bookshelves to overflowing and crammed things into the open-fronted cupboards or stuffed yet more things tightly into the deep wooden drawers that lined the circular room. With a great sigh of satisfaction he stood in the centre of the chamber and surveyed his handiwork, surrounded by drying puddles where he had mopped the stone flagged floor. Nevian would never know he had made such a mess earlier.

Drib suddenly felt very hungry. He had lost all sense of time since Snatchpurse's battle mace had struck the back of his head and he couldn't remember when he had last eaten. Memories of sitting close to Sloeberry, laughing and whispering in the firelight as they had shared a pickled flying fish together the night before the attack came flooding back to him. The hunger turned to a gnawing ache in the pit of his stomach. He felt so helplessly alone, so lost without her. Tears of despair began to well up and blur his sight. He shook his head fiercely, blinking them back: tears weren't going to rescue her. He had to be strong, he had to get well as quickly as he could and ride out in search for her. Yes, he needed to eat, but a disturbing thought occurred to him – did magicians eat? Did they eat real food or was it their magic that sustained them? He couldn't remember seeing anything that remotely resembled food in the dingy scullery. He had found the mop and bucket to wash the floor, but food? He glanced at the dog asleep in the sun on the step. Grannog had said that he could wander wherever he wanted to. Perhaps he should explore and see if he could find a kitchen amongst all the rooms and cubby holes that led off the main stairway. Surely there must be one somewhere in the tower? Nevian wouldn't mind him searching, as long as he didn't touch anything or tamper with the magic.

Cautiously Drib began his search. His footsteps echoed

on the uneven stone floors of the narrow vaulted passageways that led from the great circular chamber. It seemed to Drib that the tower was much longer than it looked from the outside, and quite easy to get lost in if he wasn't careful. It was also very old from the look of it and it had suffered from an age of neglect. In places water had leaked and dripped through the ceiling for so long it had formed into needle sharp stalactites that he had to duck beneath. The walls were damp, crumbling and streaked with an evil smelling moss. The heavy oak doors to all the rooms he found were stiff and creaked loudly on their rusty hinges. All the rooms he visited were crowded with peculiar pieces of apparatus: strange tall mechanical devices, rows of jars and bottles and yet more and more rickety piles of books – some stacked as high as the ceilings. And all of it was shrouded beneath thick layers of dust and cobwebs. Magic, he was beginning to think, required an awful lot of clutter – much more in the way of equipment than sweeping chimneys. More, even, than the tools in a blacksmith's forge.

Drib was beginning to give up on the idea of finding anything to eat within the tower. Obviously he had been right in the first place: a magician didn't need food. Just as he had decided to find his way back to Grannog he discovered a passageway that he hadn't yet explored, partly hidden by the huge wind engine with the crystal sails. His hopes were raised immediately. It was cleaner and more used than the other passages that he had been down and there was a faint, familiar, almost wholesome odour. It reminded him of the inns in the Granite City where he was sent to clean the chimneys. Yes, he could detect the smell of honey and cinnamon, and cured meats and other smells that made his mouth water. He quickened his footsteps and hurried beneath an archway at the end of the passage. He came to a sudden halt in the kitchen.

'By all the magic in Nevian's cloak!' he whispered, eyes wide.

He didn't know where to look first. Slowly he began to walk round, trying to take it all in. It was a long vaulted room and the whole of the far wall was a vast roasting hearth with bread ovens set into it. Two huge sides of smoke-cured meat hung from the iron trammels over the cold ashes. Long stone tables ran down the centre of the room, crowded with sacks of flour, windflower seeds, crushed ears of wheat and jars of herbs and spices. There were bottles of preserved fruits of the forest, baskets of bread and rounds of cheese almost as large as he was. And there were rows and rows of dried herbs, borage flowers and galingale heads, daydrum, white petals of loosestrife and countless others he didn't recognize all hanging down from racks set into the ceiling. There was enough for a King's feast! But how had all these provisions been brought to the tower? It was too remote for a wagon; perhaps the magician transported it by magic. Drib was afraid of angering Nevian and only cut a thin sliver of cured meat and took a crust of bread and a piece of cheese before hurrying back to the great chamber. If he was going to find out anything that would help him rescue Sloeberry then he had better start reading the magician's books immediately.

Drib nibbled at the hard rind of cheese he had taken from the kitchen, savouring the crumbly taste on the roof of his mouth. Cheese, in Sweepscuttle's house in Chimney Lane, was a luxury, a closely-guarded luxury. It was certainly not something to be wasted on the likes of a humble sweep's scramble. But despite his master's razor sharp eyes he had secretly managed to take a small piece that had once fallen, unnoticed, from the table. It had had the most exquisite flavour. And now he had a whole piece to himself. But the pleasure of eating it was marred for Drib by the gnawing doubt that he was ever going to be able to find what he was looking for in Nevian's library. He glanced up from the open page in front of him and looked at the countless, disorderly rows of books and parchment scrolls that climbed up and up high above his head until they almost touched the rafters. He had never realized just how much knowledge existed in the world. Why, even if he spent the rest of his life, every waking moment, reading, then he would still have barely scratched at the surface of all the knowledge stored in the magician's tower.

Drib sighed and returned his attention to the ancient book of magic that he had taken at random from one of the lower shelves. There didn't seem to be any order or cataloguing in the library. Books on bee-keeping rubbed shoulders with works on infernal siege engines; dark magic stood spine to spine with the art of butter churning and alchemy; numerology and history crowded the shelves together. One thing Drib had been quick to realize was that if there was anything written about the myths and legends of Elundium then it was always written in the first chapter and it was always written in what he thought must be the magician's distinctive script. Often passages were scratched out and rewritten in different coloured inks – perhaps as Nevian's perception of history changed, or his thoughts about it needed clarifying.

Drib read slowly through the first chapter of one book and for a while he became engrossed in the age of the Mason Kings – the architects of all that was once beautiful across the length and breadth of Elundium. He read of how they raised city after city, each one more intricate, each one more delicate than the last and each one mirroring the beauty of a perfect world. This went on until King

Mantern took up his mason's chisel. He was driven by strange dreams and feared the sunlight. Everything he built shadowed what his ancestors built. He used only dark, rough stone, and inside each citadel black marble traced with silver veins lined the walls, casting deep velvet shadows within. Out of these shadows rose the Granite City, sheer and windowless. A place of secret inner court-yards and echoing corridors: a place of strange, dark beauty. But still King Mantern was not satisfied and he sought tirelessly for the purest black marble. His quest led him deeper and deeper into the marble valleys until, amongst the blackest shadows, he found a pure seam of indigo dark marble, etched with veins of molten silver. Raising his hammer King Mantern swung a mighty blow, but greed drove the chisel too deep and it fractured the surface of the earth, allowing blackest night, with all the phantoms that dwelt within its smoothing shroud, to roar forth.

Drib shivered. The room seemed to darken momentarily and shadows lengthened. He glanced around him anxiously. There had been nothing of this in Loremaster Grout's stories of King Mantern: he had to know what happened next. Cautiously he turned the page, catching his breath. Scrawled in spiky, hard-edged capitals, one sentence filled the page:

*FROM THIS DAYLIGHT ON KRULSHARDS,
THE MASTER OF DARKNESS, THE
CREATOR OF NIGHTMARES AND ALL HIS
FOUL CREATURES, ARE LOOSED IN THE
WORLD.*

So that was how it all began. Drib frowned. The story had frightened him and he was glad to find that the next page contained a formula for base metals. There had been no reference to the dark evil that had inhabited Cawdor when time was young, unless the evil was some of those foul creatures that King Mantern had released into the world with that fateful hammer blow. Anyway it all happened so long ago and Nevian was sure to know all the answers, he would just have to be patient and wait for his return.

Drib turned the pages absently, feeling the rich, soft texture of the dusty old parchment beneath his fingertips. He paused now and then to gaze at the beautiful colours of the painted capitals or read a line of the spider-fine silver script that unfolded all manner of strange and wonderful secrets. Sometimes he would trace the intricately drawn signs and symbols or follow the rows of numbers and magical figures that marched across the pages with his finger. He knew that he really shouldn't tamper with the magic – touching the reed lamps had already caused him so much trouble. He was about to close the large leather-bound volume and place it on the pile he had already looked through when the illustration of a pot-bellied cauldron on a fire in a hearth, a vase filled with some sorts of herbs and an odd collection of other kitchen objects caught his eye. He laughed as he read out loud:

> 'Burn, burn, fire bright, with griddle, trammel,
>   chain and metal pot,
> Stir the goose, bubble boil and froth. Add the
>   lovage, evermind and purple sweet,
> Stir the goose, bubble boil and froth.
> Azote. Gaap. Zagan.'

A sudden noise, a clattering of pots and pans from the kitchen, brought Drib to his feet. What had he done? Had he not learned already how dangerous magic could be?

Cursing his own stupidity he grabbed the book and placed it beneath his good arm as he hurried as fast as his crooked legs would carry him along the passageway towards the kitchen. He had to duck quickly and step back out of the doorway – the air was full of kitchen implements: knives, long-handled wooden spoons, trammels, rolling pins – everything all swirling gracefully around. Kettles, jugs and earthenware pots were slowly moving along the stone tables, each pausing in turn to receive a measure of herbs and spices that jumped into them from the sacks and jars along the shelves. Unfortunately the cooking vessels were falling off the edge of the table and smashing to pieces on the floor as though surprised by having no-one to take them. The cold ashes in the roasting hearth had burst into life and a huge, black, iron cauldron that had not been suspended over the fire when he first visited the kitchen, was now hanging on one of the trammels and bubbling furiously over the flames.

Drib realized that he must have recited some cooking spell but somehow he must have got it horribly wrong. He had to find a way to stop it immediately, before the bottom of the cauldron melted and every pot and vessel in the kitchen was smashed to the ground. It was no good trying to catch them before they fell from the table and the cauldron was far too heavy for him to lift. He fell awkwardly to his knees in the entrance to the kitchen and wrestled with the heavy book of magic. Quickly scanning down the pages he found the one he had read the spell from: there must be a way to stop it. Suddenly he had the answer – in tiny writing at the bottom of the page:

Once all is prepared and ready to eat chant . . .
CHAMBLE. ORUNDOR. ORUNDOR. ORUNDOR.
And then begin the feast.

Drib cried the words out loud. The swirling utensils hung still in the air, the pots and earthenware vessels hovered as they marched off the end of the tables and slowly the flames beneath the cauldron shrank. Breathlessly Drib cried out the chant twice more and in a blink everything had returned to its rightful place. Well not quite everything, there was quite a pile of broken crockery for him to clear up and he would have to wait a while for the cauldron to cool down before attempting to empty it.

'Well, I won't try that again in a hurry,' he muttered to himself, relieved that there wasn't too much damage to be explained to Nevian. But by the time he reached the great chamber his grin began to tug at the corners of his mouth. He put the book back on the shelf but couldn't resist reaching for another. There was something so wonderful, so compelling, about magic. Perhaps he could find a spell, something very simple that wouldn't break or hurt anything, that he could try outside the tower. After all he might never get an opportunity like this again and he was quite sure that Nevian wouldn't really mind, not if he cleared everything up after he had finished.

He took the book outside and settled down on the top step, calling out to Umm who appeared from amongst the trees, carrying a branch heavy with young, green rowan berries. After making sure that Grannog was asleep inside the tower the Yerrak sat down beside Drib, barely giving the book a second glance. Drib tried to explain to Umm about magic, or at least the little he thought he had learned about it, but the Yerrak merely scratched his head and soon became engrossed in grubbing at the tiny berries. Drib began to leaf through the book, looking for something simple that wouldn't break anything. He came upon a short section about changing colours, or at least that was what he understood it to be about. There were a lot of long, complicated words about dyes and mixing infusions. He was on the point of losing interest when he turned a page and noticed that halfway down the next page there were some beautiful drawings of knapweed and lavender, juniper and meadowsweet, all in different colours. Below the illustrations were the words of a spell. And, more importantly, their antidote was written just below it in tiny, scratched letters. Umm shifted sleepily and nudged the boy's broken arm. Drib winced with pain and turned sharply towards the Yerrak but he hadn't realized what he had done: he carried on picking out the unripe berries from amongst the bitter tasting leaves.

'I'll show him,' Drib thought and he whispered the words of the spell.

> 'Change the colour, change the hue,
> Ripen rowan berries to a red, autumnal hue.
> Incarnadine. Opera. Opera.'

Umm gave a startled, deep, musical cry and dropped the branch as the rowan berries suddenly swelled up to a soft, fleshy ripeness and changed colour before his eyes. Drib laughed and reached down to pick up the branch. The spell had worked and it hadn't done any harm.

'You need not worry,' he smiled to reassure the Yerrak, 'I'll change it back again if you like.'

And he recited the words to break the spell. At first nothing happened so he repeated them twice more and then slowly the leaves withered into their autumnal colours and began to drop off the branch leaving the berries in brilliant red clusters. Umm gave a cry of dismay and leapt to his feet, moving quickly away from Drib. He gesticulated and repeatedly pointed across the gorge to where dense groves of rowan trees grew around the head of the waterfall. Their branches were bent beneath the weight of ripe bunches of blood red berries and their leaves were already turning to autumnal colours before dropping to the ground.

'Oh dear, what have I done?' Drib gasped, scrambling awkwardly to his feet and letting the book fall to the ground.

With a sinking feeling he realized that no amount of magic would ever put the leaves back on the trees – somehow he had ripened the fruit too early and it would rot before the summer was over.

'Oh, I'm sorry Umm, I really didn't mean to do that, it was an accident. I only wanted to surprise you by changing the colour of the berries on your branch . . .' He called out after the Yerrak but he was already hurrying away into the trees.

Disappointed, Drib collected up the book and returned to the tower, pulling the door shut behind him. That, he decided, was definitely the last time he would ever meddle with magic. But he hesitated as he caught sight of the thousands of books crammed into the book shelves. His appetite for knowledge was whetted, his hunger to learn was strong. Surely he couldn't do any harm if he only read through the parts that contained the myths and legends. There was so much he didn't know about the history of Elundium and the rest of the world. There were so many more fascinating stories that Grout had not told them in the Learning Hall. But he promised himself that if any page accidentally fell open at a spell he would immediately shut the book and return it to its shelf. He reached for another book but paused, shaking his head, perhaps he had better leave the books alone until tomorrow, just in case.

VII

Strategies and Deceptions are Formed in the Firelight

TIME RESTED HEAVILY on the boy's shoulders as he wandered restlessly through the tower, making sure that everything he had touched was tidily in its place. He made a fuss of Grannog and, with the dog at his heels, eventually climbed the winding stairway to explore the rooms above his sleeping chamber. He sneezed at the dry dust he disturbed but made especially sure he didn't touch anything or tear the slightest hole in the thick cobwebbed shrouds that covered so much of the forgotten relics hidden in the tower.

Eventually, after climbing for what seemed an age, he reached the magician's observatory at the very pinnacle of the tower. He lifted the door latch and for once the door opened smoothly on an oiled hinge without the whisper of a creak. Drib leaned forwards and peered inside. He caught his breath with wonder. Before him was a circular room completely made of glass windows that went right over his head. At its centre stood a tall, cylindrical, brass object with cogs and levers and masses of numbers and signs engraved all around it. It was at least as large as Berioss, if not taller. Beside it stood a high-backed, leather chair with the most beautifully carved head rest and arms that he had ever seen. It was covered with interlocking figures of dragons, serpents and winged beasts which had been carved with such skill that their scales seemed to glisten in the late afternoon light. Flanking the chair were two hexagonal tables covered with soft, crimson velvet, each cluttered with the most curious collection of brass and jewelled instruments and maps, the like of which he had never set eyes upon. Looking more closely at one of the maps that had been unfurled and held open by four small, bronze counter-weights on the right table he saw the stars pictured in the night sky, or at least what he thought would have been the stars if he had been lying flat on his back on a clear, dark night, and each one of them had a name of its own.

'Look, Grannog, look at this, come in here. Who would have thought that all these stars have names . . .' he began, but Grannog padded past him, barking, and put his paws up on the nearest stone window sill, his ears pricked forwards.

'What is it? What have you seen?' Drib asked. 'Is it Nevian?' He hurried across to the dog and stared out across the Runesgate to the distant mountain peaks.

The dog growled, telling Drib to open the window but the boy hesitated, afraid of breaking something.

'Friends are on their way. I sense they are close. Lift the latch, open the window wide,' the dog persisted, gripping at the boy's sleeve with his teeth and pulling his hand towards the latch.

After a moment of fiddling with the unfamiliar window catch it swung open. The thundering roar of the waterfall grew louder immediately and the air inside the observatory became heavy with the sweet scent of pine resin, jasmine blossom and wild rosemary. 'Who is coming? Is it Nevian? Come on, Grannog, tell me!' Drib cried, searching the lush undergrowth of the gorge below the tower, but the trees grew so densely and the canopy of leaves was so thick that he had no idea where to look for the path that led into the gorge.

'No, it is not Nevian, he is still far away,' Grannog

replied, stretching out and yawning. 'But there are friends on the wing. Be patient Drib.' The dog turned and padded silently out through the door.

'Friends coming indeed! There's a small chance of that with them all lost and scattered in the petrified forest!' Drib sighed, alone once more. He rested the cast protecting his broken arm on the window sill, overcome with loneliness, as he watched the sun sink behind the distant purple, hazy mountain tops. Cold, white snow fields suddenly glowed blood red and the pale azure sky was consumed with fire before night slowly darkened the colours of the sky and the first evening stars appeared. In happier daylights such a sunset would have taken his breath away. He would have stood hand in hand with Sloeberry, spellbound by its beauty, but now it just made everything he loved seem so far away, and impossible to touch. The sounds of the daylight were fading and nightshapes silently glided through the trees behind the tower, weaving their evening shadows. Beyond the Runesgate the steep, rocky valleys were already cloaked with darkness.

'How will I ever find you, Sloeberry? I'm so alone and lost here,' he whispered into the fading light.

Turning towards the door he realized that he should have left the observatory earlier while there was still enough light for him to find his way back down the stairs. He wasn't afraid of the dark: he had been forced to scramble up too many pitch-black chimney holes by his master for that, but he didn't want to blunder into anything on his way down. He was plucking up the courage to tap the fire basket that he had noticed hanging beside the stairhead as he climbed to the top of the tower, when a movement beyond the window of the observatory caught his eye. He stared out into the dark, star-filled sky, sweeping his gaze across the mountains, but there was nothing to see, not a single flicker of light.

'There's nothing there, I must have imagined it,' he muttered. Reaching out to feel his way past the tables he gave a startled cry as two silent, winged shapes momentarily blotted out the stars beyond the open window. One of them stooped through the gap and landed on the headrest of the high-backed chair; the other followed it into the observatory and alighted on his shoulder. With a soft hoot of greeting Silkstone pulled at a stray strand of Drib's untidy hair and gently squeezed his talons onto his shoulder.

'Silkstone! Silkstone! I never expected to see you again. How did you find me?' Drib cried with delight, reaching up with his good hand to caress the owl's chest feathers. With much hooting and shrieking the owl told Drib how he had been driven far away from Cawdor by a ferocious white magpie and by the time he managed to find his way back to the fortress it had been consumed by fire and everybody had vanished. He had searched and searched, flying in ever widening circles, but without finding trace of any of the company. He had been about to begin a search along the ancient road through the Emerald Mountains in the hope that some may be returning along that route when Orundus had found him and given him the news that Drib was safe in the Runesgate.

'So you have seen nothing of our attackers? You know they have captured Sloeberry and taken her along with them as their prisoner?'

Silkstone spread his wings and shrieked, 'Orundus, Lord of Owls, told me that the evil that attacked you at Cawdor has journeyed back into Elundium. If she is their prisoner we will find her. They leave a wide trail of devastation behind them as they loot and burn.'

Drib looked hopefully towards the Lord of Owls who was perched on the high-backed watching chair. Perhaps he had news of Sloeberry – perhaps he had seen her. In a small, hesitant voice he asked, 'You didn't happen to catch sight of Sloeberry in your search for Silkstone, did you Orundus? She is about my height and very beautiful, with large brown eyes, and dark, silken hair which falls onto her shoulders. You wouldn't know if she is still alive would you? I am so worried about her.'

Orundus had just spread his wings, ready to fly down to his favourite roost. He paused and slowly turned his head from side to side. 'No, Drib, your enemies move relentlessly forwards at such a pace through Elundium that they stir up high clouds of dust with their marching feet which obscure them completely. That evil magpie who attacked Silkstone has gathered many allies of the air: black, ragged carrion crows, vultures, shrikes and rooks, who mobbed me. So great were their numbers that I had no chance to fly too close to their marching column.'

Drib watched as Orundus lifted silently into the air and vanished through the open doorway and felt his hopes fading. 'With those vile carrion birds patrolling the air I'll never be able to get close enough to Sloeberry to rescue her without being spotted.'

He frowned, moving towards the door with Silkstone perched safely on his shoulder.

'Nevian will find a way, he is so wise, he is the Master of Magic!' The owl's hoots held such conviction that it made Drib laugh and for a moment it drove away his doubts. Yes, Nevian was the Master of Magic, even if he had become forgetful and had lost his glasses. He would find a way – if anyone could.

'It's so wonderful to have you with me again, Silkstone,

you have no idea how much I missed you,' he whispered, smiling as the owl guided him sure-footedly down the darkened stairway.

'Now, watch this!' Drib grinned, unable to resist showing Silkstone his trick with the lamps.

Standing on tiptoe he reached up and tapped at two of the iron fire baskets that hung down on long chains suspended from the ceiling of the great chamber. The chains rattled and the fire baskets swayed as he struck them with his knuckles. Suddenly both reedlamps burst into life within the fire baskets and illuminated the chamber. Drib looked anxiously at the other lamps, holding his breath, and let out a shallow sigh of relief when they didn't follow suit. 'There is so much magic woven into the fabric of this tower,' Drib whispered, 'that I have to be very careful what I do or say. I nearly set everything alight earlier by accidentally chanting a spell and you can't imagine the trouble I caused in the kitchen just by reading a cooking spell out loud – I was only reading one of the books. Look at them, who would believe so much knowledge could exist in the world? Who could have imagined that so many books could have been written? And another thing. I was trying to surprise Umm – he's the Yerrak who brought me here when I was unconscious and lying on Sparkfire's back but I will tell you all about that later when I introduce you – anyway I was trying to surprise him and pay him back for nudging my broken arm by using a spell to change the colour of the rowan berries on the branch he was holding when . . .'

A slight, chill breeze, no stronger than the ghost of a whisper, ruffled at the untidy fringe of hair that tumbled down across Drib's forehead, but it was enough to extinguish the lamps and plunge the tower into sudden darkness. Drib froze and prickles of fear ran up his spine.

He wished he had his sword or at least a dagger. The outer door creaked on its hinges.

'Grannog! Grannog! There's an intruder,' he hissed, hoping the dog wasn't too deeply asleep.

Silkstone turned his head and flexed his talons, painfully squeezing the boy's shoulder as he prepared to fly up in his defence. Soft, gentle laughter suddenly filled the darkness and, with a snap of dry fingers, every lamp in the tower burst into light.

'Nevian!' Drib's voice was full of relief as he saw the tall, slightly stooping figure of the magician standing in the open doorway of the tower. He seemed a little out of breath and his hair was dishevelled. There were burrs and brambleheads clinging to his beard and the sleeves of his rainbow cloak looked travel-stained and dirty.

Drib shrank back. The magician looked so fierce, almost angry. 'Nevian, I'm so glad you're back, but I wasn't expecting you tonight. Grannog said you were still far away as we watched the sun set from that wonderful glass room at the top of the tower. I . . . I hope you didn't mind me going up there. Have you found out something about Sloeberry or the others? Have you heard something that has made you travel back here so quickly?' the boy asked in a small, uncertain voice.

The old man shivered, pulling his cloak more tightly around his shoulders as he stepped in over the threshold and pushed the door firmly shut behind him. 'I have news to tell. But it is you, Drib, who has brought me back here in such haste . . .' he frowned as he cast a critical eye around the great chamber. 'And not a moment before time, that is clear to see,' he muttered advancing on the boy.

'Equestrius has galloped unchecked by the straightest road possible through those mountain passes and not, I might add, without considerable discomfort for me, and why? Can you guess?'

Drib felt the colour rushing to his cheeks. He had never thought that his meddling would get him into this much trouble. Before he had a chance to apologize or try to explain what he had done Nevian spun round and threw a pinch of quickfire into the hearth, igniting the cold ash and logs that lay there and sending flames roaring up the chimney. Grannog woke up at the sound and rose to his feet, stretched and greeted the magician. Nevian bent and made a fuss of the old dog and when he straightened up his anger seemed to have subsided. There was almost a hint of laughter in his eyes as he returned his attention to Drib. 'I had to come back, my boy, because there was no way of knowing what mischief you would be getting yourself into next if you were left to your own devices here, alone in my tower. Remember, Drib, it is all too easy to burn your fingers if you tamper with things you don't yet understand. The gift of magic requires a lot of study before you can attempt to use its power!'

The laughter had faded and his voice had grown serious. Drib felt a knot of guilt tighten in his stomach and his face turned a deeper shade of scarlet. He had betrayed the magician's trust and he deserved to be thoroughly punished. But how on earth could Nevian have possibly known about his accident with the lamps? Surely the magician had much more important things on his mind? The fate of Elundium, for instance, or rescuing the King from impending disaster, even finding out what had happened to his friends, surely all these should come before keeping track of what was going on in his tower.

'I . . . I . . . I'm very sorry. I really didn't mean any harm,' Drib stammered. 'I never intended to touch anything – all the lamps came on quite accidentally. I was just feeling

my way down the stairs when I struck one of them . . .
No . . . that's not quite true . . .' Drib was determined to
tell the whole truth. 'I was so intrigued by that first lamp
when it lit all of its own accord that I struck the next
one, only much too hard and they all blazed up, but nothing was badly damaged, not really. None of your books
were hurt, or your scrolls, even though they were lying
scattered all over the floor and the tables. Some of them
were slightly singed but I have cleared up all the mess
and found a place for everything in the book shelves and
put away loads of stuff in the drawers and cupboards.'

'Yes, so I can see!' the old man said in surprise, raising
his eyebrows as he surveyed the room again. 'Well, that
certainly explains why nothing is in its proper place. I
won't be able to find anything for goodness knows how
long. But that isn't why I hurried back, boy. Did I guess
rightly that you were somehow responsible for bringing
the rowan trees in every valley we rode through into their
autumn colours? Summer hasn't even properly begun
yet.'

Drib nodded silently and hung his head in shame. There
wasn't a single excuse he could find for his behaviour.
He tensed, expecting at any moment to be turned into
something horrible as a punishment for what he had done.

'Tampering with nature is a very serious matter, and so
is playing with fire. Is there anything else·you think you
had better tell me about?'

Drib swallowed nervously and owned up to the abortive
cooking spell he had chanted, breaking all those jugs and
earthenware pots in the kitchen, adding quickly that he
had cleared away all the mess. 'I promise I will never do
anything like that again. If you will just forgive me, give
me another chance, I promise I'll never meddle with magic
again. I'll scrub and clean, I'll polish the tower from top

to bottom, I'll sweep the chimney with my bare hands once my arm is mended. I'm really sorry.'

'You're right, boy, you certainly won't do anything like that again. Before you chant another spell you will have thoroughly understood its implications: you will know its cause and its effect. I'll make sure of that. Now, go to the kitchen and fetch me a jug of ale from the barrel beneath the right hand table, if you haven't tidied it away somewhere else by now. I'm sure you can do that with one hand. I'll just be heating the poker ready to mull it, it's just the drink for a cold night like this. While we drink I will tell you what news I have. Don't stand there growing roots, my boy, close your mouth and get going.'

The old man chuckled as Drib looked up, hardly able to believe his ears. 'You aren't cross with me? You're not going to punish me for meddling with your books and chanting those spells?'

'Cross, Drib? No don't be silly. A little irritated, perhaps, that you have so diligently tidied everything away that already had a place. But I'm delighted, yes, quite delighted, to discover that you have such a talent for magic. It's very rare, you know, and quite a responsibility. There is so much for you to learn, though – perhaps a lifetime of study. Now, be off with you, fetch that ale before it sours the barrel.'

The magician laughed as he reached down for a log to throw on the blazing fire.

'No, you must be wrong, there's nothing special about me,' Drib cried in confusion. 'I can't have any talent for magic: that's something real magicians, like you, do. I am only a sweep's scramble. When I set those lamps alight and turned the rowan berries red it was all a terrible accident. Anyway I can't stay here learning about magic. If I do how will I ever rescue Sloeberry?'

Nevian saw the tears welling in the boy's eyes and quickly crossed to where Drib stood. He put his finger under the boy's chin and gently lifted his head until their eyes met. 'Oh, but you are special, Drib, and quite extraordinary. How many other sweeps' scrambles can read and write? How many can understand the language of the owls? Your daylights of climbing chimneys are truly over. Put them behind you and grow in your wisdom. There is not a handful of people in all Elundium, even amongst the sorcerers' apprentices, who could have so easily lit my lamps, let alone tampered with nature to such an extent that she sent every rowan tree from here to the petrified forest into autumn.'

'But what about Sloeberry? What can we do to rescue her?' Drib asked. 'And another thing my master, Sweepscuttle might not agree to release me. How am I supposed to find the barter for my freedom?'

'Magic and the knowledge to use it is a great power, Drib, far greater than you can ever imagine. It will aid you in rescuing Sloeberry more than any act of reckless bravery. Trust me. Have faith. We will set out when the moon is in the fourth quarter and forget about Sweepscuttle. He is the least of your concerns.'

Drib looked doubtful and opened his mouth to speak but Nevian snapped his fingers and his face grew fierce, he seemed to grow taller and his shadow stretched out across the room. Lightning cracked between his fingers and Drib quailed beneath his penetrating gaze. 'Would you dare to argue with me, boy?' the Master of Magic asked.

Drib shrank back away from the menacing figure who now towered over him. 'No . . .'

Nevian laughed and snapped his fingers again, returning to his normal size in an instant. 'And nor will Sweepscuttle when the time is right. Now run for that ale, Drib, before I become convinced that your real talent is for idle chatter. Go!'

'Berioss alive! But that's impossible. He was driven to his death, forced at swordpoint over the cliff edge at Cawdor. I know he was. Nobody, not even somebody as brave and strong as Berioss, could have survived such a fall. I know he would have been smashed to pieces when he hit the rocks below,' Drib cried in disbelief. He shook his head fiercely and jumped to his feet from where he was sitting listening to Nevian on the opposite side of the fire hearth. Frothy mulled ale slopped unnoticed over the rim of his earthenware tankard.

'Oh he did topple over that cliff edge all right, and with a dagger plunged into his chest by his attackers. You were absolutely right about that, Drib, but he didn't fall very far before the magic saved him.' Nevian whispered dramatically in the flickering firelight as he leaned forwards to motion to the boy to sit back down again and hold his ale jug more carefully.

'Magic? What magic? I don't understand. If there was magic in the Citadel of Cawdor then why didn't it help us all in our fight against those evil shadows which attacked us? Why didn't it stop them from taking Sloeberry a prisoner? And where is Berioss now? Why didn't you bring him back here?'

'The magic that saved Berioss dwelt deep within him: he wasn't even aware of it until he called out for its help, and it couldn't have helped you and Sloeberry, or anyone else I'm afraid,' Nevian smiled as he answered. 'You see once, long ago I cast a spell in anger. I cursed Berioss and all those other warriors who refused to pledge their loyalty to King Thane when King Holbian, the last of the Granite Kings, died and . . .'

'You turned them into trees, didn't you. I remember Grout telling us the story in the Learning Hall,' Drib interjected. 'It's such a wonderful story, all those gnarled, old trees, a whole forest of them, moving slowly through the blizzards, following the King, watching and protecting him. I remember how those who had managed to flee were pursued by Kruel's shadowy army and how each time anyone fell from exhaustion the trees lifted them up, cradling them in their branches until they had recovered enough to continue their stumbling journey through the deep snow drifts towards the Rising. I remember the stories about the Rising too. How it is a great mound of earth and bones that had been raised by the Tunnellers for the first Granite Kings, long before Krulshards stole them and kept them as slaves, long before he took them deep into the City of Night. It is where the last ray of sunlight still shone, high above the shadowlight that had shrouded Elundium. King Thane stood on the top of the Rising and looked out at the sea of darkness that surrounded him and his few loyal friends and hope seemed to dwindle within him. But you gave him courage, didn't you Nevian. You pointed to the forest with its stark winter branches reaching up out of the shadows and you showed him how it surrounded the Rising, you told him to ride out and call forth all the warriors who love the daylight because their king had great need of them.'

Drib sighed, his eyes shining in the firelight. 'I wish I could have been there to see the King ride out all alone on Esteron. Did you know he is the bravest warhorse – the most beautiful beast – in all the world? I rode him once you know. Anyway, Grout told us that the King reined Esteron to a halt less than a spear thrust from those evil shadow warriors. He stood up in the stirrups and called out in a loud voice just as you told him to do. He said, "Warriors! I have great need of all the warriors of Elundium who love the daylight!" And then all the gnarled, ancient trees who were groaning and creaking as they moved so slowly were suddenly still. Their whispering branches fell into silence. The King called out again in an even louder voice and then the trees began to sway and crumble: hollow strips of bark fell from them and broke, shattered into a fog of splinters. In their place stood those warriors you had cast that spell over. There they stood, only this time they had no doubt about their king, they loved him. With a mighty roar they lowered a forest of glittering spear blades and surged forward, clearing a broad path through the shadow warriors who had closed around King Thane . . .' Drib stopped abruptly and stared at Nevian.

'That magic – the magic that saved Berioss – it turned him back into a tree didn't it? It turned him into a tree when he fell?'

The old man nodded gravely; 'Yes, luckily for Berioss, that is exactly what happened, although it shouldn't have. Magic isn't supposed to endure like that and unfortunately I can't think of an antidote to release him completely from the spell. The answer has got to be here somewhere in one of my books. But where? Which one will it be in? It could take an age to find and at the moment I don't have that sort of time.'

'Berioss turned back into a tree? How amazing. But what does he look like? How does he manage to move? Where is he now?' Drib was intrigued. He had often seen the old Marcher examining his hands and fingers during their winter at Cawdor and, come to think of it, they had sometimes looked very much like the ends of knobbly branches.

'Questions, questions, always questions, boy,' the magician muttered irritably. The boy certainly had a talent for persistent questions.

'Like a tree! How else should he look? And he moves very slowly, although I have managed to quicken his stride quite considerably and I have made him much taller, though he is still a tree. I have sent him into the petrified forest to find and gather together the survivors of the rout of Cawdor. He is to arm them by whatever means he can and then lead them back into Elundium, gathering all those loyal to King Thane as they travel. They are to meet us in the shadows of Candlebane Hall by mid-winter's day.'

'But we can't wait until midwinter! Sloeberry will probably have been tortured to death by then! We must start out tomorrowlight as soon as possible . . .' Drib suddenly paused and his face paled when he remembered what Orundus had told him about the white magpie and the flocks of evil birds that guarded the skies above Snatchpurse's marching column and with a sinking heart he told the magician all about them.

'Well, that changes everything,' Nevian muttered thoughtfully as he stood up from his chair and began to pace the floor of the great chamber. He had been formulating a plan on his return from Cawdor and had decided to journey secretly into Elundium to rally those still loyal to the King, taking Drib and Umm with him and rescuing Sloeberry at the first opportunity that arose. He hadn't worked out a strategy to get close to her; he knew it was going to be difficult but now, with this latest piece of news, it would be impossible – or would it?

The magician stopped abruptly, mid-stride, and turned

sharply towards Drib. He laughed and clapped his hands together, making the slender lamp flames flicker and sending his long, thin shadow swaying and dancing up across the walls of the tower. 'Of course there is a way to get right into the heart of our enemy's camp. We can travel freely without question and take every loyal kingsman and woman with us. Why, with enough subterfuge we will probably even get close enough to rescue Sloeberry, no matter how many sharp eyes are watching. The answer is in the simplest of riddles. Now, Drib, tell me, where is the best place to hide something?'

Drib frowned as he strove for an answer, but the harder he tried the blanker his mind became. He hated riddles and he had never been much good at them – even the easiest ones that Grout set them in the Learning Hall had left him baffled.

'Well?' Nevian asked impatiently.

'Perhaps in the darkest and dustiest corner of a chimney?' Drib offered in desperation.

'How do you suppose we will hide an army in a chimney, even if we had one. Don't be silly, boy. Anyway dark corners are the worst place for hiding anything, they're the first places to be searched. No, think again: the answer is really so simple.'

Drig shrugged helplessly. He felt such a fool. Silkstone hooted softly to give him encouragement but to Drib the owl's voice only seemed to mock him.

'In plain sight, Drib, that's the best place to hide anything. It's the last place people will ever think to look, right in front of their noses!' The magician was laughing.

'But what is it exactly that we are trying to hide? And how will it help us to rescue Sloeberry? I'm sorry but I don't understand.' Drib was at a complete loss.

'Ourselves, boy!' An edge of exasperation was creeping

into Nevian's voice and he threw his hands into the air. 'You, me and Umm, Orundus, Grannog, not to mention your horse and Equestrius, and all those we find who are still loyal to the King – we will gather them along the greenways. Remember I promised to meet Berioss in the shadows of Candlebane Hall with every loyal Kingsman I could find by mid-winter's daylight.'

'But ... but ... that's impossible! Snatchpurse will know every move we make now that those evil birds patrol the sky. They were quick to spot Orundus and he was only one owl on his own. They'll see us the moment we venture back into Elundium!'

'Yes, that's right, Drib, they will indeed see us, and I want them to. In fact our success depends on us being seen. Everybody must see us or how else will those who are secretly loyal to the King know of our presence?' Nevian smiled and moved close to the boy, lowering his voice, 'The art of our deception will be in being seen and yet remaining invisible.'

'Do you mean that we will disguise ourselves somehow?'

'Now you're getting the idea, Drib!' Nevian laughed.

The magician chuckled and bent to refill Drib's ale jug, making him hold it still while he plunged the red hot poker into it. The ale hissed and bubbled, giving off a strong aromatic scent of hops and malt as a head of froth arose dangerously high above the rim of the tankard. Drib bent forwards to lick it off before it spilled over the floor.

'But how can we do that?' Drib frowned.

'That, my lad, is the difficult part. How indeed shall we disguise ourselves? Since I have little doubt that the fate of Elundium and Sloeberry's freedom – indeed everything that we strive to achieve – rests on that question, we had better make the best possible choice. Think, boy, prove you are worthy of the talents that have been bestowed upon you. What shall be our disguise?'

Nevian resumed his measured pacing, muttering and mumbling to himself, lost in thought. He paused occasionally to take down a particular book of magic and idly thumb through it. How indeed could he disguise such a large company of people? He knew the answer he sought was so tantalizingly close and yet remained so elusive – it was almost as though it was hidden from him in the shadows. If only his power had not shrunk so much. Perhaps they should clothe themselves . . .

'We will be such an odd looking company won't we, no matter what you do to disguise us!' Drib's voice interrupted, cutting through the magician's thoughts. He glanced at the boy in irritation: there were certainly disadvantages in having an apprentice, especially one who chattered on without pausing for breath.

'Well, Umm is so large, he's almost a giant isn't he,' Drib continued, oblivious to the magician's sharp, irritable glance. 'And you are so distinguished looking. Nobody would mistake you for anyone but the Master of Magic, especially with that long, flowing rainbow cloak. Why, you both look as peculiar as the folk with that travelling circus that used to visit the Granite City before these troubles began. They used to have a magician and a giant who bent iron bars. And they had . . .'

'Brilliant! Absolutely brilliant!' Nevian cried. 'I wouldn't have thought of anything as clever as a travelling circus, not in an age of daylights. It suits our needs perfectly. It won't matter how large our ranks swell because crowds are always expected with a circus. There are always booths and sideshows as well – they could sell trinkets and cures – and there is always a lot of noise and bustle, all that will mask our true intent. Yes, Drib, it will be a perfect disguise.'

212

'But what about me?' the boy asked in a small voice. 'If Snatchpurse or any of his followers see my crooked legs they are bound to get suspicious.'

Nevian looked down at Drib's legs and slowly a smile softened his eyes. 'You, my boy, will make yourself invisible.'

'Invisible? But how? That's impossible,' Drib cried.

'By the power of magic, Drib. How else but by the power of magic?' Nevian stifled a yawn. It had been a long and exhausting journey back through the mountains to the Runesgate and he needed some peace and quiet to riddle out his strategies. 'But that's enough of your questions for one night. You look tired out. Off to bed with you now and that arm will heal all the quicker. Let me concentrate my mind on creating this circus of deceptions. Remember every part of it, no matter how small, must appear to our enemies to be the genuine thing; tumblers must tumble, jugglers must juggle, fire eaters will consume the flames.'

Nevian yawned again, ushering the boy towards the stairs, 'Sleep well because first thing in the morning your education in magic shall begin. You will start by learning the art of invisibility: you will vanish completely and that, I can tell you, is no easy task. Now, off to bed.'

Drib rose reluctantly to his feet with Silkstone on his shoulder. He didn't feel the least bit sleepy – not now, he was far too worried, he didn't like the sound of vanishing at all. 'But how will I know where I am? I will be constantly bumping into things,' he muttered to himself as he crossed the chamber.

Nevian smiled as he listened to the boy's fears. 'Orun Borat, Orun Borat, there is nothing to fear, Drib, nothing to fear.'

Drib paused when he reached the first twist in the stairs

and heard the gently whispered words as they floated out to him. He didn't quite catch them and he didn't understand so he turned to look at the tall, thin figure of the magician as he sat encircled by his flowing rainbow cloak in the centre of the great chamber. 'Don't you ever get tired, Nevian?' he asked.

The magician glanced up to him and laughed. 'No, Drib, sleep is the necessity of mortal men. Now you go to bed.'

Drib nodded silently and climbed the remaining stairs.

'Do I need sleep? Whatever will he be asking me next?' Nevian muttered, settling himself into his deep, buttoned thinking-chair after he had drawn it closer to the fire. 'Circus, now what is in a circus? Well we will need acrobats, tumblers ... mummers ...' The magician's eyelids fluttered and closed as his head slumped back gently into the soft, feather cushions. The lights dimmed and he was fast asleep before the wrought iron latch on the door on Drib's sleeping chamber had been drawn back.

VIII

A Dark Night in Notley Marsh

DAWN BROKE with an unnatural, eerie silence bringing Thunderstone, the keeper of the great lamp of Underfall hurrying to the highest gallery of the fortress. He looked out to find that the surrounding countryside of steeply wooded valleys and heather meadows had almost vanished beneath a cold, grey, drifting mist that softened the shapes of the trees and blurred the dereliction of Marshthistle. It clung in glistening, wet, spiderfine shrouds to the carpet of cobwebs that covered the Causeway Fields. Thunderstone frowned and wet the forefinger of his sword hand before holding it up as he peered out at the drifting curtain of mist. There was hardly a breath of air to chill his finger. The weather had unexpectedly turned to their advantage – now was the moment for Errant to make his dash for the tower on Stumble Hill. He could ride out under the cover of the mist: there was still a chance that he could overtake that evil horde who had attacked and burned the hamlet of Marshthistle to the ground. With luck on his side and some hard riding Errant might arrive in time to warn Kyot and Eventine of the impending danger that was advancing in a black, evil tide along the greenways through Meremire Forest towards them. It might just give them the opportunity to fortify their tower. Thunderstone knew that the King had sent Elionbel there when the troubles in the Granite City had worsened and they needed all the advance warning they could get if they were to protect her.

Thunderstone ran down the winding stairway, gathering those of his men who were on watch duty. Their armoured boots echoed along the low, vaulted passageways and through the gloomy maze of courtyards that brought them to the outer keep where Errant's mount stood, saddled and ready for the road. The keeper of Underfall strode purposefully forwards across the keep, motioning to the few archers who had remained loyal to keep up their positions on either side of the great ironwood doors in readiness for the moment when the locks would be undone, the bolts drawn back and the doors pulled open for Errant to gallop out. Thunderstone was well aware of the daunting road ahead of Errant and the dangers he was about to face if he was to reach Stumble Hill safely. He grasped the horseman's arm, pulling him close.

'If only we had a squadron of Gallopers and a strike of swift-footed Archers to accompany you,' he whispered, his eyes full of regret.

Errant laughed and shook his head. 'Fear not, old friend, we shall be all the faster for being alone. Dawnrise has the heart and courage of a warhorse: we will be safe.'

Thunderstone glanced up anxiously to the small patch of strengthening daylight peeping through the soaring archways, parapets and buttresses of the outer keep. 'The men that were lowered down on ropes from the upper galleries under cover of darkness have cleared away the last of the corpses that had been piled up against the doors to prevent your riding out. Now is the moment. The weather has turned to your advantage so go quickly before the thick mist that shrouds everything is burned away by the morning sun.'

Thunderstone paused and glanced around the gloomy courtyard that was lit by only three guttering reed lamps. He lowered his voice and his fingers tightened on the rider's arm, 'Have you decided which road to take through Meremire Forest? Remember there is no way of knowing which ones those shadowy hordes have taken and you won't know until you come upon them. There might not be a way to get past them if the undergrowth is tangled and overgrown, and don't forget that all the greenways converge on the one bridge that spans the Deepling Gorge. If they get to that bridge before you . . .'

Thunderstone let his voice trail away. The awful implications of such an event were best left unsaid. Errant lifted the saddle flaps and checked the tightness of his girths, making sure that every buckle and keeper was securely done up before gathering up his reins and placing his foot in the stirrup in readiness to mount. Dawnrise was fretting and snatching at the bit with nostrils flaring as Errant sprang up lightly into the saddle. Sparks sent up by the horse's iron-shod feet danced across the cobbles, his ears were pricked and his neck was arched in readiness for the road that lay ahead of him. Errant was well aware of the warning in the lampmaster's words, but which road should he take? He held the prancing horse on the bridle, racked with indecision. Everything hung on his choice. The keys slowly grated in the door locks and the huge bolts were thrown back one by one. Suddenly the horseman laughed as he remembered that there was one road he could take, one that his king had once dared to use when the Nightbeasts were pursuing him from Stumble Hill to Underfall.

'I will take the ancient road through Notley Marsh. It will be by far the shortest route and it bypasses Meremire Forest and the Deepling Gorge. It will save me leagues.'

'But that road is so rarely used and is overgrown with wildness. How will you find it amongst those treacherous shifting bogs? One false step and you will be sucked down into the mud. No, it is madness to use that road!'

Thunderstone cried as the last bolt was thrown back, allowing a crack of light and swirling mist to appear between the opening doors. Dawnrise crouched in readiness as the doors creaked and scraped across the cobbles.

'There is no other choice!' Errant called out as his mount sprang forward and they disappeared into the mist in a thunder of hoofbeats. He glanced back only once, when he heard the hollow echo of the huge doors being slammed shut and the grate of the bolts behind him, but the fortress of Underfall had already vanished from sight and been swallowed in the swirling mist. He was all alone now. He kept to the crown of the road with a tight grip on the hilt of his sword as he passed through the burnt out ruins of Marshthistle and onto the greenway that crossed the Causeway Fields. On he rode towards the steep, wooded valleys and undulating heather meadows that came to an abrupt stop beneath the brooding eaves of Meremire Forest.

Errant knew that the road he sought was close to the north of the first valley he would enter. It should show itself between two of the giant, black ebony trees that lined the greenway and grew up the sides of the valley – but which two? They were all clothed in such a tangle of vines and creepers since the Tunnellers had stopped mowing and trimming the greenway's edge. The ancient road should be on the left hand side in a slight dip climbing up steeply through the trees and carrying on to the rim of the valley. He was sure of his facts, he had ridden past its entrance a thousand times without giving it a second glance, but could he find it in this thickening mist? Would he even know when he had reached the first valley? He couldn't even see the trees on either side of the road he was on. Crouching low along his horse's neck he peered ahead, not knowing where he was. Beads of wet mist clung to his eyelashes and glistened on his helm and the sleeves of his mail shirt. The eerie, unnatural silence was broken only by the clatter of Dawnrise's hoofbeats and the creak of his saddle. It almost unnerved him. Had this new evil killed all the birds? Had it taken away all the beasts from the fields? Had it stolen the wind and replaced it with this infernal mist?

Suddenly he felt Dawnrise tense beneath him and snort in alarm. There was something ahead of them. Gaunt black shapes loomed out of the mist on either side of the road and he could hear a faint crackling sound. There was a bitter, acrid smell of burning in the air. He instinctively shortened the reins and raised his sword, only to let it fall back to his sides as the shapes he had glimpsed materialized into the charred remains of the black ebonies that had once arched so gracefully over the greenway and climbed up the steep valley sides beyond the Causeway Fields. Now at least he knew where he was. He slowed his mount to a cautious trot, seeking the entrance to the ancient path that would take them through Notley Marsh.

Thick yellow clouds of smoke drifted across the greenway as he passed between the trees, making him choke and gasp for breath. The wild, unkempt under-growth on either side of the road had been burned away and now lay in smouldering heaps of hot ash. Between the fire-scarred trees flames licked the charred branches, causing them to fall and explode into ribbons of bright sparks. The way dipped slightly in front of them and Errant found the entrance he sought – it had been made simple now that the dense undergrowth had been burned away. An ancient avenue of trees vanished up the steep side of the valley but the smoke and mist prevented him from seeing how much of it had been consumed by the fire or whether it was blocked higher up. He didn't want to ask his mount to risk crossing the hot ash without being sure the road was clear. For a moment he sat there undecided. Might it not be safer to ride on through the forest? But what if Thunderstone's warnings proved to be correct? What if his enemies had already reached the Deepling Gorge? After all they did have more than two daylights' start on him. He re-sheathed his sword and leaned forwards, pulling the tail of his cloak around his face and caressing Dawnrise's neck. His mind was made up.

'Run, great heart. Gallop! Go faster than the east wind and we will not stop until we reach the valley's rim. We have to take the road through the marshes.'

He turned his spur against Dawnrise's flank and gave him his head as he lurched off the road and began to labour up the steep slope. Hot ash and sparks rose around his thundering hooves, covering them in choking, black clouds. Errant clung on tightly, momentarily blinded by the tail of his cloak. He could feel hot sparks falling on them and could hear the roar of the fire as they raced through it. Ten . . . twenty . . . thirty strides, he lost count as the horse's hooves scrambled and they lurched from side to side up the steep sides of the valley. Abruptly the ground levelled out and Dawnrise slowed to a walk, breathing hard, his neck and shoulders black with sweat and ash. Errant pulled the cloak tail away from his face to find that they had reached the valley's rim. Below them the air was thick with smoke, but ahead, through the thinning mist, he could see the ancient road, overgrown with wildness and stretching away between towering oaks, as yet untouched by the fire. He slipped quickly from the saddle and eased the girths. Urging Dawnside to a trot he ran easily beside him to give his horse a chance to recover.

'Legends tell that there is an abandoned wayhouse

called the Hut of Thorns ahead of us, before the road drops into the marshes. They say that the King once took shelter there from the creatures of the night that were pursuing him. We will rest there too, and wash away the filth of the fire if the clear spring still rises beside the hut.' Dawnrise snorted and rubbed his dirty face on Errant's arm as they ran on in a silence broken only by the jingling of the bridle's bit rings and the squeak of the horseman's boots.

Errant hunted for breath and kept a light hold on the reins as the morning wore on. Above the trees the sun climbed high in a cloudless sky, burning away the last thin wreathtails of mist that lay low across the ancient road. Errant's mouth was dry and swollen with the taste of the ash and rivulets of sweat and dirt streaked his forehead, trickling down from underneath the rim of his helm. The hems of his long cloak were constantly being snagged by the brambles and weeds that had grown unchecked across their path. It was long past the noon day hour, of that he was sure, and he was about to give up all hope of coming upon this wayhouse when he caught sight of a ruined hut, overgrown with thorns and brambles, just ahead of him. Faintly he thought he heard the sound of running water and he quickened his stride. As he rounded the corner of the hut he saw the spring tumbling from a mossy fountain head into a crystal clear, shallow pool. Pale blue starflowers and pure white evermind grew in a thick carpet all around the water's edge.

Errant led the horse forward and waited, despite his own raging thirst, as Dawnrise drank his fill before kneeling and plunging his own head beneath the icy water. He gasped and threw his head back, shaking it fiercely and scattering a halo of shimmering droplets in the sunlight as he laughed. 'That tasted better than wine from the finest vineyard. We will rest a moment here and catch our breath before pressing on.'

He stripped off Dawnrise's saddle and bridle and washed away the filth and dried sweat from the horse's back. Dawnrise shook himself and rolled in the grass before moving beneath the trees to graze, allowing Errant to return his attention to the tumbledown hut. Could it really have once had the strength to protect the King from the Nightbeasts? He wondered how much of the old legends were true. There was no proper door, or not one that he could see, just a rough hewn opening in the crumbling stone work that time and wildness had all but covered with an impenetrable barrier of sharp entangling thorns with branches as thick as his arm.

'Nobody's been in here for an age of daylights by the look of it,' he muttered. He was about to turn away when he noticed that there were some partially concealed words carved in the creeper-covered lintel just above the opening. Drawing his sword he tried to hack the creepers down but they seemed to writhe and tangle themselves around the blade, causing him to step back hastily and resheath it. He remembered that some of the older, isolated wayhouses had the most peculiar door locks and defences: perhaps the words above the opening were a key. Tentatively he moved closer and reached up. The creepers parted at his touch to reveal a legend, deeply carved in the time-worn stone. Slowly he read it aloud. 'Though darkness holds the road he that seeks refuge may enter and sleep in peace until a new day dawns.'

The air around him was suddenly filled with the heady scent of nightflowers and thousands of tiny white petals opened against the thorns. 'It is a door, a magical door!' he hissed, glancing anxiously towards the hut. He had an instinctive caution towards all things magic. The thorns rustled dryly and slowly drew apart. He was too afraid to enter but he peered in over the threshold to see a dust-covered, gloomy room with a bare earth floor strewn with broken chairs and overturned tables. There was a musty air of neglect about the place and weeds and vines had climbed up the insides of the walls, forming a flowering arch above the cold, smoke-blackened chimney hole. Errant yawned, suddenly overcome by drowsiness – he remembered the tales about the power of the nightflower to bring on a dreamless sleep. There was a strange brooding power in the room: for an instant he imagined the shadows lengthening around him and he thought he could hear the echo of wolves howling on the road and the blood-chilling sound of Nightbeasts' screams. Errant shivered, despite the hot sun on his back and retreated, calling out, 'Thank you but we do not seek refuge, our road lies through the marshes.'

The nightflower petals began to close and the mass of thorns snaked as they wove themselves back across the doorway, but the scent of the nightflowers lingered, making Errant yawn.

'Come on, Dawnrise, we have a long road ahead . . .' he called out, frowning and looking up as a flock of starlings suddenly wheeled low overhead making a harsh shrieking cry, almost as one, before disappearing from sight. Dawnrise whinnied, showing the whites of his eyes, before he trotted over to where Errant stood waiting.

There was something unsettling about the flock of birds. It wasn't just the bad omen of seeing so many starlings all together – it was something about their cries that made Errant want to get out of sight before they returned. Quickly he resaddled the horse and they cantered forward beneath the shelter of the overhanging oaks. He looked back just once and raised his hand in a silent salute to the overgrown hut, glad that there was still a refuge on such a lonely and forgotten road for those in great need.

The afternoon wore on and the leagues passed beneath Dawnrise's thundering hooves. The landscape was gradually changing: the avenue of oaks was beginning to thin out into wide, grassy, sunlit clearings, but much to Errant's dismay the flocks of birds seemed to be following them, shrieking and mobbing them each time they broke cover. He unsheathed his sword and swung it in an arch around his head to drive them away. He was glad of his metal helm and mail shirt beneath his cloak as some flew directly at him and tried to peck and claw at his head and chest. Where they had come from and who had power over them he could not guess; he dreaded what he might find at his journey's end. Far away to his right he caught an occasional glimpse of the dark canopy of Meremire Forest. Thick palls of smoke seemed to hang above it in the air. The flocks of birds vanished as the road suddenly dipped between tall, whispering pine trees and they entered a narrow, shadowy gorge filled with the mist and roar of waterfalls. Ahead of them Errant glimpsed the marshes. As they reached the other side of the gorge he could see them spread out below, stretching away in dense reed banks, stagnant pools and overgrown wildness to the hazy horizon line.

Once they had left the gorge the road petered out and became a steep, muddy track overhung with dense foliage descending into the marshes. Dawnrise slipped and skidded before slowing to a walk. Errant was glad of the cover of the trees in case the evil flocks of birds returned, but the low canopy soon forced him to dismount and use his sword to clear the way. The path they were following quickly narrowed and became choked with dense banks of brambles and quickthorn. They scratched painfully at

Errant's hands and face and dug into Dawnrise's flanks with every step he took.

Everywhere dead trees leaned dangerously across their path and a stink of rotting vegetation filled the air. The ground became treacherously soft and foul-smelling, wide stagnant pools began to appear through the undergrowth, catching the sparse light on either side of them. Huge, vermillion spiders scuttled along the branches and dropped onto Errant's neck as his blade tore through their thick webs. Mosquitoes hummed in thick, black clouds around their heads, happy in the hot, oppressive air. The further they ventured the deeper Dawnrise's hooves sank into the ground – green, stinking mud oozed up around his fetlocks.

Errant paused for a moment, resting on the hilt of his sword to catch his breath. Looking up at the wildness that pressed in all around them he realized that the light was beginning to fade: the sun had set and silent nightshapes were gliding effortlessly around them – floating through the tangled undergrowth they barely touched the still surface of the stagnant pools as they brought the night's darkness to the marshes.

'I've been a complete fool – we should have made camp in that gorge and waited for morning before attempting to cross this wildness. One wrong step in the dark and . . .'

He left the worst of his fears unspoken. They had got this far and he wasn't going to turn back now – too much rested on him reaching Stumble Hill before those evil hordes who had swept down from the mountains without warning.

'We must try to find a way forward. We must get through this treacherous mire in the dark, no matter how dangerous our path becomes. There can be no turning back now!' Feeling grim, he caressed Dawnrise's sweating neck and reached for the tall, cylindrical brass and crystal staysafe lantern that every Galloper and despatch rider carried securely by its hooked handle on the pommel of the saddle.

Crackling the spark between finger and thumb he lit the lantern. 'Stay close behind me,' he instructed his mount as he lifted the torch. A small circle of soft, yellow light shone dimly into the gathering darkness.

Errant had barely taken two hesitant steps forward before they were engulfed in a cloud of huge moths. The insects whirred around the lamp in their thousands, striking repeatedly at the glass and shrouding its precious light with their wings. 'Get away from the light – get away!' Errant shouted, violently waving his free hand into the air to ward them off but to no avail. Their soft, furry bodies fluttered against his hand and flew into the top of the lamp. The fragile flame hissed and spluttered, briefly flaring up into a brilliant blue white light with each moth it consumed, but the flame grew steadily weaker as their burned bodies choked the lantern.

'It's no good, we'll do better fumbling our way forward in the dark without this plague of insects!' he cursed, extinguishing the light and securing it back onto the saddle.

'Stay very close to me,' he whispered, blindly feeling his way forward in the thickening darkness using the point of his sword to find the firmest ground.

Unseen brambles and thorns scratched painfully at his face and at the slightest deviance from the path he sunk up to his knees in the stinking, boggy ground; he would have sunk completely if Dawnrise had not backed up at his startled cry and pulled him out. Doubt dogged every cautious footstep that Errant took as they ventured deeper into the marshes. But he noticed that the stink of rotting vegetation was fading, the air was less stifling and was faintly scented with loosestrife, water lilies and willow-herb. The undergrowth was gradually beginning to thin out into clumps of tall, swaying reeds and marsh grasses, some of which grew to arch high above his head. Sometimes he caught glimpses of the stars and shafts of silvered moonlight as it shimmered on wide stretches of water where before there had been only stagnant pools. The path began to open out and the ground felt strangely different beneath his feet. He brought Dawnrise to a halt in a clear patch of moonlight and knelt down, curiously spreading out his fingers to touch the ground.

'It feels like moss,' he murmured, pressing the tips of his fingers into the tightly woven carpet of tiny, water-soaked plants and ferns. The ground rippled slightly all around them and cold, clear water oozed up over his hand only to disappear the moment he took it away. Errant slowly stood up and looked down at his feet. He had sunk almost to his ankles and his horse was down below its fetlocks. The cold water began seeping into his boots: a knot of fear tightened in his stomach as he realized that they must have somehow wandered off the true path and out onto a thick knotted layer of floating vegetation – he didn't want to hazard a guess at what might lie underneath. He turned around to find that, to his horror, the clear path they had been following had vanished: all the trees, the clumps of reeds, the tangle of tall grasses – they all looked the same. There wasn't a single footprint in the springy carpet of moss to show him which way they had come. Panic seized him. They had to find a way onto firmer ground. There was no way of knowing how long the tightly woven mossy carpet would hold their weight. He was forced to move forward, hoping that the true path lay just beyond the next clump of reeds. He parted the grasses and his heart sank. Ahead of them, stretching away in the moonlight, were leagues of wide, watery channels, criss-crossed by a maze of mossy paths similar to the one they were now standing on. Some of them were bordered by reeds or by low, misshapen bog oaks growing out of them, but which – if any – was their path? He had not the faintest idea. They were now utterly lost and he knew that their next footsteps could well be their last.

A noise in the undergrowth behind them and a rustling in the reeds almost directly ahead made the hairs on the nape of Errant's neck stand up. Were those evil creatures who had burned and massacred Marshthistle all around them or were the monsters of myth and legend who lurked in the marshes about to rear up and pull them down to their deaths? He moved in close to Dawnrise, grimly tightening his grip on the hilt of his sword. He was ready to fight to the death. Dawnrise suddenly pricked up his ears and snorted, neighing as though he were greeting old friends. Errant stared wildly around him as dozens of large, black shapes, their eyes shining amber-bright in the moonlight, broke cover. They converged on them with long, loping strides, twisting and turning constantly as they changed direction to cross the marshes.

Errant laughed with relief and re-sheathed his sword – he realized who they were and held out his open hands in greeting as the two leading Border Runners stopped in front of him. They were panting hard as if they had run a great distance, their tongues showed red between rows of fangs that glistened in the sparse light. Errant didn't recognize any of the dogs but he knew they would not hurt them. The Border Runners were wild and free, they roamed the forests and rolling grasslands as they pleased, but in times of trouble, when danger threatened, they had always rallied beneath the King's standard and formed a vital part of the great battle crescents that had once swept away the creatures of the dark.

'Are we glad you've found us. You're just in the nick of time. We're lost – hopelessly lost. These infernal marshes, we were trying to reach Stumble Hill and warn them . . .'

Errant hesitated, leaving his words to trail away, unsure whether the dogs could understand what he was trying to tell them. He knew all the legends and stories of the great Border Runners. Some warriors swore that they could talk, but he had always had his doubts. They had run at his stirrup in battle often enough and had fought tirelessly by his side; they had sat close beside him at the camp fire and he had always looked upon them as friends. They always appeared when they were least expected and demanded nothing but that they be allowed to keep their freedom.

Magadus, the leader of the small pack, moved closer and Errant knelt as was the custom, allowing the dog to scent him. The Border Runner curled his lips back as he growled a soft greeting and his hot breath ghosted the rider's cheek. They had been following Errant and had kept close watch over him ever since he had galloped out of Underfall alone. The small pack of Border Runners had been silently hunting the dykes along the edge of the Causeway Fields and had witnessed the massacre of Marsh-thistle. They had been too few to do more than crouch and watch as the evil hordes burned the village to the ground before taking the road through Meremire, destroying everything in their path. Magadus had sent the fastest of his pack ahead of Errant just as his horse had cantered up onto the ridge where the road through the marshes had begun, to check that the way ahead was clear and safe to use. He realized that only a man in great need would be using such a path. The Border Runners had been about to drop back, knowing that horse and rider were safely on their way, when Errant had taken a wrong turning in the dark and had wandered out onto the dangerous moss paths that crossed the very centre of the marshes: the true path kept to the slightly higher ground.

Errant rose slowly to his feet, his face grave as he told them how urgent was his need to get to Stumble Hill. Magadus seemed to understand. He barked and ran out onto one of the springy, mossy paths, and paused, waiting. He glanced back and two of the other Border Runners moved in close to either side of Errant, crouching and pressing lightly against his legs to guide him, while the rest of the pack crowded in around Dawnrise to make sure that the horse wouldn't step off the firm path.

Errant looked ahead nervously at the vast expanse of water that they were about to cross. One false step now and nothing would save him, but there was no turning back. 'Lead on!' he cried, summoning up all the courage he could find, and to a chorus of barking he let the dogs on either side of him find the way.

The Border Runners moved swiftly through the marshes, twisting and turning, choosing the oldest and firmest of the mossy paths. Errant soon found he was gasping and labouring for each breath in his effort to keep up the pace across the soft, marshy ground. He took off his metal helm and threw it aside where it vanished with a splash. He discarded his cloak and mail shirt. The reed and moss became a blur as he became dizzy and light-headed, barely aware of the changing landscape, but he kept mumbling to himself, 'I must run. I must run until my bones crack and my muscles knot with cramp. I must reach Stumble Hill, I must reach Stumble Hill!'

The moon had long set and the dead hours of the night

had closed in before he realized that the springy moss beneath his feet had disappeared. The dogs on either side of him had moved slightly away as the ground grew firmer. They were climbing out of Notley Marsh. Ahead of him in the first thin fingers of dawn light he could see the greenway stretching away beneath tall, overhanging trees.

'I must rest a moment. I can't take another step,' he gasped, stumbling to a halt and falling to his knees with exhaustion.

Dawnrise stopped beside him, steam rising from his sweaty flanks, and rubbed his muzzle against his rider's forehead as Magadus loped back and licked the man's cheeks with his rough, wet tongue. The dog barked.

'The road to Stumble Hill is yours.'

Errant barely had time to run his fingers through the Border Runner's thick coat to thank him before the pack had vanished silently into the undergrowth. Climbing laboriously to his feet he rested heavily in the stirrups while he checked and tightened the horse's girths, but it took him a moment to remount. Gathering his reins he glanced back to look across his shoulder at the vast, treacherous expanse of Notley Marsh that they had crossed during the hours of darkness and he smiled. Never again would he doubt that the Border Runners could understand every word that a human said.

'Come on, it's not far now,' he murmured softly to Dawnrise as he broke into a trot, breasting the rim of the steep valley that led down into the marshes. Errant saw the silhouette of the Wayhouse Tower of Stumble Hill etched in dark colours against the lightening sky and his heart lifted.

Dawnrise snorted, arched his neck and broke into a canter up the last, long uphill stretch. Errant caught sight of movement on the high platform at the top of the tower:

the watchman was extinguishing the lamp and a glint of morning sunlight shone on the metal helms. There was a sudden, sparkling flash of light as the Glass of Orm, a strange, cylindrical contraption that magnified the road, was moved on its small, oiled wheels and turned in his direction. A warning bell was sounded and the great doors of the tower were slowly beginning to open, bumping and grinding across the cobbles. A strike of archers swarmed out to the right and left of the doors lining the road, each with an arrow nocked onto his bow string, leaving the crown of the greenway open for him to canter in through the open doors. The strike of archers barely gave Dawnrise time to pass between them before they closed defensively behind him. Their arrows were kept trained on the empty road as they retreated in over the threshold of the tower and the huge ironwood doors, that in better, safer, times were left standing wide open during daylight hours for the merchants and journeymen to go peacefully about their business were slammed shut and bolted securely.

Errant could see that the tower was well prepared against attack as he rode beneath the main archway. Archers and spearmen were crouching or standing at the casement slits and an inner ring of carts had been over-turned and fortified as a second line of defence should the doors be breached. Dawnrise's hooves echoed and clattered in the gloomy, damp passageway that led into the central courtyard. He brought his mount to a halt in the bustling square and stood up in the stirrups to search and peer through the thick haze of smoke and steam that was billowing out through the open doors of the armoury for sight of Lord Kyot. He could hear the rattle of hammers on anvils and the roar of forges and could see showers of sparks arcing high in the swirling smoke above the grinding wheels where blades and arrowheads were being honed. Rows of fletchers were bent over deftly flighting new arrow shafts and coopers were whittling spear shafts. Hurrying figures appeared and disappeared all around him in the smoke, laden with bows, spears and shields. Voices called out to him from every side asking him what news he brought of the road or of King Thane who was siege-locked in the Granite City. Over and over again the question was, 'Has the City fallen?'

'I have ridden from Underfall, I know nothing of the state of things in the Granite City. Where is Lord Kyot? I have urgent news to bring him.'

Glancing up Errant caught sight of Kyot and Lady Eventine; both were armed with long bows and carried full quivers of arrows as they hurried down the main stairway towards him.

'You will know everything there is to know soon enough,' Errant replied to the anxious questions, and the archers solemnly went back to their posts.

Errant dismounted quickly and eased the girths before removing the bit from Downrise's mouth. The horse's head was low with exhaustion and his nostrils were flared, steam was rising from his lathered sides and pools of dripping sweat were beginning to form underneath him on the ground. Eventine looked at the sorry state of the horse and called out for grooms to attend to him urgently.

Errant caressed Dawnrise's neck and whispered words of thanks in his ear. 'Rest, great heart, rest while you can, I fear we still have many leagues to travel before this journey will be finished.' Dawnrise lifted his head a little and neighed fiercely as he allowed the grooms to lead him away into the stables.

'You must have ridden a hard road to judge by the look of you both, Errant, has Underfall fallen? What has happened? What can you tell us of the palls of black smoke that hang over Meremire Forest and seem to draw steadily closer? What has caused those flocks of vicious birds to repeatedly attack us? Where on earth have they come from?'

Kyot's questions came at breathless speed as he gripped the horseman's arm in greeting and began to lead him to the great archer hall. With a shout their servers appeared in the doorway and prepared a fresh fire. Earthenware pitchers of warm water and clean towels were brought for Errant to wash away the dust of the journey. A thick cloak was draped around his bare shoulders as he was found a comfortable chair at the fireside. He was given a slice of waycake and mulled ale to refresh him before Kyot began pressing him for news from Underfall.

'We are starved of news, have you anything to tell Elionbel of the King's fate – has the Granite City fallen?'

Errant frowned and was about to say that he had no news – either good or bad – of the state of Elundium or of the Granite City when Queen Elionbel appeared in the open doorway. She was breathless, she looked pale and drawn and her eyes were dark, shadowed with sleepless nights. Worry carved deep lines over her face. Her richly embroidered cloak was thrown back across her shoulders to reveal a simple, home-spun gown and the hilts of the sword and dagger that now hung at her side. Mulcade, the Battle Owl, who had accompanied Elionbel and young Krann, her half-brother, in their flight from the Granite City, was perched on her shoulder and hooted before stooping across the great raftered hall and flying up to settle on the kingpost beam to observe the proceedings. Errant moved quickly to kneel at Elionbel's feet and offer her the hilt of his sword.

'I am afraid I have no news of the Granite City, my lady. I have ridden with all haste from Underfall through

Notley Marsh to warn all those I can reach of the evil hordes that have swept down out of the Emerald Mountain and are even now spreading a black tide through Meremire Forest burning everything in their path. I . . .'

He glanced up at the darkened, vaulted galleries that overhung the hall as he heard light footsteps above him and he saw two small faces peering down over the balustrades.

'Please, wait a moment, Errant.' Kyot spoke softly, restraining the horseman as he looked up at the gallery. 'I want the children to hear all you have to tell us of this new, dark evil.'

'No, surely not – we should spare them that,' Elionbel cried, clutching at Kyot's arm. She and Thane had worked so hard to shield Krann from the knowledge of his dark beginnings and huge tears welled up in her eyes as the memories of it all flooded back.

She could almost feel the echo of Krulshards' hatred: the image of it burned into her memory. She could see the grey, bloodless strips of flesh that hung about his face in mockery of skin, the pitiless, burning eyes gloating in victory and the dreadlocks of tangled hair that streamed out from his bony crown. It was all still so vivid, concealed just beneath the surface, waiting to rear up and fill her with despair. She remembered only too well the violent rage that had possessed Krulshards as he had stood upon the uppermost ramparts of the ruined Granite City, realizing that his victory could never be complete while the last Granite King lived to name an heir. She shuddered at the memory of his rage as he had turned it against her and her mother, Martbel, his helpless prisoners. She remembered how, in hatred of Thane and fear that he would be named as the new King, he had dragged her mother into the black, smothering folds of his malice that hung about his shoulders and had cruelly raped her to spawn his own heir. And Krann had been the result. He had been torn from his mother's dying body in the City of Night.

How Krulshards had gloated as he had entrusted Krann into the keeping of two of his most treasured Nightbeasts and how the boy had grown, with unnatural speed, and developed into perfect manhood, but without a shadow – his only weakness. He was obsessed with seeking revenge against Thane for killing his monstrous father, Krulshards, and he had shrouded Elundium with shadowlight as he spread terror throughout the land, driving Thane and his loyal followers to the very brink of defeat at the Rising before the ultimate triumph of good over evil. Then Thane had seeded the boy's footprints with a remnant of Krulshards' malice, thereby giving him a shadow and causing him to shrink back into the body of a helpless baby, devoid of any trace of evil and with such a likeness of Elionbel's mother about him. As Thane had stood with his sword arm raised to make the killing stroke she had begged him to show the boy mercy and pleaded with him to spare the infant's life.

And so he had been brought up in ignorance of his black beginnings. They had promised themselves that one daylight, when he was old enough to really understand, they would tell him everything. But doubt had spread in whispers among the people and before he was even half grown it was being said that the seed of evil was somewhere deep within him and, to Elionbel's shame, when the trouble with the Tunnellers had begun even *her* heart began to have those same doubts. Even now those doubts pricked at her as Errant spoke of a new, dark evil sweeping down from the Emerald Mountains. She desperately wanted to cling onto those daylights of innocence, she so wanted to be able to prove the boy was pure of heart.

'They must both know,' Eventine's voice was soft but firm as it broke into Elionbel's despair. She blinked and looked up through her tears as Kyot's wife continued. 'One daylight the knowledge of this new evil that now confronts us all may save their lives. You cannot deny the children that knowledge – no matter how much you wish to shield Krann.'

Bleakly Elionbel nodded and wrung her hands silently as Kyot called out to Krann and their daughter, Fairlight to come down into the great hall at once.

Although nobody had been able to find the time to answer their persistent questions or tell them exactly what was happening, both children had become aware that an attack on the tower was imminent from the way it had been fortified suddenly when the first clouds of smoke had been spotted above the forest and those flocks of birds had attacked. They had been expressly forbidden to leave the fortress or to play on the watching platform unattended and, from the troubled whispers they overheard amongst the archers, they had guessed that something terrible and dangerous must be approaching through Meremire Forest, but they had no idea what it could be. Exchanging excited whispers, both of their faces vanished from the balustrade and they raced one another to the stairhead.

'Errant, you have ridden from Underfall to save us! I know you have, I heard your hoofbeats on the road!' Krann cried, recognizing the weary, travel-stained rider the moment he reached the foot of the stairs a pace ahead of Fairlight.

'I can ride Fleetfoot, the pony you brought to the Granite City for me – I ride really well now, and Fairlight has taught me how to use a bow. We wanted to ride out and investigate what is happening in the forest to cause all that smoke but we haven't been allowed to leave the tower. Can you tell us what is going on?'

'You will hear everything I have to tell, I promise,' Errant laughed, and he bent down to lift the small boy up in his arms, swinging him around before setting him down again. As he put the boy back on his feet he bowed slightly to Fairlight, a warm smile softening his eyes. 'So, my lady, you have taught Krann the skills of archery have you? A most useful occupation.'

He noticed that both children were dressed alike in long, heavy-spun cloaks and the leather breeches and tunics that the archers wore, and they were both carrying small bows and quivers full of arrows, but there the similarity ended. Fairlight's face had all her mother's beauty, framed by long, fire-gold hair that fell about her shoulders. Growing up in the tower she had a country fresh complexion with an easy infectious grin, her cheeks were hot-flushed with excitement and her eyes sparkled with mischief as she looked up at the horseman. Krann was more restrained – perhaps due to spending most of his young life growing up within the confines of the Towers of Granite in the highest circle of the Granite City: his face was thinner, paler and more serious, with a gentle but haunted look in his azure, blue eyes. He rubbed aside the untidy tangle of white-blond hair that had fallen into his eyes and spoke again, his gravity dissolving into a wide grin.

'I wish I could show you how well I have learned to shoot.'

'Please, please let us show Errant how we can split a candle flame – please! We'll shoot at that one beside the hearth – it would be perfect,' Fairlight implored, reaching back with quick fingers into her quiver for an arrow.

Kyot frowned and was about to shake his head at such childish nonsense but Eventine laughed softly and nodded. 'Do it, but be quick, we have important matters to discuss.' She remembered clearly how, when she was a girl not much older than her daughter, she had asked her own mother and father almost the self-same request the moment she had secretly mastered the Great Bow of Clatterford.

'Now, take great care, both of you, and snuff out that candle cleanly,' she laughed as she motioned to the servers to stand well away from the hearth as Krann and Fairlight drew back their feathered flights in readiness. 'Now, hold your breath, do exactly as I have taught you,' Fairlight whispered to the boy as they took aim.

Krann felt his heart pounding in his chest. What if he missed? What if everybody laughed at him – he just knew he would die of shame, but he couldn't back out now.

'Keep your bow hand steady – now do it, do it now!' Fairlight hissed.

Both arrows sang through the gloomy air of the hall and cut cleanly through the tall, slender candle flame sinking with a thick thud point-deep into the mantel beam.

'There, I told you we've been practising,' Fairlight cried, wanting to try again and pointing to another target further down the hall as Krann let out a silent sigh of relief. He wasn't at all sure he would be so lucky a second time – despite anything Fairlight said. He knew he would never be half the archer she was.

'Now, sit down quietly and listen carefully to everything that Errant has to tell us – and no interruptions!' Kyot insisted.

Elionbel sat down beside Krann, putting her arm protectively around his shoulders as Errant began to describe the hordes of hideous, half-human, half-beastly creatures who had suddenly swept down out of the Emerald Mountains and attacked them at Underfall.

'The strange thing was that we were totally unprepared for the attack. The doors of the fortress were standing wide open, virtually unguarded. Underfall could so easily have fallen and we would have been overrun. But their orderly ranks suddenly broke up and they seemed to mill around in confusion as they turned aside to loot and destroy the hamlet of Marshthistle, a little gathering of houses that stands in the shadow of Underfall beside the causeway. We were hopelessly outnumbered and we couldn't do anything save to rescue a few of the villagers before retreating and siege-locking the doors before the mob could turn again.'

Errant paused and glanced fearfully across his shoulder to the gloomy recesses of the hall and then lowered his voice. 'The destruction of Marshthistle was only the beginning – there was much worse to come. Our attackers advanced towards us beneath a forest of black banners emblazoned with a clenched, grasping claw but stopped on the causeway just out of the range of our archers but close enough for us to be able to see their vile scales and the bony ridges in their armoured skin and their long, curved claws. Then the air above their monstrous bodies began to darken and eerie, shadow wraiths and ghostly figures began to rise out of them before advancing towards us, swallowing up the daylight . . .'

Fairlight gave a frightened cry and Errant paused as she ran to her mother's arms. Krann felt Elionbel's grip tighten on his shoulders but he tried to pretend he was not afraid, although his voice betrayed the terror he really felt.

'Be quiet and listen all of you so that you will know

your enemy. Go on, Errant, tell us what happened then. Leave nothing out,' Kyot hissed.

Errant swallowed a mouthful of ale and slowly wiped the back of his hand across his mouth before continuing. 'The eerie darkness boiled up against the doors and the sheer walls of the fortress that we had thought secure. It poured through every gap, culvert, crack and crevice it could find. The sunlight in the long galleries suddenly faded and the shadows thickened into the darkest night as each one of us was isolated with our own fears. The air became so stifling that we could hardly breathe and it was full of whispering voices that seemed to be offering to satisfy all our hidden desires. Cold fingers touched us in the dark as though they were trying to find a way to get inside, to get underneath our skin. Thunderstone cried out to us to deny the evil and raise our voices in praise of everything that was good and beautiful and not to give in to the temptation, because nothing of goodness could possibly come from such evil, ugly brutes. Thunderstone was right: those swirling, ghostly shapes became frantic and seethed with rage as we denied them. They clawed so painfully at us that they left us with red weals on our skin. Their pervasive whispers rose to wailing screams, so loud that they hurt our ears, but gradually the darkness began to lift and the sunlight streamed back into the fortress. The wraith-like figures who attacked us glided back across the causeway and settled in a black, brooding cloud above the evil hordes who had destroyed Marsh-thistle and we watched them as they vanished back into their hideously misshapen bodies.'

'But what happened then? Those ghosts must have told them how few you were, why did they not attack Underfall?'

Errant frowned and shook his head. 'That was the

243

oddest thing, they did nothing. Thunderstone said that it was because we had denied them and we had won a great victory, but I am not so sure, they just seemed to lose interest in attacking us. They turned away and began defiling the dead of Marshthistle, fighting and arguing amongst themselves as they piled the bodies up against the doors of the fortress in an attempt to prevent us getting out and warning anyone of the invasion. Then they set light to everything that would burn and marched towards Meremire Forest. It took us two daylights to clear away the dead and open the doors: I feared I might arrive too late to warn you. We had no way of knowing how fast they would travel through Meremire, which greenways they would take or if they would stop to loot and burn each village on their way. We thought they may destroy the bridge across the Deepling Gorge so I had no other choice but to ride without pause and take the ancient road through Notley Marsh.'

'That must mean you rode through those marshes in the dead of night! But that's the most treacherous road in all Elundium, one wrong footstep in the daylight – let alone in the darkness – and you would have sunk without trace!' Eventine exclaimed in horror.

'Yes, my lady, and indeed we would have perished had it not been for a pack of Border Runners who found us wandering and lost. They led us across a maze of mossy paths that cross the centre of the marshes and I will never doubt again that they can understand the speech of man.'

A sudden clatter of armoured boots on the cobbles outside the great hall, the sharp ring of the warning bell and the urgent shouts of the watchers on the high platform interrupted Errant's speech: a black, shadowy horde was emerging from beneath the eaves of Meremire Forest and advancing steadily towards the tower. The news brought everyone to their feet.

'It seems you arrived just in time, Errant!' exclaimed Kyot, snatching up his bow. 'Please go quickly amongst my Archers and tell them how to ward off those ghostly shapes should they try to invade the tower.'

'No, my duty lies in warning others. I know better than anyone else how to keep this evil at bay. I must ride on and try to reach the Granite City, I must tell the King. I will go now while the road is still open,' the rider replied, striding towards the doors.

Kyot knew that Errant was right and there was no sense in wasting his time with words so he hurried out into the courtyard beside him and called for Dawnrise to be saddled. The rider barely had time to check his girth and leap up into the saddle before the sky above the tower darkened as flocks of the evil birds that had shadowed his journey all along the ancient road from the Hut of Thorns descended. Dawnrise snorted and reared, pirouetting and kicking up a blaze of sparks as the harsh, shrieks filled the courtyard. The birds wheeled and dived, emptying the bustling square as the archers fled for cover.

'Here, take my helm, it will protect your head from their claws. Keep Dawnrise as still as you can,' Kyot shouted, throwing his helm up to Errant before dropping onto one knee: a three-pronged hunting arrow was already nocked onto his bow string.

'Keep as still as you can!' he called out again as the archers crowded forwards beneath the low archways that bordered the courtyard. Sunlight glinted on the steel tips of their arrows and their bows groaned as the feathered flights were drawn back, lightly touching their cheeks before their arrows sang as they whirred across the courtyard, each one skilfully finding its mark. The surviving birds shrieked with fury as they flew up and away out of bow-shot, before the archers could reach back into their quiver for another spine.

'You see we have found a way to drive off these wretched carrion but we have to be quick. If they scratch you the blood festers in no time at all. But how did you deal with these sudden attacks at Underfall?' Kyot asked as he rose to his feet. He picked his way through the fallen carcasses to where Errant sat, comforting his trembling mount as he waited for the doors to be dragged open.

'They didn't attack Underfall,' the rider replied. 'The first I saw of them was after I had passed the Hut of Thorns on the old road above the marshes . . . no, wait a moment, I *had* seen them before. There was a white magpie with a flock of black, ragged crows picking over the bodies of the villagers at Marshthistle immediately after the massacre. We could see it quite clearly from the fortress and I remember the crows flew over the fortress just before those ghostly shapes invaded. They were making awful, mocking cries – some of the men thought they could hear real voices telling them to give up and throw down their weapons. Thunderstone would have none of it and told everyone to cover their ears and stop letting their imaginations run wild. They stayed well out of bow shot then, not that any of our archers would aim at that white magpie – they considered it would bring them ill luck.'

'We, too, have caught glimpses of a white magpie each time those birds attacked. We have heard its mocking voice in the trees around the tower. My archers are afraid of it and they say that it is a herald of misfortune, all the more so because of its unusual colour. As if things aren't bad enough already without stirring up old superstitions. So far we have been lucky that it hasn't led one of those attacks because I doubt if there is a man amongst them

246

brave enough to raise his bow against it.' Kyot muttered darkly.

The bolts on the huge outer doors had all been thrown back. The doors began creaking and groaning as they were slowly dragged open, allowing a crack of daylight to appear. Dawnrise snorted. His neck was arched and the whites of his eyes were clearly visible as he crouched back on his hocks. Errant shortened his reins in preparation to gallop out. Spearmen and archers crowded in on either side of the open doors at a signal from Kyot to cover the rider's escape.

'Wait! Are you sure there isn't anything else you can tell me about our approaching enemy? Can you think of anything at all, no matter how small or insignificant? Is there anything to help us?' Kyot pressed, grasping the horseman's stirrup leather.

Errant thought back, seeing in his mind's eye the evil horde advancing up onto the causeway towards Underfall beneath their forest of black banners. 'Their shadows!' he hissed. 'Yes, I know, it's their shadows, there is something wrong with them. They don't quite belong, they're strange. They're not like our shadows, they become all distorted and confused when they touch each other or when somebody treads on them. I can't explain but something has made them react badly to one another and they seem to lose some of the darkness that shrouds them momentarily – they almost seem to change colour. Oh, yes, and when those ghostly shapes rose up out of them their shadows changed completely – they became almost human.'

'Exactly how did they change? Tell me everything you saw. Did it appear to weaken them?' Kyot asked quickly, keeping pace with Errant as Dawnrise began to move towards the open doors.

'I don't know really. They were too far away, well beyond bow-shot. I can't be sure of anything, but there was definitely something very odd about their shadows. That's all I can tell you.'

Elionbel, with Krann only a footstep behind her and armed with his bow, suddenly appeared through a small doorway just ahead of Errant. Errant reined Dawnrise to an abrupt halt, throwing up a shower of sparks as Elionbel ran to his side and pressed a letter into his hand. It was sealed with her crest. 'Will you please give this letter to Thane for me when you reach the Granite City . . .' She hesitated and with quick fingers unclasped a fine, silver chain holding a small scuffed and tarnished fingerbowl and held it up for Errant to take. Her voice fell to a whisper that only he could hear, 'Will you tell him that although all the world separates us I still love him more than life itself. Tell him that I think of him always, that my heart is with him and that with each grain of sand that slips through the hour glass I long only to be with him again.'

Errant clasped the King's fingerbowl in his hand, closing his fingers protectively around it as his eyes softened into a smile. He knew that many stories had been woven around this fingerbowl and he preferred to believe the one that said that the King and the Lady Elionbel had fallen in love the moment their eyes first met and that drinking from the fingerbowl was a secret sign between them. From the moment King Thane's reign had begun, sipping from a fingerbowl had become the signal for feasts to begin and for journeys to start or end and for many years every kingsman or woman carried a small fingerbowl wherever they went.

'My lady, I shall carry such a treasure close to my heart. It will not leave me until I can deliver it safely into the King's hand,' Errant smiled, slipping the fingerbowl secretly into an inside pocket of his jerkin.

'The enemy draws ever closer. You must make your dash now!' Kyot warned.

Errant looked out and the swarming shadowy hordes had filled the road. They were less than a quarter of a league away now, he could clearly hear the tramp of their feet. Their snarling, bloodthirsty cries almost made his heart quail.

'Gallop away to the right, go amongst the trees, there is a little-used track leading from the back of the tower that will take you down onto the greenway. Go! Go now!' Kyot urged as Errant turned his spurs into Dawnrise's flanks and with a neighing shout the horse leapt away, with neck stretched out and nostrils flared. In moments they had disappeared between the trees.

Kyot stood for a moment, undecided, pondering all that Errant had told him of their enemy as the tower doors were hastily slammed shut and siege locked in the face of the advancing hordes. If what the rider had said was true, any moment now the advancing creatures would stop and those ghostly figures would rise up out of them and assault the tower, descending in a black, smothering cloud to search out all weaknesses in his archers, finding any sign of a gap in their defences. They would cover everybody, even the children, in a dark, terrifying, claustrophobic shadow and there was no way he could prevent them from getting in. He knew that to be forewarned should mean that he was forearmed against his foe but how on earth was he to use what he had learned to his advantage? An urgent shout from one of the watchers on the night platform of the tower warned him that the advancing creatures were coming to a halt just out of bow-shot and were beginning to spread out to encircle the tower. Kyot looked about him quickly. Every one of his archers and spearmen were at their posts. The blacksmith's forge, the armoury and the wheelwrights' yards were empty as all the craftsmen and their apprentices were crouching in readiness behind the inner barricades armed with swords, staves and battle axes should the doors be breached.

Kyot suddenly realized the value of what he had been told. It wouldn't matter if he had a thousand men to guard the casement slits – those shadowy wraiths would locate them and isolate them all in their smothering darkness. It would probe them for their fears and find their weaknesses unless he were to strengthen them with the knowledge of what was about to happen. He had to let them know before it descended. Running towards the stairway that spiralled its way up to the top of the tower Kyot cupped his hands to his mouth and called out for every man, woman and child to assemble in the inner courtyard. There was not a moment to lose. As he reached the highest platform he ordered everybody to hurry down into the square below. He paused for a moment to pull the Glass of Orm across the platform. He trained it upon the seething horde who filled the road below. He had to steal one quick look, he had to try to see those strange, distorted shadows that Errant had told him about.

He recoiled in horror when he saw the misshapen, half-human, half-beast, creatures that were suddenly magnified by the glass. Nothing that Errant had told him could have prepared him for that first glimpse of their faces. He could see their spiny ridges of scaly, armoured skin, their leering mouths that were crowded with razor sharp teeth, but most terrifying to see was their staring, almost pupil-less eyes. He barely had the time to blink or to search out their shadows before the air above them began to darken and fill with a thin cloud of ghostly, swirling shapes, but it was enough for him to know that he doubted he would ever be able to find the courage to get in close enough to tread on one of them. Shuddering with revulsion he turned and fled from the high platform, racing down the twisting stairway in leaps and bounds, only stopping when he had reached the narrow walkway above the inner courtyard. A mass of uncertain, frightened faces greeted him, bound together in a breathless silence.

'Now listen carefully, all of you,' he cried, 'your very lives will depend on understanding clearly what I am about to tell you. Each one of you must shut out these shadowy, evil wraiths that are about to invade the tower. Each one of you must find the courage to do so on your own as they will isolate you and smother you with their stifling darkness.'

Kyot lowered his bow. 'Arms and armour are no defence against them: they are as insubstantial as the wind and no more solid than the night. It is your souls – your very selves – that they wish to possess. Each one of you, I know, has the strength to resist this evil.'

Without a pause for breath and just as the patch of clear sunlight high above the tower began to grow indigo dark he recounted everything that Errant had told him. 'Stay here in the courtyard, link hands if it helps, hold onto one another, share your strengths and do not be afraid of their dead, cold touch. Remember that nothing good or wholesome can come from something so foul and evil. Raise your voices as the warriors of Underfall did and deny those shadow wraiths, or whatever they are. Sing . . . sing . . . sing of everything that is good and beautiful and do not, whatever the temptation, listen to their persuasive voices. Do not let them into your souls.'

Amidst a sudden, rising clamour of fear Kyot ran down the last flight of steps and gathered Fairlight up in his arms, reaching out to pull Eventine close and putting an arm protectively around her. 'Remember, I love you both more than life itself,' he whispered hoarsely, striving, but failing, to suppress his own terror of the dark.

'I'm not afraid,' Fairlight answered in a small, very frightened voice, trembling as she held tightly to her father's hand.

Eventine caught sight of Elionbel holding onto Krann in the crowded courtyard but she realized they looked very lost and alone amongst the people of the tower. She heard Krann call out repeatedly to Mulcade, begging him to come to their aid. 'Gather Krann up in your arms, husband. He is only a child and he needs your strength and protection more than I do. Shield him with your courage while I hold Elionbel close to me, for we are like sisters.'

Eventine made to move away, but she felt Kyot's arm tighten around her and as their eyes met she saw the fear he had sought so hard to suppress. 'There is no darkness black enough to come between us, nor shrouds of evil that can diminish the light of our love,' she whispered as she slipped away and grasped Elionbel's hand before guiding Krann to where Kyot stood in the deepening gloom as it filled with the wailing voices of the shadowy ghosts who invaded the tower.

Kyot bent down and gathered Krann up, setting him beside Fairlight in his strong arms. A sudden, silent movement in the doorway of the great hall caught Kyot's eye: he glanced across the darkening courtyard and saw Mulcade fly out. The owl flew low across the heads of the crowd, ploughing a path through the ghostly shapes that were now filling the square and sending them swirling away from his beak and razor sharp claws before he stooped onto Kyot's arm, positioning himself behind the children.

Krann turned his head towards the owl and whispered to him.

'I knew you would come to defend us, no matter what dangers threatened. I know you fear nothing that moves in the dark. You are the greatest Battle Owl!'

Kyot laughed softly and for an instant held the owl's proud, blinkless gaze. He knew what risks Mulcade was taking, he knew he would be torn to pieces by the flock of carrion birds should they attack while he was out in the open. One owl could do nothing against so many. A sudden thought occurred to Kyot and he spoke softly but urgently to the owl, hoping he would understand him. 'Tonight, under cover of darkness, slip away silently and gather all your kind. Warn them of this new evil that has invaded Elundium, reawaken their memories of the great stoops of Battle Owls that once ruled the skies in the time of the great Granite Kings before the bonds were broken. You are Chief Loftmaster, Mulcade, make them remember how they once fought beside the Warhorses and Border Runners in better daylights. Remind them how they helped to rid the world of Krulshards' black evil and tell them once more the King and all those loyal to him have great need of their help.'

Mulcade hooted and then carefully spread his wings to shield and protect both the children, covering their heads with his feathers in such a way that they saw and heard nothing of the wailing and screaming of the ghostly figures as they began to smother the people in the tower on Stumble Hill. Kyot heard their resolve falter, heard the doubt in their terrified voices and he lifted his head, forcing his own fear aside to sing as loudly as he could as he moved slowly amongst his archers and their families to comfort them. Oblivious to the turning of the hour glass, he weaved stories and tales of the sunlight, telling all who would listen beneath the claustrophobic shrouds of darkness. One by one, as he passed unseen between them, they joined their voices with his and slowly the whispers became a shout and then a roar. The indigo darkness began to lift and the ghostly shapes started to stream out through the narrow casement slits to pour down over the castellated walls of the tower.

IX

The Tower Falls

SNATCHPURSE cursed silently and spat at the ground between his feet as he heard the archers' voices rise in triumphant shouts of defiance against the Eretch, driving them out of the tower with their denial. Again his forces had lost the element of surprise in their attack. He had to put a stop to it. He had to seize back control of those of his men the Eretch had completely taken over. He saw the air above the fortress darken and boil with their enraged, swirling shapes as they began to pour down the walls in defeat. He knew they would glide effortlessly back and settle over the men they had so easily abandoned when they had surrounded the tower ready to attack. He had seen it happen each time they had approached a village or a wayhouse while they journeyed through Meremire, but why did it only happen to some of them? Why didn't it leave them all weak and consumed with the same madness? It left the affected ones so mindless they tried to kill one another and were totally unable to continue with the attack. Girrolt had suggested that it was because they were not all possessed to the same degree but even if that were the case it did not explain what drove some of the Eretch to search relentlessly for fresh hosts to possess and darken with their evil.

Snatchpurse and his most trusted followers – those who appeared not too deeply possessed and could control what they did – had been carefully watching those who were most altered by the shadows. Snatch didn't want to be wholly rid of the Eretch – he had come to realize how much power and ruthless determination they had infused into his followers and he had observed with alarm how the beautiful, scaly armour and the claws and horns that the Eretch had fused into their bodies became pale and brittle and lost their shadowy power the moment the Eretch deserted those for whom it appeared they had no further use. But why did it happen? There had to be a reason for the madness. Why did it make them incapable of carrying out an organized attack? There had to be a way they could rid themselves of those particular ghostly grave-wraiths who were causing them so much trouble. They were slowing down their advance on the Granite City to a snail's pace and seriously threatening to ruin Snatchpurse's plans to seize the throne of Elundium for himself. Loremaster Grout had been right with his warnings about the Eretch. Some of them were indeed dangerous and unpredictable allies that had to be disposed of – but how? They had to have weaknesses. His men had been quick to discover the pain and discomfort of treading on one another's shadows since the Eretch had possessed them, it felt as though someone were prodding an open wound. But it was Kush who had first noticed that it was the weaker-willed among them, those who had been the easiest to lure into the Honourable Company of Murderers, who fell victim to the madness. He had suggested that the Eretch utterly devoured their souls, eating out their minds, feeding on them until they became empty, hollow husks and they had no more use for them other than to be vehicles until they found another host. And it had been Kush who had gone on to whisper that the Eretch felt they had to kill off all the old hosts to protect the new ones from being attacked, but only once they were sure they had found new ones. The only reason

Snatch could see for the Eretch leaving the old host alive
while they searched for new ones was in case they needed
to return and use them again. They had also discovered
that two of the grave-wraiths couldn't occupy the same
host, and without a host they vanished in a wailing, haunt-
ing cry to become no more substantial than pools of
shadows dwelling in dark corners, watching, waiting for
some innocent traveller to pass by, somebody whom they
could beguile with their evil whisperings of greed and
vengeance.

Armed with this knowledge Snatch was quick to realize
that there was a way to seize back control over his men,
but they had to be careful. They had to do it gradually,
secretly. 'Watch who those grave-devils settle over and
mark them well. There must be no mistakes now. Move
into your positions,' Snatch hissed to Thorograsp, Kush
and Girrolt, a small handful of trusted followers. He barely
moved his lips with his whisper. Murder in the dark had
been his speciality and he knew that the time when the
Eretch returned to settle over them, seeking their old
hosts, was the perfect opportunity.

Snatch crept quietly behind the closest of the followers,
a man who was showing all the signs of the madness
and whose armour had lost its deep indigo colouring, and
waited. The air directly above them darkened with the
returning wraiths. Snatch felt icy fingers pass over him as
the wraith searched for its own host. The man directly in
front of him suddenly fell trembling to his knees and
reached up, clawing at the swirling shapes. Slowly one of
the figures began to descend and spread itself out, ready
to melt back through the pores of his skin. Snatch knew
he had been right in his choice. Now was the moment.
His eyes narrowed into murderous slits, his lips thinned
into a bloodless sneer of delight and he slipped a silent

strangle over his victim's scaly head. He barely had the time to give a startled, choking cry before Snatch brutally jerked the sharp, thin wire tight. The man's eyes bulged and he convulsed as his clawed hands thrashed briefly in the air before he slumped lifelessly to the ground. The Eretch screamed and scratched frantically at Snatch's hands as it appeared to be pulled away from the body of the man. Its cries became weaker and weaker as it drifted helplessly away to disappear amongst the trees.

With a pitiless laugh Snatch stepped back, well pleased with his moment of work, and glanced quickly to his left and right, nodding with satisfaction to the others as he saw the lifeless bodies that lay sprawled upon the ground in front of them. A murmur of uneasiness rippled through the ranks behind and the darkness of the Eretch was clear in their faces as they saw the bodies. Snatch turned sharply and looked hard at them as the sounds died away.

'I cannot tolerate disloyalty – remember that!'

The solid mass of half-human figures edged back a pace as one. They knew their leader's moods: they knew how quickly he could change and watched him with bated breath.

Suddenly Snatchpurse laughed in their frightened faces, a cruel, pitiless sound that could have cut crystal. Then he turned his back on them abruptly and stared coldly up at the tower. The shadows of evening crept slowly up its sheer, smooth walls and the first of the nightshapes began to glide silently out from the wayside ditches and beneath the canopy of the trees, carrying the shrouds of darkness with them. Snatch cursed the Eretch under his breath for so easily squandering the advantage of surprise and he impatiently beckoned to his captains to gather around him.

'These spineless kinglovers hate the dark so we will use

their fears against them. We will storm the tower during the dead, dark hours of night. Bring forward the siege ladders and the battering rams and we will have them! This tower will be mine before the sun rises!'

Amid the sudden flurry of activity and shouted orders Snatchpurse reached up to caress Squark who was perched upon his shoulder, busily preening his long tail feathers. 'Go quickly and gather your flocks of pretty friends, Squark. Make them fly and spread a false early darkness beneath their wings as they throw their shadows across the faces of those wretched kinglovers who hide within that tower. Bring an early night to Stumble Hill.'

Squark made a harsh cry and spread his wings. 'Tell them that they shall have the first and tastiest pickings from the dead. Remember to tell them that!' he urged, sending the white magpie up into the air with a whirr of feathers.

Squark had no sooner vanished amongst the trees than a rising clamour of harsh cries erupted and the sound of beating wings filled the air as thousands of carrion birds began to rise up out of the tree tops in a dense, black, flapping cloud that slowly wheeled and turned purposefully towards the tower. Snatch's face split into a leer of delight as he saw the sky darken. The birds were indeed proving to be very useful allies: they had cleared the skies of those wretched owls and now nothing moved in the surrounding countryside that he didn't know about. Not that he found it easy to understand their shrieking voices; why just after they had crossed the bridge over the Deepling Gorge Squark had brought word that a lone rider had broken out of Underfall and had taken the ancient, disused path that led into Notley Marsh. Anger had momentarily gripped him: why hadn't they prevented such a thing happening by seizing and destroying the fortress before massacring everybody within its walls when they'd had the chance. Now all Elundium would be forewarned. But then his anger had evaporated into laughter at the sheer stupidity of such a futile dash. Surely the rider must have known that there wasn't a road through that treacherous wasteland of shifting mud and water. Surely he must have realized that there wasn't a scrap of truth in those silly Learning Hall stories of the Thronestealer once finding a path through the marshes when the Nightbeasts were running hard on his heels. No, the rider must have perished, but who, Snatchpurse worried, had forewarned the archers of their approach? They must have had knowledge of the Eretch to repel them so quickly and easily. And who was it who had slipped out of the tower and vanished amongst the trees only moments before they surrounded it?

A light touch on his shoulder broke into Snatch's worryings. He spun round, his dagger raised, to find Thorograsp standing a good pace beyond the reach of the blade directly behind him. 'The carrion birds are massing above the tower in a solid, black cloud. Everything is now ready for the assault.'

He pointed to the forest of siege ladders and the battering rams that were being brought forward and placed in position. Snatchpurse reached for his battle mace and gripped it firmly in both scaly hands. 'Light the torches, let those within see us. I wish to strike fear into those archers' hearts. Attack on my signal!'

As Thorograsp hurried away he paused for a moment, racked with doubts about that rider. One by one the torches were lit, casting a lurid glow in the false darkness. 'Well, I will know soon enough.' His thin lips tightened into a gloating grin as he realized there was one certain way to find out. He would torture it out of the inhabitants of the tower once they had captured it. He would extract

262

the truth word by word. Glancing impatiently across the ranks of his advancing men in the torchlight he caught sight of Crimp roughly prodding and goading Sloeberry, the ugly little female Tunneller that he had captured at Cawdor, and forcing her to take shelter in a safe place amongst the trees. His smile dissolved into a scowl. Much as Girrolt insisted that Crimp was utterly loyal he couldn't shake off the distrust he instinctively felt towards him whenever he caught sight of him. And as for that female Tunneller, she was uglier than a goblin. She had given him little or no pleasure. Perhaps it was time to wring her neck and have done with her.

'Crimp! Bring that creature over here to me!' he shouted. The boy hesitated as he heard his name shouted out above the start of battle, and the anxious glance he threw across his shoulder only served to fuel Snatch's distrust even further.

'Come over here, boy, and be quick about it. Find a place on the leading siege ladder, I want you to be one of the first to scale the walls of the tower. Take as many prisoners as you can, and I want them alive – remember that! Give me that ugly little goblin's chain, I will keep her close to me where she will have the best possible view of our victory. Why, I might even let her choose how your captives are put to death once we finish with them. Hurry, you are holding up the attack. Run, boy, run!' Snatch sneered as he watched the boy break into a run, dragging the girl behind him, making her trip and stumble as the heavy iron shackles cut into her bleeding ankles.

Sloeberry didn't even have the time to whisper her thanks to Crimp for the way he had done his best to look after her since he had become her keeper. She knew the risks he had taken and that they had been made increasingly difficult by the presence of those evil birds.

'I'll keep an eye on her,' Snatch hissed as he wrenched the end of the chain out of Crimp's hands and pushed him roughly towards the siege ladders. He knocked Sloeberry to the ground and he tossed the chain down beside her with barely a glance.

'When Drib comes to rescue me he will make you pay for every time you've hurt me!' she sobbed to herself, but Snatch heard her.

For an instant he stared down at her, his hooded eyes glittering with hatred. 'The cripple's dead!' he sneered. 'Nobody's ever going to come and rescue somebody as ugly as you anyway.' Then he threw back his head and laughed a thin, humourless laugh that became a snarling, blood curdling roar as he raised his battle mace above his head. The sound drove his hideous followers surging forward, the torchlight causing their black shadows to leap up the walls of the tower.

The moment the claustrophobic darkness, filled with terrifying, ghostly shapes, lifted and vanished from the tower, Kyot sent his archers and spearmen hurrying back to their posts and ordered their families to take refuge in the great hall. He felt a sense of foreboding. With Eventine close to his side and their two captains, Thistlebow and Thornbeam, each commanding a strike of archers, they ran up the spiral stairway to the top of the tower. All hopes Kyot might have nurtured that their attackers would pass by once the shadowy figures had left them, as they had at Underfall, deserted him when he looked out over the parapet and saw the vast horde of half-human, half-beast creatures in the evening sunlight. They filled the road and had spread out to encircle the tower completely, standing just beyond bow-shot. They seemed to have multiplied since he had snatched that quick glimpse of them through the Glass of Orm. Kyot went back to the glass and positioned it carefully, taking a closer look. They were armed to the teeth with vicious-looking pikes and battle axes, and a forest of siege ladders and huge battering rams were being brought slowly through the ranks and positioned for the assault.

'Where in the world have those foul creatures been spawned? They are neither beast nor man but a vile mockery of both.' Eventine's voice was a frightened whisper.

Suddenly Mulcade stooped to Kyot's shoulder, squeezing his sharp talons through the thick weave of his cloak as he shrieked a warning, making him look up and out across Meremire towards the distant mountains.

'And they are not alone! Look over there,' he cried, pointing with his bow towards the treetops which were darkening in the pale evening sky as thousands of carrion birds took to the air and began to form a dense, menacing cloud that cast a solid black shadow over the trees as they wheeled and turned slowly towards them.

'Fly, Mulcade, fly, while there is still time. Raise the alarm among the Battle Owls!'

Kyot sent the bird high into the air. Mulcade hovered for a moment above the tower and then turned to stoop fast across the heads of their attackers and vanish beneath the trees, fleeing before the gathering storm.

'Tell Thane, if you get to Candlebane Hall and he still lives, that the tower on Stumble Hill stood firm and took the shock of battle proudly,' Kyot whispered as the owl disappeared.

'What is happening over there, to the right in the front rank? Look – quickly – pass me the glass,' Eventine called, twisting the lens to focus it on a small woman who was suddenly thrown to the ground in front of a particularly foul looking creature. 'She looks no taller than a half-starved child, and she is laden with chains. Wait, I think that's Sloeberry, yes, I recognize her now. She was one of that company of Tunnellers who used to stop here when they were gardening the greenways through Meremire Forest. Our blacksmiths used to sharpen their tools, you must remember them. Oaktangle, Blackthorn and Mistletoe were part of the same company, they were the ones accused of starting all those troubles that brought ruin and desolation to all Elundium.'

'The ones who escaped from the Granite City with Greygoose's son, Eider and old Berioss the Marcher? I remember, they fled to Cawdor. Well, she doesn't look as though she is causing any trouble now, that's for certain,' Kyot murmured as he looked down at her through the glass.

'I wonder what happened at Cawdor? Do you think those creatures came from there?' Eventine frowned, but before Kyot had the time to think about it their attackers surged forwards with blood-curdling shrieks.

The last of the evening light was blotted out abruptly as the flocks of carrion birds swept low over the tower, attacking the archers' helms with their sharp, outstretched claws and making them duck and curse as they scattered for cover in the sudden gloom. Below them the voices of the advancing horde rose to a deafening roar as one by one torches were lit in a continuous circle around the tower, casting a lurid, flickering light on their attackers' hideous faces. Kyot heard men cry out all around him as they were seized with terror at the sight of the creatures confronting them in the shifting torchlight. He felt the light, warm touch of Eventine's hand as she left his side and went amongst their Archers. Her clear voice rose above the tumult immediately, dispelling their fears and giving them courage as she took her place at the parapet, the great bow of Clatterford bent in readiness.

Kyot was quick to follow her, deploying the two strikes of Archers strategically around the edge of the parapet and placing those men whom he knew had courage to spare amongst the ones who were showing the greatest fear. He called for as many spearmen as could be spared from the inner circle of defences to arm themselves with siege hooks and come to the top of the tower.

'Be ready to clear the parapet of siege ladders!' he ordered before calling out to the Archers to hold their positions.

'Do not falter. Use the light of those torches they have lit to your advantage. Aim at the creatures holding those siege ladders and battering rams and make every arrow count. They must not be allowed to reach the tower walls.'

Nocking an arrow onto his bowstring he took up a position amongst his archers directly above the doors where he knew the assault would be at its fiercest. 'Have courage, raise your voices and show these evil monsters that we are not afraid of them. Sing out loudly and tell of the sunlight and all the beauty that lies beyond their smothering shadows. Drown out their foul screams and howls with your voices.'

Eventine sang out as she bravely loosed arrow after arrow down into the advancing creatures. One by one, starting as a trembling, uncertain whisper, surrounding voices joined her, swelling into a thunderous battle hymn as their rain of arrows shrieked and whirred out of the tower. For an instant it sent a ripple of doubt through the ranks of their attackers, making them abandon their ladders and battering rams to hide behind their shields.

Kyot laughed and pointed at them. 'Look! Look down

there! They're nothing to be afraid of, look at them. They're about to turn tail and run away!'

But the moment was short-lived.

Snatchpurse snarled and cursed as he strode forward through his cowering army, deliberately exposing himself, drawing a host of arrows that bounced harmlessly off his scaly armour. 'Look, those Archers can't harm you! On your feet all of you. Fowards! Forwards!' He snarled as he wielded his battle mace in a brutal arc.

His followers surged forward to storm the tower as true night fell and the sky was sprinkled with a bright canopy of stars. The flocks of birds flew back and disappeared into Meremire Forest, their work over.

'It's no good, our arrows are glancing harmlessly off those creatures. We can't do anything to halt their advance,' Thornbeam shouted wearily, leaping backwards as the tops of dozens of siege ladders clattered against the parapet all around them.

With a triumphant roar the creatures began to swarm up the ladders. Snarling, hideous faces and cruel, grasping claws appeared above the parapet as the Archers heard a dull boom and felt the floor beneath their feet tremble as the very walls of the tower shuddered to the base of their foundations. The Archers retreated from their positions, moving aside to allow the spearmen to rush forwards wielding their siege hooks. Many of the siege ladders toppled backwards away from the parapet to shed their vile load onto the ground far below but for every ladder they cleared away, two more instantly clattered into its place. The creatures began to swarm over the parapet in a monstrous, howling tide, driving the spearmen back. Seeing that they were in imminent danger of being over-whelmed, Kyot shouldered his bow to draw his sword, shouting to every man on the watching platform to do what they could to clear the parapet. He caught a glimpse of Eventine, her hair streaming out behind her as she rushed forward to be beside him, gripping the hilt of her sword with both hands. With a defiant shout the archers surged forward, wielding their swords against the mass of scaly, armoured creatures, stabbing and thrusting, the lurid torchlight showing the blood lying red upon their blades as they forced their way forwards, smashing helms and chopping off claws. Step by desperate step the archers fought their way back to the brink of the parapet, hurling down any of the creatures they slaughtered to sweep away the forest of siege ladders.

Kyot rested heavily on the hilt of his sword, breathing hard as they had a moment's respite and put his arm around Eventine to comfort her as he anxiously surveyed their dead and injured. 'I don't know if we will be able to repulse another attack if they come back as ferociously as that. They have killed half our men.' He had to shout to make himself heard over the thunder of the battering rams as they continued to assault the tower.

'We have to, husband, we just have to. There is no other choice, there will be no surrendering to these evil beasts.'

Eventine began to reach back into her quiver for another arrow when an urgent shout from below brought them both to the stairhead.

'Lord, the walls of the tower are beginning to crack beneath the battering – the doors are almost splintered through, their hinges are breaking and they'll be down at any moment.'

Kyot looked at the remnants of the two strikes of archers who still manned the parapet and glanced at the small company of spearmen who survived the assault and were still binding their wounds. He gripped Eventine's arm.

'No, we'll not stay here to be trapped like rats in a barrel. We will not just wait to be slaughtered. Quickly, go below and have the horses saddled and made ready in the inner courtyard. The last thing these monsters will expect is for us to try and break out – go quickly!'

Eventine hesitated, 'But what about the archers' families, they won't be able to fight their way out. I would rather die with them than abandon them.'

'Nobody is going to be left behind,' Kyot replied, his voice filled with urgency. 'No-one, believe me. Now form a hollow fighting column with the strongest swordsmen and the tallest spearmen on the outside and the women and children in the centre. Make sure that all their shields are firmly interlocked and tell them that on no account are they to break rank or slow the pace until we are well clear of these foul creatures. Sprint and Tanglecrown will lead the charge. Now hurry, my love, and have everything ready. We will use the cover of night to our advantage. Go quickly!'

Eventine ran down the stairway as Kyot worked hurriedly with the remnants of his two strikes of archers to prop up the bodies of the fallen to block the top of the stairway. They had barely reached the second landing before they heard the clatter of the siege ladders being thrown against the parapet above them.

The inner courtyard was thick with a choking fog of dust and mortar that was being pounded out of the crumbling walls. Fine stone chips crunched beneath the archers' armoured boots as, grim-faced and silent, they hurriedly formed a tight-knit flying column, their shields firmly interlocked and bristling with out-turned spear blades. The archers' families, armed with swords and staves, waited and whispered nervously to one another in the centre of the column, shuffling their feet and looking ahead through the gloomy archway towards the great doors that shuddered and groaned, their splintered cracks growing longer around the locks and hinges each time the weight of the battering rams was hurled against them. Quick hoofbeats echoed across the cobbles making nervous heads turn as Eventine, mounted upon Tanglecrown, led Sprint ready-saddled for Kyot out of the stableyard to take their place at the head of the column. The rest of the mounted Archers and a small company of mounted Gallopers armed with lances surrounded the Lady Elionbel who was already mounted on Stumble. The children, Krann and Fairlight were trotting their ponies out of the stables to take their places immediately behind Eventine.

'I wish I had Mulcade with me. He would claw the eyes out of those monsters who are attacking us. He would keep us safe on this dash,' Krann whispered to Fairlight in a small, frightened voice.

'You need not worry,' she replied in a brave whisper, 'Tanglecrown will force a path through those evil creatures. He is the Lord of Stags you know, and he isn't afraid of anything. Just look at those razor-sharp antlers, they have crystal tips; Fairday, my grandfather, armed him with them ages ago. He used to fight against the Nightbeasts with them. And Sprint is the bravest of horses, the bravest in all the world. He carried my father through the darkest shadows many times and . . .'

A rush of footsteps and the sound of an urgent cry on the stairway made her pause and look up to see her father surrounded by the remnants of the two strikes of archers with the spearmen retreating in broken order. They were stabbing daggers, thrusting spears and loosing arrow after arrow up into the howling, shadowy creatures who were pursuing them down the steps. The men ran into the places that had been left open for them in the rear of the column, drawing in close together and grabbing the shields that were thrust into their hands, forming a solid, impenetrable wall that bristled with their bloodied spear blades. Kyot vaulted into Sprint's saddle and shouted to the two doorwardens who were crouched in readiness beside the splintering doors. Immediately they released the locks and ran back to their places in the column. They all knew that the next time the huge battering ram was hurled at the doors they would burst open and then nothing but their courage and their strength of purpose could carry them to safety. To hesitate, to falter, would mean certain death.

In that moment of suspense while they waited with bated breath, poised to charge, Elionbel suddenly remembered the small leather pouch that contained the remnants of the nightflower seeds that Loremaster Pinch-face had given to her moments before he died. She had always kept them in the pouch attached to her belt and hidden beneath her cloak. She knew that the flower seeds had great power against the evil of the Nightbeasts but would they be of any use against these vile creatures? She unknotted the pouch with quick fingers and divided its precious contents, pressing them equally into the palms of Krann and Fairlight's small hands, keeping only a few of the seeds for herself.

'Now listen carefully, both of you. These tiny seeds have great power over darkness and evil. I want you to throw them into the faces of those foul monsters as soon as they swarm around us and try to prevent our escape. But remember, use them sparingly. Can you both do that for me?'

Krann and Fairlight nodded seriously but Krann, opening his hand and seeing the tiny blackened seeds cradled in his palm, doubted that anything so small and fragile could have any power against anything so monstrous as the howling creatures pressing in around the tower.

'I'll cast my nightflower seeds out to the right if you will scatter yours to the other side of the column.' Fairlight just had time to whisper to Krann before the battering rams struck and with a shuddering crash the doors broke open, tearing the hinges away from the walls. The crowd of half-human creatures carrying the battering ram staggered as the doors suddenly and unexpectedly gave way and the weight of the ram sent them stumbling to their knees with cries of alarm, trapping many of them beneath it as it came to rest across the entrance of the tower. Kyot gave the signal to charge the moment the doors flew open and the column surged forwards with a shout, scrambling and trampling over those still trapped beneath the battering ram as the column gathered speed and thundered out through the riven doors.

Tanglecrown kept a pace ahead and, lowering his head, he cleared a narrow path through the seething enemy with his huge stand of razor sharp, crystal-tipped antlers. Eventine, Kyot and all the mounted archers drew back their bows and with careful aim extinguished the lurid torches directly illuminating their desperate dash. The howls and snarls of their oppressors turned abruptly to screams of panic as the flying column ploughed into their ranks, scattering them and sending them milling into one another. But the archers' element of surprise and the speed of their dash was quickly diminished as Snatchpurse realized that they were trying to escape. New torches flared up all around the fleeing archers and he drove the full force of his army at them from both sides, screaming and shouting to his followers and ordering that not one of them was to escape.

Thus betwixt hammer and anvil the flying column

began to slow and flounder and threatened to break up beneath the sheer weight of the hideous creatures who surged in against them on every side. Double-handed axes and brutal spiked battle hammers battered and smashed against the archers' shields, splintering them and making even the strongest men on the outside of the column stagger and begin to lose their footing. Each time they faltered or showed the slightest sign of weakening hundreds of cruel claws reached out to their interlocking shields in an effort to pull them away.

Again and again Kyot rallied his desperate archers and spearmen, shouting at them, commanding them to stay together and as close as possible to those who were mounted as they sent a storm of arrows ahead of them in an attempt to clear a path through the swarming beasts. But it was all to no avail. Tanglecrown was hemmed in and overwhelmed, his huge stand of antlers were bloodied and broken, jagged pikes and swords were thrusting and stabbing towards him and Eventine. Elionbel saw the shadowy creatures close in and she cried out to the children, 'Now! Cast the seeds now!' She spurred Stumble forward through the mounted archers, past Kyot until she was riding abreast of Eventine. Dropping the reins onto Stumble's neck she flung the last of her nightflower seeds ahead of them at the same moment that the children threw theirs into the seething masses.

Flashes of pure white light lit up the night searing the flesh wherever the seeds touched the creatures' scaly skin. It blinded them and drove them back in terror. Wherever the seeds fell onto the ground they instantly took root at the crowd's feet, sending up thick, tentacles of interwoven vines armed with vicious out-turned thorns. Millions of tiny pure white, star-shaped flowers blossomed on the vines releasing a sweet heady perfume into the night air that Snatch's army could not abide. The nightflowers began to spring up out of the ground ahead of the column, cutting a clear path through their attackers and leading the archers' column to the greenway. The moon had risen unnoticed during their desperate dash and in its silvered light, beyond the last of the avenues of tangled night-flowers that protected them, Kyot caught a glimpse of the road ahead as it stretched away towards the rolling grasslands – it was clear and empty of all foul creatures of the dark.

'Run, run, go as fast as you can, safety lies but a footstep away . . .' he began to shout, but the words choked and died in his throat as huge, dark shapes – hundreds of them – suddenly and silently broke cover from amongst the trees that bordered the greenway and began to crowd forward, crouching in readiness to swarm out and block the road. He could see their savage fangs glinting yellow-white and their eyes reflecting pale amber in the moonlight.

Kyot's mouth drew into a thin, grim line of bitter despair. To have fought so hard, and to be so close to winning the road . . . but they would not go easily in defeat. They would build such a wall of those vile mon-sters' bodies around them – they would fight until their quivers were empty, their swords were notched and bloody and their helms riven. There would be no surrender.

Kyot tightened Sprint's reins to bring the horse to a halt and looked quickly about him for the best place to make their last, defiant stand. He knew only too well that the flowers with their sharp thorns would lose their power once the sun rose. Suddenly a joyous shout from Eventine made him peer ahead and his despair turned to laughter. Those dark shapes crouching and waiting to attack them were not foul creatures of the night, they were a huge pack of Border Runners who, unbidden and in the nick of time, had come to their aid. Everybody in the column laughed and cried with relief to see so many unexpected friends appear beside the greenway's edge and they all gave a great shout of thanks as they passed safely between the dogs of war who closed in behind them, snarling and growling to block the road.

'We will not stop or pause to rest until we have journeyed far into the endless grasslands. We will make for Clatterford and rally my father's men,' Eventine called as Tanglecrown forged ahead.

Snatchpurse screamed with rage as the nightflowers blossomed and the wretched archers vanished in amongst them to escape. 'There will be no archers left alive in Elundium, not a single one, when I get my hands on the throne.'

As he cursed the pupils of his eyes shrank to pinpoints of fury, 'Go – go all of you and kill every one of them. Bring back their severed hands to hang from the tower as trophies of this victory. Go!' he snarled.

With a bloodthirsty roar his followers gave chase only to be brought to a sudden halt by the huge pack of Border Runners who were now blocking the road. The dogs growled and slowly began to advance.

'You had better call them all back and get them safely inside the tower before those filthy dogs tear them to pieces,' Thrograsp warned urgently. 'The archers are not worth it. Let them go and let them take the mangy curs that protect them as well. Come on, let us examine the tower we've won and make it into our headquarters. Now that we have a centre for the Honourable Company of Murderers we can rule the surrounding countryside with ease. We will prepare well for our advance on the Granite City.'

X

The Simple Art of Disguise

DRIB STIFLED A YAWN and tried hard to concentrate on the large book of magic that lay open on his crooked knees, but his mind was beginning to wander. The hum of the summer bees beyond the open door, the rustle of the wind in the tall trees below the tower and the persistent roar of the waterfalls tumbling into the gorge were all beginning to blend together and in them he thought he caught a faint, faraway whisper of familiar, friendly voices. They seemed to swell and fill the warm shafts of dusty sunlight that streamed down into the Runesgate Tower and softly steal inside his head, drawing him away into daydreams of better times. But the voices grew harsh, they chided his inactivity and laughed at his futile attempts to create magic. 'Where are you, Drib, while the whole world falls into ruin?'

Drib tried to call out to answer, he tried to tell the voices that the magician would not let him leave the tower but the words became nothing but a whispered mumbling as sleep took him. Images of Sloeberry welled up as the voices shrank away. He thought he could hear her call out to him, he thought he could see her hands reach out through the darkness towards him, and yet he could not touch her. Drib's hand twitched on the open page and his finger, that marked his place, slipped slowly off the spidery line of complicated script that he was supposed to be learning. His head nodded forward sharply and made him start awake just in time to grasp the book and prevent it falling onto the floor at his feet. He blinked, trying to catch hold of the fading image of Sloeberry and was momentarily overwhelmed with his empty, yearning sense of despair that always filled that moment of waking. Rubbing his sleeve across his eyes he straightened up and glanced anxiously across to where Nevian sat wrapped up in the voluminous folds of his rainbow cloak waiting impatiently for the boy to finish learning how to prepare a spell properly and finally to have the formula word-perfect.

Drib let out a sigh of relief to see that the magician was sound asleep in his high-backed, leather chair and he quietly closed the yellowing parchment pages to put the book on the pile beside his chair. He needed to get out of the dusty atmosphere of the tower and breathe in some fresh air. Rising stiffly to his feet he headed for the open doorway. Grannog, who was lying sprawled in front of the cold, empty hearth, opened his eyes and growled softly as he began to rise to follow him but Drib wanted to be alone. He quickly put his finger to his lips and without intending it whispered a sleeping spell. The old dog yawned, stretched his forelegs and sank back onto the hearth rug, his huge head resting across the magician's feet, and fell into a deep, dreamless sleep.

Treading silently around Grannog, the boy hurried out of the tower and sat down on the top step. Resting his chin in his hands and staring out across the lush foliage of the Runesgate Gorge towards the distant mountain peaks he let out a sigh of despair. They looked so impossibly far away. He caught a glimpse of Umm and Sparkfire moving amongst the trees below him and he raised his hand in a half-hearted wave, hoping that they would leave him alone in his misery because, try as hard as he might, he just couldn't seem to grasp the basic principles of magic and until he did Nevian would flatly refuse to let him take one step beyond the confines of the Runesgate Gorge. Making magic wasn't really the problem – it was quite the opposite. He was making far too much of it. He had lost count of how many times Nevian had thrown up his hands in exasperation at his erratic attempt to cast even the simplest of spells.

'You are a danger to us all, boy,' he would cry, as he set about restoring his latest disaster. Drib could not help but smile as he remembered the deluge of milk he had accidentally drawn from an axe handle as its blade was buried deep in the doorpost, or how the lamps in the tower had burned with a bright, white fire for five daylights before the old man had managed to unravel the spell he had accidentally cast over them. His attempts to move things almost always resulted in their being permanently spirited away. Yes, he was a danger, and Drib reasoned that the sooner Nevian gave up on the stupid notion that he had the makings of a brilliant magician and let him get on with the real and more urgent task of trying to find Sloeberry, the better it would be. After all his wounds had healed perfectly, except for a slight weakness and tingling sensation in his sword arm whenever he tried to pick up anything heavy, but he was sure it would improve with time and use. He was sick of waiting, sick of kicking his heels and he was sick of being a virtual prisoner in the Runesgate Tower. He was beginning to think that the magician had forgotten all about setting out disguised as a travelling circus to search for Sloeberry. He certainly had done nothing about it since that night he had returned after discovering Berioss was still alive. All he seemed interested in was making him cast spells and what good was that going to do?

'You are not a prisoner, boy, and it is no good sitting there pretending you are as you revel in self pity instead of learning from the books I have given you to read. If you think you can find Sloeberry on your own and then rescue her without my help then you had better be on your way. Go on, nobody's going to stop you. There are no locks in the Runesgate.'

Drib struggled to his feet, his face crimson with guilt. How did Nevian read his thoughts so clearly, especially the dark, doubting ones? Hearing them spoken aloud made him seem so ungrateful for all the time and trouble that the old man had bestowed on him.

'I . . . I . . . I'm so sorry. I didn't mean any disrespect, but . . .' he stuttered, looking down at the ground between his crooked feet, 'it's just that I am so hopelessly bad at all this magic and I am never going to grasp it in time to rescue Sloeberry, I know I'm not, and I can't bear to think of living without her.'

Nevian looked down at the small boy and his face broke into a smile. He placed his hand beneath Drib's chin, gently lifting and tilting his head until their eyes met. 'But you are so wrong, Drib. You have such an undiscovered talent for magic at your fingertips, such power, and believe me you are going to need every ounce of it. Have patience and persist in learning how to harness it properly. We'll leave the moment you are ready, I promise you. Now take my staff and recite that preparation for a spell you learnt and make the staff grow sweet, perfumed flowerheads.'

Reluctantly Drib took the gnarled, polished ebony staff from the magician's hand and chanted the words. Perhaps this time he would get it right. But before he had even uttered half the words he had learned the staff shivered violently and grew ice-cold in his hand. The air seemed to darken and fill with threatening, ghostly shapes which swirled around him. Buds erupted all along the polished surface of the staff and barbed, sinuous vines sprouted out of them, immediately snaking themselves around Drib's fingers, trapping them to the stick so quickly he had no time to drop it. In a blink the thorny tendrils covered with small, fleshy, crimson leaves had entwined themselves around his wrist and climbed halfway up his arm. Drib staggered beneath the weight of the growing creepers and cried out in terror.

'Nevian – what's wrong? I said the first part right – I was word-perfect, I know I was. What's happening to me? Help me, help me Nevian, make it stop.'

'I don't know why this happens, Drib, it defies logic. Stand absolutely still while I chant an antidote.' The magician frowned, stepping around the boy warily as he examined the mass of foliage that had almost reached his neck. He had never known a simple growing spell to go so disastrously wrong, but at least there was one sure way to put a stop to it. 'Hold still, Drib,' he repeated before reciting the words he was sure would nullify even the most virulent growing spell.

He reached out and pulled the staff out of the frightened boy's hand as he said the words, only to gasp in pain as the sharp thorns pricked his fingers, drawing blood. At the same moment hundreds of tiny, pure white, star-shaped flowers blossomed between the out-turned thorns and gave out a sweet, heady perfume that wafted around them.

'That is the scent of nightflowers – I would know it anywhere,' muttered Nevian darkly as the summer breeze took it away.

The petals rapidly began to fade and fall in a fragile carpet around Drib's feet. The breeze ruffled them into scented drifts before carrying them away into the trees. The thorny tendrils withered and shrank back into the staff without leaving a single scratch or mark on the boy's skin. The growth vanished as quickly and as magically as it had appeared. Drib stared dubiously at the gnarled old staff, his heartbeat racing, and he gladly allowed the magician to take it from him.

'There, if that doesn't show you how hopeless I am I don't know what will. Everything I touch goes wrong. I just can't do magic!'

'No, no, I think quite the contrary may be true, boy,' Nevian murmured as he bent to examine the staff. He cast his mind back over Drib's other erratic attempts and suddenly realized that there was a common thread woven through all his disasters. He looked sharply up at the boy.

'Yes, yes, in fact I think there is a distinct possibility that the fault of your failures lie with me . . .' Nevian turned in a flurry of cloak tails as he hurried back into the tower leaving Drib standing alone in confusion, shaking his head. He followed the magician over the threshold to find him already surrounded by his books, muttering and mumbling to himself whilst making notes on a curling scrap of parchment with his peacock's quill.

'But you can't go wrong – you are the Master of Magic, the fountainhead of all wisdom and knowledge. Loremaster Grout was always telling us that in the Learning Hall. It has to be true, just look at all your books!'

Nevian glanced up over his open book and his ancient, wrinkled face softened into a smile. 'Well, of course I have not been wholly wrong, Drib, you have to give some credence to knowing how to do things properly, don't you. I can't emphasize enough how precise you have to be to practise magic properly.'

Nevian paused and frowned as if pricked by his own argument and then added gravely, 'Why, you only have to look at poor Marcher Berioss to see that he is trapped in the shape of a tree, imprisoned by my own forgotten threads of a spell, and goodness knows how many others there are like him who may have suffered the same plight. And why, you may ask? Because I cast that spell to turn the rebellious warriors on the Causeway Fields into trees far too hastily. I didn't give it a moment's thought and would not have believed that it would endure beyond the King's forgiveness. And that forgiveness, I might add, should have erased the spell completely if I had only cast it properly in the first place.'

Nevian's eyes grew serious with regret. 'Anger can make you careless, Drib, and haste is a very dangerous ally, never forget that. What happened to Berioss is a perfect illustration of the implications of not giving time and the proper measure of thought to the meticulous preparation of a spell before you cast it.'

'But, as I remember, Loremaster Grout told us the story of the warriors refusing to pledge their loyalty to the King and you didn't have the time to prepare a proper spell. The vast, angry battle crescent was sweeping across the Causeway Fields, cursing the King and calling out that he had stolen the crown. You had to do something to save him, didn't you?' Drib argued. 'You didn't have any alternative.'

'Of course I could not have stood idly by, you're quite right about that, but there is no excusing such a blunder, Drib, none at all. Remember, if you are to keep your integrity when you practise magic you have to be accountable for everything you do. You have to be willing to accept the blame for your mistakes.'

'But surely,' Drib sighed, 'Berioss wouldn't be alive today if that spell had been cast properly. From what you have told me the only thing that saved him from plunging to his death over the cliffs at Cawdor was that inadvertent spell you cast over him, so who's to know how anything we do today will affect tomorrow? Who's to be sure what benefits our mistakes might bring?'

Nevian laughed and raised his eyebrows in busy circles of surprise at the boy's unexpected perception about the cause and effect of magic. It was something he had not planned to touch upon for some considerable time due to its complexity.

'Well, yes, perhaps you have a point Drib. I will concede that, but I won't accept it as an argument for cutting short the proper preparations for casting spells. But enough of this idle chatter, there is work to do if we are to journey to Elundium and banish this dark stain of evil that is creeping relentlessly across the countryside.'

'You mean we are going to set out to rescue Sloeberry now – today?' Drib cried, barely able to control his excitement as he turned to run towards the door. Then he paused. 'Why? Why this sudden change? Was it something to do with the mass of nightflowers that sprouted out of your staff just now? What did it mean? Nothing terrible has happened to Sloeberry has it?'

The old man glanced darkly towards the doorway and beckoned Drib to come close as he lowered his voice to a whisper. 'I don't know, I can't be certain of anything these daylights. The windows of my observatory are muddled with too many dark and conflicting images. Nothing is quite what it seems since the failing of my true powers, but that incident with the staff was a black omen. Those dark, ghostly shapes that engulfed you momentarily as you began the spell have no place here in the Runesgate Gorge, or in your spell, and nor did the nightflowers. They cannot be conjured by magic – I could not have drawn them out of my staff. The Lady Elionbel is the only person I know of who has a small pouch of the precious seeds, and nightflowers only blossom and give off that heady scent when darkest danger presses in on every side. I wonder if she has been forced to cast them yet. I wonder whether the Granite City has fallen.'

'But Queen Elionbel and Krann are at Stumble Hill,' Drib interjected. 'Quencher, the blacksmith, told me. They arrived the same night as his people – they were seeking Lord Kyot's protection.'

'Then the Lady Elionbel is in great danger – that is the warning carried by the staff. I fear our presence in Elundium is long overdue. Yes, we must hurry to the tower on Stumble Hill without a moment's delay. It is time to put aside learning the intricacies of magic for a short time, my boy, and concentrate on making our travelling circus a reality. Remember there will be so many eyes watching us – hostile eyes – so our disguise must be perfect: we must live the parts we play with the utmost conviction. Now, I have been giving a lot of thought to the problem while you have been poring over your books. I, of course, shall travel disguised as a humble conjuror, a performer of simple tricks and illusions, a teller of fortunes . . .'

'But somebody will be bound to recognize you. Everybody knows what your rainbow cloak looks like!' Drib interrupted.

The magician chuckled and then whispered conspiratorially, 'Watch!'

He cast aside his rainbow cloak and, reaching into a cubicle among the towering wall of books that Drib had not yet noticed, he brought out a tattered hessian cloak and pulled it around his shoulders. Exhaling a long, dry breath that rattled in his throat he shrank in stature until he had assumed the shape of a tired, bent and wizened old man who appeared to be only half his original size. Even the polished ebony staff he still held in his hand seemed to wither into a crooked length of wormy elm.

'But that's marvellous! That's real magic. I wouldn't recognize you myself. How did you do it? How long does the spell last?' Drib was amazed at the frail, bent old man who hobbled around the tower, pausing to examine the huge, silent wind machine as though he had never seen it before.

Nevian stopped in front of him and laughed softly as he cast off his tattered cloak. Breathing in deeply he straightened his back and unbent his knees. Drib blinked as he watched Nevian appearing to grow in front of him, he then drew his rainbow cloak about his shoulders and all his strength and vitality instantly returned.

'It is no more than a trick – an illusion, it is not true magic. If you use the right disguise people will see exactly what you want them to see. Why, even you Drib, were fooled by that tattered old cloak, weren't you?'

Nevian smiled, rubbing his hands together enthusiastically, well-pleased with his simple disguise. He knew that few could resist having their fortunes told and it would bring the people very close to him: it would give him the opportunity to test their loyalty to the King before urging them to follow him into the Granite City.

'Remember,' he added seriously, 'nothing is ever entirely what it seems to be.'

'But you looked so completely different just then. It won't . . .' Drib paused and a troubled shadow passed across his eyes as he remembered Orundus warning about the evil flocks of birds that now patrolled the skies above Elundium. 'It might not be so easy to disguise the rest of us. You can't exactly dress up Silkstone, Orundus or Grannog. And what about the horses? You can't disguise Umm, can you, he is so huge and he's got all those bright orange tufts of hair all over his body. With his long arms and his seven fingers and toes he's going to be impossible to disguise – he's going to look strange even as a part of a circus.' Drib hesitated as he steeled his courage; he had left his biggest worry to last.

'Well?' Nevian asked, glancing across impatiently at the hour glass.

Drib swallowed. 'I know you said I have to make myself invisible – but how? I haven't been able to find a single spell in all the books I've read since I've been here in the tower, and I really have searched through them very carefully.'

Nevian's impatience dissolved into a chuckle. 'You won't be needing your books for that kind of magic, oh no. The power to make yourself invisible is already inside you. Why you have already touched it, you have even started to use it, although you are obviously not aware of it quite yet. Think back, boy, how many times have I sent you out to learn about the wind, the earth, the trees and the sky? How many times have you gone outside to feel them and to understand all the millions of things that make them up? Can you remember how still I made you stand so that you could hear the rocks crack and the bark grow? And for long moments you almost became a part of them, blending in totally. These are the moments you became quite invisible.'

Drib gasped and then wondered aloud, 'That's all very well but how on earth will I be able to rescue Sloeberry if I have to stand statue-still all the time? And what is going to happen to me if we stop in the middle of a town or a village – where am I going to hide then?' Drib's voice trailed away as uncertainty took over.

The magician threw up his hands in exasperation, 'Don't be silly, boy, think! Think about what I have been trying to teach you all summer long. Haven't I made you move more quickly than the blink of an eye, despite your disability? I have taught you to move just as often as I have made you stand still – and why?'

The old man seemed to grow. He towered over Drib, his eyebrows drew together fiercely as he waited for the boy to answer him.

'You often talked about me blending in. But I don't see how moving quickly or slowly will help me do that. There are too many people who will remember my crooked legs if they catch a glimpse of them.'

'Well, yes, you're probably right,' Nevian admitted reluctantly. 'Blending in won't be enough in your case – we'll have to think of another way of disguising your legs.'

Nevian fell silent as he paced around the perimeter of the great chamber, deep in thought and seemingly unaware of the small boy standing wretchedly alone. He came to a halt in the open doorway and laughed softly before turning towards Drib once more.

'We'll think of something, Drib, don't worry. Whatever we decide to do I have the greatest confidence in you. The horses and Grannog will be easy to disguise because nobody will expect the Lord of Horses and one of the Nighthorses to be yoked together to pull a humble circus cart – provided I can get them to agree to do it. And you will be surprised what a little mud, liberally spread across their coats with a few burrs and thorns clinging to their manes and tails will do. Why, I will wager my rainbow cloak that they will barely draw a second glance. And Grannog, if he will stay between their hooves, will go completely unnoticed. He will appear to be nothing more than a common carter's dog to the casual glance. Remember, boy, the trick of a true disguise is in its simplicity. You have to be exactly what people expect to see.'

'But what about Umm? Surely he will be as difficult to disguise as me?'

'No, no – quite the contrary, Drib. Umm will, in fact, be the easiest.' Nevian chuckled as a look of bewilderment crossed Drib's face.

'How? I don't understand how you're going to do it.'

'Tell me, boy, what is it you remember most about that circus that last visited the Granite City?'

Drib thought for a moment as his head filled with the sounds and smells of the circus. He remembered the tight tingle of anticipation and excitement as the performers emerged from beneath the canvas flap of their striped tent. 'There were fire eaters, and there was a man who could roll himself up into a ball . . . oh, and there was a woman with three legs who rode back to front on a green pony . . . and there was . . .'

'Exactly as I expected,' Nevian interrupted. 'What you remember from the circus are the oddities – the unusual – and that is where Umm will fit in. He will be the world's strongest man. Why with a little careful shearing of some of those tufts of hair and dress him in the right clothes he will fit the part perfectly. But . . .'

Nevian paused, his forehead creased with a sudden doubt. Would Umm be able to cope with the bustle of life in a circus? He had forgotten that the Yerrak were shy, nomadic creatures unused to the hustle of crowds. The old man looked down at Drib and gripped his shoulders. 'I'm afraid it is going to be up to you to prepare Umm for his part in this circus of deception as we journey up through the Emerald Mountains and into Elundium.'

'But why me? Haven't I got enough to do trying to riddle out a way to make myself invisible and find my own place?' Drib protested. He liked Umm, and he would be eternally grateful to him for bringing him to the tower, but it took so long to make him understand even the simplest things about the ways of men. He had only now just started to enter the tower of his own accord and he still ran away with his hands clamped over the top of his head if Grannog so much as barked. Teaching him how to stand in the centre of a rowdy, jostling crowd was going to be an impossibility.

'Impossible, Drib, surely not. Have you forgotten that "impossible" is not a word we use here in the Runesgate?'

The magician's soft but penetrating whisper cut across Drib's doubts as sharply as a razor and made him jump. He felt his cheeks flush scarlet: he had never, despite its regularity, got used to Nevian reading his thoughts so easily, especially the less positive ones, the ones he kept to himself.

'I . . . I . . . I didn't mean that I wouldn't try,' he mumbled in embarrassment, looking down at his crooked feet.

'No, of course you didn't, it's not in your nature to shirk a challenge, and who knows what part Umm might yet play in rescuing Sloeberry.' Nevian replied with laughter in his eyes as he ushered the small boy out of the tower. 'Now, go and find Umm, he can't be far away, and begin your task. Put that talent you have for idle chatter to good use and bring him to the stables; there is a circus cart to prepare for the road and little time to do it in if we are to leave here early tomorrowlight. Hurry, boy, many hands make light work and there are a million things yet to do.'

Drib hobbled out of the tower only to stop on the bottom step as Silkstone alighted on his shoulder. He turned back to call back to Nevian, 'What about the owls? You haven't said how they will be disguised. We will need them won't we?'

Nevian nodded thoughtfully from the doorway. The boy was right – he had a way of touching the truth – they would need the owls to guide them and keep a sharp look out for danger on the road. Any fool could hide the owls in the cart but the real test of their ingenuity would be to have them flying, hovering in plain sight of those evil flocks of birds who now patrolled the skies of Elundium, without them being mobbed or revealing who they really were.

'You know, just for once I am completely at a loss.'

The old man frowned, glancing up at Orundus as he flew silently out of the tower and stooped to Drib's other shoulder. Nevian was painfully aware that the sands were slipping through the hour glass. He waved Drib away impatiently, 'Don't worry yourself about the owls. I am bound to think of something before we reach the heather meadows. They can shelter in the cart until then, hidden from prying eyes. Now be off with you. Hurry and find Umm, and between you you can drag that cart out of the stables; while you are at it you can gather together all the harness and give it a thorough clean. Oh, and grease the axles.'

The old man hurried back into the tower. Gathering up his voluminous cloak, he climbed the stairs and began to rummage quickly through the maze of storerooms and cluttered cupboards in an effort to find everything they might need on such a dangerous journey. As he pushed his way through thick shrouds of cobwebs, ducking beneath low beams and tripping over unseen chests and linen presses, a pile of essential, if dubious, props suitable for a circus act began to grow around him in the centre of the great chamber. Juggling sticks and trapeze apparatus; ropes and poles; quickfire; oil for the lamps; charts from the observatory; the Eye of Arabra; a crystal sphere shot through with abelone and amethyst with veins of the purest topaz; sticks of draweasy for creating clowns' masks; weights for Umm to lift; striped canvas for the tent; and as many artefacts of magic that he thought the cart would carry. A small armoury of swords and daggers wrapped in oiled cloth were to be hidden beneath the floor of the cart and as many different clothes that he could find would cover them. While searching through a small attic room at the top of the tower he discovered some brightly-coloured jesters' costumes from the times of the first Granite King and amongst them he uncovered an acrobat's three-cornered hat, narrow-waisted padded jacket, tight breeches and a pair of soft, slender deerskin shoes. For a moment he held the dusty garments in his hands as an idea formed in his mind.

'Of course, these would make a perfect disguise for Drib! Why didn't I think of it earlier,' he exclaimed, throwing the small lattice window wide open and shouting the boy's name to the wind. He shouted so loudly that he sent startled birds flying up from the tree tops and brought Drib, with Umm hard on his heels, running towards the tower.

'Quickly – come here, boy, put on these clothes. They will make the perfect disguise for you,' the magician cried, hurrying down to meet him.

'Try them on, see if you don't agree with me,' he urged.

He barely gave the boy time to struggle into the tight-fitting yellow breeches and button up the twenty tiny silver-inlaid buttons with hooks that stretched from the high collar of the dark, bottle-green jacket to the buckle of the belt which hung just below his waist, and finish by pulling on the soft, slightly curling shoes.

'Well that's perfect! Don't you think it's an ideal disguise?' Nevian asked, jamming the hat down hard onto his head and propelling the boy across the room to the hearth so that he could see his reflection in the surface of a highly polished shield standing propped up amongst the clutter.

'Well?' Nevian pressed. 'What do you think?'

Drib liked the colour and the rich feel of the tightly-fitting costume and he wriggled his toes luxuriously in the softness of the shoes. They felt so different from the armoured boots he had become used to wearing. He had to agree, as he stared at his misty reflection in the shield, that the costume did change his appearance and made him look slightly taller, and he hardly recognized his own face beneath the oddly shaped hat; but the tightness and the colour of the breeches seemed, if anything, to make his crooked legs even more obvious. He was about to shake his head in disagreement when Nevian suddenly grasped hold of him by the belt and with a twist of his wrist turned him upside down exclaiming, 'No, no, no, you're looking at yourself the wrong way up. Stand on your hands! Walk on them like an acrobat would. Go on, turn cartwheels. I'm sure there are a dozen or more tricks you can learn to distract people's eyes from your legs. Nobody would ever dream that you could have become an acrobat, and yet why not? There is nothing wrong with your arms and hands. There is no reason at all why you can't do this – give it a try.'

'You want me to become an acrobat? But that's impossible! I've never done anything like that before in my life – I just can't do it.'

A flash of impatience clouded the magician's eyes but he continued softly, 'Yes you can, Drib, and you have done it before, what else was all that scrambling up and down chimneys if it wasn't developing agility and balance? What else is there to being an acrobat except, perhaps, a little timing? All you have to do is think about scrambling up those chimneys – only the other way up.'

Drib could scarcely believe what he was hearing. Walking on his hands? Doing cartwheels? It was nothing like climbing a chimney, but he realized that the magician wasn't going to let go of his idea until he had at least given it a try. Gritting his teeth he made a tentative effort to move one hand forwards.

'That's the spirit! Go on, take another step!' Nevian cried, letting go of him.

Drib felt himself begin to overbalance and reached out wildly with his other hand only to topple backwards. With a wail he crashed painfully onto his back at Nevian's feet.

'I never said it was going to be easy, did I?' Nevian smiled at him as he bent forwards stiffly and gripped Drib's ankles, lifting him up to try again. 'But think of all the advantages you will have when you can move as quickly on your hands as most men do on their feet. Think of the agility it will give you. Why, if you become really good at it you will be able to tumble in and out amongst our enemies and they will hardly see you at all. Go on, try again.'

Silkstone hooted encouragement from high up amongst the rafters and Grannog, disturbed from his sleep close to the cold fire hearth, padded to Drib's side and licked his face with his rough, wet tongue. Much as Drib didn't want to agree with the magician, he could see the sense in his argument. It would shift people's attention away from his crooked legs, but he doubted that he could ever become an acrobat.

'It's only practice, Drib, practice and determination. Now go on, try again!' Nevian urged, giving him a slight shake of the ankles before letting go of him.

Drib concentrated his whole mind on keeping his body

still but as he tried again to walk on his hands he found himself beginning to sway and overbalance. He tensed, bracing himself for the inevitable fall, but it didn't happen; instead a strong hand that couldn't possibly be Nevian's, gripped his ankles from behind, steadying and supporting him. He twisted his head and looked upwards awkwardly to see Umm's large, seven-toed, hairy feet planted firmly on the ground either side of him. He heard the magician laugh.

'That's it, Umm, you can help. Help Drib to become an acrobat while he teaches you all about the noisy, jostling crowds that we are bound to encounter when we set off with our travelling circus.'

'Nevian, you can't leave me upside down like this!' Drib shouted angrily as he caught a glimpse of the magician hurrying away up the stairs.

Nevian paused and looked thoughtful, 'Remember, practice makes perfect, my boy. I will meet you by the cart – when you reach it on your hands.'

With a laugh he vanished around the twist of the stairs.

XI

A Glimpse through the Eye of Arabra

MUCH TO DRIB'S SURPRISE he found that the old man was right: he had indeed, without being aware of it, developed the balance and dexterity he would need to become an acrobat while scrambling up and down those filthy, soot-choked chimneys in the Granite City. Even some of the fencing moves that Berioss had taught him helped. But it still took an enormous leap of faith and all the courage and determination that he could muster to take those first tentative steps on his hands unaided. Within a short time, however, he was walking around the great chamber and down the steep steps to the forest outside.

'There, didn't I tell you? I knew you could do it!' Nevian cried encouragingly from the stairhead, making the boy momentarily lose his concentration and fall.

The magician hurried down the stairs, carrying a precariously balanced bundle of clothes and deposited them on the floor to help Drib to his feet. 'That is enough for now. Here, take these costumes out to the cart – you can practise your acrobatics as we journey.'

'It feels so different, so peculiar,' Drib murmured, rubbing at his sore palms before picking up the bundle.

'That is because you don't have the disability of your crooked legs to contend with. Haven't you realized it yet? On your hands you are equal – more than equal – to anybody else.' The magician smiled, adding, 'And from the look of it you will be a lot quicker than most people are on their feet by the time we reach Meremire Forest. Remember Drib, nothing is impossible, not if you want it badly enough.'

A mischievous twinkle appeared in the magician's eyes, 'And if you wish to add in a little of the magic that you have already learned it won't go amiss.'

'I'll do anything – anything, if it will help to rescue Sloeberry.'

'Oh, it will, I'm sure of it. Now, let us hurry and get that cart ready for the road,' Nevian laughed, putting his hand on the boy's shoulder and turning him towards the door.

The grey hours were touching the distant mountaintops below them. Everything for their journey had already been loaded into the huge, sky-blue, painted bow wagon making it sit low and heavy on its massive coupling pole, bolsters and axles. Nevian called out instructions and between them they hoisted and pulled the large, weather-proof, striped circus awning up and over the tall, hooped frame of the wagon. The old man had told Drib that it would give them protection from the weather as they travelled and it would also hide what they carried from prying eyes. The awning flapped noisily in the chill, dawn breeze as Nevian disappeared into the stables and it threatened to blow away. Drib made Umm hold it down while he quickly threaded a rope through the eyelets that had been sewn along its edge and lashed the awning securely to the stout iron hooks that protruded along the steeply-curved side-boards of the wagon.

'That should hold it!' he muttered, stepping back and pointing up to the bold letters printed onto the canvas to read them out to the Yerrak. 'The Kindred Spirit – that's the name of our circus . . .'

'That's right, Drib,' Nevian called as he led the horses

out of the stable yard, 'I'm hoping true kingsmen will know us for who we are by that name, but whether or not it fools our enemies – that we have yet to see,' he added darkly.

The polished brass and leather harness glinted in the flickering torchlight and jingled musically as Nevian positioned the two horses between the shafts and began to adjust the traces. 'Have you ever driven a wagon as large as this?' the old man asked as he checked the breeching straps around the horses' buttocks and attached the tugs to the shafts before climbing up to sit on the high driving seat and gathering up the reins.

Sparkfire had been harnessed to the crude sledge that Drib and Eider had fashioned out of fallen branches in the petrified forest to carry the Nightboar they killed on that first daylight at Cawdor; he had dragged fuel back into the ruined fortress for their fires and he stood quietly. Equestrius, the Lord of Horses, was unused to such restriction that the harness offered and he fretted and fidgeted, tossing his head and making the wagon shudder and rock backwards and forwards as far as the drop chains would allow.

'Easy, easy, you'll get used to the harness in no time, my boy,' Nevian called out to calm Equestrius.

Half-rising he peered around him impatiently, calling for Grannog and the owls to hurry to the wagon. He could see Umm waiting amongst the trees just below them. 'Release the drop chains, Drib, and jump up. It's time to begin our journey – there is no time like the present to learn how to handle a wagon like this, is there? Once Equestrius has settled you can take the reins.'

'No, no, wait! I've forgotten something very important, I won't be a moment.' The boy limped up towards the tower steps and called out for Silkstone and Orundus to come to him as he unlocked the door and slipped inside, clapping his hands for the lamps to come to life. An idea had suddenly come to him while they were loading the cart: he knew how the owls could be disguised and hover in plain sight without anyone realizing who or what they really were. He had been afraid that Nevian would laugh at him, and he had only just plucked up the courage to ask for the owls' co-operation as they were about to set off. He might as well give it a try, it wouldn't take a moment. He would need some paint, parchment and string – there was plenty of this strewn around the chamber floor, left after the hasty preparations for their journey. Silkstone stooped down silently to Drib's shoulder as Orundus remained sitting watching him from high up in the rafters.

'Now listen, I think I know of a way to disguise you, but you will have to stand very still on the table with your wings outstretched. Will you do this while I make something?'

Silkstone alighted onto the table hooting softly and spread out his wings. 'It won't hurt, I promise, but it might take a little bit of getting used to,' Drib whispered as he dipped one brush into a pot of bright vermilion paint and another into a pot of bilious yellow to paint the shape of a flying dragon across the owl's body and outstretched wings. He then took a piece of stiff, yellowing parchment and painted on it the roaring mouth of a dragon. He cut it out and secured the shape of the dragon's head around Silkstone's neck, bending it and joining its snapping jaws together until it completely hid the owl's face and yet still allowed him to see through the cut-out eyes. From a long, curling piece of softer parchment he fashioned a scaly tail which he tied around the rear of the owl's body, joining it to the headpiece by a thin elder branch. He stepped back to admire his handiwork and then told the owl to fly up and hover in the air above the magician's storm engine.

Silkstone beat his wings and rose into the air, but the awkward burden of the dragon's head and tail and the paint which was drying stiffly onto his feathers hampered him. With a shrill cry he fluttered helplessly to the ground.

Drib dropped to his knees and gathered the helpless owl into his arms. 'It's the perfect disguise, let me alter it a little. Please, you must let me try again,' he urged, lifting the owl up.

Silkstone swayed and beat his wings harder and slowly he rose above Drib's head until he was hovering around the top of the storm engine. 'It's perfect, just perfect!' Drib cried with delight.

'What on earth is keeping you, boy? Do we have to wait all daylight for you?' Nevian's voice thundered with impatience.

'I'm sorry, I'll be just a moment longer,' the boy called out, coaxing a reluctant Orundus down from the rafters as he dipped his brushes once more into different, but no less brightly coloured pots of paint.

'Kites! Kites! You've been keeping us waiting while you were playing inside making kites?' Nevian exploded as Drib hurried down the tower steps, his arms full of pieces of parchment, string and pots of paint which he stored carefully in the wagon before tying the two kite strings to the side of the wagon.

Drib climbed up to sit beside the magician, 'Oh, they're not just ordinary kites. Look again,' he grinned.

The old man stared up at the two kites that seemed to hang motionless in the brightening morning sky and then he laughed and clapped Drib on the back. 'Extraordinary, quite extraordinary. You have such a talent for magic and invention, my boy, such a talent. I would never have thought of such a clever – no, ingenious – way to disguise the owls.'

Still chuckling, the magician released the brake and the wagon began to move forwards slowly down the steep sides of the gorge, zig-zagging down the path towards the narrow, perilous ford that passed beneath the soaring creeper-covered archway and led out into the Emerald Mountains.

The roar of the waterfalls cascading down into the depths of the Runesgate Gorge, the sweet smell of wild jasmine and everything that Drib remembered about that magical place gradually grew fainter and eventually became lost in the rhythmical creak and rumble of the wagon as their journey took them up through purple heather meadows and over narrow, echoing passes or down steep, breakneck descents into thickly-wooded valleys where elder bushes and blackthorn grew in wild profusion beside the track and soft, resin-scented carpets of pine needles deadened the horses' hoofbeats and silenced the rumble of the wagon's wheels. They forded mountain streams full of the rush and gurgle of clear water running over stones, and they rested beside high banks of knap-weed in the shade of swaying ferns, soothed by the heady scent of wild garlic, rosemary and the hum of summer bees.

Nevian made frequent stops during the hours of daylight to consult with the owls and pore over his one ancient map which told of the hidden ways through the Emerald Mountains. On a clear, starry night he would stand beside the dying embers of their fire long after Drib and Umm had fallen asleep, studying his star charts, fearful that they would lose their way. But gradually as the daylights passed they drew closer to the narrow gap between the sheer mountain walls and the high pass that would take them down into the distant, hazy landscape of Elundium.

Breasting a ridge close to the pass Drib let the reins go slack and leaned out of the wagon as he looked back across the wilderness they had just crossed and he caught a faraway glimpse of rainbows painting soft, misty colours across what he thought must be the entrance of the Runesgate. Memories of his time there flooded back and he craned his neck, leaning out further as he searched for sight of the tower perched on its high promontory, but it was lost from sight, wreathed in dark, ominous storm clouds. The wagon suddenly jolted and began to pick up speed as they started their descent and he felt a sharp tug on his belt as the magician pulled him firmly back into his seat and snatched the reins out of his hands.

Half-rising he tried to slow the horses and muttered crossly, 'Don't just sit there in a dream, boy, work the brake. Can't you see we are going too fast for the horses to hold us steady on this descent. What did you think you were doing, daydreaming instead of paying attention to driving the wagon! Do I have to do *everything* myself?'

The horses were throwing up their heads and snorting wildly in alarm as the breeching straps cut into them. Their hooves skidded and slipped on the steep rocky slope as the wagon began to slew sideways towards the sheer drop into the valley below.

'I'm sorry, I'm really sorry, but I thought I could catch a glimpse of the Runesgate, it looked so beautiful shining in the soft rainbows!' he cried as he threw his meagre weight against the brake lever.

The brake block bit hard and juddered against the iron rim of the wheel, sending up an arch of bright sparks.

Gradually the wagon slowed and Nevian eased the reins, letting out a pent-up breath of relief. He glanced across at Drib as he repeatedly worked the brake and smiled, his moment of anger melting away.

'There is nothing to be gained from looking back, Drib, save to cling onto memories. The future lies ahead of you, beyond that last high pass. You should be concentrating all your energies on perfecting your acrobatics and teaching Umm everything you know of the ways of the people of Elundium. The success of this venture and everything we strive for may depend on it.'

Nevian paused and pointed ahead, 'With luck we will reach the top of the high pass before nightfall where the ancient road from the great fortress of Underfall once ran across the mountains to Cawdor. We will make camp there for the night and begin our descent into Elundium tomorrowlight if everything goes well.'

The sun had long set in a blaze of fire to hide behind the mountains and the first pale stars of evening were beginning to shimmer in the darkening sky which drew its mantle of darkness across the vast, undulating forests and meadows of Elundium before Nevian reined the weary horses to a halt at the head of the pass. Drib looked out to the vast landscape that lay spread out below them and appeared to vanish into the distant gloom of night. A shiver of doubt crept up his spine. Elundium looked so huge as it stretched away beyond the edge of sight: what if he couldn't find Sloeberry? What if they arrived too late to rescue her? Fear and the enormity of their task made him shrink back.

'Are you ever afraid?' he asked Nevian in a small voice as the magician began to climb down stiffly from the driving seat. 'You know, afraid of not being able to achieve something that you have set out to do because you find it is a far bigger thing than you ever imagined?'

The old man paused and a smile pulled at the edges of his mouth. 'Imagination, Drib, is a powerful weapon. Use it to stiffen your resolve; never let it overwhelm you. Of course I sometimes have doubts, and I am sometimes afraid, but doubts sharpen your mind and fear focuses your concentration. Only a fool would dare to venture where we are going without feeling either of those things. Now put aside your fears and see to the horses will you, we'll talk more around a camp fire.'

Drib leapt to the ground and secured the drop chains to the wheels of the wagon before releasing the horses from their harness. He watered them and found them a safe place to graze for the night in the high pasture close to the wagon while Nevian lit a fire with an armful of kindling that Umm had gathered from the last wooded valley they had travelled through. He set a small, pot-bellied kettle of broth to bubble above the flames and then removed the owls' disguises, stowing them carefully in the back of the wagon. The owls stretched their wings and ruffled their feathers before rising silently into the chill, night air.

'Fly ahead, use the cover of darkness to gather news. See if you can discover whether Underfall has fallen,' Nevian called out after them.

Grannog, who had stretched out beside the fire, suddenly lifted his head, his ears pricked, and with a soft growl he vanished into the darkness with long, loping strides. Drib gave a cry of alarm as the old dog ran past him but Nevian merely laughed. 'It's nothing to worry about, he has probably caught the scent of rabbits and has gone off hunting for his supper. Eat yours before it gets cold, we've got a long daylight ahead of us tomorrowlight.'

They heard a muffled barking from the valley below.

'There, I told you he was hunting, didn't I?' Nevian chuckled.

Drib was sitting close to the fire, spooning up the last dregs of the wholesome broth from the bottom of his bowl when he noticed what difficulty Umm was having trying to eat with his spoon, despite the number of times he had shown him how to do it.

'Perhaps you had better show him again. That sort of clumsiness with the commonest of eating implements is the very thing that is likely to arouse people's suspicions,' Nevian murmured with concern as he sat in his old rocking chair that he had set near the fire. He rested his own bowl of half-eaten broth on the map of Elundium that was spread open upon his knees and added gravely, 'and while you are at it, Drib, you must try and impress upon Umm the importance of wearing those clothes that I sorted out for him. It isn't only a matter of covering up as much of him as possible – the people of Elundium don't go about naked, do they? Try and reassure him that he will get used to them eventually.'

The old man sighed and finished his broth before turning to stir the embers of the fire with the end of his staff before continuing, 'I'll make no bones about it, boy, we will all have to keep our wits about us and be on our guard once we descend from the safety of these mountains.'

Nevian glanced down at the map, tracing the ancient road from the head of the pass with his forefinger, 'By my reckoning we should reach Underfall by . . .'

A faint noise in the rocks and scrub beyond the circle of the firelight made the old man pause anxiously. He rose quickly to his feet, spilling the last few drops of his broth from his bowl and sending the spoon spinning away to land in the fire. The map he had been consulting slipped from his knees and crumpled to his feet.

'What was that?' Drib hissed in alarm. He jumped to his feet ready to defend them and reached instinctively for his small dagger that he had sewn into the lining of his acrobat's jacket.

Umm scented the wind and looked around wildly as huge dark shapes with yellow and amber eyes and fangs glistening whitely in the firelight began to crowd in on every side. There was no escaping them, no matter where he looked. He shrank down with a wailing cry of terror and crawled beneath the wagon.

Nevian laughed softly and took a step forwards, lifting his hands in a gesture of welcome as Border Runners, hundreds of them led by Grannog, began to leap and scramble down through the rocks and scrub. In the blink of an eye the rough-coated hunting dogs had completely surrounded Nevian and his party. They looked so large, so menacing, as they milled about in the firelight – far more intimidating than the small pack of dogs who had helped Drib and Eider hunt that Nightboar in the petrified forest. Grannog, who stood a good head and shoulders above any of the other dogs, suddenly lifted his head and barked. Immediately the dogs closest to Drib and Nevian licked their faces and hands and settled down on their haunches beside them. Grannog barked again and those who surrounded the wagon backed away.

'Drib, tell Umm it's all right – they're not going to hurt him. These Border Runners are our friends and they will help us drive out the evil that is spreading across Elundium. Tell him he can come out now,' Nevian urged.

Drib squeezed in between the dogs, making his way to the wagon where he dropped onto his knees. After much coaxing he managed to convince Umm that the dogs of war were not going to hurt him and that he really had nothing to fear from them. Whimpering softly, his gentle black eyes brimming with terror, Umm eventually crept out from his hiding place beneath the wagon and, keeping very close to Drib, he cowered down near the fire. Grannog spoke in low growls to Nevian and Drib and then, one by one, the dogs lifted their heads and began to howl and bark, each in turn telling of everything they had secretly witnessed: the looting and burning of the villages and the rape of the countryside by the hideous, half-human creatures and their shrouds of evil shadows who had swept down from the Emerald Mountains to cover Elundium.

One by one the dogs fell silent, but before Drib could ask if any of them had seen Sloeberry he felt a draught of cold air upon his cheek and he looked up to see Silkstone stoop down out of the darkness. The owl flew directly onto his shoulder and was followed by Orundus who dropped onto the magician's arm. Suddenly the night sky was filled with stoops of Battle Owls that had been gathered from the wooded valleys below. They perched all over the top of the wagon and on the stunted, wind-riven trees and high rocks all around the camp. Their voices started to rise in hoots and shrieks as they told much the same story that the Border Runners had just told, save that they had seen many people fleeing as the creatures advanced and they were all hiding in the forest.

'Are there warriors amongst them? True Kingsmen who could join us?' Nevian suddenly asked, his interest sharpening.

Orundus ruffled his feathers and spoke softly amongst the stoops of owls before crying out, 'The Battle Owls have seen many who they once knew to be proud warriors but who now shun the world and live as hermits in the forests; men who were once mighty Marchers, Archers and Gallopers that circumstance has reduced to living from hand to mouth, men who feel betrayed, abandoned by a thoughtless king who, in the heat of victory, disbanded the great battle crescents and released them from their pledges to serve him merely because he had no further use for them.'

'No . . . no . . . no, that simply wasn't true. Those warriors have wholly misunderstood King Thane. He did not abandon them, no certainly not!' Nevian protested. 'The King simply wanted everybody to be free, and for everybody to benefit equally from the peace they had fought so hard to win. His proclamation at the end of the Battle of the Rising was supposed to be a just reward – not a punishment. Surely they must have understood that!' He looked from the Border Runners to the owls but not an eye blinked nor a hackle moved in the flickering firelight.

Nevian fell silent, lost in thought. Orundus had confirmed doubts that he'd had at battle's end. He feared then that the King had acted too hastily, acted rashly in the heat of the moment, but there had been nothing he could do to prevent it. There had been no time for wise counsel or whispered caution. His powers that had been woven through the long reign of the Granite Kings had come to an abrupt end the moment that Thane had sewn that remnant of Krulshards' black malice into Kruel's footprint and thereby given him a shadow. The very moment that Kruel had been reduced to a helpless infant, the colours of his rainbow cloak had melted in the strengthening sunlight and his voice had faded, pulled away by the wind. But there was no time now for regrets, nor recriminations. Those warriors were greatly needed but how, he frowned, could he convince them that the King had not intentionally betrayed or abandoned them?

'Have you seen Sloeberry? She was taken prisoner at Cawdor and we are in desperate need of news of her,'

Drib cried looking from face to face and using the moment's silence to describe her.

A low murmur of hoots and growls broke out and then many voices reported seeing a starving, bone-thin girl such as he had described. She was dressed in rags and loaded down with chains. She was being driven with a lash and was a helpless prisoner of those evil creatures. Drib wept as he heard how they beat her and cruelly tormented her for their own amusement whenever they stopped or paused to loot and burn a village, but the fragile spark of hope that he had carried for her suddenly burned bright in his heart. The Border Runners and Battle Owls had seen her. She was alive – alive! He clenched his fists in determination.

'We must rescue her at once. We must set out now without delay!'

He ran across to where Nevian stood and grasped at the magician's sleeve, 'Nevian, you must cast a spell over all those warriors who are hiding in the forest, make them band together and meet us where the ancient road emerges from the mountains. With them and all these owls and Border Runners we could sweep down and rescue her. Come on, there is no time to lose, we must set out right away.'

Drib made to run towards the meadow where he had set the horses loose to graze but Nevian caught hold of his arm. 'Think, boy, think. You must use your head and stop listening to your heart for a moment. Rushing off to try and rescue Sloeberry will be about the worst and most stupid thing we could do. It's the best way of alerting Snatchpurse and his murderous friends of our presence that I can think of. Sloeberry's life hangs on a slender enough thread already without risking those evil creatures severing it completely. If he gets the slightest whisper that we are about to try and rescue her they would slit her throat without a moment's thought. Why, we are not even sure exactly where she is being held, are we?'

Drib looked crestfallen. He nodded. He didn't want to agree but he knew in his heart that the old man was right. A handful of warriors did not make an army and they would probably find Sloeberry a lot quicker, and even be able to get close enough to rescue her without alerting Snatchpurse's suspicions, if they continued to travel disguised as the circus than by charging recklessly through the countryside. But he couldn't stop the tears of frustration filling his eyes as he stared fixedly into the fire.

Nevian spoke softly to Orundus and Grannog and in moments the owls and the Border Runners melted away into the darkness as silently as they had arrived. The magician put his arm around the boy's shoulders and took him beyond the circle of firelight to point out across the countryside spread out below them a single, tiny light that looked like a fallen star clinging to the distant horizon line. 'Underfall. The owls have told me that it stands secure. We will begin our journey there as soon as the grey hours light the sky. The owls and the Border Runners will try to bring those solitary warriors to us secretly as we travel: perhaps we may just convince them to swell the ranks of the Kindred Spirit.'

'When will this night ever end? Tomorrowlight seems so far away!' Drib fretted impatiently as they returned to the fire. He was unable to settle in one place for any length of time.

'It will come soon enough, boy, have no doubts. Now come over here and use the time more profitably – it is no good you pacing backwards and forwards in front of the fire like this, all you're doing is blocking the warmth. Come here and help me to finalize the subterfuge we will perpetrate. Remember our performances must be both foot and word perfect: use the time to familiarize yourself with the countryside we will be travelling through.' The magician frowned, distracted by the boy's crooked shadow repeatedly passing over the map that he had picked up and smoothed out upon his knees again.

Eventually Drib paused at Nevian's shoulder and, standing on tiptoe, he looked down at the map and followed the old man's slow, erratic finger as he traced their route down from the head of the pass, around the sheer shoulder of the Emerald Mountain until it eventually descended into the meandering foothills and wooded valleys and then through the narrow gorges and dark, shadowy ravines until they passed Manterns Mountain and the ruined Gates of Night and reached the Causeway Fields and the fortress of Underfall. Drib tried to read the small, spider-fine names written on the map and work out all the places they would pass through, but there were so many and he soon gave up. The spectre of the doubts that they might never find Sloeberry began to rise again, smothering any hope that the owls and the dogs had rekindled. Elundium looked so vast.

'Don't despair, Drib, nothing is ever as black and hopeless as it seems in the darkness just before dawn,' Nevian reassured him softly.

'But everything looks so far away – and how will we ever know where to begin to look? She could be anywhere.'

The old man smiled and shook his head, 'Oh, I don't think we will have much difficulty finding Sloeberry. From what the owls and the Border Runners have told us Snatchpurse and his murderous followers are leaving a trail of ruin and devastation behind them that is so wide a blind man would find them easy to follow. Now getting close enough to rescue her. That, I am sure, will not be so easy and it will test all of our ingenuity. That is when your ability to become invisible is really going to come in useful.'

Drib felt the cold fingers of doubt tighten in his stomach. He still wasn't convinced about this invisibility business.

'But what if I can't do it? What if somebody sees me? What if . . .'

'No more ifs or buts!' Nevian snapped so sharply that he made the boy jump. 'Think positively, Drib, there isn't going to be any room for doubts where we are going tomorrowlight. No, not now, not ever!' Nevian held Drib's gaze with a piercing look that searched deep down into the deepest, most secret recesses of his soul, refusing to let him look away. 'Remember what I have taught you, Drib: nothing is beyond your reach, not if you want it badly enough. And don't be afraid to use those threads of magic that you have learned to control, there's no knowing when they will come in useful.'

'You know I will do everything I can. You know I would rather die than fail to rescue her, only sometimes it seems so impossible when I am on my own.' Drib's face suddenly flushed scarlet as he realized what he had said. 'I'm sorry, I didn't mean it quite like that, I meant no disrespect. I just sometimes wish that Eider and the others were here with me. They were the best friends I have ever had and I really miss them. I can't help wondering where they are and what's happened to them.'

The old man's eyes softened. He knew Drib didn't want for courage, for all his disadvantages, and he rose stiffly from his chair, carefully folding the map and slipping it into his inner pocket. Perhaps he could ease the boy's fears about the fate of his friends. Perhaps here, so close to the roof of the world, he could dredge up enough of his lost powers to use the crystal sphere that he had brought with them: he could search across the hidden depths of the petrified forest and find them. 'Wait here a moment – build up the fire,' he instructed Drib as he shuffled across to the wagon, his ragged cloak of hessian billowing out around him in the chill, night breeze.

'What have you got there?' Drib asked, his eyes wide with curiosity as Nevian returned to his chair with a heavy looking object wrapped in a sky-blue velvet cloth and cradled in his arms.

'This, my boy, is the Eye of Arabra,' he whispered con-spiratorially as he unveiled the crystal globe and carefully polished its smooth, opaque surface with the soft cloth.

Drib felt an invisible tug on his sleeve and almost tripped over his own foot as he was being drawn down towards the opaque sphere. 'What is it? What can it do?' he asked in a small, frightened voice as the power drew him closer.

'Stay! Come no further!' Nevian suddenly warned, put-ting out a hand to stop him. 'The Eye of Arabra is an all-seeing window. It will reveal things that are shrouded, things that lie beyond the edge of mortal sight but only to those who have the power to use it wisely.'

Drib opened his mouth to ask what sort of things it would reveal but Nevian silenced him before he could utter a word. 'Quiet, boy! This isn't the time for your idle chatter. Let me concentrate!'

He bent forwards and focused all his attention on the crystal sphere, touching its smooth surface with his finger-tips and uttering the words that would open the Eye of Arabra, but its opacity unexpectedly deepened instead of clearing and cavernous, swirling shadows moved inside the glass. It suddenly grew colder and beads of condensation formed a cloud on its surface. Nevian frowned and whispered the words again. He was troubled – nothing like this had ever happened before. But the more he persisted the wetter and colder the sphere became. Hoar frost suddenly crackled beneath his fingers and completely shrouded the surface of the glass and he took his hand away and looked up to Drib.

'I'm sorry, Drib, my powers seem to have completely deserted me. I was going to search for Eider and the others. I was going to find out what had happened to them for you, but . . .'

'I can see starlight in the sphere, it's reflecting on a frozen lake. The lake is hemmed in by tall, thickly-wooded mountains – and there is a tower . . .' Drib whispered.

'You saw a tower and mountains in the glass? You're telling me the Eye of Arabra opened for you? But that's impossible – you're only a boy, you don't know the words to invoke its power. You are only just beginning to develop your magic!'

Nevian was completely shocked. He reached forwards and grasped Drib firmly by his sleeve almost tipping the crystal sphere off his lap and onto the ground as he did so.

'I . . . I . . . I'm sorry, I really didn't mean to do anything wrong . . .' the boy stuttered, afraid of the magician's anger, 'but the frost sparkled with so many colours that I couldn't resist stealing a look at it.'

'And then what happened?' Nevian asked severely.

Drib swallowed nervously, 'Well, as you looked up away from the sphere the frost suddenly melted and the glass took on a crystal-like clarity. It seemed so deep, so vast that it was as if I was looking into the whole world and the tiny beads of condensation sort of sank into its surface and became like the stars in the sky, only they were inside it.'

Drib hesitated, 'No, that's not quite right, they *did* become stars but they weren't the ones we can see in the night sky above our heads, not at all – they were quite different. I caught a sooty smell of snow in the air and I saw steeply-wooded slopes, and then I saw the starlight reflecting on that frozen lake, I saw the tall mountains and the tower . . .'

'Did you recognize the tower? Did anything about the lake seem familiar to you?' the magician pressed.

'No, no, I have never seen them before,' the boy began, only to pause as a movement in the glass caught his eye – two lights travelling down across a snowy slope above the trees – and drew his gaze back.

'There are two riders carrying staysafe lanterns cantering down a steep, snowy slope towards the tower. They have bows slung across their shoulders – no, wait, I recognize one of the horses – it's Nightshade, yes I can see now, it's Eider riding Nightshade!' Drib cried suddenly as he leaned forwards and reached out. But the moment he touched the glass its surface became cloudy and opaque.

'What's happened? The picture has become dim, I can't see anything.' He frowned.

'You must not touch the eye. Take your hand away,' Nevian whispered quietly.

Drib withdrew his hand and immediately the glass cleared. But the two riders had vanished, the scene had changed, and he found himself peering into a huge, dimly lit, raftered banqueting hall, flanked with long, trestle tables piled high with food. Soft firelight danced and flickered in the vast soot-blackened chimney where the carcasses of two wild boars were being turned on a spit above the fire. He could hear the hiss and crackle of hot fat dripping into the flames and his mouth watered as he imagined the smell of roasting meat. The firelight reflected leaping shadows from the hundreds of mounted hunting trophies that lined the walls. Drib could hear faint voices laughing and talking and everywhere he looked in the hazy, smoky room he saw groups of figures dressed in the strangest clothes. Some of them wore clothes that were fashioned entirely from animal skins, some wore soft, knee length leather boots and silken trousers while others wore long sable cloaks that swept the ground. He thought he caught a glimpse of children playing hide-and-seek beneath the tables and he was sure he could see at least a dozen large, broken-coated hunting dogs – sleek creatures who had been bred for speed in the chase with long, powerful jaws and savage fangs, though now they lay sprawled on the flagstones close to the fire hearth, basking in its warmth and gnawing lazily at the raw, splintered knuckle-ends of a bone.

Drib frowned slightly, tilting his head as he thought he could hear a faint, but familiar, voice amongst the murmur of conversation and laughter in the hall. 'Eider, is that you? Are you in there somewhere?' he whispered, moving closer, his lips almost brushing the glass and causing tiny beads of condensation to mist its surface.

The slender figure of a young, dark-haired woman robed in ermine and talking earnestly to somebody at the closest table who he couldn't quite see caught his attention. He concentrated on them and their image moved closer: Drib could see they were holding hands. The woman laughed softly and then he overheard her saying, 'It's no use continually worrying about what has happened to your friends – starving yourself won't help them will it? I am sure my father will organize a hunting party soon and he will search for them. Come on, eat, you will feel better.'

She broke away from him and reached forward to choose the ripest purple forest fruit from an earthenware bowl that was piled high with all varieties of them and then she turned back to the young man and pressed it into his hand. Drib inhaled a sudden, sharp breath as the figure turned towards him and the flickering lamplight revealed his identity. It was Eider. It was definitely Eider but Drib could hardly recognize him, his face was so gaunt and haggard, his skin so pale and he was so thin. The self-assured young man Drib had known seemed to have disappeared. Eider hardly smiled as he took the fruit and he toyed with it rather than devouring it the way he would have done back in the Learning Hall or during their daylights together at Cawdor. He seemed to be distracted as he listened to the beautiful young woman talking about their day's hunting and the great kill they had made.

'Eider, you look so unhappy. What has happened to you?' Drib cried out in alarm, and for an instant the young archer froze and he searched the shadows of the hall as though he had caught the distant echo of something that pricked his consciousness. His eyes suddenly took on a haunted look of despair.

'Eider, you must not worry, it's all right, I'm alive, all of us . . . most of us . . . survived . . .' Drib began, but his lips accidentally touched the sphere and again it clouded over.

Drib drew back, willing the glass to clear, but it remained an opaque, swirling cloud of shadow.

'Tell me exactly what you saw this time, and make sure you leave nothing out!' the old man urged.

'I saw Eider, he was in a dimly-lit banqueting hall full of hunting trophies, but I have no idea where he is. I didn't recognize anybody else and Eider looked so miserable. His face was all drawn and thin . . .'

Drib then described every detail he could remember of

the two riders he had glimpsed cantering towards the tower and told of the scene inside the great hall.

'The hunting trophies and the people you saw were mostly dressed in clothes fashioned from animal skins you say?' Nevian murmured. He let his head sink slowly forwards into his hands to concentrate his mind on the images the boy was telling him of. He was sure he had once visited a place just like it, if only he could remember when. Suddenly he looked up.

'Yes! There is a place such as you describe, it is all coming back to me. There is a single tower perched high amongst the mountains beside a turquoise lake. But how did Eider ever find it on his own? It is quite beyond my riddling, it is so remote. Unless . . . somebody must have taken him there . . .'

'It can't be that remote – the hall was full of people,' Drib interrupted.

'Be quiet, boy. How can you ever expect me to find the answers or reach any sensible conclusions when you endlessly interrupt and drive the simplest of thoughts into oblivion?' The old man frowned crossly as he attempted to focus his concentration on the tower again. At length he said, 'The tower belongs to Largg, the huntsman, and the people crowding his hall will be his kin. I would deduce from your description of the young woman talking to Eider that she would be his daughter, Ayeshe, although I have not seen her since she was a child. As for Eider's apparent look of despair and unhappiness that you describe I think the answer to that lies in something Berioss told me in the ruins of Cawdor. As all of you galloped across the Causeway and in through the ruined gatehouse Eider's horse reared up and spun around, turning tail and fleeing back into the forest. Whether it was because the horse was afraid of the dark evil that had overrun Cawdor or it sensed Eider's heart quail, only he can know the truth of. But I suspect, from your description of his haunted eyes, that it might well be the latter and that could be why he is so eager to set out and try to find you, only he won't be able to until Largg agrees to organize a hunting party to show him a way through the mountains.'

At Nevian's mention of Berioss and the others Drib stole another quick look at the sphere, hoping it might reveal a glimpse of them. The glass became crystal clear as his eyes travelled over the smooth, cold surface and thin shafts of moonlight filtered down through a dense canopy of branches, softly illuminating countless flowerheads and lighting them blue-white in the darkness that hung still amongst the tangled vines and creepers. Drib was aware of the smells of the forest, the sweet perfume of the orchids, the pine resin and leaf mould, and there was the faint rustle of a light wind high up in the tree tops as it combed its fingers through the leaves. Where it was in the forest, or indeed which forest, he had no idea but lights began to appear through the trees. There were hushed voices and the jingle and creak of saddlery getting closer.

Drib widened his eyes and stared hard into the glass, trying to see who was coming. A gnarled, tree-like figure with an ancient weather-beaten face and long, straggling branches where his arms should have been strode into view. In his crooked fingers he gripped a crude spear and the ground seemed to shake with each ponderous footstep that he took as masses of roots curled and dangled from his feet. 'It's Berioss!' Drib barely had time to whisper before other figures began to appear on either side of the old Marcher. He could see Oaktangle, Mistletoe, Damask and the company of Tunnellers he had journeyed to Cawdor with as they came into sight carrying lanterns.

Immediately behind them were many of the people that Quencher had led over the high passes of the Emerald Mountains to bring into Cawdor in the depths of winter. The last Drib had seen of any of them was when they had fled towards the safety of the forest as Snatchpurse and his followers had attacked the ruined fortress. They had been scattered and were running for their lives then. They looked quite different now. They were well-armed and purposeful as they marched so deliberately between the trees. Drib felt a smile of pride tug at the corners of his mouth as he remembered the promise Berioss had made to Nevian as he stood in the ruins of Cawdor. Drib dearly wanted to call out, to urge them to hurry and to let them know that Sloeberry was Snatchpurse's prisoner. He wanted them to know that he was going to try to rescue her – in fact there was so much he wanted to tell them but he knew it would be futile, as they would never hear him.

Thoughts of Sloeberry welled up inside him and the picture of Berioss and his friends instantly vanished. The glass trembled slightly on the magician's lap and the gentle sound of the night wind in the tree tops became a roar inside Drib's head. The trees, the rocks, the sheer mountains and the stars – everything became a blur of light and shadow that made him reel with dizziness and clutch at the arm of the magician's chair for support. The image in the sphere began to slow, passing over Meremire Forest as it followed a silvered road in the moonlight towards a tower perched on the top of a hill. It looked exactly as he imagined the tower on Stumble Hill would look from the Loremaster's stories he had heard in the Learning Hall. Drib felt a shiver of dread run up his spine as he was taken in through the great doors of the tower and saw they were splintered and riven from their hinges.

Fallen masonry and trampled defences littered the outer courtyards whilst shadowy figures hurried through the gloom beneath a general air of devastation and ruin.

The scene changed abruptly and Drib was shown into a long, crowded, dimly-lit hall. His eyes quickly grew accustomed to the lurid, uncertain light cast by the crude reed torches that had been forced into the broken lamp brackets along the outer walls. He sensed that Sloeberry was somewhere very close – he felt her fear and knew that she was cowering down, trying to hide herself as best she could. He had to see her, he had to catch one treasured glimpse of her before the magician took the sphere and wrapped it up in his velvet cloth or before the Eye of Arabra shut. He willed the glass with all his strength to help him find her. He begged it to take him further into the room amongst the shadowy, half-human creatures who crowded and despoiled the Archers' once beautiful feasting hall with their wildness, their shouting and cursing, their fighting and squabbling over the mounds of raw bones as they grabbed for the tastiest strips of flesh, drinking noisily from the cauldrons of evil-smelling liquors and flagons of frothing brews that filled the hall with stench. Drib searched frantically to left and right, he looked beneath the tables and searched amongst the unconscious figures who lay in the filth and rubbish: he looked everywhere for her. Swallowing his revulsion he gasped as the sphere took him unseen through the seething masses towards a high dais set with a smaller table at the far end of the hall.

As Drib drew closer he suddenly caught sight of Snatch-purse, surrounded by his captains, sprawled in an ornately carved chair right in the centre of the dais. He rose unsteadily to his feet, clutching a jug of ale in one clawed hand, his murderous eyes searching the crowd behind him almost as though he sensed an unwanted intruder.

'Where is that girl? Bring her here – make her dance for us!'

Snatch blinked, shaking off the sensation that he was being watched and demanded in a snarling voice, 'Bring that ugly little goblin forwards, make her dance. Let the entertainment begin! Hurry up, Crimp, I'll not ask you twice!' He hurled his half-empty ale jug at him.

'Hurry, girl, hurry, dance for your master. You know the longer you keep him waiting the more he'll beat you – I can't do anything to stop him. Hurry, please hurry.'

Crimp hissed nervously as he made a show of tugging hard at the heavy iron fetters that snaked away into the shadows beneath the dais. Drib felt his heart quicken as he heard the faint clatter and scrape of the chains. Sloe-berry was so close to him – he could feel it in every part of his body and he could barely breathe. A tiny, frail figure began to emerge, half stumbling, half crawling from the dark recess beneath the dais and jeers and taunts of cruel laughter erupted from all around. But there was a look of hope in her bruised eyes and her lips seemed to whisper Drib's name as she looked quickly round the dimly-lit hall, almost as though she could sense him near.

'Dance, goblin, dance, dance!'

'Sloeberry, Sloeberry, what have they done to you my darling?' Drib whispered through trembling lips as tears welled up in his eyes. He saw the raw flesh on her wrists and ankles where the chains and shackles had rubbed her; he saw the mass of bloody weals across her back and shoulder; he saw her arms and legs striped from the whip that clearly showed through the filthy rags that she was dressed in; he saw the blackened bruises on her face, and he wept.

'Come on, girl, get up, I'll not wait all night. Get up

and dance!' Snatchpurse leered, grasping the chains from Crimp's hand and pushing him aside roughly. 'Get up you wretched creature, get up!'

He was swaying drunkenly as he gave the chain a brutal jerk and then tossing it aside he reached for the long, iron-tailed lash that lay amongst the greasy, maggoty remains of the feast upon the table.

'Now you will dance!' he snarled menacingly, raising the lash high above his head to strike her.

Something inside Drib snapped and a rage, an intensity of anger he had never felt before, boiled up. Without thinking what he was doing he cried out, 'No! No, you vile monster, by all the power of good you shall not harm her!' and he reached out his hand as though to stop him.

Bright flashes of lightning suddenly fizzed and crackled coldly between Drib's fingertips and he experienced a sense of power he had never felt before as he touched the sphere. The clear image of Sloeberry cowering beneath the lash didn't become opaque, nor did Drib hear Nevian's cry of alarm. Their camp site at the head of the high pass through the mountains seemed suddenly vague and shadowy as the brittle crystal orb yielded to his touch, and his fingers, then his wrist and arm, seemed to penetrate its outer surface. A rush of darkness engulfed him as the Eye of Arabra drew him into its depth, letting him enter the feasting hall of the Tower of Stumble Hill. He was there, there on the dais amidst the stench and chaos of the Honourable Murderers, he was close enough to reach up and grab at Snatchpurse's scaly wrist. Using all the strength he could muster he gripped it tightly to prevent him from wielding the lash.

Snatchpurse hesitated as he suddenly became aware of somebody, an indistinct, shadowy form who should not have been there. It was standing so close, closer than any of his captains would have dared to stand. He felt fingers, invisible fingers, close around his wrist and he heard a voice challenge him. It was no more than a whispered echo but it was loud enough to send a cold shiver of recognition through him and up the bony ridge of his spine. His self-assured leer faltered and then tightened into a snarl of hate, his eyes narrowed into murderous, glittering slits as he searched the smoky light of the hall.

'I'm not afraid of your ghost, you crippled boy. I killed you at Cawdor, you can't threaten me! He wrenched his arm free and lurched forwards, wielding the whip at Drib's faint, elusive shadow as it melted away. The iron-tipped tails of the lash sang through the air and wrapped themselves around Drib's vanishing arm. Snatchpurse felt a tug on the handle as it jerked him forwards and in a rush of swirling darkness he was drawn after Drib through the eye of the crystal. The sphere toppled off Nevian's lap and bounced across the ground as Drib reappeared, attached by the tail of the evil whip.

The feasting hall and everything that was familiar to Snatchpurse abruptly disappeared and became a faint, far-away echo. The feeling of rushing, tumbling through the darkness suddenly stopped and he found himself some-where high amongst the mountains facing the ghostly image of Drib, only now he seemed much too real to be a ghost. Snatchpurse didn't understand. What was hap-pening to him? What tricks of illusion had drawn him away from Stumble Hill? But in that instant he didn't care. Hatred of that crippled boy swelled his rage and his only thought was to kill him, his only purpose was to be rid of him forever. He saw that the flail of his whip was still wound around the boy's arm and with a snarl he gave the whip a brutal yank, reaching out with his other hand to grasp the boy around his throat. But he couldn't reach.

He couldn't quite reach. His snarl of rage turned into a cry of fear as his hand touched the invisible surface of a cold, still pond and another figure suddenly appeared on the edge of his swirling vision. The shape of a wizened old man dressed in a hessian cloak was shouting something at him, shouting at him in a muffled voice, gesticulating at Drib, telling him to unwind the tail of the whip and throw it away.

'I'll kill you all!' Snatchpurse shrieked as he hurled himself towards the invisible barrier.

The sphere shuddered and began to swell as thousands of tiny fractures spread across it. Slowly Snatch's snarling, scaly face began to push its way through its surface. Silkstone who was perched on top of the wagon saw Drib desperately trying to tear the whip from his arm as the hideous, half-human, half-beastly creature began to emerge from the crystal ball and reach out towards him. He stooped with his talons outstretched to rake them across the monster's scaly face.

Snatchpurse screamed as the owl's talons cut bloody gouges deep into his cheek and he let go of the handle of his whip. Drig staggered and fell to the ground. Instantly, Snatch was sucked back into the swirling darkness, tumbling over and over with a wailing howl of pain as the sphere shattered into a thousand brittle pieces.

'You fool! Now look what your meddling has done. Why did you have to go messing around with things you do not yet know how to control?'

Nevian threw his hands up in the air in exasperation as he trod through the sparkling shards of crystal, scattering them with his feet. He moved closer to confront the boy and, grabbing hold of his collar, he lifted him up off the ground.

'What madness possessed you to reveal us to our

330

enemies? I only allowed you to glimpse through the Eye of Arabra to reassure you that Eider, Berioss and the others were safe. Why, oh why, didn't you stop to think? You must surely have realized that there would be dangers in searching further? You must have known that if Eider sensed your presence then others were sure to. What possessed you to try to find Sloeberry – that is what you did, isn't it?'

Bleakly Drib nodded. 'But I didn't intend to do it. I think about her, worry about her, all the time: I suppose I must have been thinking about her while I was looking into the glass, and the next moment I was in that vile feasting hall and Snatchpurse was raising his whip to beat her. I tried to stop him. I didn't think – I'm sorry.'

'That, my boy, was a very foolish move and it has probably squandered our element of surprise.' The old man frowned, glancing to the east at the thin finger of dawn light on the distant horizon. Anger and recriminations were an expensive luxury and he could ill afford to indulge in them. With a sigh he set Drib down. He turned and began to kick over the shattered fragments of crystal sphere and the embers of their fire.

'I am really very sorry about breaking that beautiful crystal ball, and I wish I hadn't revealed our presence to Snatchpurse. It is all my fault: I would never have stolen a glance into it if I had only realized.'

Drib tried to apologize but Nevian hastily pushed his excuses aside. 'There is no time for regrets, Drib: what is broken cannot be mended – well not at the moment. If you want to rescue Sloeberry, you'd better look sharp and harness the horses: hurry, boy – we must be as far away from here as we possibly can be before the sun rises. I would imagine that Snatchpurse will send out those evil birds to find us as soon as he can. And throw that whip into the back of the wagon, for there is no knowing when it will come in useful. Hurry, boy, hurry – there isn't a moment to lose!'

With quick, trembling fingers and an anxious eye on the strengthening daylight Drib tightened the last of the buckles and keepers on the harness. Equestrius and Spark-fire knew they were to make the great dash for the cover of the trees in the valley far below and they snorted and fretted, champing at their bits. Umm had been sent running on ahead down the steep, winding, ancient road with Grannog at his heels to find them a safe place to hide from prying eyes.

'Hurry, boy, hurry!' Nevian urged, the reins held tightly in his hand as Drib fumbled to release the last drop-chain on the wagon's wheels.

The cart jolted forwards as the links finally separated and he had to run and jump, clinging onto the edge of the driving seat as the horses threw their weight into the harness and the wagon surged forwards. The first rays of sunlight were touching the mountain peaks above them as the horses entered the narrow, echoing ravine at the bottom of the pass, cantering hard, necks outstretched, ears pricked and nostrils flared. Sweat was already lathering their flanks as the road raced beneath their flying hooves in a blaze of sparks. Behind them the wagon rocked wildly from side to side and Drib hung on tightly, gritting his teeth as they neared the thickly-wooded valley. He knew that the fate of Elundium, Sloeberry's life, everything they were striving to achieve hung by a slender thread. The safety of the trees loomed closer, arching above the road, but the sky was darkening as flocks of evil carrion birds approached from the direction of Mere-mire Forest, soaring and wheeling as they searched for them.

'Gallop, great hearts, gallop!' Nevian shouted above the thunder of the wheels, and with one last, mighty burst of speed they vanished beneath the trees.

The daylight abruptly dimmed into verdant shafts of misty light and the thunder of the wheels and pounding of the horses' hooves diminished to a muffled whisper as they padded over the carpet of undisturbed leaf mould that lay thick upon the forest floor.

'Look, there's Umm ahead of us, over there, to the right. I think he must have found somewhere for us to hide from the way he's waving and pointing!' Drib called out just in time for Nevian to haul on the reins and turn the horses towards the narrow track that the Yerrak was gesticulating towards.

It led into dense, seemingly impassable, undergrowth and Drib let out a cry of alarm, throwing up his arms to shield his face, as the horses neighed and tossed their heads, veering between the trees to pass beneath a tracery of low, hanging vines and creepers and plough their way through bramble thickets and stands of young saplings that bent and thwacked against the sides of the wagon before springing back behind them.

'Whoa! Whoa!' the magician cried suddenly, standing and pulling hard on the reins as he saw that the way ahead was completely blocked by a massive fallen oak.

The horses threw their weight against the breeching straps, churning up the leaves and soft earth with their hooves and brought the wagon to an abrupt halt only a handspan from the fallen tree. They were completely hidden by a dense canopy of leafy branches that Umm had so cleverly woven to conceal them. The leaves rustled and the branches creaked before they fell still and the forest silence enfolded them, to be broken only by the harsh, shrieking cries of unseen carrion birds wheeling and turning above the tree tops as they searched fruitlessly for them. Drib slipped quickly between the horses, loosing buckles and keepers on their harness and removing bits from their mouths, momentarily disappearing in the clouds of steam that rose from their sweating flanks. He heard Nevian laugh softly and glanced back from between the horses to see the old man standing on the driver's seat and looking up at the dense canopy of branches above them, his head tilted slightly to one side.

'We've done it, Drib! Thanks to the speed of our horses and this roof that Umm wove to hide us from their prying eyes we have escaped! Those carrion birds haven't spotted us nor will they find a single trace of us on the ancient road. To all intents and purposes we have vanished from sight, and that, I'm sure, will sow seeds of doubt in Snatch-purse's mind. He might even think that raising the lash to beat Sloeberry conjured up a ghost. It might make him think twice before he beats her again, for fear of your spectre reappearing.'

'Does that mean you think there is still a chance that we may succeed despite everything I did to ruin things last night?' Drib asked, his hope rekindling.

'Oh yes!' Nevian replied in a hushed whisper. 'We will proceed with extreme caution and with luck, and perhaps just a little magic, our circus of deception will journey right into the heart of our enemies' camp. Oh yes, there is quite a good chance that we might just succeed with our plans.'

But Drib was not so sure. He felt the touch of the cold hand of doubt tighten around his heart. He had glimpsed Sloeberry through the Eye of Arabra: she had looked so fragile and vulnerable, a helpless prisoner loaded down with chains, surrounded by those huge, half-human creatures who had crowded the ruins of the archers' tower, cursing and fighting over their vile feast. What, in truth, could they do against so many, even with the help of Nevian's magic?

The undergrowth around their hiding place suddenly rustled; twigs snapped and cracked underfoot. Drib spun round to follow the noise and reached for his dagger. They were under attack. Umm gave a cry of alarm and shrank beneath the cart, Grannog snarled, hackles raised and fangs bared as Drib braced himself, dagger drawn. Nevian raised his staff, gripping it with both hands, but instinct warned him to hesitate and he refrained from uttering a spell that would curse an unseen enemy.

The undergrowth rustled again and slowly parted in a dozen places as ancient warriors began to emerge cautiously, their grim faces more weatherbeaten than the bark of trees in the forest and their flowing beards entwined with flowering vines and ivy. Battle Owls were perched on their shoulders and Border Runners padded at their heels. Drib lowered his dagger, his eyes wide with wonder, as the tallest warrior stepped forwards to offer the hilt of his sword to Nevian. They were all exactly like the ancient warriors from Loremaster Grout's stories and some of them were so gnarled and covered with foliage that, at a glance, he had thought they were trees.

Nevian put aside his staff and lifted his open arms in greeting as the warrior spoke. 'A new evil is treading through the countryside – the Border Runners and the Battle Owls have brought us word – and we have heard grave tidings that Elundium teeters upon the brink of ruin. Is this true?'

'Yes, everything you have heard is true. That is why I have asked the owls and the dogs of war to summon you from the secret depths of the forest,' Nevian said gravely.

Without pausing to gather breath the magician told them that the King stood alone, siege-locked in Candlebane Hall, and he laid bare the bones of the Chancellors' black treachery. Looking from face to face he asked quickly, 'Would you now put aside those old grievances and understand that the King's award of your freedom was truly meant? Will you rally once more beneath his standard and swell the ranks of the Kindred Spirit? Will you join with us to drive the evil from the land?'

Drib felt a surge of hope flood through him as he looked up at the fierce band of warriors who surrounded them. He wanted to call out and beg them to come with their travelling circus but the warriors drew back without appearing to notice him as they huddled together. There was an uncertain, whispered debate and Drib's hopes began to shrink. He took a hesitant step forwards: perhaps if he told them of Sloeberry's plight it might swing the balance, but he felt the magician's firm hand upon his shoulder.

'They must choose their own path. Be patient.'

After what seemed an age of waiting the warriors turned to Nevian and, one by one, offered up the hilts of their swords. The leader spoke again.

'For too long we have nursed a hollow grudge against the King and we have been blinded by it. We could not see that he had bestowed upon us a truly great gift at Battle's End. Yes, we will march with you but we will do so as free men, not bound by duty or pledges of loyalty, and we will fight with you for the King. We will now give him his freedom and rid Elundium of this dark evil.'

'There, what did I tell you, Drib! Good, honest men will flock to our cause as we journey forwards. Yes, from small beginnings great deeds will be done.'

Nevian beckoned to the warriors as Drib and Umm

gathered around him, 'Come closer, all of you, we have plans to make and strategies to form if we are to rescue Sloeberry and break the siege of Candlebane Hall.'

Weaveworld
Clive Barker

Weaveworld is an epic adventure of the imagination. It begins with a carpet in which a world of rapture and enchantment is hiding; a world which comes back to life, alerting the dark forces from which it was hiding, and beginning a desperate battle to preserve the last vestiges of magic which Human-kind still has access to.

Mysteriously drawn by the carpet and into the world it represents are Cal Mooney and Suzanna Parrish, two young people with no knowledge of what they are about to live through and confront. For the final conflict between the forces of good – the Seerkind – and of evil, embodied by the terrible Immacolata and her ravening twin wraith sisters, is about to take place.

Weaveworld is a book of visions and horrors, as real as the world we live and breathe in, yet opening doors to experiences, places and people that we all dream of, but daren't hope are real. It is a story of quest, of titanic struggles, of love and of hope. It is a triumph of imagination and storytelling, an adventure, a nightmare, a promise . . .

'Graphic, grotesque, and yet compellingly readable . . . its energy is unstoppable.'   *Washington Post*

'A powerful and fascinating writer with a brilliant imagin-ation. *Weaveworld* reveals Clive Barker as an outstanding storyteller.'   J. G. Ballard

ISBN 0 00 617489 2

Dragoncharm
Graham Edwards

The ultimate dragon saga

THE WORLD IS TURNING

The bones of trolls are turning suddenly to stone as nature draws apart from the Realm, the mysterious source of charm. It is a young world, but soon it will be old, and no magic is strong enough to resist the onset of a new era.

Instead, a young natural dragon named Fortune, with no fire in his breath nor magic in his power, holds the key to the survival of charm.

The malevolent Charmed dragon Wraith knows this, and he awakens the basilisk in a desperate bid to gain power over Fortune . . .

Myths handed down since the dawn of time tell of dragons, the most strange and magnificent creatures of our mythical prehistory. In this glorious epic fantasy, Graham Edwards captures the terror and the beauty of the days when dragons roamed the sky.

ISBN 0 00 648021 7

Magician
Raymond E. Feist
New Revised Edition

Raymond E. Feist has prepared a new, revised edition, to incorporate over 15,000 words of text omitted from previous editions so that, in his own words, 'it is essentially the book I would have written had I the skills I possess today'.

At Crydee, a frontier outpost in the tranquil Kingdom of the Isles, an orphan boy, Pug is apprenticed to a master magician – and the destinies of two worlds are changed forever. Suddenly the peace of the Kingdom is destroyed as mysterious alien invaders swarm through the land. Pug is swept up into the conflict but for him and his warrior friend, Tomas, an odyssey into the unknown has only just begun. Tomas will inherit a legacy of savage power from an ancient civilisation. Pug's destiny is to lead him through a rift in the fabric of space and time to the mastery of the unimaginable powers of a strange new magic. . .

'Epic scope . . . fast-moving action . . . vivid imagination'
Washington Post

'Tons of intrigue and action'
Publishers Weekly

ISBN 0 586 21783 3

A Darkness at Sethanon
Raymond E. Feist

The triumphant finale to the bestselling Riftwar saga

As Prince Arutha and his companions rally their forces for the final battle with an ancient and mysterious evil, the dreaded necromancer Marcos the Black has once again unleashed his dark sorcery.

Now the fate of two worlds will be decided in a titanic struggle beneath the walls of Sethanon, as the link between Kelewan and Midkemia is revived.

'Well written and distinctly above average . . . intelligent . . . intriguing'   *Publishers Weekly*

ISBN 0 586 06688 8

David Eddings

Domes of Fire

Book one of
The Tamuli

PRINCE SPARHAWK AND
THE TROLL-GODS

Queen Ehlana and the Pandion Knight Sir Sparhawk are
married, their kingdom peaceful at last, their union
blessed with a very special daughter named Danae. But
soon trouble sweeps westward from the Tamul Empire to
disrupt not only the living of Eosia but the dead: horrific
armies are being raised from the dust of the long-past Age
of Heroes, threatening the peace won at such cost in
Zemoch.

Prince Sparhawk is called upon to help the Tamuli nations
defeat these ancient horrors. Perhaps the Troll-Gods are
once more loose in the world! With Ehlana and a retinue
of Pandion Knights, Sparhawk will make the hazardous
journey to the Tamul Empire . . . only to discover in fire-
domed Matherion, the incandescent Tamul capital, that
the enemy is already within its gates.

Full of marvels and humour, romance and shrewdness,
above all full of magic, the resources of the epic form are
mined deep by the greatest of modern fantasy writers.

ISBN 0 586 21313 9

David Eddings

The Shining Ones

Book two of
The Tamuli

HAVOC AND WAR

Prince Sparhawk is pledged to fight the enemies of the
Tamul Emperor Sarabian with all the skill and cunning of a
Pandion Knight. Meanwhile his Queen, Ehlana, educates
Sarabian in the art of ruthless statesmanship. Sarabian is
transformed from a mere puppet ruler into a formidable
politician. But still Trolls, vampires, werewolves, zombies,
ghouls and Ogres form a vast conspiracy to take over the
Empire. Most disturbing of all are reported sightings of the
Shining Ones amongst the hordes. These luminous beings
inspire more fear than the rest combined. And Sparhawk
and his companions must resurrect the sacred jewel of the
Troll-Gods to combat them.

The enemies of the Empire know that possession of the
jewel makes Sparhawk as dangerous as any god. But gods
are among his foes. And while Sparhawk defends the far-
flung Tamul Empire, he cannot also protect his beautiful
Queen.

David Eddings, the greatest of modern fantasy writers,
unveils the hidden powers at work in the story of Sparhawk
and the Tamul Empire, an epic for our times.

ISBN 0 586 21316 3